PECKOVER'S PATERNAL INSTINCT

Clatterings from the hall below. Now on the stairs. Damn. No exiting down the stairs. Behind him, first place they'd look, the nursery, a no-go area. The bedroom opposite, equally useless. Was there a loft, a way to the roof?

Marvelous. He could see himself sitting on the roof holding a baby and a bag of necessities, trying to keep her quiet, smacking the mosquitoes, admiring the jungle view. Take a grip on yourself.

Then the gunfire erupted...

Other Avon Books by
Michael Kenyon

A FREE-RANGE WIFE
A HEALTHY WAY TO DIE
THE MAN AT THE WHEEL

PECKOVER HOLDS THE BABY

Michael Kenyon

AVON BOOKS ◆ NEW YORK

AVON BOOKS
A division of
The Hearst Corporation
105 Madison Avenue
New York, New York 10016

Copyright © 1988 by Michael Kenyon
Published by arrangement with Doubleday, a division of Bantam,
Doubleday, Dell Publishing Group, Inc.
Library of Congress Catalog Card Number: 87-22278
ISBN: 0-380-70636-9

First Avon Books Printing: September 1988

AVON TRADEMARK REG. U.S. PAT. OFF. AND IN OTHER COUNTRIES,
MARCA REGISTRADA, HECHO EN U.S.A.

Printed in the U.S.A.

K–R 10 9 8 7 6 5 4 3 2 1

ONE

"Adjust your muffs and glasses," ordered the one-eyed sergeant. His charges, three men bulkily jerseyed against the cold, did so.

"With six rounds—load!"

The men loaded their Smith and Wesson .38 revolvers. They assumed the drawn weapons position, facing the target, gun at waist level and pointing at the target, finger off the trigger.

The sergeant had to shout to be heard through the deadening ear-muffs. "This is a ten-round shoot, sense of direction, paired shots, in twenty-five seconds. Your time starts—" He looked at his watch, taking his time.

Detective Chief Inspector Peckover, grimacing, swung his arms to eye level. He gripped two-handed, thumb on thumb, the lump of wobbling metal. The thing was not supposed to wobble but wobble it did, barely perceptibly, but tremulous all the same, fluttering with maidenly vapours. Was it the arctic cold or was he victim of a muscular disorder of the arms and wrists? Something inherited, perhaps, a genetic flaw emerging only now in mid-life, and in this humiliating posture, backside thrust lewdly back, legs splayed, knees bent, arms reaching, beseeching.

If he were a shaker, a trembler, that surely should disqualify him from this obscene farce. He could get a doctor's certificate—

"—now!"

Bang, bang, bang, bang!

Peckover was unconvinced the ear-muffs made a jot of difference. The din from the three guns crashed against his eardrums. First the bangs, then the twangs as the bullets hit the Detroit bullet-catcher behind the targets. A reverberating, skull-riving bedlam of bangs and twangs. The fiber coating over the range's bricks and breeze-blocks cut the decibel count hardly at all. From a distance, from outside the range, you could even hear the bullets smack through the targets. This is what playing in a rock group would be like.

But he had kept his eyes open this time. They stared through the splinter-proof, perspex glasses, registering little. Fifteen yards ahead, plywood with paper faces, stood three terrorists, or armed bank robbers, or hit men for King Crack of the London-Amsterdam run. Whoever, they had to be dealt with instantly. Them or us, as the sergeant kept insisting. His personal foe for today was the one in the middle, and still, as far as Peckover could see, unriddled *virgo intacta*.

Already, Dews on his left, Sherborne on his right, had dropped to the kneeling position and were reloading. Peckover went on one knee, ejected the spent cases, and dug in his pocket. Like an amateur bloody chorus-line in the local pantomime, he brooded, fumbling, reloading with four rounds.

Bang twa-annng, bang twa-annng! went the guns of Constables Dews and Sherborne.

Click, went Peckover's gun.

Soddit.

Click again.

Then *bang, bang, bang, bang—twa-a-annnng!* from Peckover's gun.

The chorus-line broke open their guns for inspection. Sergeant McMaster wore the blue beret, shirt, pullover, and pants of a Metropolitan Police D11 firearms instructor. His fingers protruding from mittens were white with cold, his nose russet, his eyepatch black chamois, and the rest of his face creamish, like a mushroom. He was a Glaswegian with a line in crude patter for which pistol instruction gave him plenty of opportunity and which amused the younger trainees. Two years running he had come third in the free pistol shooting at Bisley (5.66 calibre, 50 metres, shooting arm unsupported), but that had been before the accident with the cork from a bottle of Asti Spumante. The eyepatch ought to have lent him a piratical air, but even with the red nose he was too seedy for a pirate. The result, Peckover supposed, of postcork life in classroom and sunless shooting-range at Lippett's Hill Camp.

"Two wee misfires there, Mr. Peckover. Close her in the

correct position, remember, or ye'll hae nae bullet in the chamber. Afraid that'll be another twenty p to the beer kitty." Sergeant McMaster stepped back. "Holster your guns. Move forward and check your targets."

Gunfire crackled in adjacent ranges. Peckover, advancing, blew on his frozen fingers. His colleagues on the course thrilled to all this. Annie Oakleys every one, they could core an apple at fifty paces, or believed they would one day, given the practice.

"Got 'im where it hurts that time," Dews said, elated, peering at his speckled target.

"Full marks, laddie," the sergeant told Sherborne. "You punctured his liver and lights."

Peckover's target showed one nick.

"We're still snatching with our Saturday-night finger, sir," the sergeant said. "Our Special's nae a slam-bam fornicating shotgun, remember. She's Special because she's a lady, responding to a soft squeeze, gentle but firm. Let her know ye're in control. No jerking or ye've lost her. And no jerking-off on the range either, not unless ye've a third hand—right, lads?"

Dews guffawed.

"Back to your marks!"

The space-heater was pathetic. Inside the range was five degrees colder than outside. Ventilation was an opening in the roof through which could be seen December's prison-grey sky. At least the cold killed smells. The range was reek-free, without gunpowder stench, armpit odour, or mildew.

Not, to Peckover's mind, that Lippett's Hill, in this unthrilling bit of Essex, would have been any less depressing in midsummer. Forty years earlier its acres had been a POW camp. The place was spooked by the drab ghosts of Germans with nothing to do. Before the prisoners there had been an anti-aircraft battery with concrete bunkers that now were part of the assault course. First day of weapons training you passed a fitness test, or failed. You ran, jumped, balanced, climbed a six-foot wall, sprawled under ropes, struggled over ropes, and lugged a hundred-and-fifty-pound weight on your shoulder, in two minutes. Then for one minute you pointed a revolver rock-steady at a four-inch circle.

Peckover had puffed but passed. His revolver had held about as steady as a lemon jelly. Sergeant McMaster must have shut his good eye. Peckover had wondered if he would still have passed as fit if he'd been unable to lift the gun, or dropped it, and sunk to his knees croaking like a frog. He suspected they might have found a way.

"With six rounds—load!"

The chorus-line loaded. They assumed the drawn weapons position, facing the plywood enemy, their grudging matinee audience.

"Again, a ten-round shoot, sense of direction, paired shots, in twenty-five seconds. Your time starts—"

Bang! roared Peckover's gun.

"Wait!"

Bang, bang, bang! roared the nervous copycat guns of Constables Dews and Sherborne.

"Keep at it then!"

Bang twa-annng! Fumes swirled to the gaping roof; the matinee audience shuddered; a ricocheting bullet chipped the wall.

When the order came to check targets, Peckover hurried forward. He ogled in disbelief.

"Three. Are they mine? This one's through the heart." Peckover touched a bullet-hole with the tip of his pinky. "I've killed 'im!"

"Premature as ye was, sir, likely ye have," said Sergeant McMaster, staring one-eyed at the holes. "Better too soon than too late. Some of the villains walking the streets, like your Mr. Clegg, too late in this world could be too early in the next."

"Who's this my Mr. Clegg?"

"Clegg. And the Honourable Viv. Our Old Etonian toerags with shooters, what ho. Why ye're here, isn't it? Lead the hunt?"

"What hunt? What're you talking about?"

"What I heard, sir. Thought it was common knowledge."

"Common codswallop. You must know more than I do." Untrue. He knew more than the sergeant. He just didn't like to think about it. "Put it out of your mind or you could fetch up sounding a twit."

"I will. All the same, sir, for the premature ejaculation it's another ten penn'orth in the kitty. Right, lads?"

TWO

Forty miles from Lippett's Hill, hungover, holidaying Jeremy Clegg awoke with bellringers festive in his head and no certainty as to whose bed he was in.

He'd remember in a moment. Whoever, she wasn't here. He remembered with no effort the sum he'd dropped at backgammon. Seventy thousand.

He uttered a single shout of a laugh. This proved a poor idea. The bellringers went berserk, jungling and jangling.

What the hell. He would recoup with interest from next week's consignment. Twenty-five pounds of the snowiest, mind-fusing purest from Medellin, Viv had said. Only the best for the paying Los Angelenos. His cut would have to be six figures at least.

Jenny, that was who. She'd had to leave early for Rome, or was it Rio, get herself photographed in a hat against a mountain or an Alfa-Romeo. Plenty of time to make amends if he'd behaved badly last night; he was here for the rest of the week. Could he afford London for the rest of the week? Not at the Sporting Club he couldn't. He risked the laugh again, the bells pealed, and when his head and the bells had calmed, one of the bells carried on pealing.

Damn. The door.

Clegg stepped over scattered clothes and in the bathroom wound a towel round his waist. The sitting room was passably tidy, the brandy bottle gone from the table—there'd been brandy, hadn't there? Someone had neatened up and it hadn't been him. Bloody freezing. Cheapskate bitch must have turned the heating down again. Why did she do it? She earned plenty. Worked hard for it, though, which was more than you could say for some. The favoured few. When Jenny got her next day's assignment for Tangier or wherever, she would yawn like a cave.

Walking to the door, Clegg realised that in his business London was the only place he knew where he'd go to the door dressed in a towel and his hands empty. London was his city. On the other side he'd have had his gun. Here, had he been suffering less, he supposed he'd have carried a casual something, ought to have—that vase, one of the fire-irons. Even so. London was home and unmenacing.

Except when the green baize wrapped you round like a mother and carried you away. Jesus, seventy thousand!

No spyhole. How much would a spyhole have cost her— twenty quid? Skinflint slag.

"Yes?" he said.

"Express delivery for Jennifer Patterson."

Even as he opened the door, Clegg caught himself thinking the accent hadn't been quite that of an express delivery man. Not a London express delivery man.

There were two, both pointing guns, the tall one slightly in advance walking into him, pushing him back into the sitting room. The other shut the door.

"Jeremy Clegg?"

"No!" shouted Clegg.

Five thousand miles across the Atlantic, and the Caribbean, Vivian White in a yachting cap, worn espadrilles, cotton slacks, and a tailored shirt buttoned at the wrists to keep the mosquitoes from eating his arms, entered his gun room and chose from the sporting arsenal a Remington 7400 semiautomatic rifle and a .39 parabellum automatic.

Viv had reddish hair and a beard he had grown in prison and kept. Scissoring it from time to time whiled away a half hour. His belly he had also acquired in prison, and though he wasn't doing anything about it at present, come the point when he could no longer fasten his pants he'd cut down on the vodka, he supposed, and eat nothing except filthy mangoes until he was flat again. His nose was fractionally adrift from an encounter with a shithead copper and the ministrations of a less than adroit bone surgeon who none the less had charged a Croesus ransom. A drug trafficker's ransom, Viv mused, would that be the modern equivalent?

The nose did not bother him. Only his mother and himself would have known. In a way it was a plus, a reminder of what could happen to you out there. Here there was nobody to be Mr. Handsome for. Two days ago he had celebrated his thirty-second birthday by killing a full-grown female ocelot with a single shot, and dining alone off pink beef and champagne. He had dressed for dinner because a man on his own could get sloppy. Then he had fallen asleep in front of "Dynasty."

He returned the automatic to the shelf and picked up the Smith and Wesson .38 revolver.

Boys and girls together, me and the London fuzz. Today, Viv decided, let's pretend we are piglets, see if we can hit a house with what the piglets carry. He pocketed a dozen shells for each gun and locked the cabinet. His pockets chinked as he walked.

Buffing the corridor's tiled floor with a duster tied to a broom was Papitos. She had seen the master with guns often but she still stared and stood back against the wall. Victorian days, Viv reflected, she'd have turned her fat face to the wall. I'd have dismissed her all the same for being visible. For existing. As he walked by, Papitos murmured, "Señor." He ignored her.

The living room was cool, the shutters closed over the windows in the east wall, the shades lowered on the French windows, but with light from the windows beyond the piano falling on the three Hockneys and causing them to shimmer. Inviting enough to come back to after target practice, he thought, though God knows what to do. *The Noël Coward Piano Book?* One chorus of "I'll See You Again," and he would be bored into a stupor.

He stood and surveyed open spaces of tiled floor, Indian rugs, painted screens, and wrought iron. On a shelf, a Mayan onyx funerary mask, ceramic vases, and jade figurines; on the floor, two tons of stone phallus, if that's what it was, looted with Jeremy from remains they had found near their first airstrip, before the army had blown it up for something to do, for the fun of it, because they were more bored than anyone. The spindly Giacometti on the TV probably shouldn't have been on the TV, it should have been on some custom-built pedestal, but on the TV was all right, and who cared anyway? The white doeskin suite shipped from Neiman-Marcus had twin sofas with room enough to seat a string quartet and a team of usherettes.

He could telephone August when he got back, tell her to take the first flight, bring the baby and the nurse. He'd tell her he would ring Fortnum's, have a Christmas hamper flown in. Dammit, if Christmas wasn't for the family, what was it for?

He probably wouldn't phone her. For one, they had

agreed she shouldn't ever come, not here. Running dope was high profit and low risk, but there was risk, and she didn't have to share it. She was better off where she was in spite of where she was, with his mater and paterkins.

Viv sauntered, picked up the Mayan mask, and put it to his face. It smelled of a thousand years of rot. He put it back. He wished he were in Tuscany. Siena, Florence.

Wouldn't be Augusta who would answer either, or his mother, or any of the servants. It'd be Father. What father and son had in common was that they were bored rancid much of the time. The old boy had nothing to do except keep fit and answer the phone. So all day long it would be him answering the phone, and the evil eye and a hundred lashes for anyone who got there before him, not that anyone tried. He'd spring up from his press-ups and have the phone by its throat in a wink, chuckling and shouting into it with his gruesome breeziness—until he discovered it was his son and heir he had on the line.

Almost worth telephoning just to hear the silence fall, then the fake exuberance—"Vivian, dear boy, how are you!"—and the unfunny jokes which failed to conceal the dislike. But not worth it. Daddy always won. Daddy was a competitor. The only man he knew who could terrorize as women could terrorize.

Only a few more years, the way your boy is coining it, and you might have lost the coining competition, so stuff you, daddykins.

Early morning and evening, when the sun wasn't too fierce, chances were his father would be putting on a show on the tennis court. Augusta might answer. Or if it were his father, he could hang up.

Viv wiped his eyes on his sleeve and said, "Oh damn." He believed his head wasn't right. He didn't know why he wept so easily.

He eyed with disgust *Hustler* and *Penthouse* beside the telephone on the glass and wrought-iron coffee table. For a start he would order Papitos to get rid of them. Either take them back to Jeremy's rooms or light a bonfire. Bloody liberty. Whose house was it? And get rid of the puking orchids; they knew he loathed orchids. Waxy, sickly things, they watched him, moved when he moved; they would suck his head inside them and swallow him if he didn't get rid of them.

What else he could do after target practice was he could look at the wall and carry on waiting for the next consignment. Drug-running was bursts of activity punctuated by millennia of nothing, tedium you couldn't escape because you needed to be in place if you were to get the next load, if Pushy Pat in Popacatepetl was not going to get it. The business was competitive. Daddykins would have burst into song.

His contact had said a week from today. So next Monday. That meant any day except next Monday. He would be given an hour's notice.

If Jeremy wasn't back by Monday, he'd not be stashing the stuff in the jungle this time, stowing it under banyan roots and returning for it with Jeremy to find there'd been a party, only string and shreds of canvas bag remaining, and out there stoned deer, lizards, tapirs, perhaps jaguars, high as kites, hooked, a new market but without profit. This time he had a back-up pilot, so hard cheese, Jeremy.

Believed he had one. Flight Lieutenant Lumley, ex-Falklands, currently of the lounge bar at the Fort George Hotel. His gongs included the Distinguished Flying Cross so he shouldn't be too intimidated by the U.S. customs intercept planes, if he happened upon one.

Five grand should see Lumley happy. Another grand to rent a machine because the Piper Cheyenne was still in Ventura, damn Jeremy to hell. Gongs and the Falklands notwithstanding, the Biggles of the Belize tap rooms wasn't about to borrow a RAF Harrier to shunt a bale of cocaine to California.

Vivian White put on sunglasses and walked with his rifle and revolver into the morning glare, across the patio, past the two-storey garage, the blue pool, and along a brick path which bisected two acres of lawn. Bougainvillea bloomed redly; the poincianas and tulip trees offered circles of shade. A hound belonging to a gardener snoozed under a eucalyptus. Viv walked backwards for a few paces, looking at the green-and-white house, and wondering if he might feel a morsel of regret when he sold up, moved out of Casa Verde, and on. Another three, four years, however long it took to thumb his nose at Daddy.

He had bought the place for a song from a retired major turned sugar planter. No one else had had the money to buy it, apart from rival coke carriers, a cabinet minister or two, and one bent copper he could name; and no one was dim enough to want to keep it going as a sugar plantation, not since sugar prices had collapsed and Tate and Lyle closed one of their two refineries. Jungle had already reclaimed the abandoned hectares of cane. Roots, fronds, savannah grass, viridian savagery, howler monkeys, and Technicolour parrots encroached to the rim of the lawns. He needed a moat, a

stockade. Men with scythes kept the green assault at bay but
they had to battle. Tidiest solution would have been napalm.

Up the builders' arses with a squirt of napalm. Their
chute for rubble disfigured the west aspect of the house and
was going to be there for ever. They had begun in a frenzy of
sound, fury, and dust, knocking two upstairs rooms into one
for a master bedroom with bathroom en suite. Telephones
too, because if ever the major had phoned anyone he'd had
to do it downstairs. Now the long nothing. Like London. He
hadn't seen the builders for three weeks. The fat steel tube
projected out of the window of the master-bedroom-to-be,
angled down, like a challenge in a futuristic playground, and
stopped short in a dusty yawn above a skip piled with laths,
plaster, and lumps of concrete.

Everything in this damn country was concrete because of
the termites. Foundations, walls. If termites weren't yet in
his doors, windows, and staircase, it was because they had
more sense; they'd have drowned. The doors were so swollen with damp you needed a fireman's Hurst tool to open
them.

Viv popped into his mouth the last white rectangles from
a box of Wrigley's Chiclets. He dropped the box for someone
else to pick up and walked on. Ramon, watering the blousy
hibiscus, chewing on tobacco, eyed the rifle and revolver,
grinned with brown teeth, and said, "Buenos dias, señor."

"Morning," Viv said, walking past.

Idle spic. Soon as the master was out of sight he'd sit with
his hound in the palm's shade and go to sleep.

Am I, Viv wondered, becoming like Mother? He remembered her in the brick house in Cadogan Square endlessly
whining about how you couldn't find reliable staff anymore.
She was right: you couldn't if you were Mother because no
one in their right mind would work for her.

He followed the trodden path through the high grass and
into the pines where the sun shone through in rods. He heard
flapping wings and scuttlings. Stepping lightly, he loaded first
the rifle, then the revolver. He'd swap a Hockney for the
sight of a puma but he'd seen one only once. To his right
sounded a squawk and a flurry. He swung his arm, fired the
revolver, and the bullet blew a wild turkey against the base
of a tree. The bird hung for a moment, flapping against the
bark, then dropped.

"That one's for Ramon," Viv said, while from the
branches overhead came a clatter of fleeing creatures.

Another fifteen minutes, he estimated, before anything
would stir again. His espadrilles crushed down on decayed

leaf-mould, moss, and pine needles. When he arrived at the pool of sunlight which was a glade, he stuck the revolver in his waistband, and waited, out of the sun. The glint in the grass was a spent cartridge from an earlier sortie.

He stepped into the sun, put the rifle to his shoulder, and fired skyward. Feathers whirled, floated, and the shreds of a hummingbird fell to earth.

"That's for you, Henry Shithead Peckover," he said, and fired again.

The hummingbird's mate exploded in the sky.

"How about that for you, dear Father."

Hummingbirds were legal. The turkey had been illegal. Tough shit, turkey.

People were illegal too but like turkeys that didn't stop them coming to grief sometimes, and wouldn't, ever again, if they came too close to him.

On the Caribbean's farther extremity, Sir Peter White, in sneakers and shorts, approached the cot with exaggerated stealth. Most of Sir Peter's actions were exaggerated. But for the child he would not have been tiptoeing; he would have been gusting through the house banging doors and shouting people's names. He liked an audience and knowing what people were doing.

He was tall and bony, and his bare, sweaty chest and balding head were toasted to a cocoa colour never attained by those whose efforts are limited to two weeks at the Club Med. At the Andros Island Beach Club (Strictly Members Only) he had just won in two straight sets against Tom Devon, a useful Yank half his age, so his mood was merry. Had he lost he would not have been visiting his affections on the baby or on anyone. But the club being small, a far cry from Nassau, he seldom lost, though now that he was sixty-seven his name was no longer at the top of the ladder.

"Iggle-iggle-oo," said Sir Peter.

The baby was awake but starting to suffer, mouth opening, face crumpling and reddening. The first protest was a paltry bleat, a tuning up for the symphonic variations to come. New breath was being drawn. The second complaint sliced like a cleaver through the silence of the covered veranda, insensitive to the feelings of others.

Where were the others?

"Icky-bicky-boodle-oodle. It's all right then, it's all right."

Sir Peter strode from the veranda into the drawing room calling out, "Gussie? Nanny? Someone's famished! Someone wants nourishment and gamesy-wamesy! Nanny? You there?"

He arrived in the air-conditioned spaces of a palatial hall and called out, "Hello?" Winnie, a red-and-white Irish setter, padded through a doorway and paraded inquiringly round her master's feet, sniffing them.

Sir Peter had given the hallway of his Christmas getaway house unexpected depth and interest, he believed, by recreating here reminders of past glories from English history. A full suit of armour from a Christie's saleroom, polished to a gleam by one of the indoor staff, stood on a rattan mat beside a jardiniere of lurid purple bougainvillea. On the south wall was mounted feudal weaponry, mainly swords and axes, as if in a museum. A series of sporting prints of bygone Derby winners, jockey statuesque in the saddle, hung along the length of another wall. On a third wall, in monstrous gilt frames of moulded whorls and curlecues, were grouped naval battles, oils of listing, yawing galleons spouting smoke from cannon in the act of sinking the fleets of France, Holland, Spain, Portugal, and America.

Doors led from the hall to a further living room, a library, breakfast room, cloakroom, and the briny outdoors. Beyond these rooms sprawled sun rooms, the dining room, games room, conservatory, and decks and verandas overlooking the park and ocean. That was the ground floor. At the end of a passage off the hall, narrow stairs led to basement kitchens and other empires. The stairs, which mounted from the centre of the hall, were wide, shallow marble. Here Sir Peter lifted his bony head and shouted, "Gussie? Nanny? Anyone?"

Lady May White, wrinkled as a tortoise, and proceeding at much the same speed, came from the breakfast room carrying secateurs and jasmine. Without looking at her husband she said in a monotone, "Gussie's at the hairdresser. Nanny's buying orange-juice. Granny will go."

Sir Peter watched her ample back move in the direction of the cries. Even to Lady May, who recoiled from nicknames and diminutives—or who had done so in better days, before leaving London and home with her husband, at two hours notice, and turning in on herself—their daughter-in-law was Gussie. She was Gussie to everyone except her absentee husband, their son.

On the veranda, Lady May set down the flowers and secateurs on a bamboo table. Vivian had always had to be different. Being different would put him back in prison one day.

She hoped he would be comfortable there and the food nourishing. She reached into the rowdy crib.

A telephone rang. With a premonition, and less than his usual alacrity, Sir Peter headed for the ringing. He put the phone to his ear and waited. The other party was waiting too.

"Hello?" Sir Peter shouted.

Click.

"Brat," said Sir Peter. "Whippersnapper. By jove, that one needs a tanning!"

THREE

At day's end the policemen receiving gun training un-wound in the Lippett's Hill canteen before going home to their wives, lovers, boyfriends, or a bachelor room at the station house and a beer and warmed-up shepherd's pie at the Pot and Kettle.

Sherborne was to fill a pavement vacancy at the Israeli Embassy. Dews had been assigned to the Prince Charles team. Three were bound for Heathrow, and six were transfers to the Special Branch. All twelve on the two-week course were volunteers, except one.

At forty-five, the exception was the oldest by ten years. Detective Chief Inspector Peckover was also the most senior in rank, and might have been a good deal more senior but for blots on his personal file. Limericks long ago about an unlov-able assistant commissioner had not helped, neatly felt-penned above the urinals at Cannon Row police station. And breaking a tearaway's arm. The concensus among CID of-ficers at the Factory had been that the yob had deserved his other arm broken, and both legs, but the tabloids had stormed about police brutality. Over its front page the *Sun* had spread two photographs: the anguished yobbo with his arm in plaster, and the startled face of Our 'Enry, Bard of the Yard, caught with a pint in his hand in the Duke of Buck-ingham. WEED OUT THE WANKING WORDSWORTHS! shrilled the headline. A reporter's digging had unearthed rhymed contributions from Our 'Enry in *Punch, Homes and Gar-dens, The Listener, Poetry Quarterly, Motor, Country Life, Taste, Slimming,* and *Woman's Realm.*

Nine commendations but too much waywardness, at any

rate in his salad years. Never having volunteered for gun training was minor waywardness, but that had not helped either. London policemen were expected to be versatile and willing.

DCI Peckover, drinking hot yellow tea in the Lippett's Hill canteen, resolved to have it out with Frank Veal that evening. He hadn't volunteered; he'd been press-ganged, and giving in was about the stupidest thing he'd ever done.

He would lead the hunt for Clegg and the Honourable Viv if asked, if there were fresh evidence, if either were in the country. He'd be delighted. He'd hunt at a gallop, give up his free days, seek Clegg in the Clairmont and the National Sporting Club, and the Honourable Viv wherever he might be, presumably back with his wife and child. But not with a gun. The nation was going bananas, disappearing down the plug in a swirl and rattle of cartridges, sucked under in a foaming broth of cordite and sewage which everyone still believed to be good old British phlegm.

If Clegg had killed the copper, or if Viv had, in spite of what the jury decided—or more likely if they'd had him killed, God knows they could afford to pay—fine, they had graduated to public pests number one. But they were still humdrum stuff, more sordid than most, but still ratbags, and to be handled with the humdrum methods which still were preseverance, plugging on, questions, a tenner here and an arm twisted there, surprise if you could work it, beef always, lightning flashes of sheer genius from Frank Veal at his desk, if you were lucky, and numbers. Outnumber the bleeders. Bring on every last one of London's finest, vanloads of 'em. Bring on gas, shields, hoses, horses. That was how. Not bleedin' guns.

If ever he were to collar them, either of them, and they pulled a Magnum on him, he'd still be safer without a gun. Fancied he would. Talking to them was the route. Muddle them with chat. Thump 'em, given the chance. But a gun? The rule book on this course, rule number one: It said never draw a weapon from its holster unless you have occasion to use it. Great. That catch-release thingummy you thumbed open on the holster to get the flap up, it'd be dark before he got his gun out of its holster.

Rule number two: Never point a firearm at anyone unless you're prepared to shoot.

Aye, and there's the rub. Unless you're prepared to shoot. How could you know if you were prepared to shoot, really know, until you were here with a gun, and the other geezer was there with a gun, and you were looking deep into the glaucous pools of each other's eyes, or however it was going to be?

Clegg he'd never met, never seen outside photographs in the file, but who could shoot a bleedin' playboy? Jeremy Clegg, playboy pilot, flying bales of the stuff out of the Caribbean into California with a bottle of Mumm in his hand, a whore in his lap, and two thousand quids' worth of AM/FM stereo radio with a cassette deck belting out "The Eton Boating Song." Playboy would then come back to dear old London on the Concorde and scatter his earnings on roulette and girls. Liked the bubbly and an ethnic joke, so the file's pop psychology page said. Simpleton traits, Peter Pan syndrome, classic oral and anal retardation, not obviously suited to drugs traffic.

On the contrary, absolutely suited, Peckover believed. Nothing at all on him. After the bright lights, cleaned out and giggling, back to the sunny side for the next air-lift and refill of his shopping bag with lolly at probably six figures per consignment. For a simpleton suffering from Peter Pan syndrome Clegg hadn't done badly. Palms must have been greased but that would be Viv's department. Viv would be a whiz at the wheeling and dealing if he were his daddy's son.

Peckover nibbled the skin by the nail of a forefinger, realised this was his trigger finger, and continued to nibble. He wondered if Vivian White might be one person he just might be able to shoot. A toe, an earlobe. Nothing mortal. He had bent Viv's nose when he'd made the collar, but if he'd known the jury wasn't going to buy a murder charge, he'd have gone for something more satisfying than the nose. All Viv had been handed was the sermon and eighteen months for illegal possession of drugs and a shooter. Six months remission for being a good boy; now he was out. He was probably capable of having killed a copper, and one day likely would; the odds were on it, the game he'd gone into.

"Sugar please, Henry."

Sherborne was arguing with Dews and Burton about West Ham selling to Barcelona their only player who knew how to kick a football. The canteen, bleakly festive, hung with holly and last year's paper-chains from stores, was hardly warmer than the range. Peckover imagined a Home Office directive extolling Maggie's triumph over inflation and forbidding all police dining facilities more than a two-hour trickle of heat per day. On pain of being shot at.

Shoot everyone. Twirl those shooters. Shoot up the canteen, the manager, customers, cooks, worthless radiators, teacups, sausages.

Peckover watched as two tables away, with the other two instructors, Sergeant McMaster forked into his mouth copiously ketchuped cod and chips. No wonder he was the colour of rain. What meal was this at five-thirty in the afternoon?

"What do you say, Henry? Was it them?"

"Who?"

"Clegg and the Verminous Viv. Wasted Jimmy Thornley."

"Wasted? Where do you get words like that?"

Hollywood TV stuff was where. Peckover eyed his raw forefinger. Hell's bells, two years ago, nearly. New Year's Eve, DC Thornley on surveillance outside the Curzon Street flat rented by Viv White, except he wasn't surveilling, he was dead on the pavement, a gold chain with a lump of jade engraved VW in his hand, and no one had seen or heard a thing. Straight TV, except the blood was blood, Thornley's blood, not a lot of it, and the hole small, tiny really, bullet-sized. Even the defence hadn't tried to pretend the chain was for keys to a Volkswagen.

"Back in business, are they?" Dews was creating a sugar Alp in the sugar bowl, building and smoothing with a spoon.

"Couldn't tell you."

"What's the plot, Henry? Do you go after them, the pre-emptive strike, or do they come after you? They say the Honourable Viv's the vengeful sort. Bears a grudge."

"Who says?"

"Come on. When he was inside. He talked about you. Talked about nothing else for a year. What they say."

"If they're back in business it's on the other side of the Atlantic, the sunny side. No one's going after anyone, not from here."

"What's the Atlantic?" With a deft scoop Dews turned the Alp into Vesuvius. "You can fly the Atlantic, shoot a copper, and be back for supper. If it was me going after Viv, I'd have my hand on my gun twenty-four hours a day."

"You talk a terrible load of twaddle."

"On my left," Dews said, "Clegg and Viv, two ratbags. On my right, Mr. Henry Peckover, backed by five thousand licensed London bobbies, if we happen to be there at the time."

"Triple twaddle."

"Why you're here, isn't it? Getting ready to take care of yourself come shootout-at-sunup time? I envy you. Wish the ratbags would come after me."

"If ever I see them, I'll tell them."

Dews, one eye closed, arms outstretched, pointed the

sugar spoon into the empty space between Peckover and Sherborne. "Paired shots, two for each ratbag. Pow-pow! Pow-pow!" He lowered his arms. "You're being groomed for stardom."

"I'm already a star, cock, I don't need grooming. Seen this month's *Good Housekeeping?*"

"Never seen any month's *Good Housekeeping.*"

"A sonnet?" said Burton.

"A carol," Peckover said. "Seasonal stuff. 'Bang-Bang Merrily on High.'"

Sherborne said, "Do we give the sarge a Christmas present?"

"Duelling pistols," said Burton. "Pick up a nice pair at Sotheby's for a grand."

"How about a tartan eyepatch," said Dews. "Burlington Arcade."

"'Ow about a tin mug for 'im to collect my ten-p fines in," Peckover said, and pushed back his chair. "See you darlings tomorrow."

Peckover drove along the M11 at seventy with headlights blazing and newsreaders on Radio Four telling him that French farmers at Channel ports had set up road blocks to prevent the dumping of turkeys; the U.S. dollar was thought likely to bottom out; and the weather would continue as cold and disgusting as an Eskimo husky's poop-tray. They didn't actually say that in so many words only because they weren't sure the thermometer wouldn't rise and the sun shine, but they didn't sound optimistic. In eighteen minutes he was in the East End and rush hour hopelessness. Through Bow, Stepney—*Wotcher, Stepney, scene of my childhood, cradle of genius*—the City, and along the Embankment to Parliament Square and Victoria Street took another fifty-five minutes.

He found a parking space in Artillery Row, which he considered appropriate. The street ought to have been reserved expressly for official gunslingers such as himself.

A north wind blew drizzle in his face. The street lamps shed light the colour of Camembert on shop assistants and secretaries with umbrellas scurrying for St. James's Park Underground to home in Ealing, Wembley, and supper, feet up, and television. Three number eleven buses, nose to tail, headlights and interiors shining, hissed too fast along the street. Peckover, increasingly damp, cantered along Broadway and through revolving glass doors into New Scotland Yard.

All Warrant Cards and Office Passes Must Be Shown.

The blue police flag hung overhead, the yellow flame for London bobbies dead in two world wars burned on its marble block. Behind the reception desk both girls were harassed, listening to customers, telephoning, scribbling messages. In the waiting hall, Molly Abbott from the press office was talking to a scruffy media beast in a bomberjacket. The *Times,* Peckover judged. The man was jotting something on the back of a cheque book. Her phone number?

"'Ullo, Henry." Sergeant Bernie Bright, capless and white-haired, had stood in the foyer directing arrivals and fielding questions for as long as anyone could remember, probably since the founding of the Metropolitan Police in 1829. "Been on leave? All right for some."

"'Appy Christmas, Bernie. Mr. Veal in?"

"When was he not?"

Peckover got out of the lift at the seventeenth floor and walked left. The plaque on the door read, DS Frank Veal, Cl. He tapped and went in.

"Freeze!" he cried, then beamed like an imbecile. "It's me, your friendly neighbourhood gunman."

"Jesus, where did you get that tie?"

"Like it? It's a gunman's tie. Dazzles the enemy, makes 'em shoot crooked." Peckover, no longer beaming, flapped the pink silk, glittery as a dog's tongue. "Regulation issue at Lippett's Hill, along with the rod."

"The what?"

"The gat. The piece. The heater. Gawd, where've you been? So 'appens the Smith and Wesson Thirty-Eight Special is what I'd not say no to a word about. We're talking about the Model Sixty-Four with six chambers. Think of that. Six. What it shoots is a hundred-and-twenty-five-grain, semi-jacketed, semi-wadcutter bullet."

"If it works."

"Course it works."

"Can't they misfire if they get damaged or bunged up with rust and gunge?"

"Haven't 'ad that lesson yet."

"Or if you don't load them properly?"

"Someone been talking to you?"

"Cuppa tea, Henry? I'll phone down."

"Listen. I'm not your man, old darling. Not with a gun."

"Milk, no sugar, correct?"

"Being a stripling you'll find this 'ard to understand, but I've reached an age where I'm giving things up. Sugar, right. I've also given up tobacco, fried bread, ice cream, jogging, girls, late nights, and exceeding the speed limit. At present I'm giving up guns. You send me out into the blue with a gun, I could kill someone."

"There's that risk."

"It'd be the postman. A tourist. Anyone at all comes padding up behind asking the time. I'm jumpy as the next bloke. I'm also a pacifist. Back at Lippett's Hill, home on the range, know what they call me?"

"You're about to tell me."

"Gandhi. Know what they're giving me for Christmas?"

"A loin cloth? Veal," Veal said into the telephone, swivelling right, then left, in his high-backed chair. "Pot of tea for two, skip the sugar."

Veal's chair, the only piece of furniture in the office with any sort of pretention to class, was a kinetic throne, shinily and spongily upholstered in some sort of Gucci-style material in deepest, practically black green, heat-controlled, stress-free yet stimulatory, absorbent, and certainly the treated, hand-beaten skin of a rare species of African wildlife. It had a detachable foot-rest, embedded buttons, glimmers of metal, and an interior bristling with cogs, sprockets, ratchets, and ball-bearings, which allowed it to twirl like a top and rock like Elvis.

Behind Veal a frosted glass door connected to the dark of Commander Astle's office. The two tidy vacated desks belonged to Mrs. Coulter, human reference library, and Sergeant Terry Sutton, who played lock for the Metropolitan Police B rugby team when he was not in plaster, his ribs cracked, ankles buckled.

Veal rocked and said, "You're not happy about guns."

"You could say that."

"You can probably relax. I'm not saying you should go off on your holidays, though it could come to that, in a funny way. But there's been a development. Jeremy Clegg."

"Our playboy," Peckover said. "He's just broke the bank at the National Sporting Club."

"He's just been shot. He's dead."

FOUR

"Between two-thirty and three this afternoon at his girl-friend's flat in Chelsea. Beaten up then shot. Very close range, couldn't have been closer. Powderburns on what's left of his head." Veal perused a sheet of paper with not much on it. "He was naked, might've been wearing a towel. Welling-ton Square. The girlfriend's a Jennifer Patterson but we haven't found her yet. Everyone's there including the com-mander and the deputy AC. You're right on one thing, he spent the night at the National Sporting Club—but he lost. Seventy thousand, a bagatelle. They still have sheiks lose twice that. Seventy was probably the limit on his plutonium American Express."

Peckover stood with his hands in his raincoat pockets, pink tie hanging.

"So say something," Veal said.

"Like what. One down and one to go?"

"If only. They might be coming out from under their stones after this. How about a good old-fashioned gang war, only contemporary, drugs-style, the gun artists smashed out of their skulls. Our Honourable Viv exacting vengeance. Col-ombians flying in for the fun. Did you know the Colombians don't dispose of just who's in the way? They kill the whole family. Kids, aunts, the goldfish. Where are you going?"

"Wellington Square."

"You're not. We're talking. I tried to reach you but you were off shooting your gun."

"Whose fault's that?"

"Sit down. From a policing point of view Clegg is not

exactly a disaster. True, the gaming tables won't be happy. But we're not out of the wood."

"Meaning I'm not out of the wood."

"There are ramifications."

"Thought there might be. Viv's come to town?"

"Viv's at his Casa Verde hut, according to Superintendent Campos. Presumably waiting for his next consignment, except he doesn't have a pilot to fly it any more, not as far as we know. Which isn't to say he won't find one." Workaholic Veal, in shirtsleeves, leaned back in his wildlife chair and caressed his handlebar moustache. "We're not bone idle here—see, telephones. He wants help."

"Viv or Superintendent Campos—whoever'e is."

"Their top drugs cop. He wants us to move our bums, get over there, see for ourselves."

"See what? Banana trees? Señor Campos paying the air fare?"

"He wants us to look at what they've got on Viv. He says he can give us names, people there who know Viv, have done business with him. Campos wants him off his patch. He wants him extradited."

"What grounds? If Viv's back in business, he's in business over there. He's done nothing 'ere."

"Thornley?" said Veal, and he raised both hands as if to ward off attack. "I know. But the file's open. If Campos can give us something fresh, people to talk to, we should do it."

"Why can't he talk to them himself? Got an impediment?"

"Talk to them? He's probably in bed with them. Top drugs cop in a top drugs country of a hundred and fifty thousand—what's that, Hampstead? If Hampstead had a drugs traffic worth fifty million a year. Only reason Campos is alive is probably because he talks in whispers. 'Yes sir, no sir, three bags full sir.' That fifty million is cannabis alone. God knows what Viv and Clegg make shipping cocaine."

"Campos is probably in bed with Viv building his retirement fund. What do we know about 'im?"

"He'd like to be rid of Viv."

"Why? Frightened he's getting in too deep? He's pocketed enough for the world cruise and a Rolls and a nice coconut grove and wants out before it all blows up in his face?"

"Perhaps he's straight and trying to do his job."

"So let 'im lock Viv in a cell. Or has Viv bought the judge and jury? I can see Campos could have a problem. But extradition's the Solicitor's Department, drugs are for the Drugs Squad, and matey mine, I'm neither. I'm just going to tell you about me and guns, quick peek at Wellington Square, then 'ome."

"Henry, that's a chair, stick your arse on it." Veal's chair sighed as he got up. He dug in a cabinet and brought out a cassette. "Campos isn't the only one wants Viv out of Beliz. Did we play you the call from Viv's father, July, from the Bahamas? He as good as threatened to sue if we didn't pluck Viv out of the Caribbean, cheeky bugger."

"Saw the transcript." Peckover sat. "This one of the ramifications?"

Veal put a tape-recorder on the desk, inserted the cassette, and pressed Start.

"I'm Sir Peter White, Sir Peter White speaking," Sir Peter shouted as if the telephone were still to be invented. *"I asked to speak to the commissioner."*

"You're speaking to Inspector Tregear, Fraud Squad."

"Fraud? Fraud, fellow? This has nothing to do with fraud—"

Stop. Fast forward. Stop. Start.

"—no point asking me what the falling-out's about. I do know if harm comes to my boy the police will be responsible. When thieves fall out, what? I'm not suggesting my son is up to anything illegal, absolutely to the contrary. But young Clegg is dangerous, he's—"

"What kind of harm?"

"Address that question to Clegg. Your clear duty is to persuade my boy to return to England. Before there's trouble. Preventive policing, I assume you're familiar with that? Up to you how you go about it, what? You have ways of applying pressure."

"Unless your son is engaged in criminal activity—"

"Don't be impudent, fellow! It's simply that he's keeping exceedingly bad company. That Clegg is a blighter. Now, here is what you do. I am prepared to sit down with my boy and any senior officer you send over for full and frank discussions. What about the one who arrested him last year, eh? Peckersby? Pecksniff? I might have certain facts about young Clegg—"

Stop.

"Barmy," Peckover said.

"And lucky. Loots his bank of eighty million and gets away with it. From today he doesn't even have to worry about Clegg being a bad influence any more."

"Luck or good management?"

"Fair question. But he still wants Viv out of Belize. He did last week. He phoned from Andros Island. That's the

Bahamas, one of their Family Islands—don't ask me. Mrs. Coulter checked it out and it sounds like a tourist gimmick. Probably a swamp. Anyway, not his place in Nassau. This is some cabin he takes off to for Christmas. I would guess five miles of private beach and assorted swimming pools in the shape of dollar signs, yen, Deutschemark, and sterling. He didn't mention Clegg but he still wants to talk."

"To me?"

"He didn't specify."

"Good. Send Drugs. Send Fraud. Can I go now?"

"Can't play you the tape, it's with the AC. Here's what he said, for what it's worth." Veal reached across the desk with a sheet of foolscap. "Takes the cake, doesn't it. Our richest villain biting his nails over his son, our most neurotic."

"Got good reason, the game Viv's in." Peckover scanned the paper and handed it back. "Tell 'im if he's so keen to talk to come back and talk here. Solve everything. There's a half million investors he robbed blind waiting to edge 'im off the top of a tall building."

"The AC thinks Belize might be worth the air fare," Veal said. "You'd have one of the Drugs Squad with you. Alan Moss might suit. You talk to Campos, see what he's got. Viv if he's available. Sir Peter? As long as he's adjacent, like in the same hemisphere, no harm in a courtesy call. You don't have to be courteous, you could kick his face in. Ideally, you'd drink his Chivas and coax him back to England to make amends, clear his conscience."

"Very droll."

"Still, what's to be lost? Finish the course, Henry, a few days in the sunkissed Caribbean, and home for Christmas."

"The course 'appens to be what I'm here to tell you about. The hell with Viv and his 'orrible daddy. Are you ready?"

"Shoot."

"That meant to be funny?"

Yes, probably. Inscrutable Veal in his classy chair was fondling his moustache. Not a grey hair in it, though he might, Peckover conceded, be snipping them out. Veal was his junior in years but not in rank. He was in line for commander, Cl, one of the fanciest chairs in the Serious Crimes Branch, as long as he kept out of the wrong beds. When not at his desk, he was too often between the sheets with one lady or another, including on occasion the bedazzled wives, girlfriends, sisters, daughters, and mothers of Metropolitan policemen. Never mind, Veal was to Peckover's mind living evidence of the nonsense that no one is indispensable. With-

out him the CID would roll over on its back and lie there
twitching. He'd make it to commander and beyond if he
avoided being discovered *in flagrante delicto* with the Home
Secretary's wife.

A row of books competed for desk space with telephones,
files, and loaded in-trays and out-trays. Though their spines
were away from him, Peckover identified the hardback *London AZ*, the *Concise OED, Moriarty's Police Law,* the *Police
Almanac,* and in its blue cover the *Home Office Consolidated
Circulars on Crime and Kindred Matters.* He angled his neck
and squinted, trying to read the title of an unfamiliar terra
cotta tome which lay flat apart and would have kept a colony
of termites happy for weeks.

Veal pushed the book towards him and said, "Page two
hundred and seven."

Halsbury's Laws of England, Vol. 18, Explosives to Foreign Relations. Peckover found page 207. *Extradition and
Fugitive Offenders Act, 1967.* Extradition treaties existed
with all Commonwealth countries. Plus Albania, Argentina,
Austria, Belgium, Bolivia, Chile, et cetera. About fifty of
them. Peckover, curious, examined the list. Who was missing? Where couldn't we get a criminal deported from? Not
from Brazil, too true. Thirty years after the Great Train
Robbery, getting on, Biggs still sunned himself there. Not
from Russia, Libya, Egypt, Vietnam, Japan, South Africa.
All the places no fugitive offender in his senses would want
to flee to. Footnote: *Extradition treaties between the U.K.
and the Cameroons and Togo appear to have expired.* Goodness gracious, they have? All the same, he doubted there'd
ever been a rush to the Cameroons and Togo.

"Listen to this: *Extraditable offences,*" Peckover said,
reading.

"Save your breath. I know them."

"No extradition for political offences, we all know that.
And no mention of drug-smuggling. Here's what you can get
deported for. Murder, rape, abduction, child-stealing, piracy,
sinking or destroying a vessel at sea, bribery, and genocide.
Where's Viv fit into that lot? Bribery's never going to do it.
Not by any chance a pirate, is 'e?"

"I just said, old son. Jimmy Thornley was murdered.
Right, it's a hundred to one shot, but if Campos has anything
at all on that, it's worth the effort. Meanwhile, you were
about to bitch about the gun course. What you don't know is
you're not going to tell me anything I don't know. What
you've got is weapons withdrawal syndrome. It's normal; it's
healthy. Everyone has it and gets over it."

"Don't patronise me." Peckover put the book back on the desk. "That first morning, when the instructor says if any of us 'ave religious or moral objections, now's the time to collect our hats, don't think I didn't think about it."

"Eleven years since I did the course." Veal rocked in his chair like a granny at the fireside. "I haven't held a gun since, and hope I never have to. Not that I'd be allowed to without retraining. You're unhappy; every last one of you who might have to shoot is unhappy."

"Not on my course. They can't wait."

"Don't believe it. Think they're going to hint they might be soft? Think they'll let on they wake up sweating about whether they're going to be able to manage the hairy-chested life-and-death stuff? Comes the crunch, they handle it, nine out of ten."

"I'm the tenth."

"Balls."

"I'm going to fail."

"No one fails."

"It's happened."

"Very rare."

"I've never hit the target."

"You hit it today."

"Ring you up with the tidings of comfort and joy, did 'e—McMaster? Or do you phone him?"

"He doesn't say you're a natural." Veal's rocking gathered momentum. "He thinks there's a small block. But you're getting the hang of it. You'll pass."

"The exam's Friday. What if I don't hit the thing once?"

"You'll hit it."

"If I don't?"

"Heaven's sake, you're not spastic!" Veal ceased rocking and started swivelling. Left, right, left, right. "You're getting the best training there is."

"You're not listening. What if I don't hit it?"

"You'll repeat."

"Highly irregular."

"Getting you on the course at two weeks' notice was irregular. Somewhere out there seethes whoever you displaced, and he was a volunteer."

"Viv was let out last March. If you were so keen I learn 'ow to protect myself you didn't 'ave to wait nine months."

"The calls from Campos and Sir Peter aren't nine months old; they're happening now. We didn't know it was over there someone might need to protect himself. Still don't. Nothing's certain. No point getting you excited." Veal was now swivelling and rocking simultaneously. "And the less anyone hears of this the better, Henry, you becoming a gunslinger, and Belize. They just might dream up a link. Viv will have eyes and ears in London."

"One fewer without Clegg."

"We don't know. Sir Peter says they were no longer best chums. What if when Viv was inside, Clegg took advantage, restructuring the firm, voting Viv out?"

The telephone rang and Veal answered monosyllabically, squiggling notes. Peckover stood up, tucked in the pink tie. Veal replaced the phone.

"At least two killed Clegg," Veal said. "He was held, bashed, and shot four times with probably a thirty-two. Jenny Patterson's a model and wasn't there; she's modelling in Rome. And Wellington Square's empty except for a couple of uniforms from Division getting themselves wet. The commander's on his way back if you want to tell him your troubles."

"I'll tell you one, except it's not mine, it's the taxpayer's," Peckover said, buttoning his raincoat. "Each error is another ten-p towards Friday's booze-up at The Owl when we sing gunmen's songs and wave our new pink cards licensing us to kill. I've shelled out about what Clegg would drop in a bad night at roulette. I'm charging it to expenses."

"I'll sign them. Bestest to Miriam. Henry?"

"What?"

"You don't need a passport for Belize but in case there are side-trips, check it's up to date."

Going out, Peckover met the tea coming in.

He drove through drizzle along Eaton Square and the King's Road and into Wellington Square. A man and woman carrying Safeway's shopping bags were scuttling down steps to a basement. Two wet bobbies in capes patrolled past terraced Georgian houses which no one could afford to buy except people like Sir Peter White, who could have bought the whole square, having robbed investors at his bank of £80, now worth heaven knew how much, and models like Miss Patterson, especially if her boyfriend had a starring role in drugs and was generous.

Late boyfriend. Peckover wondered why he had come, unless it was for the Markham opposite, in memory lane.

He had known the pub in his PC days but now hardly recognised it. It had gone open-plan. There were wall-long swaths of shelving you could put your pint and macaroni cheese and elbows on, and bulbous hanging lights a big bloke could crack his skull on, and rock music pounding, but wasn't there in every pub.

The customers he recognised, or at any rate the voices. The neighing and twittering of the Sloanes and Hooray Henrys quenched to some extent the juke-box roar but made him yearn for his ear-muffs. Fashions in dress had changed, but not the classics in aspic: a blazer with regimental tie, a tweed cap smelling of horse trials, a knotted silk square from Turnbull and Asser on a rosy sprig who would wear pin-stripes for his four hours a day in the pater's office in the Square Mile. The girls with tight bums and small boobs wore designer jeans and cashmere jerseys and would still have jobs in art galleries in Cork Street and estate agents in South Kensington. One or two might be clumsily raped before the night was out, though rape wasn't quite the word, because it wouldn't be force which landed them in bed with young Lord Looney, heir to the Earldom of Looney, it would be ambition and desperation. He was cheered to see two Chelsea pensioners seated like waxworks at a table near the Gents, making their Guinness last, and a group of lime-and-aubergine punks by the juke-box, soberly drinking halves of lager, but in the wrong pub.

"Why, Mr. Peckover, I've not seen you since the Flood. Did they make you commissioner yet?"

"Hello, Willie," Peckover said. "What're you doing out?"

Willie Ryan, rogue, erstwhile informant, looking respectable enough, even dapper, but when had he not? Carnation, vile polka-dot bow-tie. Peckover almost extended a hand for shaking. Instead he slapped it theatrically to his right breast, confirming that he still had his wallet.

"That's not kind, Mr. Peckover. Particularly as I happen to be your host. The four o'clock at Newton Abbott, China Girl waltzed in at twenty-five to one. Aren't I Baron Rothschild for the night? What'll it be?"

One hour, a phone call to Miriam, three pints of best, and three double Jamiesons for Willie later, Peckover had learned that yes, Willie had noticed activity across the road in Wellington Square, earlier, but he'd taken no heed of that, nor of the headlines in the last edition of the *Standard,* China Girl having skipped home like a dancer; and didn't a filly like that put everything out of your head except the miracle of existence and the goodness of God? No, he'd never heard of Jeremy Clegg, not till now. Sure, he remembered the Vivian White case, a toff, a drugs artist over in one of them places across the sea where the blackies came from, sent down for having a shooter. The eejit had to be certifiable. Hadn't the judge sorrowed and mourned about the feller's advantages, on and on, like it was all a terrible anguish, enough to make a judge break down, drop his pencil and mallet?

Crinkling his face, trying to remember, Willie said, "Did he go on too about the father, the banker boyo? I'm thinking, would that one as your father constitute an advantage or a disadvantage?"

"He didn't come into it."

Peckover suspected Willie remembered the case not only because it had been on the front pages, but because evidence had been given by Chief Inspector Peckover, the same who, during hard times, when China Girls had not always romped it, had been a source of loose change for tips unconnected with the turf. He shook Willie's hand and left the Markham. Willie had never harmed anyone who held tightly to her handbag, buttoned his pockets, and kept a decent distance on rush-hour escalators.

The traffic had calmed itself but not the weather. In Collins Cross on the other side of London, Peckover parked, locked up, and started across the road to his front door. The drizzle had become substantial rain.

The inside of a car parked ahead lit up as two men came out of the front seats and went dark as they shut the doors. They walked in the same direction, towards Thirty-two, a white door with brass numbers, letter-box, and showy, hexagonal knob from Camden Market. Peckover splashed through puddles. The car lit up again as a third man, a laggard in an orange winter-warm, emerged from the back seat.

Two he could have tackled. Tried anyway. Three was asking a lot. Were these Viv's eyes and ears? The jungle drums had drummed fast if they were.

They might of course be acquaintances of yore, traffic offenders who'd been biding their time, or some of his current informants, Willie Ryans come with the answer to the riddle of the universe.

They weren't though. Not here in his personal paddock, on his Englishman's castle doorstep—almost. They weren't carol singers either. He reached the pavement in front of the Peckover family door.

Where were the police when you needed them?

Digging for keys, not looking back, Peckover took the four steps up to the door in two strides, but he wasn't going to be in time. Once perhaps, before the break-in, but no longer, not to open up and get the door between himself and the world. (The shame of that break-in—the bobby burgled, policeman pilfered, rozzer rifled, copper clipped, pillaged, looted! They'd taken the TV, stereo, silver cream jug, Miriam's engagement ring, his policeman's pride, and left not a wrack behind, nor thumbprint.) These days, post break-in, opening the three locks of Fortress Peckover took for ever.

He turned key number one once, twice, in the top lock.

"Mr. Peckover," said a voice at his back.

FIVE

Mister Peckover?

Peckover turned. If he were thumped now, turning, with luck it would be professional, he'd know nothing about it.

Mr. Polite even looked polite, but he stood too close, on the top step, one hand in the pocket of his gaberdine, the other extended for shaking, unless he was a black belt.

Peckover had never seen him before. Medium height, hair a medium, rainy, mouse-colour. He was medium from his spectacles to his shoes, a forgettable clerk, a salesman without panache, medium-happy from nine to five, a member of Mensa at weekends, attending meetings in corduroy and sandals. As a steak he would have arrived medium.

"Can we talk inside, or in the car?" the man said, lowering the extended hand.

Peckover had never seen the hard case standing on the second step either, not in the flesh, but he was Murray. He'd carried Murray's picture with him as had most London coppers. Half his life Murray had lived at the nation's expense, bashing up the timorous who were in for fiddling the books or playing with little boys, snarling at the screws. Australopithecus Man in trawler captain's duffle coat and hood. Do Not Feed.

Number three was a long-haired smiler and another unknown, grinning up from the pavement in the quilted maroon windcheater which had been selling well at Marks and Spencer. When their eyes met, the smile became something between a giggle and a simper.

A crazy, Peckover thought. The three kings bearing gifts of perhaps a razorblade in a spud, a flick-knife or two, maybe a gun if they were mates of Viv. Murray, ruddy-faced in his hood, was weatherbeaten either from hauling in the herring or high blood-pressure. His mates had a prison pallor. By December Londoners were the colour of sliced white Sunblest, but this pasty pair looked as if they hadn't seen sunlight all year.

"This is to your advantage, Mr. Peckover." Mr. Polite's accent was north country. "Invite us in."

"What's your name?"

"Ask us inside. We're getting wet."

"You beauties ever show up 'ere again, I'll break you in pieces. Understood? Understand that, Murray?"

"You terrify me," Murray said.

"I should. Viv was lucky, got 'is nose pushed a bit. For you, every limb, promise you."

"Why not now, copper?"

"Who's the smiler?" said Peckover. "Does it speak?"

The man on the pavement grinned up at Peckover. He looked delighted with himself, the rain, the confabulation on the steps. Life was a party.

Mr. Polite said, "This is friendly, Mr. Peckover." Watery beads dribbled down his spectacles. "You're going to be able to pay off your mortgage. Take trips. A cottage in the country."

"Forgiven and forgotten, has 'e? Got his nose straightened?"

"All everybody wants is peace."

"'Ow much?"

"Ten down. That's goodwill. There could be retainers."

"Negotiable?"

"I don't have that information."

"What do I do?"

"Nothing."

"What I thought."

The bee-drone of a motor grew louder. Mr. Polite, Murray, and the happy grinner, turned their heads. A van rumbled past. Not a police van.

Peckover's difficulty was keeping his voice calm. "What did you say your name was?"

Not saying, Mr. Polite said, "You could have a very merry Christmas, Mr. Peckover."

"'Ow do I get in touch with you if I don't know who you are?"

"We'll get in touch with you. Best Christmas ever. One other thing. You fail the gun course."

"I do, eh?"

"Simpler all round."

That was probably truer than this slice of mouldy bread in front of him, this factory-reject, this squirt of pus, realised. What gun course, and how do you know about it, Peckover wanted to ask, but it would have been a waste of breath, and why give them the pleasure of not answering. Frank Veal was right as usual. Somewhere in London, Viv had eyes and ears.

He said, "When do you talk to your Honourable Viv again?"

The gaberdine shoulders hiked up.

"Because when you do," Peckover said, "ask 'im from me how he got to be so stupid. I'm not a one-man show. If I get no results, the next in line takes over."

"The kitty's bottomless."

Peckover stared. "I don't believe this. You know 'ow many police there are in the CID alone?"

"You might seem to get results. You know how to play along. It wouldn't be forever. You could become rich."

Peckover blinked rain from his eyes and held Mr. Polite's gaze. He looked at sneering Murray, and beyond him at Smiler, who winked.

He said, "When do I start?"

Mr. Polite permitted himself a medium smile, dipped the unshaked hand inside his gaberdine, drew out an envelope, and presented it.

"Ten thousand?" Peckover said, massaging the envelope.

"Why don't we go to the car, count it. Used, untraceable—I don't have to tell you. You've no problem."

"Look, you sleazo," Peckover said, and heard the tremor in his voice. He was not convinced of the wisdom of what he was saying and about to do.

"It's not that I'm not as corrupt as a boil on a baboon's arse. It's just that you don't appeal to me. Any of you. Your unbelievable moron of a Viv least of all."

Backhanded, a wristy, net-skimming stroke on number one court while the customers watched amazed, Peckover flicked the envelope past Mr. Polite's ear. It soared above Murray's hooded head, over thrilled Smiler, hesitated at the peak of its parabola, a luminous, fluttering dove, then dropped in the middle of the road. Murray exclaimed and lumbered in pursuit.

"You show up on my doorstep again, I'm tellin' you, every limb." Peckover's fists bunched the lapels of Mr. Polite's gaberdine and a section of shirt collar and walked him backwards down the steps. When the man missed his footing, Peckover held him suspended. "Piss," he hissed, "off."

"A mistake, bad—ug." Dangling and squirming, fingers round Peckover's wrists, spectacles drizzling rain, Mr. Polite began to choke. Rosiness tinted the prison pallor. "Mistake," he coughed.

"Don't talk to me."

Peckover released Mr. Polite by pushing him into Smiler, who stumbled and grinned, fizzing with pleasure at the party game. In the road, Murray was an agitated monk, his cowl askew, swearing and wiping the envelope on his sleeve. The rumble and glare of the van, or another van, approached. Mr. Polite retreated to the car, at his heels Smiler and cursing Murray. Peckover waited on the pavement until the car drove off. A grey Sierra hatchback, B996 AGN.

He turned keys, went into his house, and in the hall locked and bolted the door.

"Henry, love," Miriam called from above. "That you?"

"Better be," he called back. He hung up his coat. The wet on his face was mainly rain. On his palms and in his pits it was sweat. "Everything all right?"

"No."

"What is it?"

"Sam. He's wicked. He drew something on the blackboard. Miss Taylor made him stand in the corner."

"What did he draw?"

"He won't tell. He wouldn't eat his supper."

"Why? What was supper?"

"Yesterday's coq au vin. Mary ate hers. Come up, the news is starting."

"I will. A minute. Couple of quick phone calls."

Quickish and quiet. No point upsetting Miriam. If Sam wouldn't tell, his Dad wouldn't either. Miriam was upset enough already over the gun course.

In the kitchen he breathed a winey smell from the oven. Dialling, he breathed deeply, trying to calm himself. Barking at some uncomprehending desk sergeant would achieve nothing.

He dialled first the local cop shop because you never knew. Sierra Sue might have run out of petrol at the corner. More likely she had already been abandoned. Flinging the ten thousand hadn't been too bright; there'd be repercussions, God, wouldn't there just, but it'd been a long, bumpy day.

Then he'd phone Veal. Peckover didn't yet know whether he would be snarling at Veal or seeking comfort. Whichever seemed more likely to steady his hands.

*   *   *

The next evening white-haired Bernie said, "Message for you, Henry. Mr. Veal's with the AC and the commander and would you join them in the AC's office?"

"The commander, eh?"

In the lift, after his day on the range, Peckover wondered if he should go first to the washroom, lave away odours of cordite and gun-oil, comb his sharpshooter's locks. Soddit, he thought, let's get it over.

The assistant commissioner's office was less drab than most but it still wasn't the Savoy. There was a poinsettia but it stood on a gunmetal filing cabinet. On one wall were reproductions of Monet's waterlilies, but another was hung with maps of the metropolitan area. Veal sat in one armchair, a stack of files in his lap, and Commander Bill Astle, smoking a cheroot, in the other. On chairs of steel and plastic were Ken Long and Alex Bevans, Murder Squad; Chief Inspector Martin, Drugs Squad; and Mrs. Coulter with pen and pad. They sat in a ragged half-moon round the front of the AC's desk, turning their heads and murmuring a greeting when Peckover came in, except the commander.

If he were about to be tortured they'd have said nothing. If they were going to award him a medal there might have been a standing ovation. He spied *Good Housekeeping* on the AC's desk but had no way of knowing whether this boded well or ill, though probably the latter. No one in the office was his junior in rank so if they felt inclined they could pick on him. Astle was usually inclined. He'd pick on anyone but he was hostile to poets in particular, and Peckover being the only poet he knew, all his anti-poetry wrath had but one place to go. That was Peckover's opinion. He believed Astle to be probably the crabbiest case of male menopause in the annals of medical science, or would be if he'd been documented. One day someone would tell the *Lancet* about Astle and they'd give over a whole issue to him.

The AC's jacket and tie hung on the back of his chair. He wore a white shirt through which showed the horseshoe neckline of his vest. He picked up papers which looked to Peckover like his report on last night's sleazebags. He said, "Good to see you, Henry. How's the firearms training?"

"All right, sir, thank you." He avoided looking at Veal. "Bit parky out there. Frostbite of the trigger finger is the main 'azard."

"Excellent, that's the spirit." The AC's reputation was for being fair, informed, and not above side-stepping the rules if side-stepping might be useful. Weak on the social side. A non-person over the cocktails and canapes. "We're not much further on with Clegg. He had an air ticket. He was flying to New York today. Where his own plane is, God knows, but apparently not in Belize. A Piper Cheyenne, same as the American customs people use, which you could call an irony. Not much progress on your visitors last night either. How would they have known you're on the gun course?"

"I've wondered. It's not top secret."

"So why does Vivian White come up with a bribe now you're about to qualify? Why not last month when he might have hoped to persuade you to keep off the course altogether? Gone sick, pressure of work."

"I assume it's tied in with Clegg. Bit coincidental that Viv's partner gets murdered and next thing I'm in line for a generous payola."

"Go on."

Go where? Peckover, stroking an earlobe, inventing, trying to come across like a thinker, said, "Clegg's been killed." A safe start. "Viv's going to be expecting trouble, questions from his local lot, maybe from us if they ask us over. Either he's guessing that any visitor he gets from the Yard could be the one who nabbed him before, like me, or there's been a little leak. He's immobilising us before we start climbing the ramparts."

The AC looked sceptical and said, "Hm."

"I agree," Peckover said. "Best I can manage till someone comes up with something better."

"Why kill Clegg?"

"Must be scores of people in the drugs racket he might 'ave upset and we know there are some don't fool about." Safe again. Why the hell not kill Clegg? Anyone in his job, dealing with the people he was dealing with, they were asking for it. "Possibly Viv had it done. Sir Peter says they'd had a falling out. Can't see 'ow he'd have known that because there's not too much communication between father and son, far as we understand it. On the other 'and, Viv's wife Gussie —Augusta—she might have been up-to-date. Phone calls across the Caribbean between her and Viv, she could have passed on to her in-laws any tidbits about bad blood between Viv and Clegg." He had their attention. He wished he hadn't. He'd have preferred them yawning and talking among themselves about Arsenal and the new Ford station-wagon. "She's been at Sir Peter's place since Viv went to gaol, or she was, last we heard."

"That right, Frank?"

"Far as we know she's still there," Veal said.

"We've still only Sir Peter's word for a disagreement and we know what that's worth," the AC said.

"Might have been shenanigans while Viv was inside." Why, Peckover asked himself, did no one offer him a chair? He didn't want a chair. He didn't want to be comfortable, settle in, but why didn't anyone offer? "A little double-dealing goes a long way with their kind of money. Money, power, who's running the ship."

"Crime passionelle?"

Peckover tweaked his earlobe and said, *"Passionelle* with who—whom?"

"Come on, Henry," the AC said. "With each other—Viv and Clegg. They fancied each other at Eton, bashed each other's bishops behind the bicycle sheds, that sort of thing." He coughed, and glanced at Mrs. Coulter, who returned the look with a steadfast, woman-of-the-world expression, pencil at the ready. "You dug it up yourself before Viv's trial. They've been mates ever since, maybe more than business mates."

"Eton was fifteen years ago. They're all doing it all the time at those schools, aren't they? After they've left they discover girls." Peckover frowned. "Don't they?"

"Don't ask me."

"No sir. Well, you have a theory. The little I know of Clegg I understood he was Casanova, but he may have been both. Viv's married, not that that says anything. He's certainly different."

"Let's keep it as a theory. We're holding Murray, did you know?"

"No." Cowled, neanderthal Murray. If they were holding him, they should have had him leashed.

"Frank?"

"He's at Rochester Row," Veal told Peckover. "We picked him up at the Can-Can Club. His two mates, he says he met them in a pub last night, never saw them before. But they knew you and were off to hand you a rude Christmas card, take the mickey, so he went along for the fun. One uproarious joke. That's his story and it's so hopeless it could be true, if we didn't know it was a load of rubbish. His lawyer's Hugh Greaves, obnoxious as ever. We can't hold him much longer."

Peckover said, "Attempting to bribe a police officer with a Christmas card. No, I suppose we can't."

A meditative quiet fell, as in a Quaker meeting. Commander Astle blew cheroot smoke, and Peckover thought, here it comes.

"You didn't see this money they gave you?" the commander said.

"No. May not have been money but I fancy it was. All ten thousand of it."

"If you'd hung on to it we'd have had something. You realise that."

"If I'd 'ung ton to it I'd likely have spent it by now," Peckover said, and knew he should not have.

"You were precipitate."

"Those sleazos, they got up—" Why couldn't he just shuffle his feet and say sorry, or better still simply shut up—"my nose."

"Exactly. Seems to me we've been here before. Precipitate, reckless, self-advertising, and flamboyant. It's for you to get up their noses, not them up yours. What do you think?"

The Murder Squad looked at the carpet, the Drugs Squad at the ceiling. Mrs. Coulter doodled a slow spiral on her pad. She gave it ears, eyes.

"Well?" the commander said.

The bugger really wants an answer, Peckover thought. He said, "Yes, well." A nose is a nose is a nose. One man's nose is another man's hooter. He gazed about him as if for a chair.

Veal said, "Don't sit down, Henry. Have you got a couple of hours?"

"I'm going to be 'ung up by my thumbs?"

"You're going to see if you can pick out Murray's mates. The polite one and the smiler. Five hundred happy head-and-shoulder shots waiting for you below. Could be more. Full-face and profile. At least you're not turning pages any more. Feed the beast, switch on, tap the button, *voilà.*"

Thanks, Frank, thanks for the out, old matey. With a "Right away" for Veal, a "Sir" and a nod for the AC, and nothing for the commander—though with difficulty he resisted sticking out his tongue and wiggling his ears—Peckover skedaddled briskly.

He'd have to watch out. Any more sins and he'd be absolutely top of the list for trekking into the jungle to ferret out Viv.

Top of the list he presumably already was. Expendable 'Enry. Those who live by the rhyming dictionary shall die by the tsetse-fly and a round between the eyes from Viv's hunting rifle.

Viv's replacement pilot, Flight Lieutenant Julian Lumley, RAF, decided he would need a gun. Something that would go in his pocket. He would have to find out how to use it, unless there was nothing more to it than aiming and pulling the trigger, and he doubted that.

On looks, Lumley would have been central casting's choice for the clean, fair-haired English flyer who is shot to pieces by Messerschmitts before the film is half over. Or for the role of Rupert Brooke, pale, doomed poet and period-piece unaccountably missed by Hollywood. Not that Lumley's looks were quite so fresh-facedly boyish these days as central casting might have wished. The eyes were a little bloodshot.

Having decided about the gun, Lumley believed he felt easier in his mind. He felt nauseated too, but he could cope with that. It was the havering, the failing to make up his mind, which had been sending him potty.

He had killed people but at long distance where they'd had no faces. He had helped sink a ship. His stomach was sick because this pocket-size thing wasn't going to be at all the same, if ever he had to use it.

"Same again, Bobby," he said, sliding his glass across the counter.

The piped music in the bar of the air-conditioned Fort George Hotel in Belize was at present syrupy strings. The last time he had seen Jeremy Clegg had been here, three weeks ago. Same bar, same exemplary barman, same customers, or similar. Business types and fit Yankee tourists with snorkelling gear and underwater cameras on their way to or back from the Barrier Reef Hotel on Ambergris Caye. Jeremy had sat at the bar wearing a plaid tam-o'-shanter low over his eyes to annoy the British clientele who wanted the Fort George to be Claridge's. They had talked about flying, as they always did, each embroidering his stories for laughs.

Lumley sipped, keeping the ice at bay with his upper lip. Clegg had been a danger-junkie. No real surprise he was abruptly dead. If there hadn't been danger, drugs would not have held Clegg's interest for five minutes. It had been a game, like a night of baccarat for sky-high stakes.

It's not a game with me, Lumley assured himself. He would step into dead Clegg's boots for a half-dozen trips and that would be it. Six trips, eight maybe, would set him up. Then the weirdo Vivian White would have to look for someone else.

A chance like this, you'd have to be feeble-minded not to grab it. The RAF had taught him to fly—fine. They'd got their mileage from him and soon would be retiring him. Out on the street and with what? A bunch of gongs, a farewell

party in the mess, a pension which would take care of the
bread, but no jam, and if he wasn't run down by a bus, another fifty years to live and do what with? Martini salesman?
Insurance?

Better the bus than spend those years in prison, but it
didn't have to be either. If Clegg had carried a gun he might
still have been around, uncorking the fizz, daisy-chaining
from one woman to the next.

The RAF Regiment had guns in their armoury. No way
he was getting involved in that.

Viv might fix him up. Conversely, Viv might refuse, perhaps scream at him for even suggesting it. Rumour had it
that Viv had an arsenal at Casa Verde big enough to equip a
battalion. But he was so weird he probably insisted his pilots
go into battle nude, carrying a bible and the rules of the Eton
Wall Game.

In a funny dump like Belize you probably had only to ask.
All those natty creeps peddling the stuff and sidling up to
you on Queen Street and in Regent Square, some of them
had a gun stuffed down their shirt.

"Bobby? Same again and one for yourself."

Bobby wore a starched white jacket. He made the snor-
kellers happy with his rum Kickers, Flanagans, Beach-
combers, Zombies, Wedding Nights, and his own Fort
George Fire-Alarms, which he made a big theatrical commotion about being a secret recipe, though they were obviously
simply rum, lime juice, and too much tabasco. In Lumley's
opinion, Bobby also knew the precise moment when a cus-
tomer was too happy to look at his change. The new Villa
Hotel was making overtures, trying to lure him, so Bobby
said. But his loyalty was not for sale, he next would say.
Self-respect was more precious than dollars. The tradition of
excellence here, the dedication of the staff, the class of cus-
tomer, were second to none in the Caribbean, and he was
not to be bought.

Jesus wept, what a hypocritical snob! And a bloody good
barman.

"Bobby, listen. I've a mate at the base who's peeing his
pants he's so scared. It's over some Indian woman. Her
brothers are these cornerboys who say they're going to chop
him up. They'll do it slowly with machetes. Where would he
find a gun to defend himself?"

SIX

After failing to pick out Murray's mates, and having had to tap the button a second time for the last zillion shots because he had not, he realised, been looking at them, he had become cross-eyed and comatose, Peckover walked to Rochester Row. Murray scowled in his cell, sneered, and turning his back, told him he was wasting his time. A Christmas card was his story, and that was that.

Lumps of sleet sloshed on the windshield. From Radio Four Peckover learned that gilts were supported by the hope of lower interest rates. Jolly good. What could be nicer? Christmas was coming and Murray wasn't going to be on his doorstep.

Only empty milk bottles were on the doorstep. Inside, the heating had been turned down, if not off. Miriam, in her slip, hairbrush in hand, was on her way to bed. She came down the stairs and said, "Had a lovely day playing with your gun?"

"Please, not now."

"Drill your little target full of nice little holes?"

"Love, we've been over this. I'm a policeman. The gun is to defend myself with should the occasion arise. It won't. I'll never 'ave to use it." He felt as she did about it. The irony was that she put him on the defensive. With no one else did he find himself excusing and explaining what he was being taught to do. "I'm going to look at the children."

"Won't you be shooting those men you were outside with last night?"

Foot on the bottom stair, he halted. "Who told you?"

"Mrs. Beresford. There were three. You threw a letter or something and started pushing them about."

"They were trying to buy me." He continued up the stairs. "It's over and they'll not be back. Mrs. Beresford the one with the net curtains and binoculars?"

"Do they have guns?"

"Course they don't."

"It's to do with Vivian White, isn't it?"

"It's nothing to do with Vivian White or anyone. It's finished, done with. Leave it, please."

"If they come back, I'm leaving. I'm taking the children to Maggie's, I asked her and she said yes. I'm not having them here with you and your criminals and guns on our doorstep."

Hand on the door of the children's room, Peckover paused again. Miriam had a point but he was never going to admit it to her. He went in and bent to look at sleeping Sam, then Mary. Mary, prone, spreadeagled, uncovered, had turned through a quarter circle and slept crossways, on top of Potato, a chewed, disreputable, insanitary rag doll there was no sleeping or even existing without. Miriam picked Mary up, rearranged her direction, tucked the blankets round her, and placed Potato by her head.

On the landing Peckover said, "Is there anything in the oven? I'll get it, don't come down."

"Frightened I'll see gangsters out of the kitchen window?"

"I'm more frightened I'll plug you between the eyes, kid, if you keep on like this."

"You haven't brought it here!"

"One in each pocket, three in the car."

She came down and set a place at the kitchen table while he looked for peanuts, poured red wine, asked if she would like one, and heard the expected no.

"What's supper?"

"Hare with lavender."

"You're not joking either."

"It's your favorite."

He had never heard of it but hare with lavender was par for Miriam. With Sam at school, and down the street an unemployed philosophy graduate delighted to have money in her purse for looking after Mary for four hours a day, Miriam had returned part-time as caterer at the Royal Archeological Society, whence she would bring home cook's perks—leftovers. Usually the archeologists left—which is to say left alone, as in avoided—the experimental dish which Miriam would try to include in each day's menu. Over the years

Peckover had grown accustomed to see set in front of him such adventurings as waterzoi, which was a kind of freshwater bouillabaisse of pike and eel; a nameless but heavily seasoned salad of raw, sliced Brussels sprouts, olives, oysters, and barbecued chicken gizzards; and myhee molee. The name *myhee molee* stayed, lurching and burping in memory, after the composition of the dish had faded, though it may have been the fish in coconut milk. Sam and Mary played with these meals, eating parts of them, spitting out others. Peckover feared for their digestions and wondered if they would grow up Escoffiers or fiends for bangers and mash.

"What you said at the start, weeks ago, how you'd never be bringing a gun into the house," Miriam said. "That's still true, isn't it?"

"Yes."

"Sam's not going to open a drawer and find a loaded gun there?"

"Every gun is handed back and goes into the safe. I've told you. No exceptions. If it's taken from its holster, you report it. If it's fired, you report it in spades, you don't clean it, you don't touch it, it goes to forensics for tests. No gun will ever come 'ome with me. Most likely I'll never 'ave to carry one. All right? Now, this isn't at all bad, quite heady, but what's this?" Peckover, munching, probed with his fork. "Is it the lavender? Bit of old lace? I might mention it to Mrs. Beresford, she'll have an opinion."

He should probably have a word with Mrs. Beresford, ask her to keep her binoculars trained, because he doubted he'd seen the last of last night's visitors, whether on his doorstep or somewhere equally unexpected. Question was, next time would they be upping the ante, like to twenty thousand, or trying something different?

On Wednesday at Lippett's Hill, Peckover scored six out of ten on the sense-of-direction shoot at seven yards, three out of ten at fifteen yards, and zero on aim-shooting at twenty-five yards. Overall score, thirty per cent. He was improving. In the next practice he twice hit the target at twenty-five yards. Forty per cent overall.

Minimum percentage required to pass the firearms-training final classification shoot: seventy.

In the afternoon, Murray walked out of Rochester Row police station with Hugh Greaves, M.A., Ll.B. The police station lacked doormen for hailing taxis, but a taxi coming out of Vincent Square pulled up. The driver switched on his sidelights. At half-past four the street lights were already on. In another thirty minutes daylight would have gone entirely and good riddance, since all day it had never managed better than an opaque dinginess. Murray and his lawyer climbed in and the taxi, driven by Detective Constable Wharton in an anorak and knitted green cap, headed towards Vauxhall Bridge Road.

An anonymous Ford Escort which had followed the taxi out of Vincent Square continued to follow. At the wheel, DC Bottomley cursed a motor cyclist who cut in and slowed, forcing the Escort to slow and miss the lights at Vauxhall Bridge Road. "Bleedin' lark tailing anyone in this place," he muttered.

"Think yoursel' lucky it isn't rush-hour," DC Frith said.

"It's always rush-hour."

"Cushier than Saturday's CND demo's going to be. Wake me if anything happens."

As far as his seatbelt allowed, Frith made a performance of slumping down in the passenger seat, but he kept his eyes open.

They sighted and eventually caught up with the dawdling taxi. The lawyer got out at Charing Cross. The cab headed north with Murray, crossing Bloomsbury, skirting King's Cross, penetrating into Islington.

"Doesn't Our 'Enry live here somewhere?" Bottomley said.

"Does he?" said Frith. "Keep a distance. Not so close."

The taxi ploughed through Islington to Finsbury Park and deposited Murray outside a terraced house on Seven Sisters Road. Murray paid the driver, rang the bell, and was admitted by a teenage girl in an Aran jersey and jeans.

"See?" Bottomley said. "Molesting a minor. Eighteen months and a hard time from his mates inside. Who is she?"

"His violin teacher. They're going to do duets."

The Escort followed the taxi round the corner into Portland Rise and stopped behind it. Frith got out. DC Wharton adjusted his cap and said, "He gave me a three-quid tip. Is it mine or do I hand it in?"

"Who was the girl?"

"How would I know? There was a fish and chip shop a half mile back, you might be needing it. He's all yours, chum."

The taxi drove off. Bottomley swung the Escort back into Seven Sisters Road and parked fifty yards from the house in the gloom between street lamps, near a phone box, probably vandalised. But it worked. Frith called the Yard and was told to continue surveillance. After two hours Murray and the girl came from the house, the girl now in a fur coat, beret, and leg-warmers. They got into a black Honda and drove to Wembley.

The stadium was freezing. The breath of parading dogs in coloured jackets pumped into the floodlit air. Neither Frith nor Bottomley had ever seen greyhound racing. The punters were sparse, fewer than a thousand, most of them huddled on the lower terraces which faced the bookmakers and their blackboards with chalked, changing odds. Murray and the girl had bought racecards and queued at the Tote. Now they stood on the first ledge of the terrace. From a high terrace the detectives watched them.

"If he's meeting someone, he could do worse than here," Bottomley said.

They took turns keeping a distant eye on Murray and the girl, seeking sustenance from trips for hot-dogs and tea, reporting back to the Yard, and in the case of Frith, fluttering. Frith decided this was to be his night, bet on five of the eight races, and lost seventeen pounds. The Yard told Bottomley the address in Seven Sisters Road was the home of Sandra Clark, née Murray. Eddie Clark, her husband, was in the Scrubs for breaking and entering, assault, and GBH. She was Murray's daughter and she wasn't a minor. She was nineteen and could drink, drive, and vote.

Other than the clerks behind the windows at the Tote, father and daughter approached no one, and no one approached them. They shouted at the sprinting dogs, stamped their feet and waved their arms, jumped in the air and hugged each other, and hustled to and from the Tote.

After the last race Frith tore his ticket in two and said, "So can we go home now?"

Murray and his daughter were at pay windows at the Tote.

"Watch out," Bottomley said.

Murray had wheeled and was bearing down on the detectives. There was no evading him. Sandra, hugging herself in her fur coat, hung back.

"I ought to do you two, sue you, invasion of privacy." Murray, bruiser's face thrust into the face of Frith, then Bottomley, folded banknotes into his wallet. "You're not worth it. You're rubbish. Your 'Enry Peckover's a genius compared to you two."

On Thursday, Peckover's percentage scores in practice shoots were less than genius level but still improving. Forty-five, sixty, and twenty. Fail. Sergeant McMaster passed on a message that Mr. Veal had rung and would he stop by the Yard when he got back to London.

Radio Four described in detail Christmas customs round the world, as it did every Christmas. Children in Holland and Belgium filled their wooden shoes with hay for a white horse on which Santa arrived. Peckover didn't believe it. Today, in Holland and Belgium, wooden shoes? In Ireland, the day after Christmas, children killed a wren, painted their faces, and went from door to door collecting money to bury the wren. He believed that.

Before Veal-time, a beer. He bought an evening paper, went into the Feathers, and sat on a red velveteen bar stool with a pint and peanuts, leafing through the *Standard.* An inside page reported the funeral service and cremation at Melton Mowbray of brutally slain Old Etonian playboy Jeremy Clegg. The story recapitulated the murder and quoted a Scotland Yard spokesperson asking that anyone having seen two fair-haired men, middle-twenties, wearing dark overcoats, in or near Wellington Square at or around 2:30 p.m., Monday, contact their nearest police station.

"Going to assist us in our inquiries, are they?" Peckover said in Veal's office, taking off his coat. "Before you tell me, would you mind stopping swivelling. It'll upset your stomach. It's worse than watching Wimbledon."

Veal stopped swivelling. Studying a print-out, he said, "Patricia Wilson, thirty-two, divorced, tenant of the flat beneath Clegg's flat—that's to say the girlfriend's flat—was leaving the building at half two when she saw this pair coming in." He looked up. "Except she didn't."

"She'll make a sensational witness."

"Seems they passed on the stairs but she didn't look. She was rushing and checking her passport and stuff in her handbag. She thinks they may have had short fair hair, dark coats, and were tall, one taller than the other—that can happen. They might have been youngish because she has the impression they came up the stairs nimbly. She's spent half today with Simmonds and his Photofit magic getting nowhere. Faceless Man, Late Twentieth Century."

"She sure they were people? Couldn't they have been prize-winning marrows?"

"Only things she's sure of is one of them was wearing, maybe both of them"—Veal consulted the print-out—"Paco Rabanne."

"Where do you wear that?"

"You sprinkle it, splash it."

"Never 'eard of it. She must have educated nostrils. What is she, a cosmetician?"

"In fact, yes. She's a buyer for Selfridges. The ground floor halls with the reek of lipstick and lotions. She was off to Paris. She's always off somewhere. She'd never heard of Clegg until she got back home today."

"Quite the executive class in Wellington Square. Clegg on Concorde. The girlfriend modelling in Rome. Mrs. Wilson at scent-smellings on the Rue Chanel."

"It's something. The time's right and there were two did Clegg in."

"So all you 'ave to do is round up the usual suspects, like everyone who's bought a bottle of Paco Thing in the last five years."

"Look at these." Veal handed across the desk a shiny wad of photographs. They were about ten inches square, the size of stills once displayed in glass cases outside cinemas. "Take your time."

After studying the first few, Peckover said, "Clegg's funeral, is it?" He looked at the next photograph, and the next. There were a score. "Lovely teeth, some of 'em. Even the vicar looks like a brood mare. The Reverend National Velvet. What's 'e smiling about? I 'aven't seen Viv yet."

"You won't. He's in Belize. Campos called again. He wants help."

"Don't we all. Who am I looking for? The doorstep boys —Murray's mates?"

"That'd be manna, Henry. Just anyone you might know."

Peckover scrutinised the photographs. They showed family in mourning filing out of a church. He arrived where he started and passed them back.

He said, "Too bad. Where do we go from 'ere?"

"Not we, Henry. You. Good grief, a holiday in the sun, all paid? There's not one in the CID wouldn't give an arm and a leg." Veal fondled his moustache. "Have you told Miriam?"

"Told 'er what?"

"You're right. Nothing's certain till it happens—Veal's First Law of Life. Good luck tomorrow."

Before tomorrow, home and the evening's reheated timbale of mutton, prunes, and chopped samphire, with beets in anchovy sauce, shunned—nay, fled from—earlier in the day by the archeologists.

Miriam, eating sparingly, believed the timbale might have benefitted from capers. Her husband asked if it might bring on side effects because tomorrow he had to be fit in mind and body. Not that he wasn't always, but tomorrow would be particularly testing.

In bed, Miriam closed the *AA Road Book to France*, which she was in the habit of dreaming along with when London was at its bleakest, as now. She took off her reading glasses, put glasses and book on the bedside table, switched off her light, and said, "Do you want to?"

"Must we? You know I don't."

Peckover closed *Anna Karenina*, put it aside, and turned off his light. He hoped he would finish it before his eightieth birthday; he had a couple of other books on his list, but it was stupendously long, especially at the rate of two pages per day, sometimes per week. He hadn't yet made up his mind about Anna either, though, he was nearly halfway through. He sympathised, who wouldn't, but he didn't think he'd want to have known her.

He said, "Please, how many more times. It's for self-defence only, it'll never come into the house, and Sam and Mary will never get their hands on it or even see it. What's so funny?"

"They've seen it hundreds of times. As for getting their hands on it, it's the last thing. Aren't we at cross purposes?"

"Oh. All the same, I should be conserving my resources for tomorrow, the big event, like athletes do." He plumped his pillow, lay back, emitted a sound somewhere between a sigh and a cheerful grunt, and turned to her. "Vamp."

"Satyr."

"Scarlet woman."

SEVEN

Bang, bang, bang, bang—twa-a-annnng!

Two-handed, thumb on thumb, arms reaching, Peckover squeezed the trigger. And again. And again. His ears screamed. He was wearing the most threadbare, ineffectual ear-muffs at Lippett's Hill or anywhere in the western world. Stereophonic ear-muffs, cobweb-thin museum pieces worn to tatters from years of pummelling from volley after volley of amplified, exploding shells. Custom-designed ear-muffs for enhanced pleasure in listening expressly to Tchaikovsky's *1812* Overture, allowing the cannon-fire to resonate in its fullest glory.

Down on his knee. Reload. Get it right for once, dammit. The range was a deep-freeze, perfect for New Zealand lamb. His fingers fumbled. It had been like this when he was a boy, winter time, seeing and holding your untied shoelaces but unable to feel and tie them.

Up. Legs splayed, knees bent, bum back, arms rigid, pointing.

Bang, bang, bang . . .

The final classification shoots were two sense-of-direction at seven yards, one at fifteen yards, and two aim-shooting at twenty-five yards. Each man fired fifty rounds. Peckover was distractedly aware of Dews and Sherborne, to right and left, going great guns, ha-ha, geddit? In half an hour it was over. The instructors with their clipboards of names and scores retired to confer. The dozen policemen drove to The Owl to await them.

They knew they had passed, with the one exception. The wisdom handed down from course to course was that if you hadn't passed you would know before the celebration, so if you had nothing to celebrate you could be absent. But there had been horrifying surprises, famous in police history, where a celebrant on his fourth beer had been taken aside and told, sorry, chum. Peckover with his pint was an older, more senior, and slightly isolated figure among these babes. They were friendly, sympathetic, and suffered with smiles and shrugs the few who offered premature congratulations. In silence he cursed the Chinese, who had invented gunpower, Smith and Wesson, whoever they'd been, Colt, Winchester, Sten, Bren, Howitzer, Maxim, Gatling, Signor Beretta, Herr Luger, Mr. Browning—not Robert Browning, *The best is yet to be,* oh yeah?—and all the mischief-makers, including Nobel and his dynamite, and he hoped to God he had passed because he couldn't stomach another two weeks of this in the New Year; he'd apply first for transfer to dog-handling, or the car-clamp unit. The pass-fail assessment was on performance throughout the course, on which he had to be below average; on the written exam, where he guessed he had a hundred per cent or close, because he'd never failed a written exam, and this one had been for idiots, if you had listened and read up on your notes; and the final shoot. He watched Dews laughing and yammering, passing out pints, aching for the ninety per cent which would lift him into marksman category. When the instructors came in, one-eyed Angus McSixgun carrying a briefcase as well as a clipboard, the trainees applauded and whistled. The barmaids and regulars had seen the ritual before, but they looked on in expectation.

Beer arrived for the instructors. Sergeant McMaster fished from his briefcase an envelope, took out of the envelope a pack of pink cards, and began to distribute them alphabetically. Each presentation elicited applause and ribaldry.

"Constable Ainsley." Cheers and jeers. "Constable Dews —top marks, laddie. Well done."

Cheers, back-slapping. Top marks for this course, but not ninety per cent, not marksman status, Peckover guessed, observing Dew's forced grin, a child's suppressed distress at getting the book, not the bicycle.

"Sergeant Grimshaw." Cheers. "Constable Holt." A tepid cheer, elsewhere a cat-call, and from someone a half-heard comment best left undecoded, Holt being a snake.

Inspector Martin...cheers. Constable Partridge... cheers. Chief Inspector Peckover—

An eruption of cheering. West Ham had won the cup,

income tax had been abolished, and the Queen was coming for tea. The assembly whooped and stamped. The staff behind the bar, and regulars in corners, grinned at the source of all that was clearly clean, noble, and glorious, whom they had never seen before in their lives.

"A wee bit slow at the start, sir, but steady, building all the time, just as the lassies like it, and today a fine and stirring climax—seventy per cent for the shoot," said Sergeant McMaster.

Smiling in spite of himself, and the appalling sergeant, and not too sheepishly, he hoped, Peckover allowed his hand to be shaken, his back to be slapped. He resisted calling for drinks all round, for the moment anyway. He'd paid already in 10-p penalties for more than enough of the beer being swilled.

Two hours later, eight in the morning local time, temperature twenty-one Celsius and clammily rising, the news reached Casa Verde, Belize. Outside, mosquitoes hovered in patient squadrons. Inside, Papitos buffed the living room floor.

"Piss off," Vivian White told Papitos, and waited, holding the telephone against his chest.

He wore a kimono with a chrysanthemum pattern which Jeremy had given him three Christmases ago. Oh God. Tasteless, fake kimono from some gimcrack boutique on the King's Road which the idle bugger had gone into because it was there and he couldn't be bothered to grab a taxi to Harrods five minutes away.

Oh, the hell.

Luis had brought breakfast only moments before the telephone had rung. Now the orange-juice was warming, the toast and coffee were cooling.

Christmas together, with Augusta, here at Casa Verde, like it or not. She wouldn't like it. Sorry, Augusta. You may have no choice. We think we know a way.

He watched unhurried Papitos gathering dusters, a pail. She needed a stoat up her skirt, make her move. He switched the telephone to his left hand, picked white sleep from the corners of his eyes, demolished it between the tips of thumb and forefinger, and wiped the smear from the bridge of his nose with his ring finger, girdled by a gold wedding-ring.

"Yes, go on," he said into the phone.

"He passed."

He passed. Would, wondered Viv, the Giacometti go well

with a mate? He might phone the gallery. Meanwhile he'd try it for a spell on the piano.

"Are you there? Hello? Did ye hear?"

The Hockneys no longer pleased, he admitted it. Sheen and shine, nothing there that hadn't been there the first time he had seen them. Definitely he would call the gallery.

"Look, you Honourable steaming turd, there's no way anyone can fail if he passes, or can pass if he fails, so don't blame me. I told you, we're three of us. Every score is cross-checked. D'ye still nae get it? Here's something else. You can have your sodding money back. Are ye there?"

No, he wasn't there. Viv hung up, walked across the living room to the Giacometti on the television, and moved it to the piano. He was thinking so sanely and creatively that he knew beyond question his IQ was pure gold.

One. If Peckover or any other shithead from Scotland Yard came close to him, with or without a gun, he would kill him and bury him in the jungle.

Two. Augusta should be here for a family Christmas because she was his wife and her place was with him.

Three. He would be prepared for the mission to fail, to not even take off, because he needed a team, and people let you down. *De l'audace, encore de l'audace, et toujours de l'audace.* Who said that?

Four. The team. Priority Immediate. Lumley and a co-pilot. Papitos. Billy Ponsonby.

Papitos knew about babies. No problem there.

Lumley, if today was impossible for him, then tomorrow, or the day after. Not Monday, consignment day. After Monday was getting close to Christmas.

Gulf Air Charter would come up with a co-pilot, at a price. For this trip it was a jet or nothing because he wasn't spending a week up in the clouds in some rattletrap biplane flown by a weekend charlie in goggles and a silk scarf.

Billy Ponsonby would giggle and come in with sea and land transport for auld lang syne. He might, if he were still in Nassau. Since Eton they'd met only three or four times. He might be dead, his head broken by one of his pick-ups, pockets and drawers rifled, or more likely from the disease too dread to mention, except every day it was on the front page. Pay-off for Billy, his pound of flesh, would be eight inches of his own flesh, for auld lang syne.

Billy had better check out the abandoned military airstrip on Cat Caye, see it had not been blown up, or tourist chalets built on it. Cays in Belize, cayes in the Bahamas. Potty. The Colombians had been using Cat Caye for refuelling so it should be okay. The transport he wanted wasn't going to land on a beach, or on his father's lawn.

Viv sat by the telephone and opened his address book. After all this, target practice. This morning he would slather himself with the bug-bomb. The stuff stank and he would still be bitten but it was worth it. Nude shooting. He'd come like a cannon.

The office smelled of cheroot smoke. Chief Superintendent Veal said, "Let's see it then."

"See what?" Peckover said, though he knew.

"The pink card."

"You've seen them. You 'ad one yourself."

"I want to see yours. Seeing's believing."

"You're peculiar," said Peckover, but not without a perverse satisfaction he took out his wallet and slid from behind his blue warrant card his authorisation to carry a gun: Form 6590, pink, no photograph, date-stamped for four months. He passed it to swivelling Veal.

"You haven't signed it."

"'Aven't 'ad time." Peckover selected a ballpoint from the selection in the Dundee marmalade jar on the desk, signed, and returned the card to his wallet. "So, the gents who sent Clegg to the Golden Shore, got 'em under lock and key?"

"Who's Clegg? I've fifty other things going on here. Astle says Drugs have talked to every known dealer, pusher, importer and exporter in town, and no gang war, he's sure of it. So if it isn't that, what is it?" Veal, swivelling, stroked his moustache. "D'you ever get the feeling you've had enough, you just wish it would all go away?"

"What other feeling is there?"

"Like me to confess? I was plotting today to filch your place, take off for the sun instead of you. All right, not plotting—dreaming. The AC'd never wear it."

"And you'd have to retake the gun course."

"Dammit, why're you so sour about a miserable bloody gun? In your shoes, if I were meeting up with Viv on his turf, you'd think just knowing how to shoot straight would be a comfort."

"Thy rod and thy box of hundred-and-twenty-five-grain, semi-jacketed, semi-wadcutter bullets they comfort me."

Veal ceased swivelling and leaned forward across the desk, hands clasped in front of him. "Henry, you give yourself tomorrow off. Take the children to the zoo. Buy your salt tablets and sun oil and snorkelling gear. You don't need jabs. There's malaria, I expect you'll get it, but you don't actually die of it, not usually. I'll fix a briefing for Sunday. Mrs. Coulter has your ticket. Eleven A.M. for Miami, somewhere round eleven. Then a bit of a wait."

"Like all day. Permission to see Disney World, sir?"

"Alan Moss in Drugs will be going with you. You get along with him, don't you?"

"Wouldn't imagine so. Frank?"

"What?"

"I've this strange sensation you think you're serious."

"Ring Mrs. Coulter tomorrow about your traveller's cheques and currency. They use some kind of dollar."

"Frank?"

"What now?"

"Where the sod's Belize?"

Supper, the archeologists having hit the plaice and chips, was leftover paupiettes of lamb stuffed with chopped liver and kumquats. Peckover blamed the conspiracy of flashy young fashionable chefs and food writers who had to make their name somehow and had cornered the food space in the glossy magazines and serious newspapers. Miriam was a real cook. Her blind spot was that she read these people, and they fed her fears that she might be missing something if she did not at least go ahead, experiment, and try.

The paupiettes, in fact, tasted less bizarre than they sounded, though they would have been better without the liver and kumquats. Over the Stilton, Peckover told her he might be flying to Belize on Monday for two or three days.

She asked if he would be taking his gun. He said he didn't have a gun, he had a piece of pink paper, and if he tried to take a gun through the detector, he'd be smothered and trodden into the ground before the buzzer had finished buzzing. The smothering and treading would be performed by ten men bigger than he was who wouldn't have been there a moment ago and who would haul him off and put him in a sack and wrap chains round it, like Houdini, never mind he was a working copper.

They took coffee and cognac into the sitting room and sat on the sofa with Volume Two of the 1960 *Children's Britannica,* bought second-hand in the expectation that Sam and Mary might be thirsters after knowledge one day, if not quite yet. The entries hopped from Belgrade to Bell, Alexander Graham. No mention of Belize.

"It wasn't Belize when this was published, it was something else," Miriam said. "Honduras? British Honduras? It's tiny and has beaches and fishing. You'll eat tuna. None of the buildings are above two or three storeys high."

"How do you know all this?"

"The Queen went there. It was on television. It was the only country in the Commonwealth she'd never visited." Miriam flipped the pages. "Wasn't it one of the places that said no to that garbage barge from New York—Long Island —which sailed on and on trying to dump its garbage, like the Flying Dutchman?"

"Are you feeling all right?"

"It's next to somewhere communist which wants to take it over. I think. So anyway the army's there. Our army, and a bit of the air force."

"That's the Falklands, featherhead."

"Featherhead yourself. It's Belize. The Queen ate gibnut. That was in the papers, I've never heard 'gibnut' spoken so I don't know if the *g*'s soft like giblet or hard like gibbous."

"Gibbous? What the hell's gibbous?"

"Gibbous, for heaven's sake. You're the port. Moons are gibbous. Here, is this it?"

The entry under British Honduras included a map of Central America and a photograph of a river with mahogany logs on the bank.

"Capital, Belize," Miriam read out. "See? Falklands, honestly. How do you manage to be so ignorant."

"Hard work and a touch of luck. Guatemala's where it's next to. And Mexico, look, a corner of it."

Startled, and apprehensive, Peckover stared at Central America. Nicaragua, El Salvador. These were places one read about but didn't actually go to. He had never had the urge to go. Were they the Caribbean? He supposed they must be, geographically. But they didn't play cricket.

He read aloud, "'Chief exports: Timber, chicle gum—for chewing gum—citrus fruits and frozen seafoods.' Do we need chicle gum? I could bring you some for your archeologists, serve it with gibnut. 'Maya and Carib Indians in the interior...'"

Would Vivian White be in the interior when they met? If they met. Or on a beach, or astride a mahogany log, or in the city, dragging laundry bags of dollars to the bank?

"You won't need your raincoat," Miriam said. "December's the dry season, start of it."

Now silent, now commenting, Peckover and Miriam read the article, which was not long.

"'... hard to draw a firm line between the different races but there are not many pure white people,'" Peckover read out. "Sounds all right except for these 'stinging and biting insects.' Wish you were coming, love. If it 'appens. Doesn't say anything 'ere about gibnuts but I'll bring you a 'alf pound if I see any."

"You'll have a job getting them through customs. They're rats and they're big as pigs."

When the doorbell rang, Miriam raised herself on one elbow and said into the dark, "Henry?"

Peckover was already out of bed, groping for his dressing-gown. Hand on the banister, he took the stairs three at a time. In the sitting room the clock was chiming the half hour, though whether half past midnight, one, two, or what, he could not have said. He drew the curtain a couple of inches aside and looked out.

They wore scarves over the lower part of their faces. Why? There was no mistaking them. They knew he'd know them, so they wanted him to know, though come question-time he was never going to be hand-on-heart certain. Neither would anyone else who might see them. And they'd have alibis safe as mother love.

First the money, now the muscle. They had a new car at the kerb, a cream hatchback. This time Mr. Polite stood in the road, scarf round his face, watching No. 32, Collins Cross, through his spectacles. Murray on the top step, ringing the bell. Smiler on the pavement, maybe smiling, maybe not. No way of knowing.

Smiler swung his arm. Something crashed through the sitting room window, billowing the curtain into Peckover's face.

Peckover reached the front door knowing he would regret what he was about to do, not knowing what it would be, but he was going to hurt them so they would never leave hospital, not functioning as they functioned now. He was trembling. The locks were more quickly opened from inside than from outside.

"Henry?" Miriam called from the top of the stairs.

"Get back in the bedroom!"

He opened the door. Murray, cowled in his trawler captain's duffle coat, woolly scarf over his nose, hit him on the side of the head with something hard. Peckover fell partly on the step, partly inside the door, dressing-gown flapping, one bare leg twisted beneath him.

He hoped Murray would not hit him a second time. Murray, above him, held a wooden mallet, the sort Miriam pulverised veal escalopes with. From the way the scarf below the bulge of the nose made little blowing and sucking movements, he was speaking, telling him something. Still mouthing, watching him, Murray started backing down the steps. A car passed along the street, except it didn't pass. It stopped.

The two men who got out wore dark overcoats and hoods which were brown paper shopping-bags with eyeholes. It's a show, it's street theatre, Peckover thought. The car was a Rover. He tried to read the registration, reaching for the railing to pull himself up.

The men with hoods carried automatic pistols, which they fired in silent bursts at point-blank range. One fired first at Smiler, then at Mr. Polite. The other fired at Murray, who had started to run and had achieved four or five strides before he was hit.

The pair climbed back into the Rover and drove away, leaving Murray, Smiler, and Mr. Polite dead in the road.

EIGHT

The first patrol cars arrived in two minutes, on their roofs frost like sugar. Peckover gave the Rover's registration, AAJ 258P, and refused offers of transport to Islington General Hospital.

Within ten minutes police swarmed in Collins Cross. Lights shone from every house. Householders peeped from behind curtains or watched wrapped and shivering in doorways, some venturing down the steps to ask questions for which the police had no answers. In his bathroom Peckover washed with care, impressed by the swelling on his temple. He shaved, dabbed the raw area with Dettol, and dressed in a sombre suit and tie because come daylight, if not sooner, the brass would be having words with them. The commissioner himself, more than likely. His head throbbed. So much for the day off, showing the children the zoo.

The children were not going to be available for the zoo anyway. Miriam, not speaking to him, had already dressed. She had telephoned her sister and now was dressing the children. All she would say was, "Anyone else would have a doctor look at it but you're such a hero."

The street was cordoned off. Spotlights and searchlights from the police cars made Collins Cross outside No. 32 as bright as Piccadilly. Veal arrived and told Peckover to clear off to the out-patients and have his head attended to.

"Thought you said it wasn't a gang war," Peckover said.

"Not me," Veal said. "Bill Astle said it. Still, name me the gangsters. None of our lot fits this. They just don't do it."

"They just have." Peckover returned a wave from Ken Long, Murder Squad, across the street. "Someone has."

Commander Astle arrived in a radio-cab, and Dr. Matthews, pathologist, in his ostentatiously peasant-chic Citroen 2CV with galloping red rust, side windows swinging, and canvas roof patched with free samples of Elastoplast. Then the first night-shift reporters, soon to match the police in numbers: saturation coverage from the *Mail, Sun,* and *Mirror.* Encumbered television crews scrambled with cameras, cables, and unnecessary generators, and called to policemen to move out of the way. The commander instructed they be kept at bay, he'd speak to them later. He, no one else—understood?

Still unsatisfied, coughing cheroot smoke into the wind, Commander Astle demanded reinforcements from Forensics and Division. Into the plastic bag went Murray's kitchen mallet, labelled. Into another bag, the missile, an unopened can of Guinness, which had gone through the sitting room window. A sergeant told a constable unwary enough to mention glazing experience to get on with it then, not to leave the plot until he'd replaced Mr. Peckover's window, though where he was going to find glass at this time of night was something he might need to think about.

Two hours after the triple murders in Collins Cross, PC Golightly, walking the pavement of Camden High Street, entered a call-box to report a Rover, AAJ 258P, parked outside W.H. Smith. Unlocked, key in ignition, to all intents and purposes abandoned, PC Golightly announced in measured tones, a still small voice of calm by comparison with the theatricals in Collins Cross. PC Golightly was young and overweight, and already disillusioned, even lugubrious plodder of no observable initiative and little confidence in himself. He would probably become a bully unless rescued by fate, which seemed to him to have now intervened in the shape of AAJ 258P. Clean, sir, the vehicle, he'd not entered it, touched nothing, but no visible firearms, paper bags, baggage, nothing, PC Golightly reported. "Stand by," came the order from the Murder Room temporarily set up in the Peckovers' kitchen, and somewhat contradictorily, "Carry on." Outside the box, on the empty pavement, not a soul to be seen, PC Golightly carried on with a skip, a hop, a knees-bend, and a hopeful, falsetto ditty. "Promo-o-tion fills me with emo-o-tion," he warbled. Two cars despatched to the scene with detectives and technicians found the Rover in place, PC Golightly sternly on guard, like a commissionaire tearing cinema tickets in two.

In Collins Cross the commander told Peckover to stay out of sight. If his thumped ugly face beamed out of the front page of the final editions of the tabloids in the morning he'd have his guts for garters because this wasn't publicity day for poets, mate, this was a murder investigation, and he, Peckover, was up to his neck in it.

"You wouldn't be insinuating anything, would you, sir?"

"You said you tossed the ten thousand back. Perhaps."

"What I said was would you be insinuating?"

"All right, forget it. But let me know when you can tell us why it's outside your house we've got all this."

Veal, embarrassed, looked away. Peckover went without a word into his house. The best he could hope for was that Astle would swallow his cheroot, and it would smoulder, and in time burst into flames, barbecuing the bastard's tripes and entrails.

At 5:15 A.M., after the measuring and photographing, the scouring of the street in a blaze of man-made light for every spent shell, the driving away of the cream hatchback, and the removal by ambulance of the bodies, Dr. Matthews driving behind with billowing roof and slapping windows, the cordon was lifted. Police from the cordon joined the house-to-house inquiries. Every household was awake anyway, conferring with neighbours, brewing tea and grilling bacon, inviting in or fending off reporters, and congratulating themselves that today was Saturday, they didn't have to go to work. Pete's sake, an airport, embassies, Marks and Spencer even, all right, but Collins Up-Market Cross? What had London come to? The concensus was that the gunmen were Arab terrorists and the dead were Jewish diplomats resident in the street, though no one knew of any. IRA assassins was a dissenting opinion without serious support. A few of the street's madder pinko intellectuals—a sociology professor at the London School of Economics, a CND organiser, a vegetarian literary agent, a feminist sculptor who had won notoriety for her gross bronzes of the male nude—these believed the dead were Arab terrorists, the killers a police Swat team, but the facts were never going to come out because Britain was a closed and totalitarian society run by a network of gay Oxbridge bureaucrats, grasping bankers, and last-ditch peers for whom the greatest disaster ever to have befallen the country had been the 1870 Education Act making going to school free and compulsory. The door-to-door questioning continued through dawn and for much of Saturday. On many doors hung a wreath of holly. Some doors had silver bells and cut-out Santas.

*   *   *

Far from the brouhaha, Lieutenant Robert R. Sapolsky, Los Angeles Police Narcotics Division, slid low enough in his chair to be able to reach out his legs and lodge both heels on the window ledge. The city at midnight glittered like a birthday party.

Out there were disputes beside which the three dead on a London street was meek, workaday stuff. L.A. was something else. Cocaine Consumer Capital of the world.

Lieutenant Sapolsky said, "Pack a bag, O'Day. You're going to Belize."

"Whatever you say, sir. Where?"

"In that folder is where. The one says *O'Day, Belize.* Whatever it says. Listen, are you clairvoyant?"

"I don't think so."

"What's that mean, you don't think so? You don't *know* if you're clairvoyant or not? The word is that you are."

"I made two good guesses on the Carlotti homicide. That's not clairvoyant. I get funny feelings sometimes but who doesn't?"

"What funny feelings? Look, I don't want funny feelings and I don't want clairvoyance, not in this department, okay? Goodnight."

"Goodnight."

Instead of goodnight sounds of the rustle of a folder, departing footsteps, there was silence, or would have been had the office not been an open-plan half acre of sounding telephones and prattling cops and their clients.

Lieutenant Sapolsky twirled from the window, burrowed among papers on the desk, found one, and adjusted his half-moon glasses.

He said, "There's two limeys bringing it in from Belize. Vivian White and Jeremy Clegg. Clegg's out of it because he's dead from Monday, and the D.E.A. identified his Piper Cheyenne at Ventura, so that's out of it too. But the stuff's still going to come in because Mr. White has got himself another plane and a pilot. If they'd take their shit to their own country instead of here we wouldn't have to care, but that's the way the souffle sinks. The new boy is Flight Lieutenant Julian Lumley, Royal Air Force, Belize. Now listen carefully. You say it *Leftenant,* not *Lootenant.* Got that?"

"Sure."

"Say it."

"Leftenant."

"Not bad. It's in case you have him by the nuts some time or other and feel obliged to say something, but you want to be polite, like the Brits are before they bring the knee up and burn the stadium down. Where were we. Vivian White and his pilot, co-pilot, and one passenger departed twenty-three hundred hours Belize Municipal Airport in a rented Hawker Siddeley One-Two-Five business jet. That's their time, Central Standard. Stop looking at your watch, O'Day, you'll only get confused. Direction north north-east. That's not this way, not this time, it's like the Gulf, Cuba, Miami, that area. I've looked at maps, I'm trying to help you. Ireland if they keep going, your turf, O'Day, name like yours, which is pretty bewildering. They're up in the sky at this moment. Range, two thousand miles. Maximum cruising speed, five hundred miles an hour, but they're not going to do that. The rental people say this HS-One-Two-Five isn't a wreck but it's not factory-fresh either. Details, details. The coast guard has a P-Three Orion tracking them with radar. What they've got on board isn't coke, unless Belize customs are blind, and we don't have any reason to suppose they are. They've got a carton of Pampers diapers, milk, and a load of Gerber jars, like strained junior chicken and vanilla custard pudding. You deduce anything from that?"

"They're on the Mush Diet."

"Thank you, O'Day. Better than having mush for brains. The passenger is Papitos Lopez, twenty-six, one of his cooks or housemaids, a native Belizean, which as I understand it could mean Mayan Indian, Spanish, Mestizo, Garifuna, Creole, Chinese, East Indian, or a mix of the whole boiling. The White guy is the Honourable Vivian White, though I gather the Honourable credentials don't add up, and he's got a record. He's Eton College and Wormwood Scrubs, the latter being a slammer. Don't be impressed with the Honourable bit, O'Day. He's a cockroach. Don't bow and drool and fall on your face bleating and slavering and licking his shoes because he's an Honourable, if he is, and only two off from a king. Don't do it, O'Day. Do I have your word?"

"You've got it."

"Good. The co-pilot is a civilian, Norman Stringer, a brigand, but he has his ATR. That's Air Transport Rating. Means he can help handle a jet, if he's sober. You need two for these jets because what if the lobster's tainted, there's only the one pilot, and he's stricken with galloping salmonella? Must be occupational problems we don't even hear about. Joystick itch, landing-gear fibrosis. What do you say? Am I right?"

"Never known you wrong, sir."

Sapolsky opened his mouth, changed his mind, but kept his mouth open and tipped into it coffee, long since cold.

Belize, Bahamas, Turks, and Caicos, a score more of step-ping-stones from there to beyond, producer to consumer, a string of landing-strips, coves, and beaches across the Caribbean for pick-ups and refuelling in forsaken wasteland and tourist paradises sodden with corruption, half the time officialdom on the grab, and the kids in L.A. snorting themselves draft. Into Sapolsky's head seeped the Channel Five night-time query, "It's 10 P.M. Do you know where your children are?" Yes, in fact he did. He'd called Ellen. The youngest was in bed, the next was watching "The Cosby Show," and Laura was quickstepping at her ballroom dancing class. He didn't envy the kid dancing with her. He hoped he was wearing shin-guards.

He said, "Seems the Honourable's father is a bigger crook than his son but that isn't our worry. Your target is Mr. Viv. Watch him, look him over, look his place over, bug it—Casa Verde, it's in the folder—do whatever you need to do to convince a jury. Plane ticket's in the folder. Aeromexico to Mexico City, then God knows. Mule train through the rain forest then hot-air balloon over this fermenting volcano. Just kidding. It's TAN-SAHSA, a regular airline. If it gets you there before the Honorable is back, you could have the run of Casa Verde, maybe. We don't know he's coming back but no reason to suppose he isn't. I don't want to build your hopes but you could cover yourself with glory, O'Day. You could be leading the St. Patrick Day's parade. If we get enough on this guy to put him away for twenty years, we've zapped a piece of the Belize connection. Until next week when the next cockroach sidles in." He swallowed the cold, dregless last of the coffee. "Questions?"

"My significant other, sir?"

"Your what?"

"Who's going with me? Like Max Bierman. Or Larry."

"You're on your own. Anything else?"

"So what if I don't get this guy by the nuts but he complains I did, and ripped off his money-belt? It's my word against his."

"You're undercover. You've done okay on your own before. You're a teacher on vacation and excited about Indian artefacts. Or pineapples. Your choice. It's on your passport—"

"In the folder. Thanks. Max Bierman could be another excited teacher."

"I can't give you Bierman, he's in court. Larry's in Fresno. Milne's on crutches. Joey Garcia's taking his first two days off since September because if he doesn't his wife divorces him. I've got no one else. Name me someone else."

"Mary-Jo?"

"O'Day, that isn't even funny. Mary-Jo is eight months pregnant. It is eight or nine? They wouldn't let her on the plane. TAN-SAHSA, I dunno, maybe they would. Maybe they're baby crazy, like Italians, they'd fork-lift her on board and play accordions. Correction. Marimbas. For once try not to think just of yourself, O'Day. Think of the living, unborn life."

"I do. Mary-Jo wants to stay active to the last. She tells everyone that. If the baby's premature over the volcano, we're going where there's diapers and junior strained chicken."

"Don't give me a hard time, O'Day. Mary-Jo stays." Lieutenant Sapolsky took off his glasses. "This isn't in the folder, we only just got it, but you don't have to be on your own. A couple of hotshots from Scotland Yard are going over. Not for another couple of days, but you could meet." He folded the glasses and put them on the desk. "Liaise with them if you're lonely, if you haven't sewn it up by the time they toddle in. Their police contact is a Superintendent Campos, same as yours, and they want this Viv zapped as much as we do. They had a cop-killing in Mayfair or some place they think he was in on. So use them. One of them's a poet."

"Excuse me?"

"A poet. Poetry. You know poetry, O'Day. 'To be or not to be, that is the question.' 'Quoth the raven, "Nevermore."'"

"A poet. Holy shit."

"'By the shores of Gitche Gumee, by the shining Big-Sea-Water—.'"

"Hiawatha, old Nokomis, off they skate into the sunset."

"You've got it. Let's see if we can't hustle London a bit. Heck, another couple of days—why not now? What're they sitting on their butts for? Three citizens gunned down, for those people that's like genocide, and they're sitting in the pub, the Brewer's Balls, talking about it over eggs and crumpets and marmalade. Lift the extension, I'm calling long distance." The lieutenant picked up his glasses. "They've a cop named Veal I've almost got confidence in."

"'The woods are lovely, dark and deep—'"

"Great, terrific."

"'But I have promises to keep—'"

"O'Day, don't push it. While I think of it, don't try boarding your Aeromexico flight with your gun. You get one from Campos. You may have to rent it—buy it for all I

know. Can't help you, never met him. One of the Brits"—
Sapolsky picked through papers on his desk—"Peckchester,
Peckingham—" He selected a sheet of paper with fading in-
terest. "He's got a pink card."

O'Day nodded sagely.

"You know what that means, O'Day? Course you do, else
you'd ask."

"Peckingham is the poet?"

"Right."

"Okay, pink card. He's licensed to write poetry."

"O'Day, don't think you're unique. You are one speck in
a baffling universe. It means he has a gun. That's the exception over there. It means he's good, and Scotland Yard is
serious."

O'Day blinked, and for an eerie instant the clattering
LAPD office was gone, and in its place a Technicolour still, a
garish snapshot as from the early days of colour, of blood-
letting in Belize. Blood, jungle, people falling, everyone
faceless. O'Day blinked the snapshot away.

The lieutenant picked up the telephone, winked at
O'Day, and said, "A modest bet on how they answer? Like
one grand?"

"You're on."

"A dollar says it's either 'Pip-pip, old top' or 'Elementary,
my dear Watson.' One or the other."

Lieutenant Sapolsky returned his glasses to his nose and
with a chewed fingertip punched, 011-44-1-230-1212. Back
for an instant came to O'Day the colour snapshot, and with it
banging guns, and a stench of cordite and sugary blood. Sapolsky was sitting back with the phone to his ear, inhaling the
office air.

The woman who answered in his ear, as if from a telephone in an office along the corridor, said "Scotland Yard.
May I help you?"

NINE

Sapolsky. In spite of Agent O'Day's expressed belief that the lieutenant never was wrong, Lieutenant Sapolsky was capable of error. He had been mistaken in stating that the HS-125 turbofan biz-jet was up in the sky. It had touched down on an empty caye off Andros Island, Bahamas. Viv was already on the next stage of his trip.

Communication between the U.S. Coast Guard Orion surveillance plane and the L.A.P. Narcotics Division was fine, but not stopwatch-immediate, there being no reason why it should be. Vivian White, his maid, and his pilots were not, as far as could be guessed, on a terrorist mission. They were not violating U.S. air space. They were not necessarily acting with criminal intent, though landing where they landed, without customs clearance, without collecting a flying permit, was unlawful, therefore suspicious. Andros Island had five authorised ports of entry and tinpot Cat Caye was not one of them. What they looked to be doing was going to meet a baby.

The Coast Guard plane radioed Bahamian customs out of courtesy. Lumley picked up the message, swore, and passed it to Co-pilot Stringer, who carried it back to Vivian White. Viv was not unduly anxious. There shouldn't be customs problems, Billy had assured him. He happened to be *deeply* friendly with a perfectly *charming* captain in customs who would be able to delay intrusiveness for an hour or two at the very *least*.

The one-time military landing strip was moonlit and adequate. Beaming Billy, chubbier than Viv remembered, and wearing a windjammer and khaki shorts to his knees, was waiting in the night with *Bonnie Jean,* a forty-six-foot Hatteras motor yacht. Julian Lumley switched off the landing lights.

After they had gone, Lumley stood with his co-pilot in lumpy, dewy grass under a high white moon like a dinner plate, listening to the diminishing drone of *Bonnie Jean.* So far, so good. As long as customs dawdled.

Soliciting a pass from the adjutant had been easy, and why not. It hadn't been as if invasion from Guatemala was imminent. A ribald remark about ladies-of-the-night and keep-your-end-up, old boy. He needn't even have hinted at a Christmas case of scotch as a token of gratitude. No matter, he'd be able to afford it. And he'd be needing the adjutant's passes again.

Monday, for a start, when the crate for his first coke run into the States, Viv had told him, wasn't going to be this sleek heap, which weighed in like one of those Japanese wrestlers, and needed a mile of landing-strip, but probably a Beech Baron. Phew. No co-pilot. Stringer was a gloomy sod.

After eight hundred miles and a couple of hours in this biz-jet, no need to refuel, which was as well, there being no tanker truck, no anything except moon, strip, and ocean. Refuelling from five-gallon cans of JP-4 would have taken them until Christmas. But starting at the starboard wing, aiming flashlights, Lumley and Stringer performed the ritual walk-around. They scraped green brush and debris out of the engine air-intakes. On the flight deck they checked the controls. They looked in the passenger cabin, its ivory bar and satiny seating designed for the delectation of lady executives and the male executives' wives or mistresses. A discarded chewing-gum carton lay on the floor. Lumley was buggered if he was going to pick it up.

Anyway his hands were occupied, passing from left to right, right to left, squeezing the trigger—*click, click*—trying to become comfortable with it, his gun. He put it to his nose and sniffed. No smell. Metallic, cold metalness.

"You hear anything, it's only me," he told Stringer. "I'm shooting at the moon."

This trip he'd not be needing it. Any luck he would not be needing it Monday either, or ever. He hadn't fired it yet, but he should, and he would now, just to be sure. In case. Practice for when the cargo-runs began, just in case.

Lumley walked from the plane and the creviced, grassy strip and onto sandy grass. He worked the slide, thumbed the safety lever forward to on, back to off, then removed the magazine the way he had been shown by the fat boy, and fed into it ten .22-calibre bullets. He replaced the magazine.

Now he had better be bloody careful.

The fat, grinning youth with rings on his fingers and glittery chains round his neck had said it was a Browning Challenger II automatic, unused, as good as. Perfect condition, dead reliable, millions sold, in production up to only a couple of years ago, you check that, man, I would like you to check that. (Where would he check? If the gun was so fabulous, why wasn't it still in production? Would *you* buy an almost unused Browning Challenger from fat boy on a street corner in Belize? He had bought it. Three hundred dollars.

Belize dollars. A hundred and fifty Yankee dollars. A hundred quid plus another fifteen for the shells. Twice what it would have cost in somewhere like Houston, Texas, Lumley had little doubt, but he hadn't been about to haggle. He had expected a far higher asking price. The only weapons he knew anything about were pricier. Like a Harrier. Like the five-million quid for the Zircon spy satellite. Size counted, he could understand that. Whether you were stopping a policeman or sinking a ship.

The size of the Browning was a bastard, nearly a foot long, and a brute of a front sight which was going to rip the lining of his pocket apart if ever he needed to get it out in a hurry. Three, four inches longer than the alternative Colt Combat Commander. Maybe Commander Combat. They all sounded like children's toys, like Sylvester Stallone films. Who could take it in, fat boy's slick, specialist sales talk. But for the Colt he had wanted seven hundred dollars. Why? A gun was a gun. They all spouted bullets.

Lumley walked across the grass towards the ocean. He halted, raised his arm, waited—he could not have said why he waited—then turned his head aside and clenched his finger on the trigger.

Nothing.

He squeezed harder. Tugged. Nothing.

Oh shit. He pushed the safety forward to ready with his thumb.

Bang!

His wrist bounced, the night roared.

Bang!

In for a penny, as his dad used to say.

Bang, bang, bang!

Enough. The bastard worked. Shaking, keeping his finger clear of the trigger, Lumley gazed across the beach to the black ocean. When he had earned his retirement fund, quick bunch of trips in the Beech Baron, and he had got out from all this, he'd be able to sell the gun back to fat boy, or to someone. He wouldn't though. First chance he had, he would put it in a brown paper bag and stuff it in a litter-bin.

Later, through the windscreen of the flight deck, Lumley watched Vivian White and the woman return in sunshine up the beach, then through the grass, striding and running. When they had left the plane the woman had carried the carry-cot one-handed by its straps. Now she embraced it, both arms holding it to her chest. Viv jostled Papitos and her burden up the four entry steps into the plane and clambered in after her.

Mission accomplished. Two hours by plane from Belize, three by Billy's boat and Volvo, six minutes in his father's house, and Viv had the baby. He would acknowledge later the luck, how sweetly smooth. When it was happening you never were aware of fortune being in your pocket because you hadn't time, you were working so hard. Another fifteen minutes, surely the whole house would have been stirring, his father banging about shouting for volunteers to run with him on the beach. At six forty-five the only people up had been the chauffeur, and in the kitchen the maid, both delighted to share in the secret, the surprise visit from Sir Peter and Her Ladyship's only son. The maid had never seen him in her life—oh my, he might have been a pervert, a molester —but she had thrilled to it, whispering and tiptoeing, showing him the nursery, returning at that point to her stove and blueberry muffin mix because he asked her to. See, Nina— her name was Nina—we want everything normal, breakfast as usual, so when I walk in it'll be a stunning surprise. Winnie, the Irish setter, had frolicked at his feet. Not a yap. Some guard dog.

If his father had surprised him, if anyone had—mother, Augusta, the nanny, staff—he would have taken anyway what he had come for. They were hardly going to attack him with golf clubs, a baby in his arms. They might have called the police. Augusta would have. Billy would probably have drawn the line at a car chase back to the boat. The baby hadn't even cried until he was out of big daddy's rosy-tinted sprawl of a winter palace and back in the Volvo, handing the swaddled bundle to Papitos.

On the sea, at beaming Billy's behest, they had unzipped. He could hardly have refused. The controls on automatic, Papitos despatched below, Billy ripping at clothing, he had performed for and with Billy and auld lang syne. *Swing, swing, together, your bodies between your knees.* Jesus, he hoped he hadn't caught anything.

A Bell Jetranger helicopter of Bahamian customs arrived as Lumley and Stringer took off into the dawn. "Aircraft departing Andros Island squawk twelve hundred," crackled a voice on the distress frequency. "Identify yourself on one-two-five point zero." Lumley snapped the radio off and sent the HS-125 streaking south south-east. Within moments the helicopter and the Bahamas had been left behind.

In the cabin Viv took a tonic water from the bar. He removed his shoes, settled back, swigged, and closed his eyes. *Toujours de l'audace.* Danton had said it. Pity they'd cut his head off because it didn't have to be like that, what judges were pleased to call the full severity of the law. He would wager that those outside the law, those with *l'audace,* got away with it twenty times more often than they were caught.

Like bold Daddy-O, to name but one. He'd have given a lot to have been a fly now on the walls of the house on Andros Island.

A fly on the wall would have stamped and applauded. Sir Peter's performance was from the heart. He stormed and raged to a point where his physician, had he been present, would have feared for his heart. He was Lear without the white beard. *I will do such things—what they are yet I know not—but they shall be the terrors of the earth.* He was without the torment as well as the beard. His frustration, however, was on a par. Nanny Park wondered if his condition bordered on apoplexy. In her opinion Sir Peter was a great big baby.

Round the wrist of daughter-in-law Augusta he left a red weal, which would turn blue, where he grabbed her when she lifted a telephone to call the police.

"Great Scott, Gussie, there'll be no police here! I'll deal with this myself, see if I don't I'll have his hide! By thunder, I'll tweak the jackanape's whiskers!"

Shirtless, clad only in tennis shorts, Sir Peter railed against his son until his tanned, bony face and bald pate took on the hue and wetness of borscht. He wept for the baby. He kicked a cane chair across the floor with his bare foot. He slapped the wall as if to demolish it, dislodging, so that the glass broke, a framed photograph of himself shaking hands with the Prime Minister, Edward Heath, at Conservative Party ball at the Dorchester on April 4, 1972. He sent Nanny Park and the black butler, Dwayne Goodsir, on a search of the house, grounds, and guest cottages, in case Vivian had not been here at all, he had been a mirage, all was as it had been, and the baby had merely run off—oh, the scamp, the little mischief!—and even now was playing in an undiscovered corner, albeit Sir Peter knew as well as anyone, unobservant in such matters though he was, that the baby not only was a prisoner in its cot until lifted out, but was hardly able to take two steps before sitting with a bump, let alone run.

He sacked on the spot the maid, Nina, and the chauffeur, Joshua. He would pay their wages to the end of the month but they would pack and leave immediately, and think themselves fortunate he was large of spirit since he was not handing them over to the police, though they were criminals—by Jupiter!—accessories to kidnapping. About to demand how much Vivian had paid them for their complicity, an instinct for self-preservation caused Sir Peter to reconsider, the chauffeur being a truculent blighter and former pugilist who had fought as Josh "The Cosh" Blanco. Instead, with a bullock-call across the landscaped park, Sir Peter summoned butler Dwayne from his search of the pool area and ordered him to supervise Nina and Joshua packing, and to examine their baggage for stolen towels, soap, and silverware. Head of the household, Sir Peter was the only member of the household unaware that Dwayne and Nina were having an affair, had been since August, and that Dwayne was more likely to stuff Nina's suitcases with all the family valuables he could fit into them than to rescue the odd, aberrant towel.

"He's no son of mine!" Sir Peter shouted, beet-red, striding and gesturing. "No son of mine, I say!"

Joanna Park, twenty-four, State Registered nurse out of St. Mary's Hospital (a stone's throw from Artillery Row, where parked Chief Inspector Peckover and others, given a space), and holder of a Montessori diploma in child care, had a year ago answered an advertisement in *The Lady*, flown to Nassau to be interviewed by Augusta White, and accepted the job because never mind the sun, which gave you skin cancer, and the money, which she didn't sneeze at, it was riches compared with her survival wages in London, but because she would be three thousand miles from her mother, and from Colin, whom Mummy and everyone ached for her to marry, just like the nineteenth bloody century, but never bloody mind that Colin, besides being wealthy and handsome, happened to be a sadist who would push tent pegs up you while you slept. She had the marks to show anyone interested, which had lasted and would last longer than Gussie's piddling burn on her wrist was going to last.

Nurse Park was walking through the hall with unsolicited Courvoisier for Lady May—not that she was a mind-reader, or a waitress, but brandy would do her ladyship no harm, she certainly wouldn't say no, and no one else would think to it—when she stopped dead. Out of the living room charged Sir Peter. He halted, staring at her as if she were an intruder, someone he had never set eyes on.

"I'll have his hide, by thunder!"

Apoplexy. Joanna, standing with the snifter of Courvoisier, tried to remember. Loss of muscular control resulting from—what? Intracerebral haemorrhage? Vascular insufficiency?

Muscular control, in fact, looked good. Excellent. It wasn't apoplexy, it was the vexation of an infant, a temper tantrum. He was off again. Joanna held her breath. He was heading towards the wall hung with the Tower of London delights—the gleaming pikes, dirks, halberds, blunderbusses, executioner's six-foot swords, polished thumbscrews, spiked iron circlets with a key for crushing the skull with as much pain as possible, a bastinado cudgel, and the cords and pulley of a strappado. Joanna would have swallowed the brandy had she been capable of movement. She had never seen him in quite such a state. If he were about to commit violence, he had the means to hand.

At the last moment, Sir Peter veered from the wall-armoury, skirted the suit of armour, and plunged into the passage which led to stairs down to the kitchens. Joanna breathed out.

Lady May, wrinkled and rectangular in a basket chair in the living room, accepted the brandy without a word. She wore a straw hat, bedroom slippers with woolly pom-poms from Libert's in Regent Street, and a tartan bathrobe—her own McDonald tartan—which her sister had given her many years ago. In her lap lay gardening gloves.

Gussie wore slacks and a collarless, chartreuse shirt which clashed deafeningly with the potted orange-and-blue bird-of-paradise plants. The world was receiving from her the silent treatment, which would pass, but which meanwhile, caught unaware, the world had to suffer. Blonde and contemptuously beautiful, she sat at one end of a chintz sofa, looking straight ahead into a vast, superfluous fireplace, motionless except for her drumming fingers on the sofa's arm.

"Would you like me to make a pot of tea or anything?" Joanna asked her. "I don't think we're going to get anything from Nina."

"Not on my account."

Red-and-white Winnie circled restlessly, sniffing at feet. From time to time she would stop and stare from a distance of two or three inches into the eyes of Lady May, next into the eyes of Gussie, her nose reaching forward, tail backward, reminding them that she was a sporting dog, why didn't they take her outside where she could be sporty, chase something, gallop about.

Sir Peter marched in shouting, "If he thinks this is how he'll get Gussie to Belize for Christmas, he has another think coming, what?"

From his mouth sprayed yellow splashes of food. Instead of a kitchen cleaver which Joanna had half expected to see, he held an opened, one-pound bag of nacho cheese tortilla chips, and his mouth was full. Joanna surmised that he was frightened there might be no breakfast today. He stood centre stage, crashed his hand into the bag, and withdrew a fistful of chips.

"I have more effective ways than the police of sorting this out, see if I don't," he shouted, slamming chips into his mouth.

You probably do, thought Joanna. You're still a big baby.

Lady May, as chattily as over tea and cress sandwiches with the vicar, said, "The wages of hubris are come home to roost in the halls of the ungodly. I told you. Nemesis rides on the heels of spirtual pride."

Everyone looked at her. Not because of what she had said, whatever that had been—she was not given to quoting the Bible or Greek drama—but because this was the first anyone had heard Lady May say anything for three days.

TEN

Peckover's picture did not appear in the late editions, though his name did. That was all right because so did Astle's, and Veal's too. Less prominently than his own but he could hardly be carpeted for that. Was it his fault it had happened in Collins Cross? And the press found him more colourful copy than Astle?

MAYHEM ON YARD-BARD'S DOORSTEP, bellowed the *Mirror*, thrilled, THREE SLAIN IN DRUGS WAR—MET'S MINSTREL MUGGED, halloed the *Sun*, beside itself.

At Scotland Yard Peckover wrote his report. Light-headed from an excess of events—he was able to tot up being bludgeoned, no sleep, the Massacre of Collins Cross, the subsequent Flight of Miriam and the Children, Belize, and the pink card, though he had almost forgotten Belize and the pink card—he added a suggestion.

Mrs. Beresford, busybody at No. 27 or thereabouts, will have viewed the incident through her opera glasses, may have filmed it, and should be held for questioning.

He read the sentence over, liked it, massaged his earlobe, chewed the skin by his thumbnail, whited the sentence out, and pondered, not for the first time, on the pros of the Yard's available but menacing word-processors versus the cons of this his personal, manual, portable Imperial Good Companion typewriter, filthy but sturdy, vintage 1959, bought for a song in Whitechapel market—fallen off the back of a lorry, he hadn't doubted it then or now—when he had been but a clear-eyed sprig and setting himself for a career as Percy Bysshe Shelley.

These days, for a two-minute repair, for the measliest replacement part, the only hope for Good Companion, and he'd been lucky to hear of it, was in the alley-riddled wasteland south of Waterloo Station: an unlit, virtually undiscoverable shot in a rotting workroom on an upper floor, and inside the back door, there being no front door, a tea-addicted Rip Van Winkle, possibly the fanatic's father, swilling tea and guarding the place as it were H. M. Nuclear Research (Star Wars) Inc. Should the shop shut down, Good Companion was doomed. Tote Good Companion into one of the glass and chrome emporia on the High Street and the lolling, slobber-lipped youth who purported to be a salesman would pick at a pimple, snort his watery catarrh, and peer at Good Companion as if it were something unearthed on an archeological dig and rejected as worthless. The yob's colleague, a zombified chit of a girl, specialised only in envelopes and paperclips, for which there was still a market, unlike typewriter ribbons. A distant shelf might hold typewriter ribbons but as well expect the girl to turn up the correct ribbon as to dry and buy a decent tomato. When she saw you approaching she would turn her back to stack paperclips, or she might defiantly attempt to stare you out on the assumption that you had come to rape her. If the manager happened along in his grey suit with the paisley lining, a once-in-a-lifetime occurrence, he would pretend not to be sneering at your typewriter while being more than happy for you to understand that he was sneering as momentously as any Paris waiter. With take-it-or-leave-it gestures he might go through the motions of educating you in alternatives, pointing out this and that in his surrounding heap of garbage, electronic boxes priced at thousands of quid a throw, but his heart would not be in it, aware as he was from your Good Companion, and middle-age, and hopeless wing-tips with laces, that you were not educable, you were a terminal case, one of the lost, a person with a standard, manual typewriter.

More than once, furtively at night among the Factory's battery of word processors, Peckover had tapped and failed, punched buttons and cursed, seen his sentences gulped away, and somebody else's sentences spring unbidden on the screen to inform him that what he was doing was false and mad. What he was doing falsely and madly he could not comprehend, but he was doing it, and the winking, cancer-inducing cursor brought on stomach cramps and made his head throb and his eyes water, and soon would induce blindness. He had but one life to live. He had only recently discovered white-out, and as far as putting printed words on paper went, and correcting them, he had decided that white-out was revolution enough for his lifetime.

Liquid Paper, Correction Fluid. Warning: Deliberately Concentrating and Inhaling the Contents Can Be Harmful or Fatal.

Same as guns. Being alive was a hazardous business.

The hooded pair he described as best he could but what could he say? They'd known their job? They were effective? The paper shopping bags, they'd been effective too, and cheap, like free. Tesco? Waitrose? Their wives hadn't sat up half the night taking fittings and hemming eyeholes.

They might have been the pair noticed by scent-sniffing Mrs. Wilson on the stairs in Wellington Square, or two from a handful of hard men in the computer, or unknown imports from across the ocean. Would an itsy-bitsy outpost of empire such as Belize, Peckover wondered, have hit men? He doubted their police resources ran to much in the way of computers, though he could be wrong. Señor Campos might have a pocket calculator if he'd been pocketing benefits in return for not noticing the hanky-panky of Viv and Clegg in the interior.

Peckover bent his arm behind him and knuckled his typist's back. Clegg was dead, the Honourable Viv barely real. He never had been real. For a start he was not an Honourable. An Honourable was the son of a baron, viscount, or earl, which Sir Peter wasn't. Honourable had apparently been awarded him at school, with heavy irony, probably because he had been snobby and thought he ought to have been a duke, and it had stuck. Honourable, dishonourable, who cared? Point was, he was surely to God too remote on his Caribbean acres to be involved in this mess.

Peckover was glad he was a mere chief inspector. He didn't have to think as deeply as Veal and Astle. They were not in the front line getting hit with a mallet and watching people shot to pieces but they were expected to make sense of it.

Best of luck, men. London these days wasn't the London he had grown up in, but it was still London; people didn't get knocked off three at a time. Hadn't Veal said that? It was true, they just didn't.

They might if they were political. Murray was as political as a leg of mutton. Ask Murray to point to Belfast on a map, and he'd have been fifteen minutes failing to find it, then punched your face. Mr. Polite, and Smiler, who knew how they'd voted? It hadn't been because of Ireland or the Middle East they'd wanted him to leave Viv alone and fail the pink card.

Peckover typed a description of the guns with even less confidence than he had described the pair who had fired them, and with some guilt. His gun course had been shown, as a treat, the arsenal in the museum at D11 headquarters in Old Street, so he should have known something. The session having been for general interest, not for exam purposes, he had scarcely listened. If contemporary guns had had normal names such as Colt and Enfield, names you'd heard of, he might have given up less easily, but they didn't have names even—they had figures and letters. It was school algebra again, lobotomising the brain. "Here we see the AR-Fifteen semi-automatic rifle, civilian equivalent of the army's M-Sixteen. Here the MP-Five-A-Two sub-machine gun as carried by the lads at Heathrow." Gawd, had he got those two right? He believed he might have. "And here the MYOB demi-semi-diddle-gun with the doodad on its dinger."

The gun from the glass-fronted cabinet which had stirred him just a little had been the one hefted in violin cases, poked through the windows of high black Fords, star of the old Warner Bros. flicks, and it'd had a name, not gibberish numbers and initials. Ah, where would Cagney and Bogey and company have been without the Tommy gun?

Peckover rang Old Street and described the guns in Collins Cross haltingly to Dave Verity, D11 blue beret. "Sounds like a converted MAC-Ten," Verity said.

Peckover typed: *Gun Model: Probability of MAC-10 semi-automatic pistol converted to machine-gun. Rectangularity most striking feature. Was there a word rectangularity? There was now. Not dissimilar in shape to Cirio tomato puree carton or jumbo Pepsodent, dimensions approx. 10 ins. x 3 ins. x 1 in., grip extending below hand. Each assailant in possession of probably identical firearm fitted with silencer.*

He gazed into space, picked up a pencil, and wrote:

Masacre in Collins Cross

> Those two were bad, those two were mean,
> Their guns made a noise like a sewing-machine,
> Like the bacon-slicer at Sloppy Joe's
> (The deli where the smart folk goes),
> A sort of whirring, metallic sound
> From MAC-10s spraying bullets around
> And blowing three sleazos to the ground.

Some say it's no stupendous loss,
Three blokes who didn't give a toss.
  Fa-la-la nonny, derry jug-jug
Sing hey the bullets in Collins Cross!
The blood and the bullets in Collins Cross.

He scrunched the sheet and tossed it into the bin. From the office window he could just make out a distant outline of Big Ben, though such was the nine o'clock murk he couldn't have known it was Big Ben had he not seen it from this window a thousand times. Terry Sutton put his head round the door and said, "Henry, the super says he'll see your report any time. I think he means now if it's done. He'd like a word."

Peckover carried the report along the corridor and into Veal's office. Veal glanced through it, said "Fine," and handed it to Mrs. Coulter for the copier. He put on his jacket. "Have you had breakfast?"

"You mean we stop to eat?"

"Not for long. Viv's flown out of Belize in a rented plane. Los Angeles has a drugs agent flying in. Suddenly everything's up in the air, so to speak. You too. You're lucky, B.A. has put on some extra flights for Christmas. You're leaving this afternoon."

On foot to bacon and eggs, Veal revealed that Henry's Mr. Polite had been identified as Derek Blackett, until lately a warder at the Scrubs, and Smiler was Gordon Hale, another warder. They might have become mates of Viv while he'd been inside. Or enemies. Shouldn't be hard to find out, though, for the present the water was muddy.

"If they were Viv's men, he must be pretty nervous of you," Veal said. "First money, next mallets."

"Didn't enjoy his nose being broken, that's all. Happened once, could 'appen again."

"You don't suppose the two with the paper bags would be happy to see you break it again?"

"Why would they want that?"

"Don't ask me. Perhaps whoever killed Clegg, or had him killed, would like his partner put out of business too. Fact is, you're alive, bruised but on your feet, you could break Viv's back. Not to be squeamish, but couldn't those two have shot you while they were about it?"

"It crossed my mind."

"So why didn't they? End of eye witness. Not that you witnessed much."

"They know there'd be a fair cafuffle if they shot a copper."

"Somebody shot Jimmy Thornley."

"What's great about you, Frank, you're so reassuring. You give the workers this terrific feeling of security."

The Rubens Hotel was fancier than Veal and Peckover would normally have invested in but they felt due for linen tablecloths and pampering. The bruise on Peckover's temple glistened like a peeled plum. The waitress had a pale, elfin face, a fringe, and round eyes which fixed on the plum and grew rounder, enthralled. She took the policemen's order.

"Lieutenant Sapolsky in Los Angeles seemed to be implying we're all too damn secure here, as in smug, not taking any of this with proper gravity," Veal said. "The agent he's flying in is on loan to the L.A. police from their D.E.A. Whether that's Drug Enforcement Agency, or Administration, I've never known. They don't either. He's a P. O'Day, and I hope you're not going to be traipsing behind him with a shovel."

"*P* as in prick?"

"That's what worries me. He might know what he's doing or he could be some gung-ho twit who'll mess up everything. He's going to be there before you. If he makes Casa Verde his first stop, because Viv isn't there, Viv's going to hear about it, which is the last thing we want. Viv on the alert isn't going to be in Belize, not until it's calmed down. He'll be in Italy, where his heart is, or was. Why Italy?"

"Why not? Good place."

"Wherever, if this O'Day scares him out we're all wasting our time, and plane tickets."

"O'Day might booby-trap Casa Verde with the latest in his D.E.A.'s high-tech wizardry, blow himself up in the process, and Viv with him. That too optimistic?"

"No. We must look on the bright side."

No one was clear where Viv had flown off to, Veal said, but he might already be back in Belize because the hot news from Campos was that six hundred kilos of Colombian best were due for him any time. Tip-off from the Bogota *policia*. Not Colombian coffee best. Unprocessed cocaine best, street value over half a million quid.

Peckover said, "His pilot's just been cremated. How does 'e get it into the States? Indian bearers filing through the jungle?"

"Seems Belize has one or two spare pilots who'd garotte

each other for the job, including a Brit with the military there. Viv might already have another pilot. RAF officer name of Lumley, the one who's just taken him up in the air. Campos says—"

"Campos says. Babble babble. When does 'e lay off blathering and show us some action? After this next consignment perhaps he'll be able to retire, leave us alone."

The waitress brought juice, tea, and toast, and glanced at Peckover's red welt.

"Henry, we don't know Campos is on the take," Veal said, infinitely patient. "We do know he wants Viv collared and he's asking for our help. Talk to him nicely. Don't snarl at him, not until you know him better. If he's bent, his second-in-command is a Sergeant Montego. Snarl at Viv all you like, if he's back, if you can get anywhere near him. Sir Peter wants him not collared but coaxed or terrified onto the straight and narrow, so snarl at Papa too if you think there might be anything there. Take the side-trip. The father could have a part in this aside from genes. He and Viv don't get on, might loathe each other, who knows? Might be in competition to see who can become the filthiest rich. The ideal might be to engineer matters so father and son are face to face, and you a fly on the wall. You'll never manage that. Just see how it goes. I'd have thought you'd be swooning. It's an opportunity."

"For what?"

"Sun, an aquamarine ocean, girls in grass skirts, ukeleles."

"Wrong 'emisphere. It's oil drums."

"If Campos is about to pull off the drug bust of Belize history"—Veal spiked a butter pat and introduced it to a triangle of toast—"heavy cocaine, Henry, not the local cheapo pot, and if you're there, putting in your two penn'orth, that wouldn't do you any harm either. What's the worst can happen? Air tickets down the drain, and the swaying palms fail to ignite your muse."

"That's not the worst and you know it. It's fishy."

"What is?"

Peckover poured tea. He observed the sparse customers. They looked English: overnight, well-to-do guests up from Hampshire and Dorset for Christmas shopping, but not prepared to shell out for the Ritz or Grosvenor House. In the run-up to Christmas, foreign tourists were thin on the ground.

"I might almost say it stinks," Peckover said. "If I didn't know you, might go so far as to say I was being set up. Give

Henry permission to shoot, send 'im off to the back of beyond, and if he gets hurt, wasn't it a crying shame. If Viv gets hurt, forget he didn't pull the trigger on Thornley—he knew something about it, and no one messes London's finest about."

Spooning sugar into his tea, Veal remained silent. Then he said, "All right, you said if you didn't know me. But you do. So shall we forget this nutty concoction?" He stirred the tea slowly. "Any rate, I think you know me."

"I certainly do. You had your fling with Miriam."

"Oh no, not that." Veal put the spoon in the saucer with a clatter. "Years ago, damn you. You weren't even married."

"We were engaged."

"You were engaged thirteen years."

"Makes it worse. We were steady."

"Can you eat two breakfasts? I'm going."

"Wait. This Belize caper, it still smells. Sorry." Sorry to have brought up Veal and Miriam, ancient history, he meant, and he thought, Christ, I'm apologising, me. "What do we know of Campos except no one heard of 'im and now he's phoning every ten minutes? Who says he's not being paid mucho dinero to entice me over? Once I'm there, he and Viv fell me with a mahogany log and throw me to the crocodiles."

"First, it isn't dineros, it's Belize dollars, two to one Yankee dollar." Veal plucked from the toast-rack more cooling toast. "Second, it doesn't have to be you going over. Hate to tell you this but your fame hasn't gone before. P'raps they don't get *Good Housekeeping* in Belize. Campos had never heard of you until now. If it wasn't you it'd be someone else, and I'm beginning to wish it was."

"Someone else with a pink card?"

"Damn right." Veal smeared excessive butter on limp toast. "This isn't shoplifting at Woolworth's, it's big drugs. Colombia—Belize—Los Angeles. The Belize police don't carry guns, in theory anyway, but I expect Campos will be able to find a spare or two for invited guests."

The elfin waitress set down eggs and bacon and scurried off.

Peckover said, "What you have to know is, this Alan Moss in Drugs who's supposed to be going with me. I don't know him and I don't want him."

"You're not going on your own."

"Didn't say I was. Point is, what's become of consultation?" Peckover slid his eggs onto toast and positioned the bacon on top of the eggs. "Seems to me I 'aven't had a great deal of say in any of this. A team should know each other, isn't that something they teach in basic training? Know what to expect of each other?"

"You're not going with Moss. He's got flu and a temperature of a hundred and three. We've alerted Sergeant Taylor."

"Unalert 'im," Peckover said with his mouth full. "Taylor I know and I'm not listening to his stock market stories round the clock. Frank, are we consulting or aren't we?"

Veal sighed. His fork, loaded with bacon and dripping yellow egg, paused in its passage to his mouth. "Who then?"

"Name's Twitty. Detective Constable, L Division, Brixton. If today's his day off, he'll be prowling Portobello Road for top hats and moccasins with bells. He likes clothes. We were on a case together last year."

"I remember. He's black."

"Going to the Caribbean, aren't we? He'll be camouflaged."

"I'd have to by-pass the commander. Anything you ask for he's going to refuse. I'd say it's impossible. In fact, put it out of your mind."

"So where did Frank Fix-It Veal go? Thought you might see it as a challenge, a test of your clout."

Veal dabbed egg from his moustache with his napkin. He said, "Has Twitty had gun training?"

"Gawd, I 'ope not," said Peckover.

ELEVEN

At least the departures building was warm. Himself warm for the first time since breakfast, Peckover looked through plate glass at mid-afternoon dinginess. Icy slush and slop drizzled on the parked jumbos.

Another fifteen minutes before passengers for the BA flight to Miami were to be called. Peckover wore a wool scarf and a quilted navy parka and carried only a briefcase, having checked in what the mail order firm had been pleased to call a tote bag, a piece of luggage bristling with side-pockets, zips, buckles, grab-handles, and shoulder-straps. Not for the first time he burrowed inside his jacket pocket, making sure ticket and boarding pass were still there, because they might have combusted, or been stolen by sprites. Passport too. He might not need his passport to enter Belize, so Veal said, and technically he didn't need it to get out of Britain, though he wouldn't want to have tried, but he sure as death and taxes was going to need it to get back in. He had roamed up and down escalators, past coffee shops, got lost, read the titles on the shelves of paperbacks, not buying, and drunk a pint of bitter because it could be his last for two, three days. Who knew what they drank over there. "Señor, you try our Belize Bomb-blast, is coconut milk, papaya, mahogany shavings, crushed mosquito, and surgical spirit." Now he walked back to the check-in counter.

He stood with his back to the counter. Operation Malaria was under way, more or less, except where was his number two? He observed humanity: the calm ones who had flown many times, the fidgety who hadn't, mothers with children already fractious and the journey hardly begun, backpackers with guitars, robed African kings, Sony-sellers from Tokyo in groups, retired couples from Manchester fleeing to Christmas in the Florida sun, and purposeful aircrew. The aircrew were overpaid pilots striding out, familiar with the exits and entrances, and the tanned stewardesses they screwed, wearing jaunty caps, carrying neat, underfilled bags containing a swimsuit, a satiny cocktail number for the Sundowner Lounge on overnight stopovers at Hiltons and Hyatts, a superfluous nightgown, a diaphragm, and empty space for the cut-price cameras and cassette-decks they would stock up on in the Thieves' Alleys of Hong Kong and Singapore. Two uniformed coppers were examining documents demanded from a stick of an Arab youth without stomach, hips, or bum. Peckover wished he were going hunting for Viv in Italy. Italy was okay.

Ten minutes.

If whoever Frank Veal was lumbering him with didn't show, he would go alone, and so much for "You're not going on your own," and corroboration. He hadn't wanted to go, he'd said as much, but having got this far he was going. If Viv stayed invisible and the trip turned out to be a holiday, he'd sooner holiday alone than be stuck with some Drugs Squad ape with Montezuma's revenge, grumbling about the heat and flies.

The flight wouldn't be full this time of year, coming up to Christmas. Maybe it would. There were additional flights. Returning Yankee businessmen, students. Had he packed everything? You didn't know if you had packed everything until you needed something you hadn't packed.

Five minutes.

A black and mobile apparition, six feet four inches tall, in a yellow Panama hat and a silvery fur coat which reached to below his calves, weaved long-leggedly between clumps of travellers, soundlessly mouthing as if singing, and looking to left and right at the airline signs above the counters. On his feet were springy track-shoes, and whatever perverse trousers he had on under the Dr. Zhivago coat, their beetroot-red, elastic cuffs were tight round his ankles. He balanced a kitbag on one shoulder, and in his left hand carried a rolled magazine with which he swatted the air, beating time to silent music, perhaps Bach, perhaps Lionel Richie. Spotting Peckover, he bared white teeth in a grin, and veered, hoisting his arm and magazine high in salute.

Peckover's heart lightened, something it had not done in days, though with reservations. Remembering seniority, and to avoid smiling back, applauding even, he assembled a frown. A plainclothes copper aged twenty-four, in Brixton, wore the same daft gear as his jobless contemporaries if he was going to move among them with any sort of ease. He'd make no headway in City pinstripes. There were limits though. Last time he'd seen the lad, a year ago, he'd been decked out in a midnight-blue George Raft suit, circa 1940, and a spotted Aunt Jemima Pancake Mix bandana.

Good on yer, Frank, and ta, Peckover mused. Nothing like residual guilt, ten years of it, to prod a fornicator into shaping up and delivering.

The apparition came to a halt in front of Peckover and said, "Detective Constable Twitty reporting for the action, sir." Smiling like a Bechstein grand, he flopped the kitbag onto the floor and held out his hand.

The flight was fullish, but with paeans of gratitude and not too much disription to three girls who looked as if they hadn't slept for even longer than Peckover, the policemen acquired adjacent seats.

Twitty wiped sleet from the Panama hat with a silvery forearm and placed it in the overhead locker. The hat had a grosgrain band, a ridge bisecting the crown fore and aft, and an interior lightly sweat-stained from encounters with gum trees in Malaya, or wherever its previous owner had worn it—for all Constable Twitty knew, on the croquet lawns of Hampshire. The coat being too bulky to join the hat in the locker, Twitty folded it and tried to stow it under the seat, for which it was also too large, but he didn't have much choice. Invading areas of wet lapels and sleeves sprawled into Peckover's floor space and lay there in furry lumps like dead rabbits in a laboratory. Lissom in a borscht-red jogging-suit, Twitty was now an Olympic pole vaulter in the warm-up stage, except Peckover wasn't looking, he was carefully not looking, and suffering a further crisis of doubt about his chosen assistant. Twitty sat, turned his head to smile at Peckover, who was fishing in his briefcase, leaned forward to examine the vile afternoon through the window, leaned back, sang in a whispering baritone, "Leavin'—*on* a jetplane," bent low and foraged in the folds of the silver sprawl, surfaced with the magazine, and settled it on his lap.

Good Housekeeping. He stole a glance at Peckover. Peckover was eyeing him.

"Put that away," Peckover said. "Fasten your seatbelt. See what it says up there? Study the safety drill, it's in that pocket, and pay attention when she does 'er demo about oxygen and lifebelts. You really fancied you could bring that kitbag aboard as hand baggage?"

"Thought I was travelling light." The accent was not Brixton, it was BBC World Service. "It's got my summer cottons in it."

"'Ow long d'you think we're going for—the social season? Tell me, have you ever flown before?"

"Of course. Once. To Majorca. I was thirteen."

"Blimey. Should 'ave guessed it? That when you won the scholarship?"

"My parents took me on a package. Skyway Suntours. They went into liquidation the next month. My dad said all my new friends at Harrow would be well-travelled so I must be well-travelled too. Made me a cosmopolitan, Majorca did."

"I can see that."

"My new friends wouldn't have been seen dead in Majorca. They spent their holidays in hunting lodges in Kenya when they weren't on private yachts at Monte Carlo or huntin' and fishin' in Scotland on the laird's twenty-thousand acres."

"Didn't give you a taste for travel, Majorca?"

"Taste of olive oil. Got heatstroke and dysentery and paella-rot."

Peckover held on to his neutral, interested expression. He thought: Hell's bells and blood, if Majorca collapses him, what's the Mosquito Coast going to do? His doubts multiplied. Get off the subject, he advised himself. Put the lad at ease.

The lad was clearly as at ease as a cat on a cushion.

"Your dad still a postman?"

"Still is." Twitty's grin flashed in place. "He won his area's Most Cheerful Postman Award. Twenty-five quid and a certificate. He wouldn't have if they'd known he kicks the dogs which shit on the pavement, but he's crafty, he pats them if anyone's watching. I tell him he should keep kicking them, he is doing the state some service."

"So where d'you go for your holidays?"

"Go dancing. Cricket. I open the bowling for the Division team. Went to Paris once, hovercraft and bus, went with a girl, Shana. It was London without real food and we couldn't understand anyone."

"They didn't teach you French at Harrow?"

"Six years of it. French, German, Greek, Latin. Computers, ethics, astronomy, comparative religion, banjo, lawn care. It's an extremely well-rounded education. Four years ago, did the summer solstice at Stonehenge with the skins and hippies. That was with Jacintha. I wouldn't go there again either. We were nearly arrested. Bastard coppers."

Peckover looked out of the corner of his eye to confirm that this was a joke. Twitty was sorting through folders, in-flight magazines, and sick-bags. Perhaps it wasn't a joke. Impossible to tell.

"You've never been to Jamaica," Peckover said.

"Any chance of a side trip?"

"None." Bahamas just possibly. Unlikely though. Peckover hoped it was unlikely. "You don't by any chance 'ave a pink card?"

"For a gun? No. Why?"

"Just asking."

Twitty watched the runway move sluggishly, then less sluggishly, and eventually hurtle. The Boeing 727 rose and tilted. Through the window a grimy, angled rectangle of roofs and fields receded.

"Majorca, sir, sorry. It's not true, I didn't have dysentery. I've the stomach of a goat. What I'm saying is, I'm not going to be a drag, I'm ripe for seeing the world. You might have to feed me tranquillisers. Best thing that's happened to me since I joined the force, this, so if you had anything to do with it, thank you."

"When you've got over the thrill, read that." Peckover handed over a fat, yellow envelope. "You can wake me for dinner. Nothing else, all right? Not earphones, films, wine waiters, turbulence, nothing."

He backed his seat into the recline position, settled the flimsy pillow behind his head, and shut his eyes. He opened his eyes. "What's the smell?"

"Poverty, sir."

"What?"

"It's the coat. It needs airing. Only twenty quid, got it last week in Brixton market. The woman said it was chinchilla and belonged to Czar Nicholas the Second. I'd say it's dyed fox. Might be vole. She was right about the epoch, it's been in someone's attic for seventy years."

Peckover emitted muffled sounds of distress. He turned his head away and closed his eyes.

When nothing further was to be seen through the window, only the infinite drab smear of the sky, Twitty experimented with the overhead switches. One turned a light on and off. Another directed a blast of humming air at Chief Inspector Peckover, ruffling his hair and causing him to grunt. Twitty snapped the switch off. He regarded the sleeping figure with the raw temple. So far, all he knew of the case was what he had read in today's papers. And that he was off to Belize to question the Whites, or one of them, which made a change from questioning the blacks, or come to that, being questioned by them.

Too often from the blacks on the Brixton streets it was still—it was getting no better—"Hey, black boy, what the hell you doing being a Judas copper, man?"

The loot, he still answered, if he answered at all. A career, he might add, if he felt garrulous, and the hostility wasn't at flashpoint. Loot and a career they didn't accept, but at least they got it. They were never going to comprehend lofty notions about morality, conscience, community relations, the social fabric. Why would they? "Social fabric? Social shit, man." So you agreed with them there were ignorant, nigger-baiting coppers, but what did they expect? What were they doing about it? Twenty-seven thousand Met police, biggest force in the world, and only a crummy three hundred were blacks and Asians. How was anything going to get better when blacks didn't *become* coppers? Infiltrate, man! Come join us! So they told you those three hundred should be put in one big box and sunk in the Thames.

Twitty bought a pineapple juice from a piled cart which came trundling along the aisle. He put on a headset and twiddled the dial in the armrest, tuning channels in and out. Pop, Classical, Showtime, Easy Listening. Easy Listening was unbearable, insupportable saccharine strings. He twiddled. The voice like boots treading on cinders was Tom Waits. He'd do.

Copperdom was okay. How many bank managers were off to the Spanish Main right now? How many doctors, teachers, estate agents? How many of his Old Harrovian mates hustling at Lloyds and the Stock Exchange, dealing and trading, milking and bilking, coining another half million from inside, old-boy information while on the road to a burst ulcer and the penitentiary?

Twitty consulted the table of contents in *Good Housekeeping* and turned to "Kitchen Catastrophes and Related Crises, or, It Could Happen to You if It Hasn't Already." Gor blimey and stone the crows, two pages of it. And the name: Henry Peckover.

> O action-painted kitchen!
> O decorated me!
> O living, panchromatic art!
> O flying potpourri!

O hot and fishy particles
Of aubergine and squid!
The day I took my finger
Off our blender's airborne lid.

Not what you'd exactly call moving, or dense with insight.
Did they pay him for this or did he pay them?

Oh boy!
　　We dined, me and my mate,
　　So well that night and not too late
　　Because at nine we had to see
　　This masterpiece on our TV.

　　A salmon souffle with brown bread,
　　Then cassoulet (prepared ahead),
　　Chive salad, cheese, zabaglione—
　　When, blast it, rings the telephone.

　　"Hullo? It's Ann, and getting late.
　　You've not forgot our supper date?
　　For starters we've the freshest hake,
　　Then Irish stew, and birthday cake."

　　"Forgotten? Never! Set to go!"
　　Oh grief! Calamity!
　　　　　　　　Oh woe!

Mm. There were three longish ones, one about a bursting baked potato. Later, Twitty put the magazine aside and opened the envelope.

Xeroxes of files on Vivian White, Sir Peter White, Robert Bertram Murray, deceased, others he had never heard of. Photographs. Statements from the secretary of the National Sporting Club, from Patricia Wilson, cosmetician, Jennifer Patterson, model. Reports on the incident in Collins Cross, one of them by DCI Henry Peckover. The file on DC James Thornley, murdered. The file on Jeremy Clegg, murdered, shot four times, close range, .32 shells as from FN Browning automatic...surmise only...no murder weapon found....

Why had the guv'nor asked if he had a pink card? Twitty looked at sleeping Peckover.

No one speaks English and everything's broken, sang the cement-mixer voice of Tom Waits.

Twitty turned down the volume a little, not too much, and began to read.

Detectives Peckover and Twitty with their passports and bags filtered through immigration and customs and out of the thronged arrivals hall into seventy-five degrees of early evening sunshine. Twitty was wide-eyed and already high on the U.S.A. His springy, Nike-shod feet stepped for the first time on New World soil, which here was asphalt, there concrete; and vinyl and stained carpet, dotted with chewing-gum wrappers, back in the terminal building, into which Peckover now led him, one gulp of unseasonably warm air seeming to have been enough for the guv'nor's refrigerated London lungs. Twitty, elated and marvelling, yet with an aggrieved call-this-weather-Christmas expression, folded over his arm the czar's mildewed fox which he had donned when leaving the plane. Little wonder the unsmiling black customs man had asked him, "Where is the gold rush, brother? You got huskies to declare?"

The connecting flight was to connect tomorrow at 10 A.M. Mrs. Coulter had booked the policemen in here for the night, the Miami International Airport Hotel, atop the terminal building. They rode lifts, or elevators, and while Peckover registered, Twitty plucked Florida publicity from a rack.

"Disney World—sir, could we?" Detective Constable Twitty spilled folders over the floor of another elevator as he read aloud exotic, incomprehensible words. "Hialeah—can we go racing? What's the Orange Bowl? Sir, a Bay cruise?"

Striding a carpeted corridor, looking at room numbers, Peckover said, "Until we're with Superintendent Campos, you can drop the 'sir.'" Faintly embarrassing this, but the lad was green, and he had to say it. For the next two, three days they were a team, dependent and intimate, heaven help them. "I 'ave a first name."

"Sir?"

"'Enry. And you're, um—Jason?"

"Wasn't my choice, sir. You don't have to. My dad wanted Winston but my mum won with Jason."

They shared a limousine to downtown Miami with expense-account gentlemen in floral, open-neck shirts who disputed among themselves about giants, vikings, redskins, bears, and rams. They walked on Biscayne Boulevard, inhaling ocean ozone and petrol fumes. They took a taxi to Miami Beach and stood in front of windows in a mall in Bal Harbour, looking blankly at tweed fishing-hats, glass eggs, and platinum candlesticks, millionaire junk identical to Bond Street junk which at home they would have gone a mile out of their way to avoid.

Twitty wanted to swim in the sea, find a disco, then swim some more. Peckover said, "Sorry—sleep. Tomorrow the treadmill, could be, er"—he dared it—"Jason."

The name emerged on an unnaturally low, hushed note. Passers-by in earshot might have thought it amorous. The policemen avoided each other's eyes. "I'll buy you a hamburger," Peckover said. What they had seen of Bal Harbour looked a little fancy for hamburgers: except there across the concourse was Mario's Surf 'n' Turf Saloon.

"Hi, I'm Melinda, and I'm your hostess this evening. Our specials are . . ."

Twitty missed what the specials were, announced lickety-split by sun-kissed Melinda. He had fallen immediately in staring, slack-jawed love with her body, and even more with her American accent, the melody of its unselfconscious banjo-twang preventing him from taking in a word she said. Peckover caught random phrases and doubted them all. ". . . jerked pastrami Florentine . . . devilled catfish balls . . . snapper gumbo Mario, saffron grits on the side . . . Cuban brain fritters with Mario's au jus gravy . . ." Melinda, after her performance, did not appear to mind bringing hamburgers. They were fat, fleshy, seeping, and all in all quite a distance from items of the same name in the Wimpy bars of Oxford Street. The salad was a crisp and glittering hillock of Everglade-green. Twitty's potato skins looked like the sweepings from a carpenter's shop, and when he had flooded them with ketchup, they looked like the carpenter after an accident with his lathe.

At eleven-thirty they were back at their hotel. "There was a call for you," said the girl at reception, and she presented a sheet from a memo pad. "He said no need to call back."

Peckover unfolded the paper. Twitty peered over his shoulder. Veal's message read like a cable. *Viv consignment due tomorrow Sunday. Festina lente. Happy hunting. Frank.*

Upward in the elevator, Peckover said, "Festina bleedin' lente. So what's all that about?"

"More haste, less speed."

"I know what it means. I don't know what he's trying to say. Our flight's ten o'clock. Nothing we can do about it."

"Perhaps he's simply saying don't miss it."

"We're not going to miss it. If he's gone to bed with a dictionary of Latin proverbs, let's 'ope he's not going to be phoning every time there's one fires his imagination."

"Let's hope we don't miss the consignment."

What if we do?" Peckover wondered. Frank and the thinkers had to be right in supposing the answers to the murders of Thornley and Clegg and the doorstep sleazos weren't going to be found in London, but in Belize. But Belize wasn't going to spout answers like a fountain. What was fishy was Campos being so keen to bring in the Yard.

All right, police could be floored, they could ask for help. In this case, though, asking for help looked like an outright admission of incompetence. If Campos was straight and genuinely wanted Viv collared and put away, why didn't he go ahead and do it? If he hadn't the evidence, Johnny-on-the-Spot, did he imagine the Yard was going to ride in and conjure evidence out of the air?

If he was in Viv's pocket, stashing gratuities from Viv into his own deep pocket, why bring in outsiders who might nail him? Maybe he really was unhinged. A Campos without his compos mentis.

Maybe he intended to float a bribe in front of the white knights from the Factory.

Maybe this, maybe that. He'd know very soon, some of it. You never knew it all. The dark places of the soul. All that jazz.

They stepped from the elevator. Peckover said, "Six sharp tomorrow, lad. Press-ups and a cold bath before our Florida grapefruit segments in the coffee-shop." He took a breath. "Jason."

"Right on, sir—er—Henry."

TWELVE

A thousand miles and a few hours behind them, Miami was already cause for nostalgia. Balmy, comfy, beatific Miami.

Here was a steam bath. Belize International Airport. One runway, a single-storey terminal building of pasty complexion, to which functionaries herded them across melting tarmac, and a distant commotion of taxis, some audibly more decrepit than others. The heat pressed down and pummelled in undulating waves. Twitty carried his fur coat over his shoulder, impatient for the hotel and a chance to change into his summer cottons. Wearing them for the flight had not seemed to be quite the thing, an opinion of surprising propriety for Twitty, which he would soon regret.

In the customs hall Peckover's spirits lifted when he believed they might be refused entry. Which was to say that Twitty might be refused, if he weren't dragged in and gaoled. But they were a team, so to reject one was to reject both. Good, Peckover thought, smiling a hopeful smile.

Several passengers in the line straggling ahead were receiving an unhurried going-over, their suitcases opened, possessions strewn, shaving-cream tested with a squirt and a sniff, shoes shaken, snorkels blown through—and these were middle-aged tourist types of blameless aspect. Peckover thought Twitty unlikely to escape. He was too tall, too young, possibly the wrong colour, wore a red tracksuit and yellow hat, and carried the czar's mink, *Good Housekeeping*, and a World War I kitbag stencilled, Cpl. T. J. Wilson, R.E., 6038714. If asked to remove his hat, his hair would be revealed in its dubious glory, bound by elastic bands in corkscrew clumps, Brixton-style, and resembling nothing so much as the charred remains of a forest after a fire. The customs officer with the Mexican bandit's moustache who appeared to be totally idle had, in fact, twenty-twenty vision. He beckoned to Twitty.

Twitty stepped to the bench, dumped the kitbag, and accepted a large card listing a thousand prohibited items. The customs officer looked sorrowfully at the kitbag. "You open please," he said. Relieving Twitty of the fur coat, he began a leisurely scruting: sleeves, collar, hem, pockets, lining. Peckover judged they could be in for a long wait.

"Excuse me, Mr. Peckover?"

Peckover regarded a man closer to Twitty's age than his own. Milk-chocolate-coloured, big shoulders, the long eyelashes of a silent-screen vamp. He wore a cotton safari suit and held sunglasses. Sergeant Montego, Belize Police, he said, and returned the sunglasses to his nose. Goodbye eyelashes.

They swapped, read, and returned warrant cards. Superintendent Campos was detained, Sergeant Montego said, but he sent greetings and would be happy for them to join him.

"For the consignment?" Peckover said.

"If it happens. If it had not already happened." The sergeant looked up at the clock on the custom's hall's wall. "Two, three hours drive, depending. We make good time, we'll be there before Mr. Campos."

"We're not going to be out of here for two, three hours depending. This is Detective Constable Twitty."

Twitty looked up from his browsing through the list of illegal goods. His customs officer with the Viva Zapata moustache had turned the czar's sleeves inside out and was examining the stitching with the hawk eye of a quality control inspector. He was light years from starting on the kitbag. Sergeant Montego leaned across the bench, shook hands with the customs man, and talked to him. The customs man dropped the coat on the bench, chalked a hieroglyph on the kitbag, and sauntered away.

"That it?" Peckover said.

"That's it."

Peckover and Twitty followed the sergeant into the glare of early afternoon and across blistering tarmac to a Land Rover with a yellow stripe and the word *Police* along its side. Under a canvas roof held up by struts the sides were open, windowless. Dusty license plates, black letters and numbers on white, bore the word *Belize*.

"Sorry, you arrive at the hottest time of the day," Sergeant Montego said. "Sling your bags."

Peckover sat in the front passenger seat, Twitty in the back. The sergeant drove from the airport onto Northern Highway and after a few miles took the left fork onto Western Highway. Western, Northern, the highways shimmered identically in the heat, their surfaces here and there scarred and holed. If Land Rovers are what coppers use here, they don't anticipate much chasing about, Peckover reflected. In this weather he was not surprised.

On each side of the road were haphazard shacks with red-ribboned wreaths on the doors. There were cut-out Santas, children playing in the dust, chickens, and goats. Youths in jeans were kicking a football. Mad dogs and Belizeans di-dum da-da dum-di-dum. Women in bright skirts and blouses walked singly or in groups holding baskets and babies. Two men in straw hats worked with hoes in a field. Peanuts? Rice?

Now there were only the vivid greens and browns of trees with hanging vines, and once a glimpse of disappearing scarlet and black which Sergeant Montego said was probably a macaw or a toucan. Peckover took off his jacket and folded it on his lap. He wished he could be sharing this with Miriam and the children. On the other hand, the children would have been floppy and cross from the heat. They were better off where they were with sleet and central heating. More dilapidated huts hove into view, and at the roadside a knot of 'people looking down on what appeared to be a dead or sleeping cow. But dwellings were becoming rarer, the jungle denser, the road emptier. Twitty in the back had put on his walkman. He swayed and jiggled as he observed the panorama of afternoon in uninhabited, inland Belize.

Peckover had the impression the road climbed, gradually but continually, through mile after mile of hot, empty landscape. Forest, scrub, a marshy area where the trees had roots like bent stilts. Mangrove trees? How was he to know? There were no mangrove trees in Hyde Park, and he wasn't going to start asking question after question about stuff everyone knew the answer to except himself. The white-haired driver of an approaching BMW with its sunroof open saluted and waved. The sergeant waved back.

He said, "Freddie Carballo. He's in the House of Representatives. Been visiting his ladyfriend."

"You can tell by the dreamy, sated look?"

"You can tell because he's given his chauffeur time off."

"Don't we go through Belize—Belize City?" Peckover said.

"Fifty miles behind us, opposite direction," said the sergeant. "Handy if Mr. White and his like would conduct their business out of the airport, or the municipal airport, but they prefer the interior. Must be nature-lovers at heart."

"Bugger, I've been bitten," Twitty announced from the back. "Twice. We've only been here five minutes."

Peckover looked at his Swatch, a birthday present from Sam and Mary. It had a white face and rare, honest-to-God numbers, one to twelve, not four dots, or an aperture with clicking figures. They had been on the road more than an hour. A glint of river or swamp appeared through the trees, and was gone.

"What's that?" Twitty cried, staring, plucking off the walkman.

A bristly brown rump with short legs crashed into the undergrowth and vanished.

"Boar," said the sergeant.

"Sorry, I'm sure," Twitty muttered. "We can't be fascinating all the time."

"Gibnut," explained soothing Peckover, turning with the information. "The Queen eats it. Not all the time, I expect. You'll 'ave to try some."

He turned front. Gawd, we're like tourists, he thought. I ought at least to have a map. Before the sun goes down we could have the cuffs on Viv. Might have them on Campos too. Then hit the highspots. Belize City Palladium, bout of the local reggae for the lad, forty pints of beer. Home tomorrow.

What counted was that the sun went down.

Peckover wiped his dribbling forehead with the back of his hand. The plum-red temple protested at his salty touch. What counted was that the sun went down and he saw Viv before Viv saw him.

Sergeant Montego pointed. "Road for Belmopan, the capital." The Land Rover continued past a wide, signposted turning. "The government, police headquarters. You'll see it later. No one lives there if they can help it. We commute. Heard of Hurricane Hattie?"

"Should I 'ave?"

"Nineteen sixty-one. Flattened Belize—the city. Two hundred dead. So we build Belmopan, away from the ocean. Still building, still wondering if it's a good idea. See the poles?"

At intervals on each side of the road stood poles without wires.

"The army put them up." The sergeant swung the wheel to avoid a small squashed carcass on the road. "Traffickers used to land here. Now they can't or they get their wings torn off. You know the Honourable Viv?"

"A little." Here, too, Viv wore the courtesy title to which he was unentitled. "You?"

"Not yet. Soon maybe. If I find the track."

Track, hell's teeth. Peckover sponged with a Kleenex, avoiding the plum. "Your Señor Campos, he know Viv?"

"Sure, Benny knows everyone."

Benny? Benito? Frank Veal had never said Campos was Benny. *Benito adoremus, do-ho-mi-num,* Peckover hummed in his head. Gawd, Christmas a-coming.

The Western Highway was running out of steam, and repairs. It could have used a gang of functioning Irish navvies. The Land Rover bounced in and out of potholes, creating its own breeze. To his left, beyond the green roof of the jungle, Peckover observed a mauve haze of mountains. Whether five miles away, or fifty, or what country, he could not have guessed. He'd have given half his December pay for a gallon of tea.

"Our Maya Mountains," tour-guide Sergeant Montego informed. "Guatemala if we keep on. The road stops at the border."

Peckover thought it had already stopped. The vehicle ploughed through a litter of fallen branches.

"North is Mexico, but there is no road north, not from here. We must get off the road soon, but where? I don't know here." The sergeant, as he drove, peered at the jungle to his right. "No one knows here, only a few Indians. And smugglers." He braked with vigour and wrenched the wheel. His passengers lurched. He said, "We try here."

Where, Peckover wanted to know. They were aiming at impenetrable jungle.

But the Land Rover had already penetrated at five miles an hour and was accelerating, or trying to. The sergeant had found some sort of track. Someone had been this way, first perhaps with axes, next with vehicles. Looking out and down, Peckover saw lopped, crushed branches and wheel-flattened leaves. Where the ground became soggy he saw the serrations of tyre tracks.

Gloom and reeking vegetation pressed in. Springy branches struck the windshield and whipped into the Land Rover. Here was no sun, no breeze either. If there were jun-

gle screechings they were lost in the engine-roar. The trail
was a tunnel, a sunless twisting past tree-trunks which only
chain saws and elephants would ever fell. The front fender
picked up a leafy bough which wedged itself upright like a
banner, further obscuring the way ahead. Sergeant Montego
followed the track at ten miles an hour, trying for twenty, but
defeated by jungle.

He shouted above the din of second gear and crunching
wheels, "Hope all this leads somewhere! The area's roughly
right but we could still be miles out!"

Peckover held fast to one of the struts supporting the roof.
Twitty wedged himself lengthways, knees bent. The vehicle
pitched and tossed, and Peckover's head hit the canvas ceiling.
A helicopter would have made sense here, he thought, but for
want of a helicopter the Land Rover was making probably
better progress than any other vehicle he knew, of apart from a
tank.

"Listen—hear that?" Twitty called.

"What?" shouted the sergeant.

"Stop, kill the engine," Peckover said.

The Land Rover slowed, stopped, and the sergeant
switched off. A pair of silent eyes looked down. The eyes
took off into darkness streaked with blades of sunlight.
Emitting falsetto howls, the monkey orbited the Land Rover,
swooping and swinging through the trees.

"Probably been with us for miles," the sergeant said.

"That's not what I heard," said Twitty.

"What did you hear?"

"That."

They listened to thuds and their echoes. Wherever the
monkey had got to, it had ceased its jabber. Again came
sounds of spaced, metallic thuds, as from pistols. Next, the
vibrato of an automatic weapon.

"*Mierda,*" said the sergeant.

"It's ahead," Peckover said. "How far?"

"Not far." Montego's knuckles tightened on the wheel.
"Your guess good as mine."

"Go on then, keep going."

Twitty jumped to the ground, pulled the banner from the
bumper, tossed it aside, and climbed back into his seat as the
Land Rover jolted forward. Peckover put on his jacket. One
thing he knew, he pretty certainly wouldn't be telling Miriam
about any of this, whatever it was.

Maybe it was nothing. Jungle noises. Campos and his
troops passing the wait in gun practice.

Dream on, copper.

He would have understood if the sergeant had dawdled, even driven gently, accidentally, into a tree. But he drove as if they were needed. The needle rose to twenty, the vehicle bumped and swung, scraped by branches, smacked by leathery fronds. He hadn't liked to ask the sergeant if he were armed. It seemed too personal a question, something he was not in the habit of asking.

Perhaps the sergeant was armed. He might have something under the safari jacket. Would he have been so eager if he hadn't? In front, without warning, appeared a patch of sunlight.

As unexpectedly as the track into the jungle had begun, now it decanted the policemen into sun and space. Sergeant Montego brought the Land Rover to a stop. He slid the gear into neutral, keeping the engine running.

What seemed to be going on was a small war.

THIRTEEN

The makeshift landing strip was a lumpy oblong twice the length of a football field but little wider than the fifty-foot wingspan of an executive jet.

Sergeant Montego reached down and dragged a padlocked steel box from under the driver's seat. He had seen similar strips, clandestine airfields hacked from the jungle, a rendezvous for expert pilots only, until the strip was discovered, as this one now was, and blown up by the army, which had not happened here yet. At either end the otherwise geometric swathe bulged untidily where additional forest had been bulldozed and filled with many tons of cleared trees and stones.

Two aircraft were on the strip: an olive-drab Cessna at the far end, blending with the backdrop of jungle, and here where the Land Rover had arrived, a Beech Baron with a pastel-pink stripe and markings. Both planes were moving bumpily through the field's stubble, maneuvering as if for a jet-age joust.

Not that these were jets. The faraway Cessna had jumped the gun by starting already its charge along the strip. The baron, one lone figure in the cockpit, was still lumbering into position, slewing in a semi-circle to point its tail at the jungle, its nose and twin propellors along the strip. The shadow of its near wing passed over the ground in front of the Land Rover.

Neither Peckover nor Twitty knew a Cessna and a Beech Baron from each other or from a kilo of Belize calabashes, though given the name *Cessna* they would have been able to say, with everybody else, that a Cessna was what a West

German teenager had once flown into Moscow's Red Square. All Peckover knew was that they had arrived too late.

Or too early, if he had been hoping to arrive in the calm of aftermath, and to pick up the pieces from there. He was not sure what he had hoped.

Most of the activity was at the far end of the strip. Four or five figures were scattering from where the olive plane was beginning its take-off.

Muffled by the din or jet engines, a clatter of automatic fire rang out. Peckover could not see who was firing, from where, or at what.

From behind the olive plane appeared a black pickup truck, gathering speed, and heading for the wall of jungle where either it would turn away or crash. It did neither, but continued on and vanished, gulped by the jungle.

Into view on the far side of the accelerating olive plane came a matchstick figure on one knee, firing either at the plane or the scattering men. The rattle of the weapon was barely audible through the crescendo of engines.

Sergeant Montego unlocked the padlock on the steel box.

Midway along the strip, close to the jungle wall, stood two empty Land Rovers, or more probably Range Rovers, or some Japanese copy. Near them lay two men a dozen yards apart, keeping their heads down. If that is what they were doing. Peckover wondered if one of the men lying doggo might be Viv.

A sprinter in jeans, denim jacket, hunting-cap, and sunglasses was racing along the near edge of the strip towards the vehicles and the two prone figures. Peckover did not recognise this one either as Viv, the visor of the hunting-cap, and the glasses, masking the upper part of his face.

Sergeant Montego brought two pistols out of the box. "Present from Benny Campos," he shouted above the jet-plane din. "You didn't bring one in?"

Peckover gave a shake of his head.

"They're set to go," the sergeant shouted.

The barrel of the revolver presented to Peckover, grip first, looked to him longer by several inches than that of the Smith and Wesson he had trained with at Lippett's Hill. At the barrel's tip the sight jutted up like a tooth. The grip was not wood but metal, and from it dangled a ring like a wedding-ring.

He could say no.

He heard Miriam ask, *Have a lovely day playing with your gun?*

Frank Veal told him, *What you've got is weapons withdrawal syndrome.*

Sergeant McMaster adjusted his eyepatch, announced Seventy per cent, and all the world burst into song.

Peckover took the revolver and a cardboard box of bullets. When the sergeant reached back to Twitty with the second revolver, Peckover grabbed his wrist. The sergeant stared at Peckover, and shrugged. Piston-engines deafened. Peckover let go of the wrist.

"Your funeral—and his," Sergeant Montego mouthed, unheard, and returned the revolver to the box. He took out a gun from inside his jacket and laid it on the shelf above the dashboard.

Twitty stowed his walkman in his kitbag. The matchstick man on one knee at the far end of the strip rose to his feet and fired burst after futile burst at the departing Cessna. The Cessna lifted from the stubble and flew overhead, clearing the pink plane, the police Land Rover, and by a whisker the rim of the jungle.

"There go the Colombians!" shouted the sergeant.

Close to the Land Rover, the pink Baron paused as if taking breath before following the Cessna's example and quitting the strip, though in the opposite direction, into the sun. Peckover could see in the cockpit the silhouette of the pilot. If the Colombians had gone, this one was Viv's man.

He saw at the field's distant end several of the scattered figures running in the direction of the two abandoned Rovers and the prone men adjacent. Others stood their ground as if undecided what to do. The Baron, roaring, pointing along the strip, started to move forward. The engine of the sergeant's Land Rover idled inaudibly, ladylike.

"Can't we stop that thing?" yelled Peckover. Impede it, worry it. Christ, do something. Bash its tail, throw sticks and stones into a propellor. We're sitting here, we're useless.

"Go!" cried unexpected Twitty, the charred battlefield of his hair thrust between Peckover and the sergeant.

"You want to kill us?"

"Block it!" Twitty cried. "Get in front of it!"

"Get in front of it yourself!"

Sergeant Montego grabbed his gun and climbed out of the Land Rover. Peckover shoved the gun he had been given into his jacket pocket, stowed bullets into his trousers pocket, and slid into the driver's seat. He put the vehicle in gear and drove after the taxiing pink plane, thirty yards ahead. He would catch up with it all right but what then?

The plane paused momentarily. The engine-note was a

bellow, a beast hugely in heat. Cue for take-off?

Peckover drove in a wide arc round the wing and over-took the plane. He twisted the wheel, U-turned, and looked head-on at the brute's nose, belly, wings, and wheels, moving again, bearing down on the Land Rover, veering slightly right as if in a last-ditch attempt to avoid trouble. Those pro-pellors would shred you. Between and beneath them, Peck-over judged, was space for a Land Rover, its bonnet anyway, to snuggle against that front wheel beneath the belly and bring matters to a halt. Twitty was clambering from the back into the seat beside him. He held a Phillips screwdriver and a needle file from the vehicle's tool chest.

"Keep your head down!" Peckover shouted, and drove forward.

The angle was wrong. The plane was veering right and was no longer head-on. In avoiding the port propellor he was also going to miss the nose wheel. He braked as he and Twitty, riding shotgun, clinging to a strut, left the sunshine behind and entered into shade beneath the snout. The bon-net of the Land Rover cleared but its roof hit the belly of the conical, pink-striped radome. The canvas split, struts buck-led, the windshield cracked. The plane, booming, moving at a crawl, pushed the wedged, stalled Land Rover sideways.

Peckover turned the key in the ignition, put the gear into reverse, and swung the wheel, trying to be free of the two-and-a-half tons of aircraft above his head. He could jump, hope he didn't jump into a propellor. Twitty had already jumped. Not that the plane was advancing at more than walking pace, but it was on the move, like a bulldozer.

Through the cracked windshield Peckover saw Twitty, berserk, attacking a fat wheel with the Phillips screwdriver. The Land Rover lurched backward into sunlight, liberated, and stalled again.

The ripped roof had settled on Peckover's head like a grotesque sun hat. He could see ahead only by leaning side-ways out of the vehicle. He switched on, reversed, then drove from behind the wing for more shade and the port wheel. He stamped on the brake.

His bumper hit the wheel, the cracked windshield shat-tered. Peckover, hanging sideways out of his seat, could not imagine why. He had driven too brief a distance to have got up speed. The aircraft had come to a stop. A hand grabbed the scruff of his collar and he was pulled bodily from his seat.

He fell backwards on top of—he guessed—Twitty, who he'd be damned if he'd call Jason ever again.

Or Viv? Arrived at last to settle with a certain London copper?

"*Carajo!*" cried his assailant as two hundred pounds of policeman landed on him. He was Sergeant Montego, one leg bent beneath Peckover's hip, but holding him down, and shouting, "Stay down! We're being shot at!"

A bullet twanged against the other side of the Land Rover. Peckover hoped it was the other side. He could see nothing except earth and a segment of Michelin tyre. If a bullet was what had smashed the windscreen, it could not have been far from his head. He rolled off the sergeant.

"Where? Who?"

"The pilot—from the flight deck!"

You could open those cockpit windows? Evidently. A pilot might have to talk to his ground crew. Peckover chose not to get up and go and check.

"All right?" he shouted.

"All right what?"

"You!"

"Yes! Maybe!"

Sergeant Montego had released him. They lay side by side by the Land Rover, awaiting the next bullet. As long as they stayed put, and the pilot kept to his cockpit, bullets would be wasted, unless they were the armour-piercing kind which could pass through one side of the Land Rover, out the other, and into any random characters stretched out here on the ground.

Peckover breathed in thick smells of earth and something powerfully like paraffin which he guessed was not paraffin but whatever fuelled the plane. By turning his head he had a worm's view under the Land Rover and along the ground to the nosewheel, Twitty's nosewheel where the lad had stabbed and stabbed, and which seemed to have sunk. Unless he was being pathetically wishful, the whole belly of the noseeone had tilted forward and down. Where was Twitty though?

Tackling the wheel under the far wing perhaps, making a thorough job. Peckover could not see the far wing and its wheel. Twitty had to be there. Give the lad the *croix de guerre.*

Not posthumously, please God. Dammit, where was he? He'd be staying down, out of sight. Tackling wheels out of sight of the cockpit. Peckover sought Twitty but the Land Rover's wheels hid much of his view.

"D'you see Twitty?" he shouted at the sergeant, who was

no longer wearing sunglasses. The words bombarded the air and hung there in stifling silence.

Whether the pink plane's engines had ceased their roaring at that same instant, or earlier, Peckover could not have said. In the sudden rush of silence his ears continued to boom and his head to throb. Narrow steps appeared on the far underside of the fuselage, lowering themselves to the ground.

"He's leaving," the sergeant said. "Come on."

As far as his own leaving went, Sergeant Montego was over-sanguine. He was having trouble with his knee and climbed to his feet only by hauling himself up the side of the Land Rover. His sunglasses lay splintered on the ground and his vamp's eyelashes glistened with sweat. The man in smart blue trousers and a blue shirt—he could have been a policeman, or a Royal Air Force flyer—came down the steps with no knee problem and sprinted from the plane like a hopeful for the gold in the hundred-metres dash, though ahead were no finishing-tape, timekeepers, and frenzied crowds. Only jungle, and considerably closer than a hundred metres away.

Peckover climbed to his feet and shouted, "Stop!"

In the absence of the lamed sergeant, and Twitty, and Campos, and police reinforcements from Belize's best, if they were here, Peckover judged that he was on his own. He chased round the nose of the crippled pink Baron and after its fleeing pilot.

FOURTEEN

Peckover was acutely aware that he was not dressed for this.

The sun over Central America sneered down on him in contempt, hissing slightly, its lip curled. He was not wearing his parka or tie, which were in the Land Rover. Otherwise he could hardly have been less appropriately clad.

He enjoyed clothes, and as long as Miriam was not looking too closely, he was capable of being adventurous, though not in the same league as Twitty. He owned ample summer gear for holidays in France: lightweight slacks, shorts, cheerful short-sleeved shirts, a pair of sandals with thongs, another pair with buckles, an apricot-coloured cotton jacket, and among three warm-weather suits, one in chicken-fat-yellow linen (Puro Lino, Made in Italy) from a bygone January sale at Simpson's, a sickeningly expensive purchase, never mind it had been half price and subject to ineradicable creasing the instant it was put on.

None of this he had brought to Belize. Miriam, as was her wont come summer's end, had stowed all such trappings away in one of the trunks in the attic. She had not been available to hunt it out for him, he had been too pressed to look for himself, and anyway it would have smelled of fermenting must, camphor, last July's wine tastings and spillings in Provence, and picnics of goose liver pâté and reeking Munster cheese.

He had not been that pressed; he could have hunted something out for himself. He had avoided doing so out of defiance and resentment. He had not asked for Belize. He would be here only a couple of days. Let the tropics do their worst.

So Peckover gave pursuit wearing the grey worsted herringbone with the heavy lining, cuff buttons, and sporty vent, which he had worn at breakfast with Frank Veal yesterday. Only yesterday? Come to that, he had worn it in sleet and slop most of last week. Plus black brogues which could have done with a polish.

The lump of metal in his jacket pocket was doing nothing for the pocket and slammed against his hip as he ran. The sergeant had said the gun was set to go. Peckover hoped its slamming and bouncing didn't cause it to go off in his pocket. Shoot off his appendages. He was tempted to fling it.

"You—stop!" he shouted. "Police!"

How banal that command, how sheerly silly! Worse, how dated, like a plea from some cockles-and-whelks Victorian peeler puffing along the Mile End Road in pursuit of the Artful Dodger. Time the idle layabouts on the airstrip got their fingers out, shifted themselves, helped collar the pilot.

"Police!" Peckover shouted. "Stop!"

Running, he looked about him for Twitty. The nearest figure, friend or foe, was the character in the hunting-cap, some forty yards away, and loping in his direction.

From the area of the two abandoned vehicles, others were starting to move his way, though with no great sense of purpose. He supposed they were Campos and his troops, some of them anyway. They could hardly be expected to know who he was. For all they knew he was a Colombian drugs artist with a grease gun up his jumper. Wipe out the lot of them. They probably hadn't a clue about the pilot either.

"Stop!" Peckover called pointlessly after the pilot.

The pilot glanced back: fair-haired, a pleasant enough face, or it might have been but for the agape mouth. The fellow looked front and raced harder. He hurdled a prostrate tree, jumped over a wall of bulldozed debris, forced his way through a screen of branches bearing brown, dead leaves, and vanished from sight into lopped, living jungle.

Peckover would have liked to have hurdled the tree, but its girth was wide, and his two legs were his only legs. The sergeant bloke already appeared to have been left with only one good leg, wherever he was. Peckover jumped onto the prostrate tree, balanced, dropped into a compost of vegetable matter on the other side, then clambered through the hewn, spikey mass of dead boughs.

Stone the sufferin' crows! Skinny branches like wires whipped his face. Underfoot there'd probably be snakes.

Scorpions. Bleedin' lurkin' tigers and crocodiles waiting to sink their teeth in you, swallow you down. A branch jabbed into his calf, probably piercing the worsted, and an artery, giving him malignant mangrove fever.

Stinking sun, who wanted it? An insect had flown into his mouth. Gawd, London. He'd have given a leg. Well, a finger. Just the tip. Spitting out insect life, he swung his leg over a log which had a green, sappy bark.

"Mr. Peckover!"

Twitty.

Astride the log, Peckover looked back to his left and saw only the running hunting-cap, who was a bloke, had to be, but not Twitty. But it had been Twitty who had called. Not "Mister Peckover," as normal people say it, but the cut-glass Harrow and BBC bleedin' "Mist-ah Peckov-ah" which can splinter glass. The twit, the innocent, misplaced, misbegotten, black, bleedin' toff. So much for roots. You'd have thought out here, bleedin' Caribbean, there'd have been some sort of ancestral welling up, he'd have called out "Mister Peckover" like a local, or in Rasta. "Hey, you jiveass honkie Mister Peckover, man!"

Peckover looked to his right and saw Twitty in his borscht tracksuit bounding toward him along the hem of the jungle, waving an arm as if hailing a bus.

"Mr. Peckover—sir!"

Peckover pointed and shouted, "Get in there!"

Twitty, puzzled, broke his stride, but kept cantering on.

Deaf.

Peckover gesticulated, arms brandishing, one rigid, stabbing finger pointing Twitty into the jungle, now right where he was. The fingers of his other hand danced from his chest to the route the pilot had taken, demonstrating as clear as day a pincer movement. Twitty slowed to a trot, offered a bewildered ivory smile, and kept coming.

In a moment we'll be able to sit down for a leisurely talk, Peckover thought. The pilot is going to get away while we get out the billy-can and stew up a python.

He stood waveringly on a bulldozed tree. A copper on traffic duty, he pointed one arm at approaching Twitty, the other into the jungle, and bellowed, "Get in there!"

Twitty wheeled and vanished into the trees.

Peckover ploughed onward. I'm not sending the lad to his execution, he insisted. The pilot went this way, not Twitty's route. The lad would be fine. The pilot had probably left his gun in the plane.

All academic anyway. Where was the pilot?

One black brogue on a pile of rubble, the other about to push down on a branch across his path, Peckover held still, listening. From the trees into which Twitty had plunged came thrashings and crunchings punctuated by a different note, possibly human, which may have been Brixton oaths.

Wisest might be to leave to Campos and his local knowledge the flushing of the pilot from the forest. Give the pilot half an hour, he'd come out without being asked. No one in his senses was going to swan about indefinitely in forsaken horrible jungle infested with cobras and giant rats and lions and cannibals and yellow fever. Pilots particularly, free spirits, their home the wide blue yonder.

On the other hand a copper plugged on. Peckover crashed through the leafy barrage of lopped trunks and branches and into vibrant black jungle.

Straight on? Left? Right? A boy scout would have looked for spoor and followed the pilot's tracks.

Peckover couldn't see tracks. He couldn't see much of anything in the jungle's gloom. He waited, and saw and heard nothing. Even the scrabblings from the direction of Twitty had ceased. His underwear stuck and one eye smarted from salty trickles.

He picked his way between packed roots and trunks encrusted with lichen. Visibility was a few yards. Did he press on or write off the exercise as profitless and dangerous? He could hardly retreat, having sent Twitty in. A woolly liana brushed his face. He recoiled, swiping at it. The merest touch of the thing probably killed you.

All about him was dank, decaying sunlessness, a mite cooler than on the landing-strip, but suffocating. A bloke could suffer severe claustrophobia. Underfoot was now a squelchy mat of leaves and needles invaded by roots and high ferns which concealed who knew what creeping horrors. Believing he heard a scampering, a swift rustle in the dark, he stood still, chest deep in ferns.

Silence.

He trod forward, striving for stealth, but achieving the slow, magnified *chomp chomp* of one who has not learned to eat with his mouth closed.

Bank jobs on the Edgware Road, tarts and pickpockets at Covent Garden, crowd control on the Mall—none of it had trained him for this caper. Closest he had come must have been vice patrol in Hyde Park, treading on lovers. Bleedin' Frank Veal, saying he'd dreamed of filching Belize for himself, a jaunt into the sun. He was welcome.

Peckover threaded on, peering round tree-trunks, alert

for the least movement which might be that of a pilot in hiding. How, he wondered, fared Twitty? No sound from that direction. He placed his feet with as much delicacy as he could muster, not wanting to step on anything which might squirm. Float like a butterfly, sting like a bee.

Some butterfly. *Chomp. Squelch.* The brogues sank up to the ankles in swamp. Much of the time it was impossible to see where he was putting his feet.

If this were the start of the dry season, it was only just the start. There had been rain. That or he was heading into the primeval ooze. Or on the edge of some putrid, stagnant river swarming with piranha and septic, venom-squirting jellyfish. There'd be quicksand. Leeches. Gawd, like the sucking brutes all over Humphrey Bogart in *The African Queen*.

Though he had penetrated no more than twenty or thirty yards, when he looked back the jungle had closed in. Not a chink of sun to show that the strip was there. If he were to be revolved three times as in blindman's buff—without the blindfold, no need for it—he would not have been able to say which way was the strip, which way Guatemala.

He heard distant thrashing sounds. Again he stopped dead, listening.

The pilot? Twitty? Jungle wild life? The thrashings stopped. They had come vaguely from the direction of where Twitty might have got to if he had not progressed far, and likely he hadn't. Twitty had no more experience than himself of Indian-type trackings. All the lad knew of jungle warfare would be surveillance duty on Clapham Common, disguised as a sapling, standing under a dripping oak tree watching the pushers and dealers.

Would a pilot be versed in guerilla, jungle stuff? That didn't seem likely either.

From the region of the thrashings, Peckover believed he heard voices. They were muffled, percolating through walls of foliage.

The pilot—with Viv? They might have been the voices of apes with bananas. A murmuring gobbledygook. Peckover discovered that he had taken the gun from his pocket. ". . . cover . . ." a voice seemed to say.

Cover? There had been a voiceless, velar *k* sound and a couple of syllables, with other syllables and blurred plosives and fricatives. "Take cover"? "Undercover"? "A cobra"? "Come over"?

"Peckover"?

Voices or whatever, they had shut up. Hard to say how distant, but not far, a saunter to his left. Peckover was undecided whether this were an occasion when it would be better to do something than nothing, or nothing rather than something. He peered into the shadows, and while he saw no one, someone might have been there.

Someone decidedly was there. Voices were discoursing again, or one voice. Twitty talking to the trees? Peckover pointed the gun into the gloom: waist level, finger off the trigger.

Six cylinders. Loaded, ready to go. Dangling lanyard ring but no lanyard. Who used lanyards—the mounties, admirals? The barrel was five inches, making the whole thing about nine inches. Roll over, Buffalo Bill. He'd have it back in his pocket before Twitty spotted it and had a seizure. He felt scared—he wouldn't have cared who knew it—and feverish. Malaria, he guessed.

"Twitty," he called softly.

He wanted the call to be heard by Twitty but not by the pilot, and he grimaced, now knowing beyond a shadow of a doubt that he must be certifiable. He wished he were away from here. Oh, London.

"Constable!" he called sharply.

No answer.

"Jason? Jason Twitty?" Still louder, "That you? Hello?"

Not a rustle.

"Police!" Peckover barked, to discourage pilots. "Come out with your arms up, hands open!"

Rien de rien.

With infinite caution, Peckover stalked to his left. One step, two, three . . .

Waist level, the drawn weapons position, the gun should have pointed at the target, but there being no target, he moved it from left to right, right to left. Something moved, or he heard something. He turned his head and saw beside a tree, ten paces away, the pilot pointing a gun at him.

The pilot thumbed the safety-catch forward. Peckover watched him do it. Pale thumb on grey gun.

The gun was a .22 Browning Challenger automatic—not that Peckover had this information—bought for a hundred and fifty American dollars in Belize City from a fat boy who wore gold chains and rings. The pilot had tested it on a caye off Andros Island in the Bahamas. He held it one-handed, level with his chest, arm bent at the elbow.

Not the Lippett's Hill way. The closest cover was a tree several yards away.

Peckover screamed, "Don't!"

He dropped into a crouch and swung his arms to eye-level. Later, if there were to be a later, he would recall that he had reacted correctly. Sergeant McMaster had done a decent job. Two-handed, thumb-on-thumb, finger on the trigger, Peckover sighted his gun.

Seventy per cent and the pink card. He couldn't miss. Neither of them could miss. It was a matter of who first. What were they waiting for? Through the jungle's murk, in the jutting tooth of the sight on the revolver handed to him by Sergeant Montego, the pilot's cheeks were shiny and wet.

"Sorry," the pilot said.

Surrender?

It was over, bloodlessly. Peckover held his breath. In a moment he would disarm the good-looking fool, arrest him, and jump in the air. He'd be able to tell Frank Veal, tell the world, guns were not the answer. Miriam would kiss him.

Detective Chief Inspector Peckover held none the less his position, as well as his breath, aiming his gun at an imaginary penny between the pilot's eyes, above the streaming cheeks.

"Please, I'm sorry!" called the pilot.

His gun wavered as Peckover's had wavered on the weapons course. Mistrustful of wavering guns, Peckover danced sideways. The pilot's gun flashed and banged.

Peckover thought, I'll feel it in another second or two, it takes a second or two.

Feeling only tingling eardrums, he dashed for the tree. Jesse Owens, was it, who had said his secret was that his feet never touched the ground? Before he could reach the tree, the pilot's gun banged again.

Missed again. Christ, the bugger was serious!

The tree was the leanest in the jungle. Peckover had not chosen it; it had chosen him. Again the pilot's gun fired, louder, closer, from somewhere to the right.

Hugging the tree, Peckover stepped to his left, and chanced a look. The pilot had chased right and was running towards him in an arc, intending presumably to come up behind the tree and his quarry. But on which side would he arrive? The pilot ran sobbing and shooting. A chip of bark clipped Peckover's ear.

Peckover whirled back behind the fatuous tree and raised his gun two-handed in front of his face. The air reverberated with relentless, non-stop bangings. He could not point the gun with straight arms because of the tree, and not knowing on which side the pilot would arrive, so he held it in front of his nose. His finger was on the trigger. One more milligram of pressure, the instant the pilot's face appeared.

Christ, how many bullets did the maniac's gun have?

The pilot came spinning past him, a flailing blur of arms and legs, as out of control as an airplane shot from the sky. He plunged to the jungle floor and lay motionless.

Peckover did not move either, apart from his eyes looking beyond the gun in front of his nose to the sprawl of smart blue trousers and blue shirt in the ferns and muck.

"Sir?" said a voice.

The spreadeagled pilot clung to the automatic pistol which had done him no good at all.

"Mr. Peckover? Er—Henry?"

With Twitty was the hunting-cap character in the denim jacket, who was a woman. Peckover could not imagine how he had ever supposed she must be a man, except that here was no place for a woman. She was young, black, and sweaty.

"Your ear's bleeding," Twitty said.

Peckover nodded. He put his gun in his jacket pocket.

Breathing hard, with nothing to say, Peckover, Twitty, and the woman looked down at Lumley. Beneath the fair-haired head a widening puddle of blood was painting the ferns. More blood seeped from under the blue body and legs.

She must have emptied her gun into him, hit him every time, Peckover thought.

"Henry, this is Agent O'Day." A look of bemusement passed over Twitty's face. "You know, Los Angeles—in the file? We just met. In the woods."

"Woods?" Peckover said.

"Back there. P. O'Day, Drug Enforcement Agency, right?" Now Twitty was enthusiastic, proprietorial, like a theatrical agent showing off his personal discovery. He snapped his fingers, Lumley for the moment forgotten. "We heard you yelling."

"I was not yelling."

"You were yelling, you were—"

"I was *not* yelling."

"Not yelling." The snapping ceased. "No sir."

"You call this leprous 'orrible inferno of a piss-hole *woods?*"

"Yes sir. No." Twitty gulped. He told the woman, "May I introduce Chief Inspector Peckover?"

She did not raise or tip her hunting-cap but her expression was passably respectful. She looked about Twitty's age, and she wore sunglasses, as did everyone in Belize, Peckover had decided, except the London contingent. He wondered how, in sunglasses, in this sunless jungle, she could see her hand in front of her, let alone hit a running pilot. Her forehead was high and her upper lip long and convex, suggesting possibilities of a smashing smile underneath, should she smile, which she was not doing.

"Hi," she said, stepping forward, her hand outstretched. "You the poet?"

FIFTEEN

Before they reached the airstrip they were met by three blue and khaki Belize policemen with guns, jungle-chopping machetes, and obligatory sunglasses.

"Peckover, Scotland Yard, liaising with Superintendent Campos," Peckover announced peremptorily.

Their guns could blow him to pieces. They had no cause to shoot but they did not know that. They did not know him from Adam. They looked jumpy enough to shoot anything that moved then chop off its head with the machetes. He hoped he bore a charmed life, like Macduff.

They eyed him with suspicion. They regarded lofty, beetroot Twitty with contempt, and Agent O'Day with lust.

"Get on with it then, he's back there," Peckover snapped. Leadership, orders of command were what they needed. He trudged on, slashing backhanded at dangling kianas in his path.

O'Day and Twitty followed in Indian file. "Peace," murmured Twitty at the Belize trio, palm upraised. The closest of the three took a step towards him, and Twitty scuttled, treading on O'Day's heel.

They emerged into the blaze of the airstrip. Sergeant Montego and a uniformed policeman drove up in the wounded Land Rover. They both wore sunglasses, the sergeant having dug up a spare. The second policeman was brown and lined. He looked beyond retirement age. Police in khaki shirts and navy-blue caps and slacks were mounting the steps of the Beech Baron. Others were descending, carrying the roped bales of the consignment.

"Sounded like you found him," Sergeant Montego said.

They set off across the strip towards the two abandoned Land Rovers, one of them now clearly a Range Rover, and neither any longer abandoned, the area being alive with police. Other vehicles had arrived. The two doggo figures who had been keeping their heads down kept them down still. Someone was photographing them. Someone else knelt with a glinting forensic instrument.

Peckover, O'Day in the middle, and Twitty sat wedged in the back of the Land Rover. The ripped roof sagged and flapped, a breeze buffeted through the windowless windshield. Everyone wanted to know everything at the same time.

Peckover wanted to know first: "Where can I get a drink?"

Sergeant Montego, working the pedals with his left foot, said, "Sam Aragon usually has a bottle of scotch, but we're not supposed to know, and he'll charge you."

"I don't want scotch, I want a gallon of tea." Second question. "Viv?"

"What about Viv?"

"I 'aven't seen him yet."

"You expected to?"

"His consignment, isn't it?"

"Not any more." The sergeant braked and halted. They watched the bales being unloaded from the pink Baron. "Best of my knowledge, your Honourable never comes near. He's not stupid."

The implication seemed to Peckover to be that he, the intruder from the Yard, might be.

The sergeant said, "What happened with Lumley?"

"Lumley," said O'Day, as if to herself. *"Flight Leftenant."*

Nobody heard, or if they did they took no notice. Questions were being put, answers given or guessed at.

Peckover: What was the plane which left? The black pickup truck which left when we arrived? How's the leg?

Twitty: Guv, is the gun a write-off? I mean, if you couldn't defend yourself? Rust, is it? It was hairy, sir, I don't mind telling you.

O'Day: You really write real poetry like Gitche Gumee and the woods are lonely, dark and deep? I took a writing course in college, got a C-plus, but I never met a real poet before.

The olive plane had been a Cessna from Colombia, landing, delivering, and leaving. It had delivered early and the police had set up their ambush late, not from idleness but for want of information. They had been only marginally late. If the main purpose of the exercise had been to keep another six hundred kilos of cocaine from reaching the street, they had been on time.

"Any earlier we'd have lost more than two dead," the sergeant said. "We'd have been having it out with the Colombians. A bloodbath."

How many, wondered Peckover, constituted a bloodbath? Two dead were two dead. Three with Lumley.

Three misbegotten sleazos on his doorstep. Clegg. Long-ago Jimmy Thornley. Eight tied in one way or another with Viv. Not bad going, Viv. Peckover watched the bales being brought from the plane and lifted into the back of a police van.

"The Colombians?"

"The Colombians what?" Sergeant Montego said.

"On the plane, killed your two."

"They killed no one. They'd helped Lumley load—presumably they did, because that's a weight of coke. They were back in their plane when Benny Campos and our lot arrived. What I understand. Bruce?"

Bruce, due for retirement, said, "If you'd found the right track off the highway, you'd have been here as soon as us, pretty much."

And come under fire too, Peckover refrained from saying. He said, "So who?"

"Viv's men," the sergeant said, and put the Land Rover into gear.

"Lumley?"

"The two who cleared off in the pickup."

"You saw them?"

"Saw the pickup. Saw what you saw."

"Did anyone see them?"

"Everyone except us." The sergeant started the Land Rover off across the strip. "Bruce?"

Bruce took off his police cap. He turned his head and said, "They had MAC-Tens. Sam Aragon and Alec from Drugs were first here, saw the loading. Soon as Benny and the rest of us arrived, these two came out of the pickup and started blasting."

"Blasting you?"

"They weren't blasting each other. Their job was seeing the transfer was made and the planes got off. Anyone in the way was to be disposed of." Bruce sounded weary. "They didn't have to shoot. We weren't shooting. They were enjoying themselves."

Weary, bitter. He was entitled. Sooner he retired to a nice

hut on the beach, better for everyone, Peckover thought.
Name like Bruce, the beach ought to be Bondi. Bruce massaged his scalp. His other hand rested on the back of his seat,
holding his cap. Peckover angled his head to see the badge
above the peak. A shield with two men, one holding an axe,
the other what looked like a paddle. The axe to chop mahogany with, he supposed. The paddle for why? Because everyone who had settled in Belize had arrived by boat?

MAC-10s were what the pair in Collins Cross had murdered the sleazos with. Correction: MAC-10s may have been
what. Description of weapon courtesy of Henry Peckover,
CID. Identification from the gospel according to Dave Verity, blue beret.

"You'll collar them," Peckover said.

"If they're not already across the border."

"And how many more of us get killed if we try?" called
back Sergeant Montego.

"Christ," Peckover said. "We're going to try, aren't we?"

Twitty said, "Sir, I was thinking—"

"Just a moment," said Peckover. Hell's bleedin' coals and
kindling, what's going on? He leaned forward. "Sergeant—*if*
we try?"

"We're trying," said the sergeant over his shoulder. "It's
just that we don't need any of this. This country's okay. Why
don't you put Viv and his gorillas on a plane and take them
away with you?"

"We get any assistance?"

"What do you think you're getting? It's us disposable natives, the local yokels, it's we who've lost two dead—not
you."

Since you mention it, right, not me personally, by a
whisker. Peckover sat back, his face fairly stormy. Lumley,
dead in your filthy jungle, he wasn't exactly a local. Probably
from Piddletrenthide, every cottage gasping with roses. Or
satanic Stoke or West Hartlepool. He had never seen Piddletrenthide or West Hartlepool, but he had been in Stoke once
and he hoped Lumley had known better, poor bastard.

The sergeant had a point, of course. But let it go. He
sounded wearier than lined Bruce, and on the edge of mu-
tiny. Let that go too, Peckover decided. We're all weary.
Time for making allowances. Frank Veal would have made
allowances. Bill Astle would have made no allowances, he'd
have engineered the insolent sergeant's instant demotion,
first inserting red-hot needles under his fingernails. Peckover
sighed for London, both the okay bits and the rubbish.

Sergeant Montego had stopped to talk to a policeman on

a motorcycle about the alert put out on the pickup.

"Sir?"

"What is it?"

"That plane. I can't see it moving until the tyres are replaced, two of them."

"You going to replace them?"

"Well, no, I hadn't thought so."

"So don't worry about it. You did all right." Pauline? wondered Peckover. Pamela, Patricia, Polly? "Miss, um— can't call you O'Day. What's the *P*?"

"Peachy."

Peckover dabbed his nicked ear with a tissue. Perhaps he could learn to call her O'Day. The blood had dried, such as there was. He supposed it would be on his collar. As well he wasn't due at Buckingham Palace to collect his knighthood. What he sighed most for was his hotel room, if it existed, if Mrs. Coulter hadn't cocked it up, had one of her bad days, muddled Belize with Belgravia, or Belgrade, or Belgium. Booked them in at the Brussels Hilton.

Hilton. He should be so lucky. Even now, reception at the Brussels Hilton might be shrugging and snorting, erasing their names from the computer. *Mais où sont ces flics anglais, ces deux Sherlocks? Zut, l'Albion perfide!* He yearned for a drastic clean-up, a tank of tea, and horizontalism. Silence and solitude.

The motorcyclist varoomed off; the Land Rover moved on.

He looked at Twitty, who was looking at Agent O'Day. Peachy? Was she pulling his leg? She was gnawing a knuckle and had slumped.

Shock, both of them, Peckover judged. Like himself. They were in shock if they were human, and certainly Twitty was. He knew nothing about the girl except she should have been more shocked than anyone. She presumably didn't kill a man every day.

"This is the first?" he asked gently. She was young enough to have been his daughter, had he started his fathering at twenty instead of forty.

He had to repeat the question. Agent O'Day looked away and shook her head.

Christ, he thought.

They pulled up beside the Range Rover and climbed out. Sergeant Montego climbed most of the way out and stood on his left leg. He held on to a buckled strut while alternately swinging and massaging his other leg. Police were milling about, some with plastic cups of something liquid. Peckover would accept whatever it was.

An ambulance drove out of the same jungle gap into which Viv's men had driven in the pickup. Behind the Range Rover a policeman was draping a jacket with epaulettes and a police badge over the head and shoulders of one of his dead colleagues. Bruce from the Land Rover looked on. He had acquired one of the cups, from which he sipped what might have been tea. Peckover approached.

"Where do I get some of that?"

"Back of the wagon."

"Which one," Peckover said, looking around, "is Superintendent Campos?"

The Belize policeman gestured at the draped body. The jacket lay lumpily over the contours of the head and shoulders.

So, the hot line from Belize, cold, kaput. Frank Veal, are you listening? Do you know your hot-line amigo, here in the tropics, your Señor Campos, he's gone?

Sergeant Montego had not mentioned Campos being one of the two dead. Peckover suspected more than a pinch of surliness. Not that he could give a hoot but what had become of teamwork? He about-turned and started back to the Land Rover.

"Sir—Henry?"

"In a minute, lad."

Sergeant Montego, having swung and massaged, was hobbling in little circles.

Peckover said, "Mind tellin' me who's number two 'ere?"

"Two?"

"After Campos." The sergeant was more and more a pain. Every question answered with an echo. "Benny Campos, who 'as passed on to a better world, we certainly hope. You didn't think it worth telling me. Who's 'is deputy?"

"Deputy?"

Sergeant Montego hobbled, and Peckover of the plum temple and chipped ear breathed in deeply. He would still make allowances. If they couldn't work in some sort of harmony, what was the point his being here? Understandable, in a way, if this berk of a Belize flatfoot resented interlopers.

"His assistant. Next in line. The geezer who's in charge when he takes—used to take—the missus and kids to the beach. What I'm suggesting is, a bit of organisation might be no bad thing. And co-operation. We've got dead coppers 'ere. Who's in charge?"

"Me."

"You?" Peckover had half expected this. He should have soft-pedalled the incredulity but it was too late. "After Campos, you're next."

"Amazing, isn't it."

"I didn't say that."

"Didn't need to. Our Drugs Unit is a rabble. We're bumpkins, buffoons."

"What's the matter with you?"

"Same time, Peckover, I could probably have you thrown out. Out of the country. Thought about that? It wouldn't take much."

"Best Christmas present I could 'ope for."

"You goddamn English."

"So that's it."

"You and your Viv and Clegg and Lumley and the rest of you. Your marines. Your big strong Harrier jets. Know what you are? Pigshit stinking up the country. Why don't you all just get out and leave us alone."

"If you're actually asking, probably nothing most of us would like more. Thought it was your lot wanted us 'ere. Keep you getting gobbled up by Guatemala."

"Fascist!"

"Oh, grow up. I'm not 'ere to talk politics. I'm 'ere for Viv. At your request as I recall. That's to say, Campos. Because you don't seem to be making much headway. Can we call a truce and get on with it?"

Sergeant Montego had halted his hobble and stood sullen and one-footed, glaring, though Peckover would have agreed the dark glasses made it hard to be certain he was glaring. He probably wasn't twinkling, fluttering the eyelashes.

"What makes you think you can help, Peckover? Where do you start? You know nothing. You and your apeshit Twitty—"

"Careful, sergeant."

"—and that Yankee nigger tart—"

"Sergeant!"

The two glowered as if about to square off, gouge each other's eyes. Twitty, advancing with two steaming cups, almost stumbled, his foot stepping in a hole left by some burrowing beast. Milky coffee slopped over his fingers. He had not heard such wrath in a while, and never from Our 'Enry. He heard the guv'nor say, mildly enough, "Who, might I ask, is the fascist?"

Unless it were pressure-cooker mildness with the heat up

and the lid on. Twitty presented the coffee urgently before the mosquitoes drank it.

"Sir?"

"A moment." Peckover took the coffee. He told the sergeant, "I've already started. Now I ask questions, with your permission. Don't worry, I'll not be asking you. I'm not interested in the Brits in Belize, or your politics, and you can't help because the party was over when we got 'ere. Except for Lumley."

And you didn't exactly go hammer and tongs at stopping Lumley. Peckover's upper lip tested the coffee for temperature. He took a swallow and shuddered.

He said, "A few questions for those who saw anything. Then I find Viv."

"He'll kill you," said Sergeant Montego.

"Won't lose you any sleep, will it?"

"Chinga su madre."

"Up yours too, mate."

SIXTEEN

"Sir?"

"So what've you got?"

"Tall, one of them around six-six, and athletic, like commando types. They could run, swerve, duck—and shoot."

Twitty in his Panama hat turned a page in a notebook. His instructions had been to take the half dozen coppers beyond the Range Rover, those who had seen anything, and be sweet, sympathetic, and not take all day. The guv'nor would talk with those returning from the plane.

Agent O'Day had gone independent. She had talked with Sergeant Montego, unless it had been he who had talked to her, discovering about the happening in the jungle. Now she stood alone, reloading her gun.

Peckover had unloaded his and wondered whether he should return it to the sergeant. He thought he might as well. He had not proved so hot at using it.

"Stocking masks," Twitty said. "Must have been pretty steamy inside. But they do the job. We've no knowledge pertaining to facial particularities—"

"Like a squint or suppurating pimples."

"Sir?"

"Get on with it."

The concensus among those who know guns, or like to think they do, is that they were MAC-Tens, as that bloke said."

"Bruce."

"Bruce. They didn't speak or yell, they just came from the pickup shooting. Far as language goes, nationality, we just don't know. Could be Brits, Celts, Indian, Ruthenian—"

"Who?"

"Ruthenia, in the West Ukraine, not that I've been. It's just south of the Carpathians—"

"Please, don't. Anything else?"

"Not too much."

"Tallies with what I've got. Not a great deal, is it? They could be from outer space. Pity the stockings weren't Sainsbury's shopping bags. Would 'ave been nice."

"But unlikely."

"Gawd, what is this muck!"

Peckover spat. A jet of coffee spurted, a khaki arc which sparkled in the sun and hit the ground to the left of Twitty's feet. Twitty took a brisk pace to the right. The liquid foamed, then expired, seeping into the earth. Peckover reversed and voided this his second cup. The first had moistened the Death Valley of his lips and tongue, irrigating the parched fissures until such time as he could find something to drink, but enough was enough.

Twitty thought the coffee not at all bad. He was on his third. Slightly spicy, and still sourish despite the sugar he had heaped in to help boost the Belize economy. As palatable as anything he had been served at Harrow, or at home, or anywhere in Brixton. Not, he supposed, that that was saying much. He had never so far tried the coffee at the Savoy. Here being so close to Colombia, where coffee came from, as well as cocaine, this might be the first proper coffee he had ever had. He just hadn't developed the palate.

He said, "What they were wearing was—"

"I've got what they were wearing. What d'you make of it?"

"Dead boring. Straight out of Marks and Sparks."

"Thanks. 'Alf my wardrobe's straight out of Marks and Sparks. Nothing else?"

"Yes. A thought." Twitty studied his notes. "One had grey flannel trousers, the other blue corduroy. Routine, boring shoes. The grey flannel one had on a tweedy brown jacket, no tie. The other, no jacket, white shirt with the sleeves turned up. No headgear unless you call stockings headgear. Other words, much like us."

"Speak for yourself, cock. Nobody's like you. Spotted someone else in a bilious jogging suit, 'ave you?"

"Exactly my point. Wait till you see me in my Hawaiian costume."

"Got pineapples on 'em?"

"I'm not saying this couple have dark overcoats somewhere, like the two in the report on Clegg, the ones the perfume woman saw, or the other two with the paperbags outside your place, if they weren't the same two. Might have blush-pink overcoats. But I bet they have overcoats. Where's your parka and my vole? In the Land Rover. You don't wear your polar gear in a place like this. You wear dhotis and saris and a necklace of orange blossom. If you don't, it's because you've just arrived and haven't had time to change. They were probably on our plane. Flannel pants, hairy tweed jackets, and not a short-sleeve shirt between them? What beats me is why they weren't wearing leg-warmers and fur hats with ear-flaps."

"You made a meal of that."

"I did?" Twitty, deflated, closed his notebook. "Thought I'd managed some detecting. In a minor way."

"Don't sulk. Nothing else?"

"Nothing I'd want to make a meal of."

"You're sulking. I'm going to try and pry some transport and a driver out of the sergeant. Wish me luck. Find out what the O'Day girl plans to do and where she's staying. We don't want'er with us at Viv's place. What're you looking like that for?"

"Like what?"

"As if I needed psychiatric help."

"Sir, unfair. It's just that she's hardly exactly, well, in the way. She came in handy in the woods—excuse me, the jungle."

"I could have handled the pilot." So why, Peckover wondered once again, didn't I? He flicked too late at a mosquito chewing his earlobe. "We're not all trigger-happy. Some of us might 'ave a higher regard for the sanctity of 'uman life than others."

Blimey, did he say that? Vote for Peckover. He sounded like a sanctimonious politician chasing the left-wing youth vote. Get off the subject.

"This Yankee, Peaches O'Day—"

"Peachy."

"Peachy. You in love with 'er?"

"Have pity!"

"Why 'Have pity'? That's not very nice. She's all there, isn't she? Active, nubile, earns her living, probably a sensational smile if ever she smiled. Not much cause at present, I'll give 'er that. You'd like 'er along, right?"

"Why not? Jesus, am I in love with her, honestly."

"Are you gay?"

"Naughty." Twitty flapped his notebook in his guv'nor's face. "Let that be *my* little secret."

"You drive on the right," Peckover said.

Twitty drove on the right, Peckover beside him holding a pencilled sketch map. Though the sun had drooped, the late afternoon was still as hot as hades. The wind through the absent windshield helped, blowing in coolly, laden with dust and bugs. After the turning to Belmopan the empty highway became freer of craters and bunkers. Twitty held the needle on sixty. Not that there was any rush, thought Peckover, when they might be heading to their death.

He had been tempted to escape first to Belize City and check in at the hotel, wallow awhile in the tub. But Viv's Casa Verde was apparently on the way, if Sergeant Montego's hand-drawn directions weren't the route to the Lost Tarantula Trap of Belize, white with the bleached bones of earlier Brits he had directed there.

If Viv were home he would kill them. Well, he probably wouldn't, but then again he might. Sergeant Montego thought he might and seemed to hope he would. Out of old-world Etonian courtesy—Brits together, far from home—he would surely allow them first a decent cup of tea. Whichever way you sliced it, Casa Verde would have something to drink quicker than the city's hurly-burly, another fifty miles on.

Peckover kept one eye on the map. The sergeant could not have been more helpful in sending them off to find Vivian White. He had drawn the map and pressed on them the Land Rover. He had said no to a driver, escort, marksman, or a single one of his own force, but that was his right. His only demand had been for a full written report. His only request, that Peckover return the gun, since he had no use for it. He had questioned O'Day about Lumley's death and got the rough picture.

Sole reason why Peckover had said no to the gun, had kept it in his pocket, was that Sergeant Montego had asked for it.

"Can I see it, Henry?" said Agent O'Day, leaning forward from the rear seat. "Is it the same one they gave me?"

Peckover forgave her use of his first name. She was American; she knew no better. She had said little enough so far, though he had put questions. She had already visited Casa Verde, she had said, but not from this direction, so don't count on her.

Peckover said, "We're looking for a turn-off to the right a half mile beyond a lake or pond which we're not going to see because it's through the trees, but it floods the road in the rainy season, which isn't now."

So fat help that is. Without turning round he passed his gun back to O'Day.

She had apparently arrived yesterday, in good time, like a yacht in the America's Cup. Alone, because in her opinion her chief, Lootenant Sapolsky, hadn't thought the Viv Connection worth the personpower for more than one, no matter the coke coming in from the Belize staging-post was enough to sprinkle a powdery highway from L.A. to Canada and on to the Yukon. The lootenant, she had said, was pretty jaded and old, like thirty-four, pretty much a dinosaur, and only sending anyone at all so as to cover himself. Her brief: Viv. A consignment was due. Superintendent Campos would be expecting her. Liaise, if she felt the urge, with the Scotland Yard whizz-kids, one of them a poet, for Pete's sake.

First thing she had done had been to call Campos from her hotel, tell him she was renting a car and looking for Casa Verde. Campos himself had taken her. A burly, cheerful guy who hadn't been expecting a lone female but who hadn't put his hand on her crotch either. Casa Verde had been shut up, kind of. Doors locked. No Viv. There'd been a gardener who'd said no one was home, and no, he didn't know where, when, he was only Ramon, try again tomorrow. She'd had a feeling someone may have been home. Maybe watching from the house. Most of the shutters had not been tight shut but held a few inches open with a hook doodad, letting air in but keeping heat and insects out, the way the big houses did their shutters in Mississippi when they were home, not off to Colorado skiing. Not that she was an expert on Mississippi.

Sure it had crossed her mind that Campos might have called Viv to let him know he was about to show with a DEA agent. It hadn't been something she had thought she should ask him.

Today Campos and two of his men had again given her a ride. "Boy, was a consignment ever due," she had said. She had been in two shoot-outs in L.A., one in Philadelphia, but nothing like today.

Now she said, "Looks okay to me," and passed the gun back to Peckover. "Webley Police Model, the official Brit revolver for fifty years, right? You should be at home with it. A hundred and fifty bucks in L.A., if that. Is the trigger mechanism gunged up? I don't see rust. We should test it."

"We should," Peckover agreed. He raised his voice above the din of the engine but the words echoed weakly in his ears: a plop of sugar lumps dropped into tea.

"I was given this Walther P-Thirty-Eight," O'Day said. "Your basic nine-millimetre parabellum, but I'm not wild about automatics. The Germans dropped it at the end of the war. You know, the one with the holocaust and Eisenhower and the D-day beaches."

"How much in L.A.?" Peckover was making conversation. The road was monotonous, Twitty preoccupied, watching for the turn-off.

"Three-fifty. Double-action mechanism. Some people like them."

"You like guns?"

"Like guns? What's to like? That's a weird question."

Twitty said, "This could be it. What d'you think?"

He turned onto a narrow but navigable road of compacted dirt. At first the vegetation to either side was maggoty, stunted trees too threadbare to be dignified as jungle, but the undergrowth became thicker, the trees more dense. A bird in absurd primary colours flapped squawking out of the foliage. After a half mile they were driving through three-star jungle.

"Could be it," O'Day said. "See one rain forest, seen 'em all. Watch out for King Kong."

Peckover believed she might have taken out and been nursing the Walther, which she was not wild about. It had hardly had time to grow cold. He did not turn round to look. To reload his own revolver might be intelligent but he could not bring himself to. Certainly not with Twitty beside him. The procedure would have been theatrical and embarrassing.

The dirt road ejected them onto a gravel driveway amid flowery, watered spaces.

O'Day said, "That's our baby."

"Slow it down," Peckover told Twitty. "Keep going. Try left."

The house was white stucco with faded green pantiles, portico, door, and closed or partly closed shutters the colour of Boston lettuce. Peckover watched for life but saw none. Casa Verde was big, square, and plain, apart from the phoney-baloney columns and roof over the front door. Peckover assumed this was the front. No cars though. Nobody.

"Keep on round the side."

The driveway circled the house. When they reached the back, Peckover motioned Twitty to stop. They looked at a two-storey, low building standing apart, probably a garage. The upper floor had windows behind which was perhaps a workshop or storage space. On the far side of the house a builders' chute snaked from an upstairs window and down into a skip. They saw a blue pool, a brick path, and two acres of lawn with occasional shrubs. The patio was without furniture as if Viv did not go in for entertaining, or he had packed his bag and gone off to tour Italy.

Come to think of it, when was the last time anyone had seen Viv?

"Where did you find your gardener?"

"Down the garden," said O'Day. "Past that red and yellow stuff."

"Bougainvillea," Twitty said.

"If you say so."

"Look for 'im," said Peckover. "We'll 'ave a word if he's here. Lad, park round the side by the skip. No sense advertising ourselves. Point 'er the way out. I'll try the garage."

The steel doors of the garage were locked. A side door, probably to stairs up to the floor above, was also locked. An adjacent shed was open, filled with gardening tools.

Peckover walked along the driveway, looking up at the back of the house. Only one of the eight sash windows, an upstairs window, was bared to the day, its Boston-lettuce shutters flat against the wall. Two other sets of shutters were ajar, held by hooks, invitations to a housebreaker, which he suspected he might be about to become. Also ajar were the shutters across the french windows which led into the house from the patio. He beckoned to Twitty.

They walked round the house to the front door. Peckover tugged on a Dickensian bell-pull. They heard mild clanging and waited, side by side, in the portico. Peckover tapped a green column with his knuckles. If it wasn't papier-mâché it was not far off. Mail-order job, like the bell-pull. Assemble it yourself. He preferred Collins Cross.

He rang again, then walked backwards, surveying empty Casa Verde, if empty it was. He shared Miss O'Day's impression that it might not be.

"We'll try the french windows," he said. "If we don't 'ave to smash them, so much the better."

Peachy O'Day in her hunting-cap and sunglasses met them on the patio. No gardner. She had found instead a gaudy yellow blossom and put it in her buttonhole.

Peckover lifted the hook which held the shutters apart across the french windows. If Viv were on the other side of the windows, looking out, he would see them before they saw him. Peckover swung the shutters back against the wall.

They put their faces to the glass and saw a living room with white sofas, a piano, paintings on the walls. They had no need to smash the glass, though Twitty succeeded in splintering the wood a little. Before slipping the catch, he said, "If this sets an alarm off we could have the police here."

"Don't build your hopes," Peckover said. "Open it up."

Twitty pushed open the left-hand door. They entered into coolness and stood on a tiled floor with scattered, woven mats. The paintings were probably Hockneys, the spindly sculpture a Giacometti. There were flowers and geometrically overlapping magazines: *Harpers & Queen, Esquire, Punch, Country Life, Field & Stream*. No *Good Housekeeping*, Peckover noted.

He supposed the gross, weathered cylinder of stone was Mayan or Aztec and possibly valuable. Unless it were a thousand years old and valuable he could see no sense to it.

No Viv. Nobody. O'Day had brought out her gun.

"Put that away," Peckover said.

"When I'm ready," said O'Day.

Twitty said, "Quiet. Listen."

From somewhere in the house sounded a baby's crying.

SEVENTEEN

Without the wailing somewhere of a baby, Casa Verde would have felt empty to the point of being uninhabited. The sound seemed to have come from above, though Peckover would not have sworn to it.

First, downstairs. If they were going upstairs, he didn't want to be looking behind him all the time, guarding his arse.

Apart from a lived-in feel to the living room, downstairs was the bleak pad of an uninterested, largely absentee bachelor with staff who shone and buffed to excess rooms which were furnished but no one entered. A dining room in aspic with candelabra; a glassed-in conservatory with pots and wicker chairs but sparse plants; a Puritan's spotless parlour, the room used once a year at Christmas, and for funerals. Most of the rooms were in half-dark behind closed shutters. In the kitchen Peckover opened the fridge. Eggs, milk, orange juice, exposed butter in a silver dish, a half loaf of sliced bread, a bowl of leftover something covered with cling-wrap.

Cold comfort. Viv wouldn't actually starve though, if he were in residence. Peckover believed he was. He might have eaten here very recently, like today. The expiry date on the bread was December 28 and the fibrous, burnt-sienna splodge beneath the cling-wrap had not greened with fur. Peckover dipped a finger and tested, expecting Etonian steak-and-kidney.

Chili. Made sense. If Viv had someone local in to cook for him, chili was what he might get seven days a week.

Peckover lusted after the six-pack of a beer named Belikin but he forswore. In the freezer compartment were a chicken, a bag of peas, and copious ice-cubes. Even as he opened the door the automatic ice-maker clunked forth a volley of ice-balls. Since the box into which they dropped still was not full, someone had been at the ice not too long ago.

Like a matter of hours.

The larder had staples of Cooper's Oxford marmalade, pasta, tuna, and Bird's Custard Powder. By the sink, chrome surfaces shimmered as if for the colonel's inspection. In the cupboard were glasses.

Peckover, Twitty, and O'Day gathered wordlessly with glasses at the sink and it cold running tap.

Exceptions to the aridity of downstairs Casa Verde were a basement, and to a lesser extent a gunroom. In the gunroom, Peachy O'Day took off her sunglasses, goggled at a glass-fronted cabinet of weaponry, and said, "Hot shit, it's a war museum."

Peckover accepted that he was jaundiced on the subject but he surmised that O'Day might be envious. He remembered the arsenal in the museum at D11 HQ in Old Street. O'Day would love that. Here in the gunroom were dust, gloom, and on the floor an empty box of Wrigley's Chiclets, as if the cleaners had instructions not to bother, indeed to stay out. The cabinet was locked. Good. No ammunition that he could see, unless it was in the steel box. Two padlocks. Good again.

The baby's wailing had stopped. Peckover paused at the head of the steps leading to a basement. He told Twitty, "Wait in the hall and watch the stairs."

"Me?" Twitty pointed a forefinger at his chest. "If there's a baby, wouldn't Peachy—er, Agent O'Day—"

"You 'eard."

"If a baby comes charging down, what do I do? Arrest it?"

"If you 'ave reason to believe it has committed a serious offence, yes. Move, lad."

The basement had a sitting room, bedroom, kitchen, and bathroom. High windows looked onto the driveway at eye level. A damp towel in the bathroom, clothes in a laundry basket; in the sitting room, armchairs and photographs. The photographs were of sunny weddings and children. Nothing of Viv. Staff quarters. Ice-eaters perhaps. Chili-makers. O'Day took the disc from a record player and read aloud, *"Mariachis del Oro. La Negra, Cielito Lindo, Las Chiapanecas."*

"You know Spanish?"

"You'd know Spanish if you were a cop in L.A."

In the hall, at the foot of the pine stairway, Twitty was fanning himself with his Panama. They climbed the stairs slowly, noiselessly, looking up and around, wondering which would be the stair that creaked. Peckover led. O'Day held her arm against her leg, pointing the Walther down. Twitty held his hat against his chest as if out of respect for the hush and a possibility of babies. When they reached the wide, halfway stair where the staircase turned, O'Day stepped ahead.

Twitty put the brim of the Panama between his teeth, bit it gently, and watched the switching slow trim bum of O'Day in her tight jeans. *Jordache,* they said across the right cheek. Peckover reached up and took hold of her arm.

"Darlin', be nice, put it away," he whispered. "That wasn't the warcry of a nutter. That was a baby."

"Viv's got a baby. You know for a fact he's not up there with his baby?"

"Miss, please. Guns, accident, you know? There's a baby."

"Any accident, it's going to happen to Viv, not me."

"Just keep behind, if you don't mind."

"You're weird, poet, you know that? You were weird in the jungle. Now you're beyond weird, you're scary. If you go first with your hands in your pockets, I'm leaving."

"Your privilege."

Peckover sidled in front and climbed the last steps to the landing, Twitty behind him. Corridors with panelled doors reached to right, left, and directly ahead. In an angle of the landing lay, as ornament, a five-foot plaster woman: nude, supine, hospital-pale, and no wonder. Rampant atop her, tail erect, a paw on her tresses, stood the rest of the sculpture, a crimson lion with fanged, drooling jaws. Was he about to eat her, or yawning? Has he killed her or was he protecting her? In the air lingered a lilac sniff of cleaning-lady's aerosol. Peckover and Twitty stood on the landing in anticipation of they knew not what. From a room off the passage to the left came the faintest sound. Again, not a warcry, and not a wail. More a gurgle.

Peckover and Twitty advanced with slow strides, at each step testing the floor for squeaking before allowing their weight to bear down. Across the landing, along the passage. O'Day too. For whatever reason she had chosen not to leave. She held the Walther in front of her. They waited outside a door. From its other side, silence.

Wrong damn door, Peckover decided, and regarded the

door opposite. Then, from the other side of their door, concert noises, neither anguished nor threatening, but a muted solo of hiccups and slurps.

O'Day took a pace back and levelled the Walther at the door. Peckover looked from her curled finger on the trigger to her eyes, screened by sunglasses, watching the door. In a moment he would feel the sweat crawl. He might gesture that she stick the gun away, depart the premises, go swim in the pool and cool off. She wasn't going to.

She had a point. Viv had a baby, he could be with his baby, and armed. He could have watched the Land Rover arrive and recognised Chief Inspector Peckover, nose-breaker. He could be eager to meet the nose-breaker again.

Moreover, Christmas was coming, water was wet, and the longer he dithered like a dog at the sea's edge, the longer he would keep dithering. He motioned to O'Day and Twitty. They backed to the far side of the door, O'Day with her gun levelled. Peckover stood against the wall on the near side, reached across the door for the round, wooden handle, and turned it. He didn't see what more he could do about O'Day and her gun. If there had to be a gun, better she had it than he did.

Maybe. He pushed the door open.

When nothing happened, he risked a look. He put his head into the open space. Viv could have blown it away. O'Day, in a crouch, hurtled past him into the room and flung herself flat on a shaggy beige carpet, gun arm extended and swinging in an arc.

But not shooting. The room had a double bed, dressing table, sink, bin with a lid, chairs, fitted cupboard along the length of one wall, baby's crib, and a carry-cot. The dressing table was against the far wall beside a sash window. The window was closed but the outside shutters were open, and light flooded the room, which was a makeshift nursery. On the table were jars of baby food and a packet of Ultra Pampers. Sole occupants were a plump young woman with a pretty face and glossy black hair, and a baby.

At first look anyway. The sliding door of the built-in closet was a couple of inches ajar. The quilt on the bed reached to the carpet.

The woman wore a black and red dress and sat on a bentwood chair with the baby on her lap, feeding to from a bottle. She sat rigid, round-eyed with fright. The baby sucked and its eyes swivelled in the direction of the eruption through the door.

Peckover had a hopeful feeling about the closet and under

the bed. More so than about O'Day and her gun.

"Get up," he told O'Day on his way to the closet.

He slid the empty closet's doors open at one end, in the middle, and at the far end. He went to the bed and plucked up the quilt. Hello, Viv —*bang*. Hello, Saint Peter, sir. He bent to look, dropped the quilt, and straightened up.

"Satisfied?" he asked O'Day. He was soggy with sweat.

"More than," Peachy O'Day said, and she stood up grinning, tucking the gun away somewhere beneath her jacket. "Oh boy."

She means it, Peckover thought. She wasn't aching to spatter the walls with blood and brains, put more notches on her gun.

Twitty had put his hat on his head, leaving both hands free. Now he held it to his heart like a swain and approached the woman with the baby. He said, "Police, ma'am. May I have your name?"

The woman stared in fear at Twitty. The baby looked about and began to circle its arms as if warming up for callisthenics. A watery bubble appeared between its lips, grew, and popped. "Bluh," said the baby.

"Everything's all right," Twitty told the woman. "You the nurse?"

The woman shook off paralysis sufficiently to return her attention to the baby, offering the teat to its mouth.

Peckover moved in and told her, "You work 'ere. You live below. You work for Mr. White. You make a good chili. Correct?"

She looked up. The baby wore only a nappy and plastic knickers and it didn't want the bottle. It wanted to get down and play: dribble over Peckover's brogues, roll on Twitty's Panama.

"Is this Viv's baby?" Peckover asked.

She nodded.

"Where is he?"

The woman tried to reorganise the baby, lifting it, settling it on her lap with its back to the police, offering the bottle.

"Is 'e here?"

She was busy with the baby and the bottle. Peckover wondered if Peachy might have better success in getting through, woman to woman. She was at the window, watching the back of the house as if for a sight of the gardener.

"Madam." Peckover, squatting, stroked the baby's knee with a finger. His voice was a dove's coo. "It's important. Is Vivian White here?"

The woman shook her head, meaning no, or she wasn't saying.

"What's your name?"

"Papitos."

Breakthrough.

"Papitos, when did you last see Mr. Viv? D'you call him Mr. Viv or Mr. White?"

If it weren't for the baby having taken hold of her nose and begun to twist it with every intention of removing it from her face, she might have answered, though Peckover doubted it. He straightened up.

"Papitos, why don't we all 'ave a cup of tea. You'd like tea or coffee?"

"Coffee, thank you."

"Iced?"

She shook her head.

"You like ice though? Nice long clinking iced drink with cubes and lime and bubbles and clunking chunks of ice to the brim"—Peckover began to feel dazed with thirst—"with perhaps a spot of rum, leaf of mint—"

"Ice makes stomach pains. Makes heart pump. Only Americans eat ice."

"True." Was it? Not the occasional Etonian? "Does the gardener or anyone use the kitchen?"

Papitos shook her head. She had at last interested the baby in the bottle.

"Papitos, is there a telephone?"

"Downstairs."

"Constable, see if you can't manage a pot of coffee. While you're down there ring the police in—in—"

"Belmopan," Twitty said, and put his hat on his head.

"We're at Casa Verde and wouldn't say no to seeing one or two of them here. There's Viv's baby and probably Viv. Doubt you'll reach Montego, he's probably still mopping up on the airstrip, but if you do I'll 'ave a word with him."

"Sergeant Montego is good man," Papitos said.

"The best." Peckover watched Papitos, who was watching the baby, who watched different points in space, and pushed the bottle away. "You know 'im well?"

"Oh, *sí, Simpatico.*"

"Come 'ere often, does 'e?"

"*Sí, sí.* He drive BMW."

"Great. Bring you roses? Sangria?"

Peckover, warmed by thoughts of true love, beamed down at Papitos. Into his ken swam a vision of Cadbury's

Dairy Box, bribe of his youth for nights at the flicks and on
Stepney Green with the Helens, Angelas, and Sylvias of his
time. Wine and roses would have devastated the best part of
a week's wage. Dairy Box was affordable and with shapes,
flavours, and centres as assorted as the girls—marzipan,
nougat, coffee cream, Brazil nut—which you identified from
a chart. Anyone too small or backward to grasp the chart,
like lively junior here, puked up the marzipan then bit into
each chocolate in turn until hitting on something edible. He
remembered imaging that if people only came with a similar
identifying chart—serious, frivolous, choleric, mad—everyone would know better what to expect and life would be
simpler.

"Send you a Valentine card, does 'e? February four-
teenth?"

Papitos bowed her head towards the baby. She was shaking. When she lifted her head, her face was red, her eyes
wet. She was laughing.

"Sergeant Montego not come see me! He come visit
Señor White!"

"I know. Only joking." Peckover gave her a laugh of his
own. "Often, was it—is it? Five times? Twenty?"

"Oh, *sí*,"

"Campos come too?"

"Quién?"

"Superintendent Campos."

"Who Campos?"

"He was 'ere yesterday with our colleague." He nodded
in O'Day's direction. "Perhaps you weren't."

It was a question. No answer.

"How d'you know the sergeant's car is a BMW?"

"'Ow not know? Is BMW, very beautiful. Before BMW 'e
has Mercedes, but not new. Is rust, I think. He 'ave caye too,
next Ambergris Caye. Not big but plenty enough for airplane, 'e say. Papitos hear."

Evidently. Peckover bestowed a benign smile. Good ol'
Montego, good ol' sarge. Twitty watched his guv'nor for a
sign that now he should go, brew coffee, summon the locals.
From the window Agent O'Day swivelled and beckoned.

"Guests," she said. "It's the pickup."

The men from the Yard looked blankly across the room at
O'Day.

"Damn limeys," said O'Day. "Are we watching the same
channel? The black pickup from the airstrip."

Peckover scowled. That pickup. He went with Twitty to the window.

Not for the first time, O'Day dug into her jacket and brought out her gun.

EIGHTEEN

The pickup had stopped by the patio with its engine running and an undecided air. No one got out. O'Day to the left of the window, Peckover and Twitty to the right, peered down. They were unable to see into the cabin.

The pickup made a three-point turn, paused to regard the garage, then returned the way it had come round the east side of the house.

"Leaving so soon?" murmured O'Day.

"As well they are," Twitty said. "If they'd carried on, they'd have seen the Land Rover."

"Who says they haven't," said Peckover. "Papitos, stay put. Everything's going to be fine."

O'Day and Twitty followed Peckover across the wide passage to the room opposite. The door stuck, as if gummed, and Peckover had to put his shoulder to it.

Viv's bedroom? Someone slept here, or had done so probably not long ago. Stereo, television, a folded something silky and navy on the bed, a paperback Peckover hadn't time to look at on the bedside table. He turned the screw which fastened the window sashes, pushed the window up, and opened slightly the left-hand shutter. The pickup arrived at the front entrance and halted, like a prospective buyer on a tour of inspection.

The doors of the cabin opened. Two men got out and stood one on each side of the pickup, looking about them, and at the entrance.

Twitty murmured, "Bags me not answer."

"Answer what?" said O'Day. "You think these people ring doorbells?"

From the angle of the high window the men's features were hidden. Both wore their hair short. One was unusually tall and had on a brown tweed jacket and grey flannels; the other, no shorty, a white shirt with sleeves rolled up.

"That's not the only black pickup in Belize," Peckover said. "I don't see guns. No masks. Who knows who they are?"

"Dream on," said O'Day. "They're Skip and Shep."

"You know them?"

"Never seen them, only on the airstrip. Look at those cute haircuts and the Brooks Brothers tweed. They're killer yuppies. They vote Republican, if they're old enough to vote. They look like Mormons."

"You can't know they're even American."

"They're Skip and Shep and they shot two cops dead on that strip like they enjoyed it. Question isn't who, it's why. And why're they here?"

"Viv's men reporting one aborted consignment," Peckover said. "Everyone's looking for Viv. If Skip and—if those two are looking for 'im here, here's likely where he is."

Twitty said, "They're not Viv's men—oops!" He swayed back from the window. "Watch it!"

Peckover and O'Day stepped back as the one in the white shirt lifted his face and surveyed through sunglasses the upper storey of Casa Verde. The one in the jacket climbed back into the pickup.

"Blrrp-p-p," announced the baby from the nursery across the passage.

Peckover said, "Who says they're not Viv's men?"

"One," said Twitty, "if they're Viv's minions and they're here to say hello, what's stopping them? Why don't they get on with it? Two—two doesn't matter. I just don't think they're Viv's men."

"Don't upset me, lad." Peckover peeked down through the open shutters. Both men were back in the pickup. "I'm listening."

"On the airstrip," Twitty said, "if they were Viv's men, why didn't they help with the loading?"

"Why would they?"

"They're able-bodied. Why wouldn't they?"

"The Colombians helped."

"One Colombian. And Lumley. They had a trolley but they had to struggle. Viv's pair in the pickup didn't lift a finger. All they did was shoot coppers. They shot Campos as if they had him singled out."

"Where did you get all this?"

"You told me to be sweet and talk to coppers."

"But you've not mentioned it until now because—"

"Hardly had the chance, sir."

"—you were sulking."

"That too."

"Blr-r-rgh!" shouted the baby.

The police watched the pickup reverse from the entrance.

"I'm probably wrong, sir."

"You probably are." Gawd, the lad had gone on and on about what the two in the pickup had been wearing, how they weren't wearing summer shirts with pineapples. All he'd told Twitty was don't make a meal of it. He remembered the lad as a fairly sensitive plant but not to this extent. "Remind me to punch your nose."

"Yessir."

The pickup had paused. It might now leave Casa Verde, which made little sense. If it investigated round the house to the right, the first item it would find would be a police Land Rover beside a skip.

"Campos is dead," Peckover said. "Montego sounds pally with Viv, but those two down there might not be. So who are they? Freebooters? Did your chatty friends see them try to snatch the consignment?"

"All they did was shoot policemen."

"'Things are seldom what they seem, skim milk masquerades as cream.'"

"That's good, poet," O'Day said. "That you or Shakespeare?"

Looking down through the shutters, they watched the pickup drive forward and to the right.

"Bugger," breathed Peckover.

"Shrrrulp!" rejoiced the baby across the passage.

Peckover and O'Day went back into the nursery. The baby lay naked on a rubber mat on the carpet, waving its legs. Papitos, kneeling, was changing its nappy. Life goes bleedin' on, thought Peckover.

Twitty veered off along the passage to the last door. With luck he would see from this room what Skip and Shep made of the Land Rover. Blow it up and dance a jig? Did Mormons jig? The room was a shambles of bricks, planks, sacks of plaster, and not worth the effort. He was not dressed for a ball, he was too scuffed for even a joggers' ball, but to have waded through this would have left him looking like one of the labourers the pubs in Knightsbridge put up signs saying no admission to. He shut the door.

At the nursery window Twitty joined Peckover and

O'Day for the view of pool, lawns, and a roof of hazy jungle reaching to the horizon, there to be sliced off by a strawberry rim of sky. Somewhere beyond the corner of the house the sun was setting. Below, between pool and patio, the pickup had halted.

Can they see, Peckover asked himself, the forced french windows? Of course they can. He glanced at the pistol in O'Day's hand. He found himself without objections.

"Here's what we do, just in case," he said.

Both doors of the pickup swung open.

"I stay with the baby," Peckover said. "Jason, you call the police if you can. Phone's below, probably that living room where we came in. Don't be a hero. You listen, you stay out of sight. Whatever else you do, you don't meet them. If you get to a phone, we don't need Montego either. All right?"

"Right on, guv."

"Miss, um—Peachy?"

"Poet?"

She watched him questioningly. She wants orders, Peckover thought. She's not sure. Below, Skip and Shep came from the pickup carrying guns.

He said, "The other thing we don't need is a shoot-out."

"Tell them that, not me."

"If Jason doesn't get to the phone there's the short wave in the Land Rover. Reinforcements would be welcome."

Skip and Shep with their MAC-10s levelled walked across the patio, parting company to go one to each side of the french windows. They're cautious, they'll be a minute or two yet, Peckover thought.

"And put the gun away?" O'Day said.

"Do what you do," he told her. "Just stay out of their way. Be invisible."

"Invisible or invincible?"

"Both. Questions?"

No questions.

Was he sending them to kingdom come? Shouldn't he hunt down the phone himself, post the lad and lass as watch over the baby and Papitos? Was there some alternative plot he had missed? Set fire to the house? Be archeologists assessing Viv's Mayan rocks and crockery in the living room?

From the nursery's doorway he raised a hand in salute as O'Day and Twitty reached the landing and without looking back at him ran down the stairs.

Running, or simply hurrying, the baby had not learned to do. Peckover, watching, was hard put not to applaud. Under other circumstances he would have crouched and exhorted.

C'mon, Tarzan. Attaboy. Go, baby, go. The baby was walking.

No it wasn't. It sat with a padded bump. It took hold of a fistful of toes, considered them, lost interest, stood, surveyed the world, spotted the big bloke in the door, completed a military left turn, if a little drunkenly, and in Peckover's direction resumed its bandy-legged hike.

"Brgbl," the baby announced, and sat again.

"*Magnifique,*" whispered Peckover, and swooped.

He gathered up the baby and hoisted it high. The baby voicelessly screamed, eyes ablaze, froth gathering at the corners of its mouth, ecstatic. Peckover would have liked to toss, twirl, and swing it upside down by the ankles, piling ecstacy on ecstacy. Before Papitos could scream, he presented the baby.

"Great little feller. Smashing walker."

Papitos kissed and smothered the baby, which wriggled, preferring ecstasy.

"Is 'e ready to sleep?" Peckover whispered. He listened for sounds from below but heard nothing. "Can you get 'im to sleep?"

Papitos was too busy succouring the child to answer, if she had heard. Peckover knew anyway the answers were no and no. Any moment now the infant would be screeching from excess of succour.

"We're going into the cupboard," Peckover said.

Papitos was uncomprehending, or not listening.

"Closet," he said. "Just for a minute or two."

He hoped just for a minute or two. Might be much less if junior yelled, and why wouldn't he? The baby battled in the arms of Papitos. Left and right hooks, uppercuts, penalty kicks.

"Bring its bottle." Peckover was whispering again, his hand on the arm of Papitos. Jesus, bring something—dummy, rusks, teething ivories, Valium. "Papitos, down below are two men we don't want to meet. Bad men. We 'ave to keep very quiet. It'll be all right."

Peckover guided Papitos towards the cupboard by way of the table which bore jars and diapers. He pressed a spoon and Gerber's vanilla custard pudding into her hand. When he ushered her into the cupboard, she still did not protest, as if every day she were put in a cupboard.

The sliding doors were white wood. No louvres, no light inside, no hanging clothes, but numberless hangers which the baby would be happy to rattle. For air and a chink of light he left the door fractionally open in front of Papitos and the baby. He went to the other end of the cupboard and stepped inside. He pushed the hangers away from him, slid the door almost closed, and peered through the gap. He could not see much. Wall, the table with jars and nappies, the closed sash window on the other side of the table.

He had enough headroom. Through the gloom to his right, fifteen feet away, beyond the hangers, he could dimly see Papitos rocking the baby.

"Blaa-b-blb," said the baby.

Why didn't she feed it or something!

He lifted his revolver from his jacket pocket, and bullets from his trousers pocket. The bullets came out with coins, which he returned to his pocket. More by touch than by sight he started loading the gun.

Unless Peachy O'Day shot them both through the heart, Skip and Shep would be visiting any minute.

From below sounded a crash. And barely audible voices.

NINETEEN

"What was that for?" said the one in the tweed jacket.

"They spooked me," said the one in the white shirt. "This whole place spooks me. I feel better now."

They regarded the wreckage of Mayan artefacts which the one in the white shirt had swept from the shelf. The jade and onyx masks and figurines had bounced and skidded across the tiled floor of the living room. The ceramic bowls and vases had shattered.

"That'll bring those asshole cops out from under their stones," the white shirt said. "If they're not deaf as well as assholes."

"If they're here."

"They're here. They're upstairs."

"Could be outside."

"Wherever. Let them stay under their stones. They come out, they're dead assholes."

"One day, champ, you'll be yammering on about asshole cops and you won't even smell the one spreads your brains across the sky like oatmeal."

"What're you, some kind of fortune teller?"

They had reconnoitred the downstairs and basement and arrived back in the living room. Enough for their purposes had been throwing open doors and looking into each room, guns pointing. They were looking for a person, not for the Koh-i-noor.

They were not interested in Vivian White either, or police, though they would have killed police had they met any.

Had they penetrated further into the kitchen than the tap at the sink they would have found Detective Constable

Twitty, rigid and holding his breath, in the alcove beyond the refrigerator.

Now they would have found him a half-dozen steps away, squatting and coiled, foetus-like, behind the stone phallus.

Twitty's palms ran with sweat; his forehead pressed against cold stone; his ears strained. Their feet click-clacked on tiles, they talked, and Twitty listened and shifted position.

They were talking to his left. Twitty inched to his right round the tumescent tonnage of stone mushroom.

He could not believe they had returned here, where they had started. Why not upstairs? They hadn't seen upstairs.

An error, they had taken a wrong turn? The crazier of the two had an urge to smash antiquities? They wanted, as he did, the telephone? The telephone was beside magazines on a glass coffee table.

Twitty had not seen or heard Agent O'Day since they had parted in the hall without a word or sign, though he wondered about her.

Peachy. Bum like peaches. Oh.

He had wondered about the guv'nor upstairs. Was he any wiser about who was doing what to whom and why than before they had left Heathrow? What had been accomplished, other than killing?

Right now, who cared? All that counted now was survival. They were talking again. Peachy's Skip and Shep. He hoped they would not hear the drops of sweat detonating on the tiles.

He edged another millimetre to his right, willing himself invisible, a flyspeck.

"How do I look?" said the crazy one who had done the smashing.

He had retrieved from the debris a mosaic onyx and turquoise mask with eyeholes and bone teeth in a grinning mouth. He held it to his face. Masked, he made lunging movements with his head and shoulders towards the one in the tweed jacket.

"Trick or treat," he said, lunging.

"Let's get on with it," said the one in the jacket, and picked up the telephone.

He tugged the spiralling cord out of the handset and base and put it in his pocket. For good measure he tracked the lead to the wall, ripped it from its socket, and stamped down with his heel, smashing the plug's casing and mangling its twin prongs. Then he headed back through the living room.

The one in the white shirt followed, passing between the sofa and a hunk of rock, holding the mask to his face, and saying, "Trick or treat, grandma? Trick or treat or I'll puree your face."

"Shut yours, champ."

They reached the hall and started up the stairs. They were an effective team but sometimes they got on each other's nerves.

Agent O'Day had let herself out of the house by the front door, which she left off the latch and closed behind her. Outside, all was peace and harmony, apart from a multi-coloured bird which she had disturbed. The bird uttered a yawp and flapped from the driveway and into the trees. If the baby was squawking inside the house, she could not hear it.

She had walked along the front of the house, shoulder brushing the wall, gun pointing, and ducking and creeping when she came to windows. At the corner of the house she waited, her back to the wall, and gulped air, before peeping round.

She was not convinced the poet had been right to split them up, though she'd had no better proposal. But together, three against two, mightn't they have handled Skip and Shep?

Crouching when she came to windows, she started along the west side of the house. The sun to her right was a low red blob which soon would go plop into hiding.

Not three against two. Two-and-a-half against two, because how the one with the classy accent was able to handle himself she had no way of knowing. In bed sensationally, could be. He had the health and the look, watching her like a puppy wanting playtime. But against these two beauts with their MAC-10s? Presumably he'd know something or he wouldn't be here. But no gun! Baffled, crouching beneath a window, O'Day looked about her, and listened.

What it came to was not numbers but a Walther and a Webley against two machine guns, two Ingram MAC-10s converted to automatic. Forty-five-calibre slugs, twelve hundred a minute, and at a whisper if you wanted. Not that they'd bothered with silencers on the airstrip, or would here, middle of nowhere.

Worse, what it came to, Skip and Shep were serious. She had watched them enjoying themselves and they took their fun seriously.

She walked on, hugging the wall. The poet might be serious about Gitche Gumee and I wandered lonely as a cloud, but far as defending himself, he was a joke. He hadn't even tried. He was a suicidal nut. He should have been dead, blown away by the pilot. Thanks to the good old DEA he was alive still, and as dangerous to Mr. and Mrs. O'Day's little girl as Skip and Shep.

More dangerous. Skip and Shep you could predict. They were as obvious as the arches of a McDonald's. But come destiny-time, Skip and Shep with their fingers on the trigger, what would Poet do? Shoot? Take out his pen? Lay his gun down and think up rhymes?

Peachy O'Day felt sweat tickle between her breasts. She stood motionless, swivelling the brim of her hunting cap to blot out the sun. "Wouldn't you know it," she muttered, squinting ahead.

She reached the Land Rover. An unsightly but functioning heap until now, it had been turned into an unfunctioning heap. The air had been let out of the tyres. She knew what the state of the radio would be but she looked anyway.

She had been mistaken supposing they would not bother with silencers. They had bothered, and the fun they'd had with the radio must have been so hilarious they'd presumably extended it to the engine's vital organs. O'Day doubted this heap would move again except behind a tow-truck. They'd enjoyed themselves with the gear on the back seat too. Baggage, coats, all had been a target for high humour and .45 bullets.

Agent O'Day walked under the builder's chute, its maw propped above the dumpster, and on to the southwest corner of Casa Verde. The sun had gone, leaving a ribbon of smoke for a horizon.

Lieutenant Sapolsky, what now please? Give me a sign, you dinosaur.

She shunted her gun to her left hand, rubbed its clammy grip on her jacket, and wiped her palm on the Jordache-jeaned bum so dear to Detective Constable Twitty, who did not at that moment have her bum in mind, but stood alone and dismayed in the living room, regarding the wreck of a telephone.

O'Day regarded the pickup on the driveway between the pool and the patio. To her left, the open french windows; diagonally beyond the patio, across the driveway, the locked garage with storerooms above. She frowned as she gazed at the storeroom windows.

Yesterday, here with Campos, hadn't the windows been bare windows without shutters or curtains? Sure they had, which was why she had supposed nothing was behind them, only storage space. There were still no shutters or curtains but venetian blinds had been lowered.

Papitos maybe, with instructions to keep the sun out. Maybe Viv White stored coke up there and believed if it weren't kept cool it would deteriorate or explode. Or a gardener lived there. Or it was Viv's computer room and he was there now doing his tax return.

Or the blinds had been down all the time and her brains were melting. Damn Lumley, poor jerk. Damn Peckover. If she allowed herself to think of the paperwork, forms, interviews, and inquiries which lay ahead, she would go out of her mind.

She switched her attention back to the pickup, which might have a radio, but nothing you were going to get through to the cops on. You'd get Belize country-and-western. Caribbean rock-me-daddy-with-a-ganja-and-rum. But the truck functioned—it was mobile wheels, for what that was worth.

Not a lot. As they'd shot the Land Rover's short-wave dead, they'd have dealt with whatever phones were in the house. The poet wanted police help and she couldn't fault that. Supposing she made it to the pickup then away from Casa Verde to hunt down the closest phone. That left two fun machine guns versus one revolver which Poet wasn't even going to point. Not judging from his performance in the jungle he wouldn't.

They'd have taken the pickup's keys but that shouldn't be a problem. Come to that, she could blow the lock off the garage. Viv probably had a Rolls or two in there.

One problem was she couldn't see into the house, and Skip and Shep could see out. If they happened to be seeing out when she was fooling with the pickup, they would have as much fun as they'd had all day.

Vivian White sat on the white board floor, one hand on the Remington hunting rifle across his lap. From time to time his hand lifted from the rifle to pluck at his beard. Forefinger and index finger of his other hand held apart two slats of a venetian blind. He watched through the gap.

Who the hell was she? Whoever, she didn't know what she was doing, standing with her popgun, doing nothing, gawping.

Go on, you whore. Get in the truck and piss off, why don't you? One fewer of you.

A pig, she had to be. She wasn't a tourist. She'd come

with Peckover and the other sambo. The Jamaican contingent by way of Notting Hill and Lambeth. His home, three thousand miles from home, infested with nig-nog pigs.

He let go of the blind and wiped his eyes with the back of his hand. He pried open the slats again with his fingers.

Unless she was the Yank. Montego on the phone had mentioned a Yank. The drop a disaster, He'd said. The coke seized. Campos snuffed it, and another local, by two lunatic pros no one knew beans about, except they came out of a black pickup. And Lumley. Incompetent prick, probably boozed out of his tiny pilot's head.

The whore below with the popgun, was she the Yank had ended it for Lumley? Bitch. Everything bitched to hell.

Tribes of visitors. Why couldn't they just leave him be? He'd done nothing. Sweet Christ, the only one he knew, of all people—shithead, nosebreaker Peckover!

News for you, Peckover. You are out of your depth. What you may not realise is I am not going back to the Scrubs. Nor, with you, to anywhere.

To paradise possibly, the only exception, both of us together, if you get a shot in and you can shoot straight. Depends, doesn't it? Got your nice pink card from Sergeant McMaster. But here isn't the classroom and paper targets, old boy.

Viv, cramped, released the slats, and shifted position, leaning his shoulder against the wall. Montego might not know beans about the pair from the pickup who were now in the house with a handy MAC-10 apiece. But I do, Viv thought.

He had never seen them in his life until ten minutes ago, didn't know their names, but he could guess where they came from and what they wanted. He surveyed the jumbled room. Jeremy's room. The wardrobe doors were open, as Jeremy had left them. The bed was unmade, socks and underwear just dropped anywhere.

Viv shifted, and opened two slats. The whore had gone. Back along the side of the house? In through the french windows? She wasn't in the pickup.

Go screw yourself, madam.

Watching the house and the grounds below for signs of life, of which he saw none, Viv began to weep.

"Oh, mummy," he said.

The babe had been as good as gold.

Not twenty-four-carat gold. It hadn't chosen to sleep. There had been slurpings, and one monstrous burp like a toot on a posthorn. But no yelling. Papitos in the gloom at the other end of the cupboard was doing her stuff, rocking and cuddling. She deserved a medal. They both did.

So far anyway.

They hadn't reached this far yet, Skip and Shep. Peckover could hear them. Doors being pushed open, sometimes shut again, comments. Faintly he heard a growling noise and one of them saying what sounded like, "Puddy puddy puddy-tat." From the thumps and creaks, some doors fit poorly, swollen with damp, and had to be opened with a shoulder. The pair were not going out of their way to be quiet as mice.

They were in the passage to the nursery now. *Creak. Thump.* One of them said, "I wouldn't give you ten bucks for this place."

Peckover in the cupboard's dark tilted back his head and breathed through his wide open mouth. Shoulders hunched, elbows squeezed to his sides, he held the revolver two-handed, chest-high, its muzzle a millimetre from the sliding door.

Praying time, but he could not. Even to think of prayer was insulting, it had been so long. Afterwards, yes, a thank you. After they'd gone. He heard a door handle turn across the passage from the nursery and the door thumped open.

The door into the nursery was already open. Has to be good, the door open, Peckover tried to tell himself. Fleetingly he closed his eyes. They'll look in. No one. They'll call it a day.

They had already looked in, moved on—had they?

"Why, lookee, what have we here?" declared a voice. He was in the room. "Crib. Diapers." He was crossing the room. American. "Babykins stuff."

"But no babykins," said the other.

No babykins, Peckover agreed. He wanted to tell them. No one, can't you see? Give it up. Please. On your way.

"Pshla-a-abl!" shouted the baby.

TWENTY

Having slid the cupboard door aside, the one with the jacket had to decide whether to defend himself against the woman or the baby.

He did both, first pressing the muzzle of his gun against the woman's temple, next putting it like a steel teat to the baby's mouth. The baby spluttered. Reasoning that the woman, in spite of her silence, posed a greater threat than the baby, he placed the muzzle under her chin and forced her head back.

Light from the nursery invaded the woman, baby, and gun, washed along the cupboard, and lit Peckover, who levelled his revolver at the jumbo-Pepsodent rectangle of the MAC-10, and the hand that held it.

I'm out of my mind, Peckover thought, and tried to take his finger off the trigger. The finger seemed as if stuck, paralysed.

"Step out, lady."

Peckover saw the gun withdraw. The man's other hand took hold of the woman's hair and yanked her from the cupboard.

"You're Papitos." That was the other voice, the one in the white shirt.

"And babykins. Ain' you de cudest li'l babykins? Where the cops, Papitos *muchacha?*"

No answer. A slap. Papitos squealed.

"Where did you say?"

"They go 'way."

"They no go 'way, you lying spic *muchacha.*" Slap. "Where's Viv?"

"Not know!" Her voice was shrill. "Not see!"

"You like to see babykins hung out the window, *muchacha? El bambino suspendo de la ventana, olé!*"

No answer.

"*Fantastico*. Love your way with words. Observe real close, *muchacha*, how we hang babykins out to dry."

There came a grunt, a slap like a stick snapping. The baby began to wail.

Papitos, you don't have to do this, Peckover wanted to tell her. I'm coming out. A moment more. He's bluffing, Papitos.

Peckover doubted it was bluff. The bloke was sick in his head. Gawd, Peckover coming out of the closet—smashing London headline, sell another ten thousand copies. Coming out for what bloody good? He might kill one of them if the gun didn't shake out of his hand. The other would kill him. What would be won?

But he was coming out. A moment. What were they doing now?

"Stupid dumb *muchacha*! Where are they?" The shout was from a spoiled brat who couldn't find his football boots. Who had lost his marbles. "You want to see that baby thrown out the window, that what you want?"

Only answer, the baby's wailing.

"Speak, spic! Say something! Say *caramba!*"

Through the inch opening in the cupboard door Peckover saw the one in the white shirt arrive at the window. He was in profile and agitated. Mid-twenties, sandy hair cropped short, little dinky snub nose, pink complexion glowing from Belize sunshine. He started twisting the screw which held the sashes.

"Hold it, champ," the first voice said. "What difference where? Why don't you watch the door?"

"I'm hanging that kid out the window is why. You watch the door."

"I will. Calm it. Papitos, you're taking a trip." The voice was further away, nearer the door. "You and the baby. Get its stuff together."

The one in the white shirt put his gun beside the Pampers on the table and jerked the window up, jolting and forcing it.

"Not tomorrow—now," the voice near the door said. "Get its stuff."

"Stuff?"

"Stuff! Don't play dumb!" The voice by the door was shouting now. These two were equally unhinged. "Move!"

"Don't move!" shouted another voice from the door.

Peckover swept the cupboard door open with a wallop which splintered it. In the doorway into the nursery, Twitty stood behind the gunman, throttling him with a forearm like a car jack. His right hand, out of view, dug into the man's back a gun, or Phillips screwdriver, or maybe just knuckles.

"Police—drop it!" yelled Twitty in the man's ear. He shouted across the room, "You—don't touch it!"

The throttled one dropped his gun to the carpet. Above the gun beside the Pampers hovered the hand of the one in the white shirt. The hand grabbed, its fingers wrapped round the grip. Peckover lifted his own hand, chopped down on the wrist, and slammed his revolver into the side of the man's head. He put the revolver in his pocket and picked up the MAC-10.

The one in the white shirt slid to the carpet and sat askew beneath the open window, holding his head. Peckover placed a foot against his face and pushed him flat. Planting his other foot in the man's groin, he leaned out of the window and flung backhanded the MAC-10. A memory surfaced of an envelope flung over three sleazos into the night and the rain in Collins Cross. He was becoming adept at this.

The gun struck the pool with a satisfying splash. Pink card in weapons-throwing for Henry Peckover.

He frisked the squirming goon on the carpet, taking from an ankle-holster and defenestrating an automatic. This time his direction was off. The MAC-10 had made it into the pool by a yard. The automatic bounced and skidded along the pool's tiled surround.

He frisked the tall, throttled one held by Twitty. The man's face was a mottled Wedgwood blue above Twitty's jack-handle forearm.

"Easy, lad, 'e's not going anywhere," Peckover said.

He extracted a pistol from a shoulder holster and collected the MAC-10 from the carpet. The pistol soared wide into grass. The MAC-10 hit first the tiled edge of the pool, next the water, joining its partner beneath widening ripples of concentric rings. Throwing away weapons might not be correct procedure, and Bill Astle would beat the soles of his feet with a truncheon, but Bill Astle was a cross-eyed turd. Peckover believed he could argue that guns were better off full fathom five than around babies.

The baby was howling like a force ten. It had not stopped, and Peckover sympathised. But where was it? Where was Papitos?

Back in the womb of the closet was where, a tactical withdrawal, cowering and unashamed. Peckover guessed they might now have been half a mile away, fleeing into the twilight, had not Twitty and his prisoner been blocking the door.

"It's all right, ma'am, it's over. You were"—*Fantastico?* Was that a word? It was not one of his words—"brave. Would you like to lie down? Shall I take the baby?"

Peckover did not want the baby, and Papitos was not about to give it to him. She held it closer. But she came from the cupboard and stood hugging and trying to comfort the raving bundle.

Twitty kneed the thug with the blue face into the nursery and released him. This one was six-six or so, taller than himself. He bent double, choked, and vomited on the beige carpet.

"Yuck," Twitty said.

The weapon in Twitty's hand was a jagged, spindly, blunt instrument eighteen inches long which looked familiar to Peckover, and not all that blunt. The policemen regarded it and each other in wonderment.

"So what is it?" Peckover asked.

"My guess is it's a Giacometti."

"Who?"

"You know. It was on the telly."

"'The Giacometti Show'?"

"Guv, you are having me on. You know Giacometti."

"I know if that's what it is it's worth thousands and should be in a gallery with the 'Enry Moores and guards tellin' you to keep your fingers off."

In low voices they talked for talk's sake, winding down, waiting for an end to tremor and breathlessness before talking to the hoodlum pair.

Skip and Shep were in fairly poor shape, though not to be relied on to stay that way. They were young and recovering. Papitos had retreated to the foot of the bed and sat there cooing at the infant, who was calmer. Peckover wanted them out of the hoodlums' company.

He asked Twitty, "You didn't raid the gunroom?"

"Didn't try. No pink card."

"Get the police?"

"They'd smashed up the phone."

"The Land Rover?"

"Couldn't say. I'm not hopeful."

"Peaches?"

"Peachy. Haven't seen her."

"'Andcuffs in the Land Rover presumably."

"Want me to get them? You go if you like. I can take care of these two."

"Right now the baby could take care of these two. Don't misunderstand, you did all right. For a black in funny clothes." Peckover was looking thoughtful. "What rhymes with Giacometti?"

"Spaghetti?"

"Betty, jetty, sweaty, Donizetti. Blimey, everything rhymes."

"Can I lend you a pencil?"

They watched the one under the window lever himself to his feet, holding the side of his head. Blood dappled his white shirt. He stared back at the policemen and grinned, as if letting them know that this was the worst they could do to him, but he would kill them. If not soon, then someday.

The vomiting one had straightened up and was turning from blue to lava. Lava with a hint of Belize russet, a shade which looked to Peckover less serious than blue, not that he had any intention of becoming anxious. This beauty killed people. He, too, had short fair hair, and the featureless, unmemorable face of someone who rings the doorbell to sell you something you don't want, so you don't remember him because you hardly look. Except this one he would remember. Both of them.

Peckover glanced obsessively round the nursery for guns. The only gun was in his pocket but knowing it did not help. He should probably fling it along with the others. Great headline if anything went amiss: YARD BARD SLAIN BY OWN GUN.

Papitos was more unsettled than he had realised. Unless she cooled down she was going to need attention. The drawn-out sounds she uttered were less cooing than keening, and she rocked to comfort herself rather than the baby, who was in fine fettle, dribbling and clucking and tugging the woman's hair.

"Libretti?" said Twitty, holding the Giacometti, eyes on Skip and Shep. "John Paul Getty?"

"Get over by the wall," Peckover told Skip, or Shep, and shoved him. "You too, squire. Face this way. Further apart. 'Ands on your 'eads. Do it! Look at me." He did not care for the way they looked at him, estimating distance. If he hauled out the gun, they would think again. But guns went bleedin' off. "Blown is what you are. Kaputski. All right? Only question, far as I can see, is what country you go in the dock. Whether you get ninety years or executed. There's not much

we don't know but just for confirmation why don't you give
your side of it?"

They weren't going to give any side of it. At the Yard they
would have been separated, individually squeezed. This was
Casa Verde. Coppers were in short supply.

Whether they said anything or nothing was not the immediate concern. The trick would be keeping them subdued
until troops arrived, and without fooling with the gun. When
and if friendly faces showed up depended on O'Day. If they
didn't show soon, he was going to have to think about ferry-
ing them to the police.

Handcuffed in the back of the pickup was probably the
best bet. Have Twitty drive and the woman and baby ride
with the lad up front, because he wasn't leaving them here
on their own.

From the bed behind him Papitos keened. She was getting
on his nerves.

He said, "So which of you is the chatterbox? Like where
would you suppose Viv might be right at this minute? And
what salary are you on? See, we've still one or two loose
ends."

Loose ends? He didn't even know their names. He wasn't
about to admit he didn't know.

"Empty your pockets on the floor."

Neither moved.

"Constable, would you mind? They need 'elp."

"Don't come near me, you black monkey," said the one
with the lava hue.

Peckover stepped forward and punched his jaw. The man
staggered, bumped into the crib, and fell against the head of
the bed. The keening from the foot of the bed rose an oc-
tave.

"Know why?" Peckover shouted at the man. "Want to
know why? Because the constable wasn't going to! Right,
constable?"

"Sir!"

"Because 'e's soft! Soft in the 'ead! But I'm a brute, got
it? And you're past hope, you suppurating cowpat, you burst
boil, you pitiful—"

"Sir!" cried Twitty above the comments and the keening.

The keening was close to a screech. Peckover looked
round. Papitos, everything evidently too much, was disappearing into the passage, hugging the baby.

"Papitos!" shouted Peckover.

Shep, or Skip, in a bloodied white shirt, punched Peckover on the back of the neck, then the side of the head. His

hand scrabbled at the policeman's jacket pocket.

Peckover wheeled, flailing and kicking, and received a thump on his cheekbone. He tried to smother the white shirt in a heavyweight clinch, to headbutt him senseless, but he butted air, and for the clinch only his left arm was available. His right hand, defending his pocket, grappled with the man's hand. A borscht blur arrived like a train and knocked pirouetting Shep and himself off balance. The shaggy floor rose to greet Peckover at remarkable speed.

He struggled on the carpet beneath company both white and red. His skull absorbed another bump. He recalled a pool of puke and hoped it was elsewhere. Nothing he could do about it. He could twitch. Otherwise he was pinned.

A yelp from Shep, a gasp from Twitty. After many years, this was the rugby field again, immobilised at the grunting bottom of the scrum. Mauling limbs, buttocks, torsos, weighted him down.

Torsos? Torsi? The pit of the scrum gave time for reflection.

Whichever, they lifted and were gone, as in rugby. Unless the referee's whistle blew, which it was not doing, what you did now was get up and battle on. Peckover, sprawled, felt his pocket. The gun was there. He felt his head.

That, too, was there. Some stickiness, much throbbing. Lumps and pains in other areas. He got up.

No one to battle. He had the nursery to himself.

Peckover reached the passage in time to see distant Twitty, solitary on the landing, stooped almost double and whirling his arm, playing-fields-of-Harrow style, aiming down the stairs. He was still stooped over when Peckover reached him.

Winded. He must have progressed this far like a hairpin. Probably hadn't managed a breath since Shep's shoe or knee had hit his stomach.

"Easy, lad. Head between your legs."

"Get"—*gasp*—"after them!"

"More 'aste, less speed. You see the woman and the baby?"

Gasp. "No."

"Then we look. Soon as you can move. They go below?"

"God forgive me, I threw the Giacometti!"

"You missed. It's down there in the 'all. And Skip and Shep are outside looking for their guns." Peckover supposed they were. He was leaning over the banister, looking down the stairwell. "As well you did miss, mate. That thing, you could've killed the bleeder."

"Wanted to. I think I did." Twitty elongated himself to six feet four and breathed and puffed. In, out. In, out. "It was all I had. I didn't think." He thumped his forehead with the heel of his hand, a bit theatrically in Peckover's opinion. "It's like using the Venus de Milo to crush grapes, or a Rembrandt for a tablecloth, and sending it to the laundry. I mean—Giacometti!"

"Bugger Giacometti."

"Philistine!"

"Me philistine? Who threw the bleedin' thing?"

"God, you're a mess!"

"Now wait a minute—"

"Your face, up on your cheek, head—oh, sod everything! You all right?"

"There they are," Peckover said, peering down the stairwell. "Quick!"

He was gone down the stairs. Papitos, cradling the baby, had appeared in the hall, then hurried into the passage to the gunroom, kitchen, and basement. Peckover did not have the topography of Casa Verde mapped in his mind but as far as he could tell she had arrived in the hall from beneath the stairs, some hidey-hole where she had waited until the cavalcade of hit men and policemen had passed by.

She was closing the door to the basement behind her when he slid a brogue into the gap.

"Papitos!"

Instead of tugging on the door, and accomplishing nothing against the brogue, she pushed it open. She was grimy and teary.

"You kind cop," she said. "You strong, take good care. For baby's sake." Not gingerly, but thrusting it at him, she presented the baby. "Papitos weak. For Papitos—enough."

"No! Papitos—"

"Enough for Papitos!"

The door slammed shut. A key turned.

"Papitos!"

Peckover twisted the handle. He rapped on the door, but delicately, for fear of frightening the baby he held to his chest.

"Papitos," he whispered through the door. He glanced down. The baby was warm, wriggling not to excess, and looking up. It was naked except for Pampers and plastic pants.

Twitty arrived smugly, having recovered the Giacometti in one piece. He looked in wild surmise at the baby, at Peckover, and again at the baby.

"Papitos?" whispered Peckover. "Please, madam— miss?" He pounded noiselessly on the door.

"I can probably get it open," Twitty said. "The locks in this place are rubbish."

Peckover hiked the baby higher on his chest. "I'm not sure what we'd gain," he said. "We'll let her be."

"Brrrlp," said the baby.

TWENTY-ONE

Agent O'Day lay propped on her elbows in the long grass between the garage and the garden shed, watching. Like an Apache, she had decided.

Did Apaches have grass? Wasn't it all cactus? Maybe she was a Sioux. Chances were she was a Comanche, or at any rate one which began with a C. Most Indians began with a C. She started adding them up. Comanche, Cherokee, Cree, Creek. She had nothing else to do, only watch.

She watched Shep scouting the lawn, and lofty Skip on his hands and knees beside the pool, gazing into the water like that guy in the myth. Narcissus. They kept looking towards the house, to the french windows, and up at the open, unshuttered nursery window.

Don't get excited, jerks, O'Day would have been happy to advise them. Poet isn't going to shoot you. He could come out and crack your skulls, and kick your nuts into ground beef, and drop you in the pool, but he doesn't do shooting.

Crow, Cheyenne, Choctaw, Chippewa, Chickasaw.

They weren't going to find the gun from the lawn or the one beyond the pool because she had got there first. She was armed like a bandit. Where to get rid of them was the tricky part. Lugging them was a sweat, like being a bricklayer with a full hod.

Not that she had ever been a bricklayer. Maybe scrape out a crater right here in the soil, cover them with grass. Her fingernails were pretty much beyond hope anyway.

She watched above the rim of the grass. Shep had given up on the lawn and joined Skip by the pool. Together they stared into its depths. They looked like a canvas in an art gallery. *Jerks in Quandry over Sunk MAC-10s.*

So what do you propose, jerks? That's the deep end you're at. Do you swim? Are you wondering if they're going to work now they're wet? They'll work, but maybe you don't know that, all you know is shooting them.

Creole, Colorado, Costa Rica. Now wait a minute. Chicano, Chihuahua. Christopher Columbus.

O'Day looked at the side door into the garage and probably up stairs to the storage or whatever was above. Skip and Shep had come running from the house at the moment she had been about to try her luck with the door, and she'd had to flop or be seen. The lock on the door was garbage. She could get in. Someone was up there.

Rats and cockroaches, sure. The gardener, Ramon? Could be.

Could be Viv.

Viv White was who she was here for. If it was Viv up there, and if she made the collar—no, too much. Dream on, Peachy baby.

But this was Viv's pad and where was he? No one knew.

Christmas. Chrysler, Cadillac—Cadillac could have been an Indian chief, unless he was some guy with a musket in the French Revolution. Clytemnestra. Boy, that was one spirited lady, butchering her husband with a sword. Those Greeks were something. About all she remembered from high school, Mr. Spiegel's myths and legends class. Spacey Spiegel with his spirals of hair like springs burst out of a clock in a cartoon.

Skip, the one in the jacket, was taking off his jacket.

Not a murmur from the house. 'Twas not the night before Christmas but all through the house not a creature was stirring not even a mouse. Poet and his partner sleeping off the excitement, she supposed. Piggy-backing the baby.

Viv, how dangerous was he? She knew nothing about him except he was a Brit middleman between the Colombia moguls and too many poor hooked assholes in L.A. And Kamikaze O'Day was right in there, in the world's most dangerous job open to ladies, after locker-room attendant at the Sisterhood Personal Enrichment Bath House at Sunset and 39th. Until she learned different she would assume Viv was dangerous. That was quite an arsenal he had. As well he didn't leave the shells lying around or those two wouldn't be dithering at the pool.

Grass tickled her chin. Carson, Kit. Cash, Johnny. Chanukah sounded Indian but it was a Jewish holiday, unless she was muddling it with something else. Cholesterol. Coke. Constable Twitty.

Musing, smiling, scratching mosquito bites, Peachy O'Day bit off a blade of grass. Jason, was it? This Jason wasn't after any golden fleece, he was after hers, which was as black as his, and knew it because every time he looked at her he stripped her clean as the sky.

Come on over, Jasey boy, you pretzel, you salty peanut, you horny bonebag. Quit the piggy-backing. Hands across the ocean. Here I is.

No I ain't.

Skip had taken off his shoes. Shep was walking in her direction. O'Day wriggled backwards on elbows and knees.

"'Jolly boating weather,'" sang Viv, throatily tuneful, "'and the hay harvest breeze . . .'"

He sat cross-legged on the white board floor by the venetian blind. He had opened the window six inches and wedged a spearmint box between two slats to hold them apart. His hands were free. As well as see out he could shoot if he wanted.

He could not see the Song of Solomon harlot who had run with the guns into the grass between the garage and the shed. Jeremy's flat had no window that side. But she was there somewhere, sniffing around, he was fairly sure of it. If the joker in the white shirt heading this way spied her . . .

So what if? He didn't have the guns. She did. Apart from the two that bully-boy Peckover had landed in the pool.

The joker seemed to be aiming for the shed. Hoping for a rod and line, a shrimping net, to haul up the guns? You'll be lucky, you prick.

Prick trespasser. Who d'you think you are?

Daddy's help was who, the two of them, had to be. Where did Daddy find these people—the Yellow Pages? Daddy always found what he wanted, paid the going rate, or above if he had to. Probably advertised in the *Times* classified, got a reduced rate because he knew someone who knew someone. Wanted: Gunmen willing to travel to the very arsehole of the world.

Though here wasn't the arsehole, or soon wouldn't be. It would be the asshole. The Yanks were coming with their scuba gear and deals for land and hotels. Only a couple of years ago, a trickle, and now a surge.

Viv caressed the Remington's trigger with a fingertip. Warm, slim inch of trigger. Astonishing but for once he wished success to the pigs. Come on, shithead Peckover, what's keeping you? Squelch Daddy's help, extirpate the vipers, wipe them away. They're not such great shakes or they'd have been out of it by now, gone with the babbie.

As long as the pigs stayed away from himself. Too bad for you, harlot, if you approach even close. I might not see you coming but I will hear. Every stair creaks, did you know? No real foundation, no solidity, see, same as people. No carpet either. Jeremy couldn't have cared less about carpets.

Viv's finger stroked the trigger. His other hand lifted to his lips the bottle of Taittinger. Nothing but the best for Jeremy, except it was tepid. Jeremy couldn't even put a couple of bottles in the fridge. Probably hadn't known he had a fridge.

Oh, Jeremy, you bastard.

Viv blinked wetly. He swigged lukewarm Taittinger and watched through the window. Who could want to kill Jeremy. An absurd mistake, an error in the computer.

Daddykins in a fit might kill anyone. Everyone. Sodding Genghis Khan, Daddy, he had it in him. All right, not actually kill, but get the sod sacked. Burn his house down.

Mummy.

The help in the white shirt with what looked to be blood on it, and blood smearing his ear, went into the shed.

"'Blade on the feather,'" Viv sang, "'shade of the trees . . .'"

He knew every verse. He would have to be quiet between verses and listen. Listen for creakings.

After the Eton Boating Song there was the whole of Noël Coward, Gilbert and Sullivan, and *Rigoletto*, *"Bella figlia dell'amore."* A medley round the British Isles, he could let that rip.

He looked forward to the medley; he could hardly wait. Loch Lomond. All Through the Night. Mountains of Mourne, blub blub. The British Grenadiers.

Viv stroked, blinked, chugged warm champagne, saw the upstairs window of the house fill again with the bulk of shithead Peckover.

"'Swing, swing, together,'" sang Viv with a throb and resonance which he thought not bad at all, "'your bodies between your knees . . .'"

The first time Henry Peckover, holding the baby, looked from the nursery window, Ship was scouting the lawn and Skep was peering full fathom five.

Or vice-versa. Peckover saw no profit in trying to tell the beauties apart. They were different but there was no difference. They were obnoxious, murderous excrement to be scooped up and disposed of soonest. Which was not quite yet, encumbered as he was.

"Brlph," said the baby, hopeful for playtime.

"Shurrup," Peckover said. He tickled the baby under its chin, transferred the finger to his lips, and waggled it, blowing. "Brrrrrlph yourself, mate."

The baby grabbed Peckover's nose. Peckover freed his nose and pinched the baby's nose. The baby chortled with rude rapture, blew its nose into Peckover's fingers, and said, "Shlpf."

"Get 'is stuff together," Peckover at the window told Twitty. "There could be an electric bottle-warmer, we'll want that. Fill it, but be sure you can pack it upright. There might be a cover. Look for the cover. When I say fill it, that's an inch of water. Likely 'alf an inch. The bottle's got to go in. There's displacement. Use your judgment."

"Sir?"

"Get on with it. You'll pack most of the stuff in the end of the carry-cot—that there." Peckover turned from the window and pointed. "Leave room for 'is nibs, 'is royal majesty 'ere, and don't get it top-heavy. You listening? Leftovers you can't get in, if there's no more room, you pack somewhere else. Find a box. All the jars, nappies. Don't forget a spoon. You report to me specifically we've got a spoon, understood? Oils, ointments, unguents, all that. What we've got to avoid is nappy-rash. What're you standin' there for? Gawd, you 'old the perisher, I'll pack. No, wait. You ever held a baby? Listen—once in your life, just listen, all right? First, you don't drop it. Worth mentioning because if you drop it from up there, you beanstalk, it's got quite a distance to go. Other 'and, you don't 'old it so bleedin' tight you squeeze the breath out of the perisher and burst it like a haggis. It's a question of equilibrium, finding the correct balance. They're fragile. Look at the size of it. But they're not that fragile, they'll take a certain amount of buffeting, being cushioned, up to a point. Not the 'ead. Gawd, take care of the bleeder's 'ead. Think procelain, Ming, like in the Victoria and Albert. Skip's taking 'is shoes off. Gerronouta that, that's my ear, little perisher. Don't you 'ave a rattle or trumpet or anything? Lad, find it a toy. I'll 'old it, you pack. You'll probably 'old it upside down. Funny thing, they like upside down. Mine did. Mary still does. Not all the time, naturally. Blimey, what're we doing 'ere? If Frank Veal could—hell, what does 'e know? Miriam would know. Listen—"

"Henry, would you calm down?"

"Eh?"

"I'm the second of eight brothers and sisters. Might be nine at this rate, time we get home, you going on and on. I grew up holding babies."

"You did?"

"I just said I did." Twitty carried baby food to the carry-cot. "You pack if you like. That way I'll not be responsible for the bottle-warmer, which I don't see. You find one, I'll give you a fiver."

"A fiver?"

"You keep asking what I've just told you. I'll watch Skip and Shep. Sit it on the carpet if you're anxious. He's not going to run off."

"Might. You 'aven't seen. Goes like a racehorse when he's in the mood."

"Where're we off to anyway?"

"Don't ask. Out. You want to stay, watch 'im grow to manhood? Celebrate 'is twenty-first?"

"You have children?"

"Not as little as this one. Odd 'ow you forget. Like they walk before they talk, that's easy. But when does the tooth fairy come?"

"Seven or eight months. How little?"

"Sam's four, Mary two-and-a-'alf. Let go my nose, you bleeder, or I'll tell Commander Astle about you. Shep's going to the garage."

They watched from the window. Twitty held Pampers and a spoon.

He said, "Do we collect Papitos?"

"Questions, questions. Ideally, yes. Probably, no. Can't force 'er if she's had enough. 'Ere, I'll pack that junk." Peckover wrestled nappies and spoon from Twitty in exchange for the baby. "Your turn, big brother."

The baby kicked and spluttered in the arms of Twitty, who told Peckover, "You horror. He's done a poo."

"Poo?"

"You're a bloody echo-chamber—sir. Sorry."

"Dunno what you're on about."

"What do you call it then with your Sam and Mary?"

"Number one and number two."

"Awesome." Twitty carried the baby to the middle of the room, sat it on the carpet, and walked away. "We know which number this is. Unless it's number three. What's its name anyway?"

"'Ow do I know what's its name?"

"You mean you don't know? You've got the file—"

"You read the file on the plane. Doesn't say."

"—you talked to Papitos. What did she call him?"

"Nothing, not that I 'eard. Spot. George. Lord White the Third. Bleedin' 'ell, what's it matter what's its name? You want 'im to sign a cheque?"

"You're amazing. You don't even know it's a boy. You keep calling it 'him' and 'it' but you know nothing about it."

"Know it's Viv's. And I know you're about to change its nappy. Don't argue. You grew up 'olding babies, you changed nappies too."

Peckover watched the white-shirted one go into the garden shed. He heard behind him Twitty grouching. A tap gushed in the sink, the lid of the bin opened and closed. The baby was perfecting a staccato piping sound—"Eeh, eeh, eeh, eeh"—which numbed the skull.

"George happens to be Georgina," Twitty said. "Or Georgette."

"He's got a rake," Peckover said from the window. "And a power-drill, is it? What's 'e want with a drill?"

"Bust into the ammunition if they don't fish up their guns."

"They can't swim or they'd have fished 'em up ten minutes ago. Why doesn't 'e take all his clothes off? Why stop at shoes and jacket? You'd think he'd welcome a dip."

"He's modest. The criminal classes are extreme in pudency."

"What's pudency?"

"Shame."

"Really. Not like at 'arrow, I'll bet. Flaunterers all. Jason, lad, just in case, I want one volunteer to spirit away that ammunition box, if that's what it is."

Skip, holding the rake, was lowering himself, and being lowered, into the pool. Shep held his arm.

"I'd like this kind volunteer to get rid of the ammunition box, hide it—"

Bang!

Slivers of tile and an invisible, ricocheting bullet flew up at Shep's feet. Shep looked towards the garage. Skip, waist-deep in the pool, started to struggle out. The rake began to sink.

Peckover and Twitty stared at the windows above the garage. One was slightly open.

"Bloody 'ell's bells!"

Bang!

More slivers and a puff of powder. The sniper was an excellent shot if what he wanted was to scare the twosome at the pool. If his purpose was to kill them, he was not a hundred per cent, but he was still pretty good.

Skip was out of the water, snatching up his shoes and jacket, and running after Shep across the driveway, past the pickup, towards the patio and the french windows. Shep carried the drill. The rake had joined the guns on the pool's floor.

"Lad, no—Jason! Stop!"

Twitty had too much momentum even to want to stop. He shouted, "Watch Georgie!"

The baby, freshly clad, was on her feet, marching nowhere in particular, but proceeding with dour, scowling determination. Left, right, left, right. She sat heavily as Twitty raced by, out of the nursery.

"'Swing, swing, together,'" Viv sang under his breath.

Next time he would put a bullet through their feet. Trespassers. Daddy's houseboys. The one in the white shirt had gone through the french windows into the house. The tall one had stopped to put on his shoes.

Barely an inch of Taittinger remained. Extraordinary. The rest had evaporated, must have. Viv giggled.

The one in the wet shoes and trousers ran across the patio and into the house.

"'Your back between your knees . . .'"

Ssssh, Viv shushed himself.

No mistake, there it was again, the creak. Not on the stairs. He hadn't heard the stairs. She was on the landing outside the door.

He stood up, walked from the bedroom into the hallway, and waited there, facing the door, pointing the Remington.

TWENTY-TWO

Detective Constable Twitty had somewhere recovered his hat. He cornered into the gunroom, braked, and came to an emergency stop. He was lifting the ammunition chest when he heard feet running his way along the corridor.

He put the box down and went to the door. Why it should have a key on the inside he might wonder later at his leisure. He put the key in his pocket. Shep ran into the room, took the constable's fist in his belly, said "Aagh!" and dropped the drill. Twitty was most of the way to pinning him with a nelson when the slapping of more feet sounded in the passage.

Unarmed, the two were not instantly lethal, but they were two, if the new feet were Skip. Twitty projected Shep hard into the gunroom, turned to the door, and heard rather than saw Shep come to some sort of grief over the chest and into the wall. Skip arrived too fast. Twitty accelerated his passage, grabbing his hair and an arm and propelling him in his partner's wake.

In the corridor, Twitty slammed and locked the door. He bounded along the corridor, up the stairs, past rampant Leo on the landing, into the nursery.

"I couldn't, there wasn't time! What's happened? Is it all right?"

"She, cock, not it. Mind your manners. She was walking but she wasn't looking. She 'ad a bump."

The baby was wailing. Peckover, holding her, was dabbing her nose with a blotched red tissue.

"I'm sorry, they were there soon as I was—"

"Course they were. Told you, you thick—"

"—and they're there now with the box and guns and drill! I locked them in!"

"You what?"

"I don't guarantee the lock for a minute, even if the drill's useless. They'll bite their way out."

"I've 'eard of setting a fox to guard the hen house. You've put two soddin' foxes inside the hen house."

"Said I was sorry!"

"Shut up. You've done all right so don't get boring. Listen." Peckover turned his ear to the door. "D'you hear drilling?"

"How can anyone hear anything with that brat bawling?"

"Watch it! She's not a brat. She's Georgie-Porgie. Just 'ad a bit of a bump, bumped into the sink, didn't you, George." He plucked a fresh Kleenex from its box and dabbed. "Naughty sink. Silly George."

"She's not George, she's a girl. You don't call your— Mary is it?—you don't call her Arthur. Or Basil."

"George is happy with George. We've discussed it, haven't we, George." Peckover hiked the baby full-stretch above his head. She stopped wailing but looked startled rather than thrilled. Her nose was grazed and red. He lowered her. "Listen."

They listened. George listened. The sustained vibrating from below was presumably a drill.

"Take the carry-cot to the Land Rover and wait for us," Peckover said. "Find the cuffs. We're right behind you."

He sat the baby on the floor and started stowing into a plastic bag items which Twitty had not got round to. Clothes, cotton wool, baby oil, Play Wipes with Aloe—what the hell were they?—and Sit 'n' Sip, a contraption for putting in or on a bottle which he would work out later.

He said, "Don't stand there—go!"

Twitty grabbed the carry-cot, skidded in Skip's spew, swore, and fled.

Peckover was not right behind because while he foraged, and came upon an indestructible box which at a twist of a dial tinkled. "The Farmer in the Dell," the baby stood up. Out of time to the music, she resolutely plodded, and before Peckover could swoop, plodded into a chair.

"Waaaagh!" What was hurt was her pride.

Peckover scooped her up. "Ssh, quiet! Good ol' Georgie-Porgie." He rewound the box.

Had the drilling stopped?

Yes, and in its place thuddings, clatterings. Too much clattering for a lone Twitty with a carry-cot. Peckover put the music-box in the bag, headed with bag and baby out of the nursery, and stopped to listen.

Clatterings from the hall below. Now on the stairs.

Damn.

No exiting down the stairs. Behind him, first place they'd look, the nursery, a no-go area. The bedroom opposite, equally useless. Was there a loft, a way to the roof?

Marvellous. He could see himself sitting on the roof holding a baby and a bag of necessaries, trying to keep her quiet, smacking at mosquitoes, admiring the jungle view. Take a grip on yourself, you berk.

"'Heigh oh the derry oh,'" tinkled the box in the bag.

The box did not tinkle the words but Peckover knew them. He had never been devoted to them. Or to the tune. Or for matter of that to any children's tunes and songs, which mashed your brains to a pudding, come the seven hundredth hearing. The grisliest aspect of being a father, a mum too, more than likely, was the stultifying repetition of "Eentsy Weentsy Spider," and "Twinkle, Twinkle, Little Star," and "Old MacDonald," and "Baa Baa Black Sheep," and "Here We Go Looney Loo." You bet we go Looney Loo.

He ran left, away from Leo and the landing, to the end of the passage, and into a blitzed room where there should have been builders sitting drinking tea from flasks. There were none. Peckover closed the door, striving for silence. The door scraped over grit and plaster.

No key.

"'. . . the farmer in the dell . . .'"

"Waaaagh!"

"Shurrup!"

Peckover planted George on a low hillock of rubble, snatched the musicbox from the bag, and failed to find an off-button. He shook it in the hope that its entrails might fall out. He beat it, tried to silence it by twisting the dial in reverse, a route the dial refused to go, and to smash it by overwinding, but it would not be overwound, and in trying he gave it another four hours of playing time. He threw it across the room.

Along the passage, thudding feet. Then quiet.

Peckover put his ear to the door. Investigating the nursery? The closet? That would take them the better part of three seconds.

George, impressively calm, probed chubby fingers into the rubble and put plaster in her mouth. "Pflp," she said.

"'. . . we all pat the dog . . .'" tinkled a distant heap of bricks.

Peckover dragged a hundredweight sack of cement through debris and set it against the door. He dragged another sack, and at the second attempt lifted it, straining and gasping, and placed it on top of the first. He heard voices in the corridor, indistinct, but perhaps reasoning that they were too late, the cops had gone, taking the baby.

Perhaps. 'Enry the optimist. With the merest whisper of a scraping sound he dragged a third sack, in case they were reasoning nothing of the kind. One more should hold the fort for a moment or two. If he could lift the bugger high enough.

Lifting sack three gave Peckover lumbar spasms, surely a hernia, torsion of everything, and numberless sprung discs. Attempting tiptoe, trembling from stem to stern, he hobbled towards the window. He skirted rubble, and the hillock where sat George, profoundly occupied with riches of laths, plaster, and rusty nails. He poked his head through the space where the window frame would have been had someone not removed it, and the chute's dusty, circular mouth.

Dusk. A beauteous evening, calm and free, quiet as a nun. Twitty was climbing from the Land Rover.

"Lad!" Peckover called in a whisper. "Jason!"

Gawd, wash yer ears out. But he dared not shout.

"Constable!"

Twitty, regarding the Land Rover, took off his Panama hat and fanned himself. Peckover reached down for a fist-sized lump of concrete, of which there was ample. He eased his head, shoulders, and arm through the window, aimed, and threw. H. Peckover, thrower from windows, by appointment.

He aimed away from Twitty but not too far away. He could have killed the lad. The concrete struck the ground. Twitty looked round, then up. Peckover, waving, heard behind him the door handle twist and rattle.

The small, rustling, sliding noise was George setting in motion an avalanche of concrete chippings down the crust of the hillock.

"Glmph."

"'. . . the farmer wants a wife . . .'"

Twitty waved his Panama, a shorebound lover bidding adieu to his beloved on the poop deck. High up, Peckover held one forefinger to his lips while vigourously jabbing up and down with the other, indicating the filled skip thirty feet below. The Panama stayed aloft, motionless, while Twitty looked blankly from Peckover to the skip and back at the guv'nor.

The chute was a generous three feet across. Peckover

placed a broken brick in its mouth, released it, and threw in two more bricks, a piece of hardboard, and some linoleum. He waited, watching from the window. If the chute was blocked, he could forget it. Shoes and shoulders thudded against the door.

He should forget it anyway. Never was he going to fit in the chute or slide with a baby down the outside. Even without a baby. Bricks, hardboard, and linoleum spouted from the chute onto the muck in the dumpster.

In the corridor a gun fired. The door splintered. The gun fired again. The baby started to bawl.

Peckover put his own gun in his trousers pocket and took off his jacket. He picked up baby George and presented her struggling at the window.

"Catch 'er!" he yelled down, quietness no longer serving any purpose. "She's on 'er way!"

"What?" called Twitty.

You 'eard. A gun banged on the other side of the door. Peckover wound his jacket round howling George, tightly round her body, less tightly round her head. He folded her like a package for the post office, wrapped the sleeves round, and knotted them. In the corridor they were enjoying themselves, alternately shooting at the door, then slamming against it and shoving. The bags of cement held, so far.

"*Bon voyage,* Georgie.*"

Peckover put an arm out of the window and signalled. A benediction, like the Pope from his balcony, he thought.

The banner headline read: YARD BARD ACQUITTED IN BELIZE INFANTICIDE HORROR.

At least he had been acquitted.

He positioned the package in the mouth of the chute. What else could he have done? Deliver up George to Skip and Shep? Throw himself on their mercy?

What else, Frank? Commander Astle, sir?

Oh Miriam.

At the moment Peckover released the package into the chute, the guns in the corridor, probably reloading, allowing rival gunfire to be heard from the direction of the garage.

Agent O'Day with a bloom in her buttonhole had reached the top of the uncarpeted stairs when the first shot had rung out.

The gun had fired from somewhere the other side of the door, the only door on the landing. It hadn't been aimed at her. Who knew she was here? She had climbed the stairs like a ghost and they had taken an eternity. Built into each damn stair had been a creak. A born-again, state-of-the-art, hands-on—wait, feet-on—creak.

The gun fired again. O'Day stood against the wall beside the door. She reached out and tried the handle.

Tucking her gun away beneath her jacket, she brought out her American Express card and slid it between the door and the jamb, beside the lock. The latest payment on the card was overdue. She'd not be sending a cheque today.

She shouldn't be attempting this, even thinking of it. No one else would, not in their right mind, only maybe Superman. She needed help, including psychiatric. Poet and Pretzel, where are you?

Viv was it, in there? She guessed so. The only people he could be sniping at had to be Skip and Shep, probably. Jason the pretzel, he of the ogling eyes, he'd made a fair case for Viv White not being buddy-buddy with Skip and Shep.

Unless Skip and Shep had busted out and Poet and Jasey-boy had made an appearance with tennis rackets. Top hole and pip pip. Or Viv or whoever was simply practicing, or he had just committed suicide.

You didn't shoot yourself twice to commit suicide.

Sure you did if you missed the first time. You might miss if you changed your mind. If you changed it once you could change it twice and next time shoot straight.

Going to be opening this door all night, Peachy? You're scared, you don't want to open it.

Because he hadn't committed suicide. He was singing. Unless it was a radio.

O'Day listened at the door. The radio hadn't been playing before. Hot shit, the guy really was singing! Lieutenant Sapolsky, sir, any special procedure for a singing sniper?

Not clear, the words. Nothing she recognised. To work the card she had to stand in front of the door on the creakingest board in Belize. Keep singing, mister. More vibrato. Heavy please on the bo-do-da-ree-bop.

Click. If she turned the handle the door would open.

"'. . . swing, swing together,'" sang the voice, "'your body, between your knees—'" The voice cut off in mid phrase.

O'Day stood back against the wall breathing hard, holding the loaned Walther P.38 which had killed once today already. He was on the other side of the door. She had sensed him there. Now she heard him. A small, indeterminate noise as from someone in his sleep.

He was waiting and listening as she was waiting and listening.

Do it, Peachy. Chrissake, do *something*.

"Police!" she shouted. "Put down your gun!"

Her voice echoed and bounced back and forth off the board walls of the narrow landing.

"Open the door real slow! You come out like a zombie, your arms in front of you! You hear?"

Hear, hear, reverberated voice and walls. From the other side of the door, nothing. The door stayed shut.

"I see your hands first—okay?" O'Day called. "They're going to be empty!"

She waited. He was there but he was not coming out. What he had in mind, O'Day could not guess, unless it were that she lose patience, come in for him, and get her head socked off.

Back to the wall, head turned to the door, she talked to him for what seemed to her hour after hour, though she would have agreed it was more in the region of five minutes, and as conversations go, one-sided. Normally, talking was a specialist aspect of terrorist hijackings, and the armed crazy person holed up in an apartment on the nineteenth floor, but the alternatives to talk—crash in, or wait till doomsday—failed to appeal. So she remembered what she could of class instruction in Hostage Situation Procedure, and talked to calm him, or as the text had approximately put it, to verbalise a conflict situation between enforcement officer and subject with a view to establishing a meaningful, one-on-one dialogue from which each party might enter into a supportive, caring relationship leading to the development of a mutually inter-personal growth and enrichment situation conducive to resolving of the hostage situation. As she understood it, that meant that when you'd got his trust, you moved in and smashed him to a pulp.

The guy on the other side of this door had no hostage, as far as she knew, and he was so calm he was comatose. But she asked him about himself, told him about herself, gave him drugs statistics, because she knew many, and drugs was what all this was about, or what Sapolsky and the file had given her to believe it was about. She was starting to wonder.

"So let's have no one get hurt," she called out.

The bozo didn't answer. He hadn't opened his mouth once, nary a peep. All O'Day heard was gunfire from the house.

She switched the Walther to her left hand and wiped her damp palm on her pants. Doubt that anyone existed on the other side of the door began to mount.

Doomsday sucks, O'Day decided. So we crash in. With

care, and a prayer, though now her guess was that there was no one. At least there'd been no witnesses to her gabbing into air and making a horse's neck of herself.

She switched the gun back to her right hand, reached out with her left, turned the door handle, and allowed the door to open a fraction.

Perfect peace.

She pushed the door wide and snatched back her hand before a resurrected Viv or anyone could shoot it off.

Continuing peaceful nothing. O'Day put her head into the doorway. There he was.

He stood at the end of the hall, pointing a rifle, and gazing vacantly at her. Scrubby, reddish beard, beginnings of a belly, wet unfocussed eyes, short-sleeved shirt, slacks, espadrilles. Meet him on the street you'd never notice him, thought O'Day, apart from the rifle, a semi-automatic, maybe a Remington. He held the rifle vertically, pointing at the ceiling, one-handed against his cheek. His arm was bent at the elbow, his finger on the trigger.

"Do I know you?" he said.

Kind of languid, not really interested. A Brit though, that at least was resolved. He had been swaying, now he almost lurched. To keep his balance he planted a foot diagonally in front of him. O'Day put her gun behind her back and stepped into the doorway.

Viv shouted, "Go away! Please go away!"

He began to fire the rifle, drowning the hall in flame and din. Plaster and powdery flakes snowed down on him.

Twitty vaulted onto the muck in the dumpster at the moment the package shot from the chute. He dived, caught the package like a rugby international, and fell sideways on bricks and plaster, hugging it to him.

He looked up as if for applause. No applause. An empty grandstand, except for the guv'nor, who was too busy to be applauding.

Peckover was on his way down, backside first, arms and knees embracing the chute, and arriving perilously fast, straddling, sliding in jolts, not too much in control. Twitty scrambled out of the skip. The human package in his arms was still and silent.

A gun banged from the window. And again, again, again. For the time being the bullets twanged off the chute. Some missed even the chute, singing into the skip and onto the driveway.

Constable Twitty did not care where. What did it matter

or anything matter? He lay against the wall of the skip, sheltered from meaningless bullets, holding the grey herringbone parcel.

He tilted back his head so they would all hear, up there, up in the house, up in the sky. He shouted, "Get on with it! Get it over! Kill! Go on!"

TWENTY-THREE

Had Twitty or Peckover been free to contemplate such matters, they might have contemplated how dusk, and next dark, herald of inkiest night, hit quickly in the Caribbean.

Twitty, against the skip with his package, passingly wondered what the time was, but without interest enough to find out from his watch. Seven o'clock, eight? He could not have seen to read a newspaper but he could still see beyond the house to the pool and a wedge of lawn. To the right, driveway in a jungly frame curved round the front of the house.

In Brixton it would be after midnight. Now was tomorrow. The last tubes, mind the doors, thrumming to Morden, Upminster, Ealing.

Shells twanged off the chute. Peckover, sliding with tearing clothes and burning fingers, swung in a half circle and continued ape-like down the chute's underbelly, hopeful that bullets now would find not his head but only hands and knees, such as was left of them. The chute was fitted in sections, each join, though blunt, being a sickle at the rate he was going. He fell on his back onto bricks, rolled off the skip, and onto Twitty and the package.

Twitty failed even to swear. He closed his eyes.

"What's the matter with you?" Peckover growled. He snuggled against the skip. "She all right then?"

Twitty presented the herringbone package, which squirmed as Peckover received it, and emitted muffled sounds.

"Hey!" Twitty whispered.

Peckover unknotted the sleeves and folded back the worsted, which was no longer grey but plaster white. George's outraged face was rhubarb red. The grazed nose glowed like a reflector on a bicycle. From her hand Peckover extracted a four-inch nail.

"Gaaagh!"

"Boojie oojie woojie," soothed Peckover.

"You could have killed her!"

"Don't tell me. Put it in your report. And stick it up your arse. We're getting in the Land Rover. Ready?"

"It's all yours, it's scrap, they've shot it up. Next suggestion?"

A right bleedin' pair of prima donnas I've got 'ere, Peckover thought.

He told the constable, "Sorry, lad." He soothed, smoothed, and tickled the baby.

"Boojie woojie." Her screaming was abating but she was not yet ready to see the comical side of life. "She's 'ad a bit of a fright, 'aven't you, girl. She'll get over it. She's got like jetlag. Wooshie ooshie bm bm bm." He lifted his head. The sky was muddy and starless. "Gone a bit quiet, 'asn't it? Like to take a look?"

"Not desperately," Twitty said.

He took off his Panama, inched his head above the skip's parapet, and looked up. The top of the silver chute entered an empty window. He stood up.

"They're going to be with us any second. Permission to piss off out of it? What about the pickup?"

"What about it? You 'appen to have the keys?"

"You shoot your bloody gun for once, hold them off, I mean just for the noise—sir—I'll start the pickup."

"On our way then."

Peckover with the baby ran after Twitty along the side of the house and across the drive to the pickup. As they reached it, gunfire erupted. Peckover dropped and crawled under the truck, clutching babbling George.

Twitty had already opened the cabin door. A bullet struck it. Having nowhere else to go, he went in head first, fast, cupping a hand between his legs, and falling as flat on the floor as the gear shift allowed. He inhaled fluff and dust from the floor.

Beneath the truck Peckover shielded the baby with his body as best he could. The baby, displeased by everything, wailed monstrously. "Baptism by fire, Georgie," Peckover murmured, and he took the revolver from his pocket. He was unable to remember if it were loaded. He would have to look, if he could maneuvre it to where he could see it without crushing Georgie into a paste.

Fading light, cricket commentators would have called it. Fading light? The captains would have appealed against the light long ago, the umpires would have upped stumps, and the teams would have trooped off for steak and chips. Beyond the front wheels Skip and Shep were visible enough.

They had fanned out and were walking across the patio to the pickup, pointing but not firing their guns.

Viv's guns, Peckover assumed. Whatever breed they might be they were less dramatic than the MAC-10s in the pool. Nothing you could go berserk with, as on the airstrip they had evidently gone berserk, and in Collins Cross. He would have bet his house that these two had once worn paper shopping bags and made a slaughterhouse of Collins Cross.

No slaughterhouse here, so far. They might be low on shells. They weren't to know that the copper under the truck was not the Yard's top shot. They had seen him with a gun. He had cracked Shep's head with it when he had sprung from the closet like a faun.

The next shot fired was by neither Skip nor Shep. They were more startled than anyone, the bullet smacking the patio midway between them. Peckover heard her before he saw her.

"Throw down that shit!" she shouted.

Peckover held noisy George more firmly, ready to move. Don't think about it, just do it, she kills, he urged Skip and Shep under his breath.

They didn't do it. Shep in his white, red-smudged shirt levelled his gun. She was standing with a rifle at the corner of the house, across from the garage. As Shep fired she stepped back, out of sight.

She reappeared, the rifle to her shoulder, firing shot after shot at the paving at Skip and Shep's feet. The pair seemed incapable of movement, as if even to flinch would be to invite being hit. They still did not throw their guns. But when the shooting paused they turned from O'Day, and the pickup, and ran.

Skip ran in a zigzag, ducking and weaving, though he was no longer being shot at. Shep looked back once. They sprinted across the lawn, Shep's whiteish shirt allowing them to be watched—Shep anyway—for a fair distance across the lawn. The white disappeared, emerged briefly, fading and diminishing, became lost in a curtain of umbrageous, one-dimensional trees, and did not reappear.

Standing by the pickup, rocking the baby, Peckover said,

"Ratbags who fight and run away, live to fight another day. Any justice, the crocodiles will get 'em."

"They're oiling their guns," Twitty said. "Five minutes, they'll be back."

"Five minutes, we'll be gone. Make it ten, time for a wash and a beer. What d'you say, Georgie? Leave Skip and Shep to Belize's best, shall we?"

"It's like the two world wars," Twitty said. "Twice that Yank's saved the day. The new world belting in to rescue the old. From the halls of Montezuma. The rockets' red glare, bombs bursting in air. We'll give him a hearty welcome then, hurrah, hurrah."

"What're you blathering about?"

"Just blathering. Who's that with her?"

Including baby George, the reunion on the patio numbered five. The Casa Verde Mixed Quintet. O'Day accompanied Vivian White, his hands handcuffed behind him.

"'Ello, Viv," Peckover said.

"Don't bother," said O'Day. "He's wrecked."

"I can smell. Lucky bloke."

"Champagne. Don't ask what he's celebrating. I asked and he doesn't know. Take over, I'm going to the bathroom."

They all wanted the bathrooms except George, who had been.

"Over-excitement, luv, innit," Peckover told her.

He appointed Constable Twitty sanitation officer in charge of natural functions, nursery class. Eyes alert for Skip and Shep, Twitty returned from the Land Rover with carry-cot contents.

In a bathroom cupboard Peckover found TCP and Band-aid for his fingers. In the kitchen the ice-maker was silent. He brought the six-pack of Belikin into the living room where manacled Viv slept on his Nieman-Marcus sofa, twitching from time to time, and grunting in champagne oblivion. Twitty lay cruciform on the floor, nappy duty done, his hat over his face. By his upturned, plaster-coated jogging shoes the baby sat and gurgled.

"Guurlph," she said, dutifully busy with a toy found for her by O'Day: a thousand-year-old jade figurine.

Peachy O'Day stood in the french windows, snatching randomly at mosquitoes, and looking out at what still could be seen of Casa Verde's darkening grounds. Viv's rifle, loaded, lay in reach on the piano beside *The Noël Coward Piano Book*, away from the baby, and of no interest to sleeping Viv. Any assault out of the night, she would be ready.

Except she was tired, tired. She accepted a beer and said, "Thanks, Poet."

Peckover said, "Thank you, and not for the first time."

They drank, gasped. Ice-cold anaesthetic.

Peckover said, "You made a nice collar, Miss, um— Peachy. You'll be upped to three-star agent. Should be. You'll be a guest on your whatsit show. Johnny Carson."

"Viv was no problem. He needs help."

"Help? Blimey, 'e'll get 'elp. Twenty years occupational therapy sawing mahogany, if that's what they do here." He watched the baby beating the floor with her toy. "Course, if money gets spread round, Montego writes 'im a nice reference, chats up the judge, he might be back in business next week."

"What business? You know something I don't, like what his business is? You've got evidence? Any evidence at all?"

"Don't remind me. What we're in Belize for, and we haven't started."

"So we nail him for resisting arrest, which he didn't. Big deal."

"And firing an offensive weapon thereby endangering the life and limb of Skip and Shep."

"So did I. That's not a crime, it's a public service. Look, I'm not pessimistic. Why would I be pessimistic? We might be able to tie him in with that limey pilot, though the pilot won't be able to help us. We see his bank records, if they're not in Switzerland. We enlist the services of the local bluesuits, if they're allowed, now we've lost Campos. We talk to everyone, including Montego. Worst comes to the worst, we get a loan of a couple of sacks of coke, plant it under Viv's bed. Shouldn't take more'n three months. Maybe Easter. For the record, the guns you missed the pool with, the bozos' reserve artillery, they're a Browning thirty-two and a Colt Combat Commander, and they're in the grass back of the garage. Right now and frankly, my dear, I don't give a damn. I'm weighing the odds on Viv waking with a smile and giving us a ten-page confession."

"Finished?"

"Finished what?"

"Bleedin' Miss Cheerful you are. Did you say a Browning thirty-two?"

"The Nineteen twenty-two model. FN. That's Fabrique Nationale de Guerre, and that's French. They're made in Belgium. Suddenly you're interested in guns?"

"Jeremy Clegg was shot with a thirty-two."

"Find me a flashlight, it's all yours. They're still in production after seventy years so there can't be more than a million of them. That bunch of shooting in the house, was that you?"

"Them. I was encumbered."

"Neat word. Rhymes with outnumbered, cucumbered. Whassit mean?"

"Means George."

"Who?"

"Georgie-Porgie. 'Er there smashin' up the tiles with what looks as if it ought to be under glass in the British Museum, if there's going to be anything left of it."

"Surprised there's anything left of you. Mind if I ask how you made it out?"

"Down the chute. Like your Coney Island."

"Excuse me?"

"George went first."

"Natch." Mystified—the poet was too weird—O'Day sipped her beer. "He's a lively fella."

"She."

"She, sure. George. Our star witness. Your honest opinion, how's she going to stand up under cross-examination? She should probably wear grey, nothing sexy, a dab of powder on her nose, cover up that knock. Our other witness, Papitos, if Montego—"

"Papitos. Damn."

Peckover left the french windows and kicked the sole of Twitty's shoe, causing him to sit upright like a cadaver in an Edgar Allan Poe story. "On your feet." He called to O'Day, "Watch the baby."

Twitty forced the door to the basement and followed his guv'nor down the stairs. Papitos was sitting in semi-darkness in a room stuffed with china cats and birds less than a thousand years old. There were wicker baskets of plastic flowers, family photographs, and holy statuary and prints in primary colours. She fingered beads in her lap.

"*...fruto de tu vientre Jesus Santa Maria de Dios ruega por nosotros los pecadores...*"

"Papitos?"

She looked toward the policemen, then away. "*...de nuestra muerte amen Dios te salve Maria...*"

"It's over, Papitos." Apart from two psychopaths somewhere out there in the night. "The baby's fine. We're all leaving. You'll be better spending tonight in Belize. What about family? Who could you stay with?"

"... *el Señor es contigo bendita tu eres entre todas las mujeres* ..."

"Pack a bag. Come up as soon as you're ready."

On the stairs Twitty said, "Best news I've heard today. Bedtime soon?"

"Let's hope so." Peckover, hoping so, doubted it.

"We deposit Papitos somewhere quick and easy—nearest bed-and-breakfast, family, whatever—and we hand Viv over at the lock-up. Ours is the Fort George, right? Sounds like a lock-up but if there's hot water I shan't complain. Question is, who drives?"

"Who drives what?" Peckover said. "What're you talking about?"

"The pickup. Here's the plan." Twitty wondered if he might not be sounding off too much like a chief constable, Peckover his green cadet. He ploughed on. "I drive with Peachy up front. She could have the baby except, you know—safety. So you have her in the back. Papitos could hold her. Or why not Viv, he's her father—except we'd need to take the cuffs off. Next we knew, he'd be jumping overboard. Anyway, the rest of you al fresco in the back with the gear, breathing the air. Like claret, guv, this air."

"Sod the pickup. Viv must have something."

"Want me to cripple the pickup?"

"Leave Skip and Shep to the tigers? You're heartless. See if you can find Viv's passport. Try his bedroom."

"Think he might try to hop out of the country?"

"Might not be the worst thing if he did," Peckover said cryptically.

Twitty went up the stairs. In the living room, O'Day on her haunches held hands with George on bare, flattish feet. Who was walking whom was not easy to tell.

Peckover shook Viv awake. "Car keys," he said.

"Srrrsh," Viv said, sibilant and unawake.

Peckover slapped the bearded face. He stooped over Viv and smelled sour champagne. The nose at the bridge was fractionally askew.

"You've got wheels in the garage?"

"Sod off."

Peckover smacked the face.

"Kitchen drawer," Viv said.

"Why didn't you say so? Going to be a few more questions, sport, later, so get used to the idea. Just one more for now. What's the baby's name?"

Apart from Miss White.

"Name?"

The echo-chamber factor. Did nobody listen any more?

"Name. 'Andle. Moniker."

"Genevieve."

Blimey. Anyway, thought Peckover, I got the initial right.

TWENTY-FOUR

Twitty would have preferred the bespoke Jaguar XJ6, surely the only one in Belize. If he did not drive this one now, he couldn't see life's whirligig presenting too many chances to drive another.

He deferred to the guv'nor's motioning towards the roomier, white Silver Cloud. Not vintage but a fair bit older than himself and heaven knew how many miles on the clock. Cars excited Twitty less than clothes and girls, but a Rolls was a Rolls was a Rolls, and this was the first time he had sat in one. He switched on—*purr*—and checked the petrol gauge.

Impressed with himself, he drove none the less nervously, but without incident, to the Land Rover. They transferred to the boot of the Rolls a carry-cot, tote bag, kitbag, briefcase, parka, scarf, and the czar's winter ermine, all except the carry-cot chewed by bullets. Headlights gouging a yellow tunnel out of the night, Twitty pointed the Rolls away from Casa Verde. He funneled along the narrow jungle road and onto the highway to Belize. The steering wheel was on the wrong side, meaning the right side, incorrect for this country, which might be awkward for overtaking, if traffic showed up. The Rolls had the highway to itself.

Peachy in the front passenger seat sat in a slewed, ungainly posture, and silent. She had taken off her cap and sunglasses and shut her eyes. She kept sprawling into yet ungainlier positions. Twitty supposed that wherever she had her revolver, it couldn't be comfortable. He recalled reading or hearing years ago about Madame Mao, on trial, adoring the attention, saying, "Wearing a pistol in front for a long time can cause internal damage to a man's pelvic area."

Something to that effect. Women had a pelvic area too. They might not admit it but they did, and it couldn't be good having a gun lunging about there. He didn't quite see himself passing the information on to Peachy.

Behind, in a corner, Papitos had dressed the baby in a pink romper suit. She fussed and clucked, trying to feed Genevieve-George from a bottle which the baby kept pushing away, whether as a game or from an adequately full stomach.

Distracted by splutterings, Peckover turned his back. He held his jacket on his lap, wondering if it were salvageable.

He told Viv, "Let's get reacquainted, start at the start. Curzon Street, January before last. Jimmy Thornley shot dead, a medal with the initials VW in the road. Old stuff but I'd still like to know who put the medal there. You too, I wouldn't wonder, unless it was your mate Jeremy and you can't believe it. All right so far?"

Viv had turned his head away and was looking through the window into the night, giving an impression of not listening. Peckover's experience was that toffs, many of them, carried off the top money and gold cup for not listening, especially not listening to the lower orders. Sometimes they turned their head away; other times they looked past the upper curve of your ear to a yonder horizon. Peckover advanced his mouth still closer to Viv's ear.

"Now we 'ave Jeremy, three sad sacks outside my place, today Superintendent Campos and another copper, and we know who put them all to rest. Where those two crawled from, what's in it for you, apart from money, little details like that, you can 'elp fill them in now, or later, but now seems reasonable. Know something else? We're not in London. No weepy tabloids and telly crews getting themselves choked up over a little police brutality, like a busted nose, which is kiddie-winkie stuff, you've got to agree. This time round could be a broken back. You and me, Viv, and the law of the jungle. I've not forgotten your misbegotten pilot either, you're morally responsible there, not that morality weighs much with you. 'Ere's what's nice though. It doesn't with me either. All that fair play junk, it's not cricket, don't kick a man when 'e's down, you're presumed innocent until the jury says different. Bugger that. See it out there, the jungle? Survival of the fittest. You and me, old sunshine. Not that we're going in there, I've been, it doesn't appeal. Give me four walls and a chair leg, that's 'ome sweet 'ome to me. Which of us would you say was fitter? You can give me a few years but you're growing a belly. So let's start with Skip and Shep.

Names, addresses, business income, why not. What would you guess they put down as occupation on their tax forms? My colleague in front there, the American lady, she says they're Skip and Shep, but that's 'er sense of fun, she doesn't really believe it."

Viv sat without answering, his head turned away, one arm stretched in front of him, the limp wrist handcuffed to a fitted chamois strap beside the window. Peckover had every confidence that as a Rolls chamois strap it was secure as any iron ring set in the stone of a Tudor dungeon. This strap would have been hand-cut from the skin of the Serbian chamois with bronze shears forged in the Rolls foundry, cured in a secret blend of brine and whisky, stitched with raw silk from Shandong province—Shantung, older employees still called it—feathered, granioned, bracillated, and finally molloxed by Rolls craftsmen—men, not a woman for as far as the eye could see. Peckover, eyeing the dangling wrist, wondered if Rolls Royce had ever envisaged this use for its passenger strap. Whatever might befall the rest of the carload if Twitty went off the road into a green and greasy river thrashing with crocodiles, Viv was a goner.

"How good a marksman are you, Viv? Hot stuff, very hot stuff, or every time the bull's-eye?"

Viv reached forward and massaged his wrist.

"Don't be modest, you were number one in your officers' training caper at Eton. Presumably you've kept it up, that arsenal of shooters you've got. Skip and Shep, your minions, you could 'ave killed them if that's what you'd wanted. One bullet apiece. Bravo and huzzah, frightfully pukkah shootin'. Saw you from the house, heard you anyway, saw the bullets creatin' alarm and despondency in our lads by the pool. So if you weren't shootin' 'em dead, and if you weren't simply 'aving a bit of a giggle, you were telling 'em something, like warning them off. You personally don't kill. Killing's risky, it can backfire—so to speak. Look at the Colombians blasting each other into gloryland, and the Mafia. Likely you don't quite 'ave the stomach for it, not for real people. You arrange for it to be done and you pay out like the chairman of the board, only in grubby notes. So what were you telling Skip and Shep? Watch out, we've got coppers? They knew that and you knew they knew. So 'ow's this, you were warning them about yourself. They didn't know you were on the premises. You thought it time they did know and pissed off out before they did what they do not at all badly, because bodies piling up in London, that's one thing, even on that airstrip, but at Chateau Casa Verde, bad publicity, old boy. On course so far?"

Viv said nothing.

"Whether you know it or not, I doubt they're still your flunkeys, your fags—that the word at Eton? The children in top 'ats who come scampering when you yell. Not fags as in faggots, perish the thought. Gawd, language, who can keep up? F'rinstance, grieves me to inform you, if you haven't heard, but they were less than useful on the airstrip. You were ambushed by Belize's best, your consignment was being shifted, speed and muscle of the essence, and what do Skip and Shep do to 'elp? Nothing. They shoot coppers. If they were asked to decorate the Christmas tree, mow the lawn, present the Nobel Prizes, what they'd do is shoot. Viv, old darlin', you've lost them, they're in someone else's pocket. They've switched and why not. They're mercenaries, they belong to the 'ighest bidder. A Belize banker, a mahogany mogul, a—psst, whisper it—a government minister? What about an electronic evangelical with shiny cheeks, d'you have them here? One of the TV God Squad, the leeching charismatics, they could afford Skip and Shep, employ 'em as God's executive arm, the Lord's hatchet men, blowing away the godless."

"How you talk, Peckover. Why can't you shut up."

"Before you lost 'em though, you had them murder Jimmy Thornley because he was a good detective and he was on to you. You had them kill Clegg because the old school tie got a bit frayed. Jeremy wanted a bigger cut, or he was ripping you off, or—sorry about this—perhaps a lovers' quarrel, you and 'im. No question 'e was indiscreet. The green baize, booze, bedrooms, sooner or later he'd find himself under the covers with an undercover copper and *finito* for both of you. Those three poor sleazos who came at me with your ten thousand quid, same thing. Ever get that ten thou back? Maybe you did. I'm not interested. Problem with your racket is loyalty. Can't trust your friends, can you. When the stakes are high, blokes will die. Because you'll be shopped unless you get in first, send in the Skip and Shep brigade. Problem now is who do you find to remove Skip and Shep? Except it's too late. You're finished. You've no problem, had you thought of that? Only coming to terms with spending the rest of your life in a cell. Probably put your daddy in his grave but too bad. Can't imagine there'll be many go into mourning."

"You're a shit, Peckover."

"I try, I do my best. Still, your papa in his sunset years,

exactly what he didn't want, the son and heir back inside for the next twenty or thirty years. We've both failed 'im."

"I don't know what you're talking about. Neither do you."

"Talking about the pater, Sir Peter the Pater, swindler and expatriate."

"My father's got nothing to do with any of this."

"Any of what?"

"Anything."

"All you know. Keeps ringing us up requesting we remove you from Belize because you're in bad company, though he doesn't say 'ow we're supposed to go about it. Got an 'orrible loud voice, your daddy."

"You're merciless, aren't you. You don't let up."

"Know who's going to be company for you in goal? Might even be cellmates, who's to know, grease the right palms. You'll be able to reminisce about the good old days. That's if you don't beat each other's brains out. Your copper friend, Sergeant Montego."

"Never heard of him."

"Course not. As a regular visitor to Casa Verde he's heard of you though. Done 'imself nicely out of you too, dollar-wise—until now. A gabby old soul, the sarge. Head full of names, dates, places, balance sheets. Not as loud as your daddy but he talks as much."

"Jesus, you're so obvious."

"Well, you'll find out. Be kind to 'im inside because he'll have a dodgy time of it. Never understood why but the inmates don't take to coppers."

"Who does."

"Since you ask, your baby for one. Sorry I can't allow you to hold 'er but disabled as you are, manner of speaking, that's 'ow it is. She and me, we've been getting along famously. Over for Christmas, is she?"

"I don't have to talk to you."

"Some Christmas. Shame, innit. Always the kids who suffer—villains' kids. I'll grant you one thing, you creep, the baby's okay. I mean she's like a normal human baby. She can walk, yell like someone on top of a mountain, enjoys a joke. Beats me but you did all right there. We just 'ave to pray her genes are ninety-nine per cent her mum's and they skipped a couple of generations on the male side, because if not we're going to need some chromosome splicing or whatever it is they do, if it's not too late. Dreadful if she turned out like you. She supposed to be coming to Belize, your wife—Augusta is it? Or were you hoping to be all festive together in the Bahamas with mummy and daddy?"

Viv said nothing.

"If you're waiting for me to read your rights, you'll 'ave to wait. You've got no rights, sunshine. You threw them away with Jimmy Thornley and Clegg and the others. Wall-to-wall lawyers is what you need and much good they'll do you."

Peckover sat back and silently sighed. The least bright lawyer ever to have squeaked through his law exams, one who cringed from law books and lawyers and had never set eyes on a criminal, who wouldn't have known buggery from barratry—Peckover believed barratry was something nautical, perhaps not so different from buggery in that case, but he would need to look it up—whose speciality was farm sales, and wills, all later disputed because of his incompetence, this or any other pale, trembling lawyer whose wife had left him, whose hopelessness reached into every sphere and was matched only by the despair of his clients, when he had one, this lawyer, even he, would have had Viv free and out of the police station in five minutes.

He said, "Your lawyer a local or do you fly 'im in from London?"

Viv ignored him.

Papitos dozed, awoke, dozed again. She had sisters and brothers in Belize where she could stay. They had never liked her working at Casa Verde. She did not know whether she would be working for the señor again. No one told her anything. She was glad of that.

The baby had taken hold of Peckover's shirtsleeve and was scrunching it and burbling as if to say that livelier conversation lay with her. O'Day had slumped from sight, all but the curve of one denimed shoulder. Twitty drove the Silver Cloud at seventy along the empty highway, leaning back and angling his head to catch the wisdom from the back seat.

Peckover said, "If your lawyer geezer is the demon Demosthenes 'e probably thinks 'e is, and you hope he is, first thing he should advise you is to come clean on Skip and Shep. If he doesn't, sack him. I'm giving you this for free. Can't honestly say I 'ave your interests at heart, on the other hand, what did someone say—Lincoln—'with malice toward none'? This'll all be blood and giblets under the bridge for you and me, one day, but I'd still like to be carrying a reasonably clean, malice-free slate when I nip through the pearly gates. Gawd, that'll be an event. Like carrying a 'ighly suspect packet through the green channel at customs, wearing a face as innocent as a rose, and hoping the uniforms are all gabbing between themselves and looking the other way. So no malice. Noses broken only in good 'umour, right? Not that I intend parting these shores for another fifty years, and when I say shores, I don't mean Belize. Out of this place tomorrow now the cause of it all's in custody. That's you, cock, riding in state. Thanks for the transport. You listening?"

"Pity's sake, do I have any choice?"

"Good. So stab Skip and Shep in the back before they stab you. Shop 'em. Shop 'em from 'ere to closing-time in the cocaine gardens of the west, because they'll shop you, they won't think twice. That is, if we're unlucky enough to take them alive and talking, which I'm not betting on. Goes for Montego too. A right twister, that one. You owe 'im nothing. May not help you that much to become Mr. Supergrass of the Belize drugs-drop but it won't do you any harm. A little co-operation sits well with some judges, like five years off your sentence. You'd be surprised. Don't tell me it's sneaky to snitch, we all know that. Forget the code of the Woosters and the playing-fields of Eton and the honour of the regiment. Okay, thousands of your lot from the playing-fields are dead on Flanders fields, and Normandy, and everywhere, but Skip and Shep have never heard of that playing-fields stuff. Weren't at Eton, were they? I mean, were they? Talk to me. Who are they and where did you meet them?"

"They're not Skip and Shep for a start. They're Luigi and Marcello, accordion players I met in the revolving restaurant on top of the Leaning Tower of Pisa."

"That's rich. A shattering experience. Very risible. Go on, more please, but you can keep it dull, I don't mind. They on drugs? Do they 'ave friends, go to the theatre? What do they spend their money on? What excites them? What do they do when they're not killing?"

"Why ask me? Can't we finish with this bilge?"

"Not bilge, mate. You know them, I don't. Don't want to know them but it's the job. They talk posh like you or knees-up-Muvver-Brown like me?"

"No one talks like you except red-nosed comedians."

"Better 'n talking like Maggie, or Noël Coward, sticks of asparagus up their nostrils. Noël Coward one of your favourites?"

"Yes. I don't know. More than you are. Can't we sleep?"

"You'll 'ave plenty of time to sleep. So, Skip and Shep, no regional accent like Welsh, look you, or hoots och-aye, or by-gum-there's-trouble-at-t'-mill. One of your messengers

they shot dead, the polite one, he was from Yorkshire or
Lancashire, sounded like it. But Skip and Shep, nothing,
that what you're saying? The Queen's accentless English,
right?"

"Yes. Whatever you want."

"Not what I want. What you heard. No accent?"

"Pity's sake, no accent! I don't know them!"

"Know why they're here?"

"I've told you—no!"

"Try. To kill Campos? Not to kill me too, is it? Couple of
days ago they killed three sad suffering sacks outside my
'ouse, they could have included me. Unless something's
changed. What's changed? You agree they're not 'ere to help
you shift consignments?"

"If you say so."

"I do. They're not porters. They're your staff, or they
were, and they're here to shoot their guns. Talk to me.
You're at the centre of this rancid mess. They here to kill the
brat?"

"What?"

"This one here, Genevieve—that 'er name?"

"Christ, you're ill!"

"It's possible. Me or you. Does she inherit if you fetch up
in gaol again?"

"You're absurd!"

"What's absurd got to do with it? What isn't absurd? Is
your nutcake daddy cutting you out and settling his looted
millions on this mewling and puking scrap of a grandchild?"

"No!" Viv leaned his forehead against the window. His
voice dropped to a murmur. "He could. Could do anything.
Leave it alone. I've told you I don't know."

"Here's something you should know. We know a sight
more than you'd ever guess. Your daddy's a garrulous sod
and it's all down on tape."

Viv lifted his head from the window and looked front. He
tilted his head back against the window. Let him stew, Peckover thought. I've stirred something. To either sight of the
cones of light flung forward from the Rolls, the black curtain
of jungle hung from the sky.

Viv said, "Like what?"

"Sorry?"

"What's down on tape?"

"You mainly, his hopes and fears. Your wife. His wife—
your mama, the Lady May. Now there's a character. 'Ow
does she live with him? Talk about loyal beyond the call of
duty. Whether to believe it all, that's something else."

"What does he say?"

"Family matters."

"What family matters?" Viv was rubbing his temple in small, slow circles against the window. He was hard to hear. "What about us?"

"I ask the questions. Tell you one thing though, your old man must 'ave colossal misplaced affection to be so set on us coming 'ere to talk to you, get you out, back on the straight and narrow. Now, Skip and Shep. We were speculatin' they might be 'ere to carry the baby off into the banyan trees, one tap on the 'ead, bury 'er deep."

"You know nothing."

"Learning though. They shoot Campos dead, then on to Casa Verde. Why?"

"Don't ask me."

"Who do I ask? Skip and Shep are exploring the jungle."

"Ask the fairies. Ask the man in the moon."

"I did. They suggested I ask your father."

"Ask him then."

"I intended to. Meanwhile I'm asking you. Who were they looking for? You, me, or the baby?"

"I don't know."

You truly don't, Peckover thought, and he sank lower in the seat, and chewed at the skin round his thumbnail.

But I know, because Skip and Shep said, and I am in trouble. I'm in the wrong place. The answers aren't here and never were. Viv isn't the centre of this, Sir Peter is. The answers are in the bleedin' Bahamas.

Think, 'Enry old son. Cerebrate. Take it from the beginning. Jimmy Thornley . . . Was that the beginning? What about Sir Peter scarpering with eighty million?

Peckover closed his eyes to think. For a moment, when he opened them, he believed he was in the sitting room in Collins Cross and had fallen asleep in front of television. Something urban and rowdy was on. A commercial for Shell, or bottled Bass.

He had slept but there was no television. Outside were lights and traffic noise. The Rolls crept, competing cars honked, people in vivid shirts and skirts strolled, and Bing dreamed cracklingly, barely bearably dinful through amplifiers, of a white Christmas. Twitty was calling out, "Which way to the police station?"

TWENTY-FIVE

Detective Constable Twitty supposed that Papitos should know the way, being a native. Viv probably knew too. Twitty's guess was that no one would need to be long in Belize, like half an hour, to know where everything was. After five minutes tooling around he was sure they had seen it all. Albert Street, Queen Street, Regent Street, a few low Victorian buildings, government stuff built on mahogany logs, rum bottles, and pirates' bones, a greater number of ramshackle wooden constructions standing two or three inches above sea level, shops and bars, docks, open sewers arrowing seaward, a swing bridge, a statue of someone. A place for buccaneers with bandanas and cutlasses to roar into, set fire to, rape whatever moved, and get out fast before insects and tedium hewed them down. He drove salivating past a Kentucky Fried Chicken. The guv'nor might get away with it, but he had decided it would be inappropriate for himself to ask Vivian White the way to the penitentiary.

"Señor Campos," Peachy O'Day said, "he said the gaol was on Gaol Street, would you believe?" She was sitting up, alert, watching through the windows, and rearranging her shirt and the equipment under her jacket. "Hey, the Villa—my hotel. Drop me off, will you?"

"In a moment," Peckover said from behind. "Keep on, lad. Papitos, where do you want?"

They decanted Papitos near the docks at a shack held up by adjoining shacks, and waited until the door opened. A woman in an apron appeared, kisses were exchanged, and Papitos went inside.

"Peachy's hotel then," Peckover said. "Not the front. Somewhere off the street."

"Prlmp," said the baby on O'Day's lap.

"Doesn't this one ever sleep?" O'Day said. "You'd think she'd be exhausted. What's it about, Pop? Been feeding her uppers?"

Viv, limp wrist drooping, said nothing.

Twitty drove to the Villa Hotel and drew up in the parking lot. He switched off the engine and lights. Peckover fingered the chamois strap, handcuffs, and wrist.

"Fancy me, pig?" Viv said.

"Wondering if there were any pulse. Never was, was there." He told O'Day, "Bring George. In fact, I'll 'ave her."

They stood at the front of the Silver Cloud, by winged Mercury. They could see into the car to manacled Viv and he could see them. A car reversed with grating gears and drove from the lot.

"Tonight being slopsville as well as decision time, I don't mind tellin' you," Peckover told the baby, hoisting her high, "you'll always be George to me. 'Struth, I ask yer—Genevieve!'"

He lowered her. The baby squealed and flailed.

O'Day said, "The desk will know where the slammer is, then he's all yours. Got to call my lieutenant. And a shower, oh boy, an hour of shower. See you guys tomorrow. Have a fun evening."

"You're leaving?" Twitty said.

"Leaving you two. Leaving Belize would be nice. Came to get Viv, and he's got, but I shot someone. If they have rules in this place like back home I'm going to be here into the next century. There'll be inquiries you wouldn't believe. I'll be up before a grand jury, the politicians will be scoring points, the civil liberties people will flay me, they'll be very polite—"

"It won't be like that," Peckover said. "You 'ave two witnesses. You'll fetch up commended."

"Great witnesses. Who believes cops?"

"You'll see. Either of you hear the chat with Viv in the back seat?"

"What chat?" said O'Day.

"Some," said Twitty.

"So?"

"You touched a nerve when you got on to Sir Peter," Twitty said. "It was in his voice. What did he say—his father could do anything? A son should know. But meaning what? His father's rich and crafty enough to accomplish anything, get away with anything, or he's capable of anything?"

"Why not all that? Brace yourself for a visit to Sir Peter and his kin, lad." Peckover eyed the graze on the baby's nose. "Anything else?"

"Yes," Twitty said. "Viv says he's never heard of Sergeant Montego, but I believe Papitos. When he says he doesn't know Skip and Shep, I believe that. Except it makes a non-sense of Jimmy Thornley, Clegg, your three in the road, probably Campos—they're hardly all one meaningless coin-cidence. So don't ask why and how I think I believe him."

"I'm asking."

"Thought you might. How can anyone be positive some-one's lying or telling it straight. I'm useless at it, should never have been a copper. Should have been a shepherd." Twitty looked through the windscreen at Viv, a bulky shadow in the back seat, one arm extended. "Unless you trap them. You nearly did that with your palaver about accents, and Viv agreeing Skip and Shep's were Her Accentless Majesty's. Then again, he might simply have been saying what he thought you wanted to hear. Only way to shut you up. I'd probably have done the same. Still."

"Still what?"

"I still don't think he knows who they are, That they're American, or they sound it. If he'd hired them he might never have met them, but he'd have known their credentials, proba-bly talked to them on the phone. Never a hint in anything he said of Yankeedom. So there wouldn't be if he was making out he didn't know them. And yet—block your ears, this is Dr. Twitty, psychologist, speaking—how quick and smart and guarded is Viv? He's dopey with champagne and all he wants is to sleep. Who, you ask him, are Skip and Shep? They're Luigi and Marco from—"

"Marcello."

"—Marcello from the Leaning Tower of Pisa. Very risible. Why not Boris and Ivan, or Paddy and Rory, or Yin and Yang—or Buster and Hopalong from the revolving McDon-alds in Huckleberry Gulch? Because he's not switched in to other places, like America, never considered they might be American, he isn't interested. He doesn't know Skip and Shep. Italy is what he knows, and loves, his file says so, and Italy's where his mind is."

"Not a 'undred per cent. Giacometti isn't Italian, if that's what you're thinking. He's Swiss."

"And Hockney's from Leeds, and Noël Coward isn't Verdi, and the big stone prick—" Excuse me, Twitty nearly excused himself, but Peachy was a grown girl, more living behind her than he had, he didn't doubt it, including men dead in the line of duty. "—that fine fellow of an object in his living room isn't Italian either. Look, this is your fault, you asked. I'm not apologising. It's vital because if Viv isn't running Skip and Shep, somebody else is and it's back to the bloody drawing-board. When you said Skip and Shep were at Casa Verde for the baby, perhaps to kill her, all that bit about inheriting, Viv sounded surprised. Stunned, I'd say. Whatever he thought they might be doing here, he didn't connect it with the baby. Though now he might."

"Could be a better actor than you give 'im credit for. You realise, Dr. Twitty, counsel for the defence is going to 'ave you and your impressions in the washtub, through the mangle, and 'ung out to dry?"

"More than you do, chum—sir—because here's something else for the washtub. Who's the baby's father?"

"Go on."

"Viv doesn't like the idea of her being put to rest, but who would? He doesn't have to be her father to throw up at that. He's a nasty. He runs drugs. But he's halfway human. What Peachy says, he's too pathetically human, not that I'd know, being a child myself—"

"Don't start the sulks, you 'orrible newt. Get on with it."

"He weeps, he sings, he gets stewed, and he doesn't shoot Peachy, he shoots the ceiling." Twitty looked at O'Day for confirmation.

"We've got a guest," said O'Day. "Now, is he the manager of the Villa coming to woo me with chocolates, or is he a retailer?"

From out of the night and somewhere behind a Chevrolet Malibu parked beyond the Rolls strolled a fat, smirking young man with rings on his fingers and glittery chains round his neck. Peckover, Twitty, and O'Day watched in silence. When the youth arrived he looked at each in turn, seeking eye-contact, and receiving it from all three.

He said, "Can I help you?"

O'Day said, "On your way."

Fatty glittered and smirked. "Name it, I can get it."

"On your way or I'll slice your nuts off," said O'Day, "if you've got any."

Fatty's smirk slipped. He put his hands in his pockets and strolled fairly briskly into the night, maintaining dignity, and preserving his manhood.

Peckover was amused. He said to O'Day, "But you're the DEA. Thought you might 'ave, I mean out of habit—"

"I went off duty five minutes ago."

"She asleep?" Twitty said, peering into Peckover's arms.

"She's 'ad a long day, 'aven't you, Georgie-Porgie." Peckover reassembled her head on his shoulder. "What you were saying was, who's her father?"

"Viv hasn't asked to hold her," Twitty said. "He hasn't said one word about her. He didn't ask what happened to her nose. He hasn't even looked at her."

"I know fathers like that," O'Day said.

"Dr. Twitty rides again," said Peckover. "Nothing else?" Twitty pouted.

"Bleedin' should be something else, mate. 'Ow old's the baby?"

"How the hell do I know?"

"You should, you've read the file. How old does she look?"

"Jesus. She looks like a baby."

"Tiny baby or big baby. Be daring, 'ave a stab at it. You've got all those siblings you've dandled. Here's a clue. She's starting to walk."

"I left my Dr. Spock at home. I never remember whether they walk before they talk or talk before they walk." Twitty uttered an animal sound some-where between a sigh and a groan. "A year."

"Close. She's eleven months. Born January sixth."

"Capricorn," O'Day said. "A deep thinker but misunderstood."

"So conceived when?" Peckover said. "Assuming a normal pregnancy, give or take a couple of weeks. Go on, lad, count."

Twitty muttered and started counting backwards on his fingers, pressing each in turn against his leg, scowling, and voicelessly mouthing months. O'Day did not join in. She looked at her watch.

"April?" Twitty said. "Oh no."

"Oh yes. Far as I know, visitation rights at the Scrubs don't include a private room. The fair Augusta wasn't in London anyway. She was in the Bahamas with 'er in-laws since before Viv's trial."

"You've known all along and never said a word?"

"Worse 'n that, mate. I've known five minutes. Didn't work it out either, I dreamed it. Don't tell anyone. May not be worth much, some other bloke as dad, but the blindingly obvious under my nose and I miss it. Some bloody sleuthing."

"Some bloody Scotland Yard," Twitty said. "We're not the only ones. What about your genius man, Mr. Veal?"

"Promise me, never mention it to 'im. It'd be too embarrassing."

"Goodnight, you guys," Peachy O'Day said. She kissed her finger and touched it to the top of George's head. "Sort it out and enlighten me tomorrow."

"I'll phone you," Twitty said.

"I know," said Peachy, and flashed him a smashing smile.

She loped through the parking lot towards the lights at the entrance to the hotel. They would not see her tomorrow, with or without enlightenment, but none of them were to know that.

In the back of the Rolls, Peckover shook Viv awake.

"You're for the clink, old son. Murder, conspiracy to murder. Anything you say may be taken down and none of it's going to do you any good."

"I look forward to this. Biggest boob of your career, Peckover. I'd say it could end it."

"You'll miss the farewell party. You'll be slopping out. Meanwhile, I'm returning George to 'er mother."

"George?"

"Genevieve."

She slept prone in her carry-cot on the floor, arms above her head in the I-surrender position. Behind the wheel, Twitty tried the radio to see if it worked. A cannonade of sound rocked the Rolls, possibly reggae, possibly the Prime Minister calling for spending cuts. Twitty switched it off and mumbled, "Sorry."

Peckover asked Viv, "Like me to say 'ello to the pater for you?" He watched an outline of manacled hand twist upward, grip, and tighten on the chamois strap. "It'll be a flying visit, no wordplay intended. But any message you'd like to pass on, in reason, I could pass it."

"You have her passport, of course."

Passport. Ah, that. Thought there might be a hitch, thought Peckover. How long since I thought straight about anything? Maybe babies didn't need passports.

Oh but they did.

He said, "I 'ave yours, mate."

"Brilliant. She's on her mother's."

"So 'ow did she get into Belize?"

"Privately."

"I know that." He had not known it. He had not even got round to considering it. "Your job, isn't it, smuggling. You collected 'er in what?"

"Hawker Siddeley."

"Pink stripe?"

"That was a Beech Baron, now out of commission, I suspect. There's something almost charming about your ignorance."

Thanks, but correct, out of commission. While you, Viv, seem to be in commission and functioning for the first time tonight. Something I said? Peckover watched his prisoner through the dark. Something in mind, sport? Same as I have in mind? Like a little confab, father and son eyeball-to-eyeball, gloves off, clearing the air, eliminating the poison, or injecting another dose of it, sorting who's putting the knife in whom? Seems to me, Viv old cock, you are not in the same league as your daddy. You are for prison. Charges to be decided but drugs certainly. Game, set, and the whole sorry shooting match to papa, you poor bugger.

The ideal might be to engineer matters so father and son are face-to-face, and you a fly on the wall. Wit and wisdom of Frank Veal. At some other epoch, on some other planet. Over bacon and egg.

Vivian White sat upright, looking back at him. His white eyes and his voice were free from champagne slump.

"Where the pink one came from, the Hawker Siddeley, there might be others," Peckover said.

"I wouldn't be surprised."

"One which might fly out now, wouldn't need wait till morning?"

"No flying out or in except daylight hours."

"We'll 'ave to wait then. Bring in the Kentucky Fried, get to the airport, sleep in the car. Can't have you braceleted in the 'otel all night, plus George. Your Mr. Montego would be round in a jiffy with 'is *habeas corpus* and lawyers."

"We?"

"Highly irregular. This really could be the end of a career. End of every bone in your bleedin' *corpus*, you don't behave. I'll not be caring too much. Your trip with the baby, that naturally was all daylight hours."

"Emergency arrangements can be made."

"Bet they can. 'Ow long do emergency arrangements take?"

"It's not the time, it's the money."

"You'll manage that. Chance like this, tellin' your dad what you think of 'im. When did you two last talk?"

"We don't talk."

"So now's your chance. Ask 'im what kind of father wants 'is son in gaol for always. What kind of father fits 'im up, frames 'im for jobs in Curzon Street and Wellington Square and Collins Cross and an airstrip in Belize—tries to. Frames 'im in bleedin' steel like a window in a cell door. You might even get a chance to punch 'is face if you're that way inclined. I mean, what kind of father?"

Viv seemed to be embarking on another weighty silence, but after a moment or two he said, "My kind."

"How long have you known?"

"I haven't, not for certain. You said he'd been phoning you, he wanted a Yard copper here to talk to me. Why didn't you add he wanted the copper killed and me put away for it?"

"Didn't need to. You've worked it out for yourself."

"Hope you're happy. Any copper would do, even one of the natives, and he's had to settle for Campos, but one from the Yard would have been the ideal. Create the biggest fuss, get me the maximum. Those two, Skip and Shep, they pull the trigger. But I'm supposed to have arranged it."

"He nearly succeeded with Jimmy Thornley."

"Damn you, Peckover. I told you, told the court, last time I saw that VW medal was years ago, in my room in his house in Nassau. Believe me now?"

"Don't expect us to apologise. Life is 'ard. You were always going to be suspect numero uno, your daddy knew that. He's been a mile ahead of you, setting you up. Nearly succeeded again today."

"Nearly but not quite, am I right?"

"Beginning to look that way. Clegg, your father's three messengers at my place, dead simply to impress us this is serious, time we got off our bums and went after you. That how you see it?"

"No. Christ, I don't know."

"Yes you do. Quite a lad, your daddy."

Behind the wheel, awaiting chauffeuring instructions, Twitty tilted back his head but for a while heard nothing more. One indeterminate sound from Viv in the corner: throat clearing or a little moan.

Peckover said, "The baby's father is your father."

"Bastard," said Viv.

Peckover was unclear whether the bastard referred to was the sleeping baby, Sir Peter, or himself. But he took it that Viv's answer to the question was, as his own Stepney mum used to say, in the infirmary.

TWENTY-SIX

Sir Peter roared, "Out! Fifteen-forty! Too bad, old boy! Close though! Nice! Quite close!"

Tom Devon stalked chafing along the base line, bouncing a ball, grinding his teeth, and restraining himself from performing handsprings and howling with laughter. Close? It was in by a yard.

But it was only a game, ho ho ho. Something to get up a sweat with, keep the joints moving, the belly flat.

Some game. War to the knife the way the limey toff played it. He was good, must have been quite the champ in his day, back in the days of long pants and William Tilden and Helen Wills Moody. But what a hilarious, cheating, obnoxious, sonuvabitch.

Tom Devon served. Ace. You'd have had to be one-eyed and looking the other way with it to have been in doubt about that one. No protest from the other side of the net. No compliment either. Thirty-forty.

He served to the right-hand court. Sir Peter returned to his backhand and stormed the net. Tom Devon lobbed. Sir Peter chased back and salvaged the ball on the bounce, achieving a marshmallow return which might or might not clear the net. The ball hit the top of the net. Tom Devon had to change direction and lunge for it. The ball dribbled along the top of the net and dropped one centimetre beyond his outflung racket.

"Game, set, and match!" bellowed Sir Peter.

The rest of Sir Peter's household on Andros Island was scattered when Peckover and his entourage drove through the gates in the swelter of the Bahamian sun. Scattered yet within loudhailer distance, had they carried loudhailers, and wished to hail one another, which none did.

Lady May in a flowing chiffon garment, bedroom slippers, pith helmet, and gardening gloves, moved through the rose garden like a box-shaped wraith, a ghost tank which had taken a wrong turn on maneuvres. She sniffed and snipped, secateurs in one hand, basket in the other, and in the basket, cut roses, a can of bug spray, and a silver flask of Courvoisier, thoughtfully filled by Nurse Park.

The household carefully left her ladyship's daughter-in-law alone. Gussie had elected to be poor company until her baby was back.

She knew the baby would be back, Peter never failed, but it had been two days. She did not drape herself on a fainting couch like Elizabeth Barrett Browning, because she was not ailing, she did not have the vapours. Neither did she live in front of her mirror doing her eyes and legs like the Duchess of Windsor. She lay in a deckchair under an umbrella by the pool, with no intention of entering it, wearing a visor, headband, shorts, and Spiegel T-shirt with unshy cream and zucchini-green stripes and bateau neck. She had suncream, a bell for summoning Seltzer, and a new hardback by Gail Godwin, open at page six after two days. She was going to survive this, she and the baby, if they were the only ones who did. She was going to live another fifty years at least, free, fulfilled, very rich, and beloved and respected by grandchildren and great-grandchildren. She wondered why she was the only uncomplicated person she knew and why everything had to be such a shitty mess.

Winnie, wearing her red and white splotches, sloped off from the pool in search of she was not sure what diversion, but it could hardly have less zip and frolic to it than this rejection beneath the umbrella, not a touch or a word. She nosed and piddled around the base of numerous high evergreens, looking about her to see whether anything worth socialising with might be in view.

Nothing was. The tennis courts were empty, and in the rose garden, only madam. Had Winnie, an Irish setter, heard tell of America, she would have chosen to emigrate there, apply for legal alien status, sooner than hang on here, ignored and unappreciated.

* * *

Joanna Park, seeing Winnie picking up momentum towards her, and now galloping, reversed through the servants' door from which, for no particular reason, she had emerged, and shut it. Winnie was a pest. Joanna was neither so numbed by loneliness that she had to have Winnie knocking her flat and slobbering her hot, wet, smelly, leathery tongue all over her face, nor sufficiently aware to grasp that she and Winnie had elements in common.

Without the baby, Joanna had little to do except go through doors, bringing with her the faintest of dwindling hopes that on the other side might be diversion. Apart from new cooking duties, the cook having been sacked, Joanna was as idle as the dog, and she worried about the stolen baby whom she had been teaching to walk. Not that it would not have walked anyway but they had begun together. Step, step, sit. Step, step, step, step, stop, start —oops—sit.

Soon she would be walking as if in a marathon and every insecticide bomb, brandy flask, bunch of car keys, and Fabergé egg in reach would have to be put out of reach. Joanna was glad of the cooking, which was basic—salads, tinned gazpacho, baked fish—and guaranteed, she assumed, continuing wages for services performed, though not the services she had been hired for.

The loot was piling up nicely thank you. A tidy saving for when she got back home. Down payment on a nifty little Fiesta, a flat in London somewhere affordable but not too disgusting, perhaps Baron's Court, or by the river at Chiswick, looking out over low-tide sludge. She hoped the money would still be worth something. Sir Peter was reckoned to know about these things, and often he would bang through the house, high on gloom and doom, ranting about recession, the markets, gold, foreign exchange, deficits, and Dow Jones. Dai Jones she believed she might have grasped—a Welsh golfer, or an important banker in Cardiff, a friend of Sir Peter, wearing leeks and singing hymns. But Dow Jones? How now brown Dow.

Dwayne Goodsir in his underwear was dealing himself poker hands in what boss man was pleased to call the butler's pantry when a light over the door came on. Ninth light on a panel of twelve. He inhaled pot and dealt. Pair of eights. To his left a pair of knaves, to his right he didn't know, he hadn't looked. Probably a royal flush. As well this wasn't the ring-a-ding Tuesday-night-is-cut-throat-night session.

No rush. Arrivals took two minutes at least from the gates to the house. Dwayne turned off the television and pulled on his white ducks. Shirt, tie, blazer. Since Nina had been fired, time hung pretty heavy. The food hadn't improved either.

Two minutes if the visitor breezed straight in through open gates, or opened them himself. Might be four or five when the gates were shut and Joshua used to come from his gatehouse to open them and look the visitor over. But Josh the Cosh and Nina both, out on their asses. He'd have been out himself if he'd been awake, and failed to scream, the morning Mistah Vivian had dropped in to collect the fruit of his loins. There were rumours, of course, that the babe might be the fruit of other loins.

"Nevah!" Dwayne exclaimed. "An English nobship playing around? Impudence! Pistols at dawn, man!"

Some butler if he didn't know who boss man had been screwing the past couple of years. Her ladyship knew, must do, but she was loose in the attic, lotsa loose junk sliding round up there. Knowing had loosened more of it, no question.

Shoes. Comb. Last suck on the ol' Aca-aca-acapulco gold. Ready to meet and greet, *sah!*

Dwayne went up the stairs, through the hall, past armour, swords, and dim paintings of po-faced jockeys on horses, and out of the front door. From here could be seen the driveway's final approach through lawns and parkland. The rest of the drive, given to twists and kinks, was obscured by trees.

He stood musing on what might come to pass should he put the screws on screwsman Sir Peter. Screw him for how much—a half million?—as reward for silence.

What would come to pass would be Dwayne Goodsir, butler, black boy, Christian, non-smoker—joints didn't count—would be in deep, deep sneakers. Like dead.

He believed that. Man, Sir Peter was strange. He had spooky strange outside staff it was best to be polite to, like the two who came and went. The son did time in the slammer, but the father, oh man, such was justice. The race was to the richest and spookiest.

None of his business but why didn't her ladyship divorce him? He guessed at that age, their generation, they didn't. Boss man wouldn't permit it anyway. Worse, he might, then what would she do?

Go back to London and live serenely. She hadn't lost all her marbles. Maybe she wanted to stay on to be with the baby. How could she? How did she stand it? What was she anyway, her relationship—step grandma. It was sick.

When minutes went by and no one arrived, Dwayne had to decide whether to take the Honda and investigate, or go back to his poker. He had already more or less decided. That electronic eye at the gate was of the female persuasion. You could rely on it like you could rely on some ladies he had met. It might switch on and burn for no reason, or you could come up to it like at a sweet jiving party in a crowded room, man, breathe all over it, and it wouldn't blink.

When Detective Chief Inspector Peckover and his retinue of three passed through the gate and by the empty gate-house, the butler in his pantry had been about to deal himself a pair of inadequate eights. Peckover looked through the window at the gatehouse and said, "Who lives there?"

"The chauffeur usually," Viv said.

Twitty drove the rented, beat-up Lincoln along a serpentine avenue lined with tulip trees and swamp magnolias. It wasn't so different from Belize, perhaps a mite less steamy, but he'd had enough of sunshine. Debilitating cancerous stuff. He was sorry for people who had to live in places like this.

Behind him Viv sat with his hands handcuffed on his lap, there being no strap. Our 'Enry was spooning something from a jar into George.

"And there?" Peckover said. He looked at a clearing which had aggressive red bushes, a lawn for clock golf, and a pastel-pink, one-storey chalet.

"Guest house," Viv said.

"Any guests?"

"Wouldn't think so."

The shutters of the guest house were shut. There was parking space but no car, unless someone was round the back.

"Pull in, lad. Pit stop. If we can get in."

"We usually seem to," Twitty said.

"If you're interested, we're announced," said Viv. "They'll know we're here. They'll know someone's here."

"The gate?" said Peckover.

"Yes."

"Good. Give 'em time to get the cocktails and canapes together."

The guest chalet was locked but not a fortress, perhaps because it was for guests, not for Sir Peter. Twitty forced a rear door and led the way in, switching on lights. On and off, in Rolls and rented jetplane, he had slept for about twelve hours and believed he felt dopier than if he had stayed awake listening to his Walkman and catching up on the Yard Bard's bursting baked potato in *Good Housekeeping*.

208 Peckover Holds the Baby

He had wanted to phone Peachy from the airport, say hello, or goodbye, he wasn't sure which, but the guv'nor had told him to stop panting, she would keep, they'd be reunited in Belize in a couple of days.

The municipal airport at night had looked like an airfield once under construction but abandoned for lack of support, though better light would have revealed a clutter of half a dozen light planes and one business jet parked near the perimeter. With the guv'nor in attendance by the public call box, Viv had negotiated for the jet. After delivering him back into the Rolls, now reeking of Kentucky Fried, the guv'nor had called his wife—Miriam her name was—then the Yard. Back in the rancid Rolls he had opened the windows and told Viv that a Sergeant McMaster, firearms instructor, had been suspended from duty pending inquiries, and what did Viv think of that?

Viv had shrugged, said all coppers were crooks or sadists or both and that McMaster had been clueless too, he hadn't been able to deliver. The guv'nor had said that Sergeant McMaster had delivered up to his masters in D11 a fee received from one Vivian White. Seemed he'd been stricken either by conscience, which sounded unlikely, or the horrors that Vivian White might shop him, since he'd failed, Mr. Peckover had passed, and so the sarge had got in first, preempted Viv, and sort of semi-confessed.

Viv had said it was only money and Peckover probably couldn't hit a bus at ten yards in spite of his pathetic pink card. The guv'nor had told Viv you never knew, he'd never aimed at a bus, but he might hit Viv at fifty yards, gravely damage his vitality, and it was worth keeping in mind.

Now, in the sitting room of the guest chalet, Peckover said to Viv, "If you want the bathroom, hurry up. Shout if you find a second one."

He removed the handcuffs.

TWENTY-SEVEN

The chalet had no guests at the moment, but there had been guests, and they had been less than diligent in cleaning up: two cloudy glasses with a tidemark which might have been milk, a crumpled packet of Pepperidge Farm hazelnut cookies, unplumped cushions, last Wednesday's *Nassau Times* open at the crossword, half completed. Of course they might be coming back.

Viv was as unfamiliar with the place as were the policemen. They heard him opening and closing doors. Twitty, perturbed, and snapping his fingers, glanced at the door through which Viv had gone, and eyed the bulge in his guv'nor's jacket pocket. In error, Peckover had put the handcuffs into his left pocket, which already held a revolver. The result was a weight of ironmongery which caused the jacket to slide and list as if caught in a nor' easterly.

"It's your career," Twitty said. But do I, he wondered, sink with you?

"Bugger career." Peckover transferred the handcuffs to the starboard pocket. "The game's become the nailing of Sir Peter, which is what it should 'ave been all along if I hadn't been so thick. Nailing him with his son's help, witting or unwitting."

"The son's not going to be much help if he scarpers off. I prefer him in the cuffs."

"The cuffs are psychology, lad, keep 'im insecure, and they've served their purpose." He knelt, watching the baby. "Viv's trapped and 'e knows it. He's for gaol. Right now he's even more terrified of meeting 'is dad than he is of gaol but he's going to do it. He wants answers. He wants a yes or no to whether his daddy loves him. He wants to know if daddy kills to try and put 'im back in gaol. He believes it and 'e can't believe it. I'd say Viv wants us listening in, in case."

"In case what?"

"In case answers is what he gets. We have with Viv a rare example of a villain in pursuit of the truth. Desperate for it. He's on the edge. Haven't you looked at him?"

"I've been driving. Watching the sodding road."

"Drugs he's stuck with. Murder charges are something else. Daddy just might get gabby, do some explaining, if he gets excited. Put the two of them together over afternoon tea and the anchovy sandwiches, my guess is they're both going to get excited. Yer, go girl!" Peckover was kneeling with his chin on the floor. "Atta girl! There's a Georgie-Porgie!"

The baby was back in her nappy, plastic pants, and nothing else. Pot-bellied from strained prune dessert, she had set off on a walkabout. This allowed not only for walking but for crawling at brisk speeds, with time out for investigating the legs of a coffee table, a canvas butterfly chair, and the pattern on a Navajo blanket which covered much of the floor.

Twitty said, "Where are we when they're getting excited? Under the table? Do we but the teapot?"

"We will see what transpires. We might invite ourselves to partake with them of the Lapsang and Lady May's home-made coconut slices. On the other 'and, we might not. We wouldn't inhibit Viv, he's beyond it, but Sir Peter we might. Further questions?"

"Yes, two." Twitty stepped to the coffee table and disinterred the baby's fingers from soil in a plant basket containing defunct, brown vegetable matter. He pointed her in Peckover's direction. "First, when we can go home?"

"What d'you want to go 'ome for? Gor, some people. Rainin' in London, mate."

"I know. I hope so. Second, this whole business has nothing to do with drugs. Right?"

"Wouldn't go that far. What're you suggesting it has to do with?"

"Sir Peter's pulsing prick."

"Easy, ducks," Peckover told the baby, who had swayed and sat in front of his nose. He patted the prune-filled belly. She looked like Buddha. "Can't entirely throw Viv's drugs out of the window. Why we're here, dupes of Sir Peter. It's 'ow he got us serious—drugs, Viv, Clegg, all the killing—and how he hoped to get us dead and Viv locked up for it." Pat-pat. The babby gurgled. "But I'd agree the thrust, shall we say, is that old devil sex. The pulsing prick, as you delicately put it, doesn't 'ave to be pulsing out of simple lust. Might be the power thing. Or showing everyone the rules don't apply in your case, like with that American who wanted to be president, forget 'is name. 'O bed, what crimes are committed in thy name!' Who said that?"

"Some *madame* in the French Revolution. Thought she said 'liberty,' not 'bed,' but she was French, you're probably right."

"You're right, lad, the drugs smuggling is tangenital." Peckover paused for a response but was coldly denied one. "Hard to credit but Sir Peter isn't the first to kill for sex. Billionth? Not all this week, but since Old Testament times. Either it's there isn't enough, or there's too much, or it's the wrong sort, or the right sort with the wrong person, like someone else's property. Ladies too. Hell knows no fury. Arsenic in the bedtime cocoa. Agatha Christie fantasyland, innit, that sort of thing—except it 'appens."

"We talking about sex or love?"

"Jason, old sweetheart, don't muddy the waters. We've got Sir Peter coming up fast and we need clear heads. He is a bloke who will have people snuffed and his son locked up in prison so 'e can flog on poking the son's wife with no 'assle, let, or hindrance. Since you ask, can't see it's our business, or it matters, but it sounds to me like eros. Gonads. The old Adam. The old Eve too. Takes two."

"I imagine it would."

"Viv's Gussie isn't being raped, far as we know. She's gone ahead and had big daddy's child. Does she prefer big daddy to Viv? Does she enjoy the act of darkness but Viv isn't so hot at it and daddy is? Does she like money and stand to inherit the looted millions if she hangs on, pleasuring 'im? Perhaps Georgie-Porgie inherits. Sir Peter might enlighten us over the goat cheese barquettes—ouch! George, you are no lady!" George was pulling Peckover's hair with both hands like a seaman hauling on hawsers. The pair wrestled, the baby squealing in ecstasy, holding her own. "Bloomin' liberty."

The gush of a flushing cistern sounded from within the chalet.

Twitty said, "Sir Peter paid for every murder?"

"Looks that way to me." He offered the baby handcuffs to teethe on but her zeal was for his hair, nose, and eyes. "Paid for everything except me to fail the firearms course. That was Viv. He didn't want us in Belize. Daddy did. Daddy didn't care whether I passed or failed as long as someone from the Yard got over to Belize, and got killed, and Viv

got put away for it. Our other bent copper, Montego, he's
been salting it away from the two of them. From Viv for
keeping quiet about consignments, from daddy for keeping
up the pressure on Campos to bring in the Yard."

"How do you know all this?"

"Natural brilliance. Unless I'm still getting it all wrong, so
don't start taking notes or go quoting me. Mostly I've talked
to Viv. You were asleep. Adorable you were. Viv doesn't
know it all. He still hasn't grasped that his very own daddy is
an evil man. But he knows bits and pieces, like why he stole
George."

"Stole her so his wife, whassername, Augusta, so she'd
come after her, the baby. For the baby. To Belize. I mean,
obvious." Twitty was slowing down. "Family Christmas. Well
sort of family. In a way."

"Exactly. You don't believe a word of it. Viv does though,
he's pretending to 'imself he does, because he can't accept
it's all to get back at daddy. He kidnapped the baby out of
defiance, malice, I dunno—hatred. Not a bad route to go if
you want to let your father know that you do, in fact, exist.
Ask 'im yourself."

Viv was walking back into the room, his face shiny, beard
damp, sighing, nodding, shaking his head, avoiding the policemen's gaze, perhaps unaware of it, but looking for a place
to be, apart from them.

"Don't ask 'im," Peckover murmured. "He's on his way."

"On his way where?"

"Round the twist. Still want the cuffs?"

"No."

"Watch the baby. I'm 'aving a shower. Six minutes. Time
me. Then your turn, if you insist."

Peckover pointed the baby in Twitty's direction. "Leave
Viv be," he said, his voice low, not that Viv was straining to
hear. Viv stood against a far white wall, facing it, occasion-
ally jiggling his head.

"His prospects are dim," Peckover said. "He's under what
we might call filial stress, putting it mildly. Into the jaws of
death, into the mouth of hell. Probably preparing 'is lines."

"Man, do you exaggerate—sir." Just the same, Twitty's
voice, too, was hushed, apprehensive lest it distract Viv from
preparing the address to father. "It's Sir Peter should be wet-
ting himself, preparing his defence."

"Son, you may be tall, your hair rages like a fire in an
oilfield, and you know cricket and Pythagoras from 'arrow,
but you are naive." Peckover kept one eye on the baby, the
other on Viv. "Me exaggerate? Your dad is an amiable, law-

abiding buffer who you like, correct? The whistling postman.
The kids and dogs come out and whistle with 'im, everyone
actually feels better seeing 'im striding along Gladstone Place
and Churchill Terrace. He's not even throwing the string
round the envelopes over his shoulder, he's putting it in 'is
pocket, and they greet him by name—what's 'is name?"

"Yodel."

"Yodel? Christ, he's Swiss? George, stop that!" The baby,
after wanderings, had climbed up Chief Inspector Peckover,
with assistance, and was demanding to insert a fist up his
nostril. "Yodel, eh."

"From Yodel Point, where he was born, in Jamaica. He's
never been able to find it on any map but he says it's near
Starve Gut Bay."

"Jason, are you a Jew?"

"Sir, go have your shower."

"Yodel sounds like the masculine of Yentl. Unless Yentl's
masculine. I saw some of *Yentl* on the box once, I was enjoying it, but Miriam got restless and switched over to something more gripping, like 'Farming in Wales.' You sure your
dad's not from Geneva?"

"Henry, the water's getting cold."

"Your affable dad, Yodel—I still don't believe it—what
I'm saying is, he's civilised. He's not Prime Minister, though
we might all be better off if he were, but he's got these mobs
of dreadful offspring who don't in fact recoil from 'im, or
him from them—do they?"

"You've made your point."

"Being that not everyone has the good fortune to 'ave a
dad like Yodel Twitty, so don't tell me I exaggerate. Sir Peter
is a basket case. He is homicidal by proxy. So far he 'asn't
put out a contract on his son—he's reasonable, all he wants
is Viv gaoled to the end of time—but that was before the
baby was stolen. He might resent that, wouldn't you say?
Take it as a personal affront?"

"He shouldn't have had the baby. He stole his son's wife.
It's hideous. It's Aeschylus and Sophocles."

"Don't give me bleedin' Aeschylus and Sophocles. Look,
if this turns out to be a doddle—marvellous. We don't know
how Viv's going to behave and I'm damn sure he doesn't
either." He watched Viv pacing alongside the white wall,
cracking his knuckles. "I rather expect Sir Peter to put on a
show, like resistance. Put yourself in his place. His son walks
in with the stolen baby. Repentant? Or perhaps demanding
to keep it, demanding the return of the fair Augusta, and
Jesus flamin' O'Reilly, he is flanked by Scotland Yard. I sug-

gest you empty the grit out of your shoes, lad, get comfort-able, a few loosening up exercises. Keep an eye on his Honourableness. And 'ere, take George."

The bathroom window and shutters had been opened by Viv and left open. Peckover looked out at a private pool for chalet guests. On a shelf above the washbasin was shaving tackle, dental floss, and male lotions. He shaved and showered. The water was barely warm before he started. For Jason Twitty it was going to be cold. Serve him right. God's sake, Aeschylus and Sophocles.

He should have brought a clean shirt and underwear from his bag in the car. Getting again into this tramp's uniform, this scarecrow uniform he had been wearing for two days, since leaving Miami, was like being sunk back into compost. Still, they weren't off to visit the Queen. They were off to visit Sir Peter White, a prominent stinker of modern times. Peckover combed his wet hair in readiness for the next combat with George. In the mirror, either the bruise on his temple had calmed down, or the sun had turned his whole face flame-red. Ever the masochist, he dabbed his chin and cheeks with after-shave. Paco Rabanne Pour Homme, the bottle said.

Very pongy, very astringent. They presumably expected to return for it some day, if the alligators hadn't got them.

Viv stood against the white sitting room wall holding a glass of either water or gin. The condemned man with his last liquid request, facing the firing squad.

While Twitty showered—yelps and gasps issued from beneath the cold spray in the bathroom—Peckover and the baby toured the kitchen and bedrooms. Two beds had been slept in and left unmade. In drawers and closets were clothes, shoes, a generous supply of ties, and that was it. No guest book with their names, addresses, and a rave comment. No letters, tax returns, birth certificates, autographed photographs: "Kindest regards, Skip and Shep." No MAC-10s.

They were ready. Peckover closed the door of the chalet behind them. Behind the wheel of the Lincoln, Twitty followed the avenue towards the house. Finally he had managed to change into his Caribbean gear, causing Peckover to turn away in envy: a lemon-yellow tank top and matching cotton shorts so indecently short that at any moment accoutrements looked likely to ease or pop into view and a half mile of legs were exposed from crotch to ankle. Twitty had

overdone on free Paco Rabanne, not dabbing but deluging.
Peckover mashed the button which slid the window down.
The Lincoln was not in its first flush. Through the paint
showed rust, and now the interior reeked like twenty French
courtesans gathered for business in a house of assignation off
the Rue de Rivoli.

Viv was docile almost to the point of stupor, though his
lips moved in little staccato bursts, either rehearsing his lines
or singing to himself.

Peckover attempted to organise the baby in the carry-cot
but she protested. He sympathised, supposing her to be in
the throes of asphyxiation from the boudoir stench of Twitty,
as was everyone else. He found a pinprick of blood on her
back. A travelling Belize mosquito? On her hand was a min-
uscule scratch, and another on her shoulder. He rummaged
down the sides of the cot and brought forth the Giacometti.

"Constable, what the bloody 'ell's this?'"

"This what?" Twitty looked in the driving mirror. "Christ,
I didn't know."

"You put it there."

"Forgot!"

"Idiot." Peckover believed him. He passed the sculpture
to Viv. He had to nudge him with it. "Sorry. This is yours."

"Keep it."

"Can't do that."

"Do what you like."

The last hundred yards to Sir Peter's sprawled, rosy palace were through a mini-Versailles of flower gardens, lawns,
and closer to the palace, a parkland of monstrous regimented
evergreens which seemed to be too close to the palace. Perhaps the intention was to shield the sun. Peckover did not
see statuary and plashy fountains but he expected they might
be lurking somewhere. Down steps from the entrance to the
house gallivanted an Irish setter. She was berserk with simple
joy at possibilities of fun, or with simple-mindedness, unless
of course, Peckover cynically reflected, they were much the
same thing.

Number nine light winked on in the butler's pantry. This
time Dwayne Goodsir had only to know his tie, put on his
blazer, and stub out his mild fix. He climbed the stairs. The
last time the light had gone on, a half hour ago, no one had
arrived. If no one arrived again, he would call the electrician.

Someone had already arrived. They must have come from
the gate like a missile. They hadn't, though, or he would
have heard. He had heard only the last fifty yards. They had

arrived like a Lincoln, and not the latest model. Getting out of the Lincoln was a character dressed like a bum and holding a baby, and someone in a straw hat and a yellow top and shorts. Then from the car came—oh boy—Mistah Vivian.

The baby was The Baby? Babies all looked the same, but this one, Viv here and all, she had to be it. The other two were bodyguards? Hardly lawyers. The soul brother dressed for a walk on the beach a lawyer? Social workers maybe? Reporters?

Cops?

Whoever else had just come through the gate, the priority was not meeting and greeting. Not this bunch and not the new lot on their way. Oh boy, Vivian, the baby. A word in the ear of Sir Boss Man who paid the wages was the priority.

Dwayne backed to the door.

"You, wait," called the beefy bum holding the baby.

Dwayne reversed back into the house at a speed not generally associated with the stately departings of butlers.

They entered the guest chalet with a key, found the back door forced, water on the bathroom floor, and a smell of Paco Rabanne in spite of the window being open.

In the kitchen they took from the oven an orange Creuset casserole, and out of the casserole two .357 Magnum revolvers, the same as many American police carry, and the U.S. Secret Service.

"This may not be what Sir Peter has in mind but screw him," Skip said.

"Unless you want to flip a coin, you take the blackie," said Shep. "Peckover's mine."

TWENTY-EIGHT

A tall blonde woman in shorts, T-shirt, and visor stood by an umbrella beside the pool, watching the party from the Lincoln file up the steps to the entrance and into the house, Winnie alongside, leaping up, requesting games. The woman walked a few paces from the pool, towards the house. She quickened her step then started to run.

Neither Peckover nor Twitty saw in the hall the man in the blazer who had stood on the steps outside, though they had to turn and peer to be sure, the hall being airy and spacious, like the foyer of a museum, but also home to a ten-foot Christmas tree, potted shrubs, a suit of armour, feudal arms and dingy paintings on the wall, a marble staircase, a passage leading to the casino or chapel or private zoo, and doors everywhere. Peckover counted five doors, which might be imported English oak, or they might be some fancy foreign wood like pecan or gingko. Peckover did not know wood. He knew the purring, which was air conditioning. The dog woofed and charged at a tanned miss in a sundress who came from the passage and halted, partly to ward off the dog and tell it "Down, Winnie," party from surprise at the motley, unannounced visitors. She recognised two, though Vivian White only from photographs.

Peckover said, "Police. You are?"

"Joanna Park." She came forward, eyes on the baby, hand swatting at pesky Winnie. "Thank God. I'm her nurse."

"Better nurse 'er then." Peckover handed over the baby. "She's all right. Bit of a bump on 'er nose, no worse than she'll get when she starts playing 'ockey. Walks a treat until she stops. We'd be grateful for a word with Sir Peter if you can rustle 'im up."

The blonde from the pool ran on slapping, sandled feet into the hall, took the baby from Nurse Park, and shot a shrivelling look at her husband. Viv smiled vaguely. He opened his mouth as if to speak to her but said nothing.

"We're police officers, ma'am. You'll be Mrs. White, I take it? Augusta— ah, ma'am? Ma'am, would you 'old on a moment?"

She would not. She had started up the stairs with the baby and did not look back. Winnie accompanied her in the mistaken belief that anything moving held out greater promise than whatever remained stationary. Nurse Park dithered, unsure who might require her most, if anyone, then followed up the stairs. The man in the blazer and tie came down the stairs, accosted her, and they whispered and cast glances. She continued up, he down.

"Your father's in the shower, sir," Dwayne said. "Who will I tell him these gentlemen are?"

Peckover said, "Scotland Yard." He was opening doors. "We'll wait in 'ere."

He walked into a living room the size of a Lincolnshire potato field and furnished in the manner of a manor in the same county: chintzily, florally, and in Peckover's view, inappropriately for this tropical spot. Here was milady's domain for bridge with the colonel and the finch-Fotheringays: Laura Ashley curtains, vases of gaudy blooms, antique tables bearing silver-framed photographs, a silver tray with sherry glasses and Bristol Cream, and in an overwrought fireplace iron firedogs, brass fireirons, and a basket of geometric, dusted logs. Except for the light he might have been at the Vicarage, Fitzpugh Magna. Just the place for tea and confession.

He opened a sash window, which started at knee level and rose almost to the ceiling, and looked out on gardens, parkland, and lurid, twittering birds. The pool shimmered beyond the driveway. Casa Verde on a far grander scale. As son, so father, cushioned runaways both. Peckover felt a pang for monochrome London, dark at tea time, grey rain on grey roofs, the heating kept low enough for you to function, if you kept your jacket on, and not drip and gasp. The only life, birds apart, was a slow woman in a flowing dress and a helmet such as was worn by soldiers of the Raj in Sunday afternoon re-runs of films like *Gunga Din* and *Lives of a Bengal Lancer*. She moved in the direction of the front entrance carrying a basket of flowers. Not a glance at the Lincoln.

"Think she might accept an offer for that hat?" Twitty murmured.

Peckover said, "Ideally we'd organise things so as to somehow so scare Sir Peter that he just buggers off out, runs away to Brazil before we can stop 'im. Then we can go home. I mean, think. What if he, say, loses 'is rag with Viv and admits everything, not giving a hoot, gives us every detail—looting his bank, the killings, being George's father. What if we get chapter, verse, and footnotes. Can you imagine the red tape and endlessness and 'opelessness of having to deal with it? This abroad, lad, and abroad is a pain. One, can 'e be deported from here? Two, can we arrest 'im? What power 'ave we and where are we? Bleedin' Andros Island. Where's that? Bleedin' Bahamas, wherever they are. Don't assume the natives are going to be friendly. If they weren't happy for Peter to stay, they could have told him to go. We're not even legal, you and me, we've come in through the back door like refugees looking for a job. Any deporting, it's going to be us. So all right, bring in the lawyers to sort us out, then to get stuck into Sir Peter's confession, which we're not going to get—I'm not totally bonkers yet, lad, though not far off. What lawyers, do I hear you say? Do I?"

"What lawyers?"

"Good question. Any lawyers 'ere, what's the betting Sir Peter owns them. Can you imagine the inquiries and affadavits and reviews and committees and grind and trips back and forth between London and this boilin', bug-ridden Caribbean, month after month, year after year. These things drag on, mate. My dream, want to hear it? It's to flush Sir Peter out to Brazil, or Tibet. Let them take care of it. Don't tell anyone I said that. I like the sound of Tibet, all those monks and lamas, they'd find a cell for 'im."

"We've flushed Viv out. See where he went?"

Viv was not to be seen.

"Damn," Peckover said.

A voice was distantly trumpeting. "Where are you then? Hello? Hello?" It trumpeted closer, louder. "Let's see you! Hello?" The voice reached the hall. "Yes, I'm here!" Doors slammed. "Great heavens, boy, show yourself!"

Into the room strode, and stopped short, a tall bony man in shorts to his knees, a white monogrammed shirt, and bare feet.

"Who the devil are you!" he shouted.

"Police. Chief Inspector Peckover. Constable Twitty. You're Sir Peter White?"

"By thunder, Peckover, eh? Stay where you are."

He left the room. In the hall he shouted, "You, ah! In here, boy!"

Wherever 'in here' was, it was not back into the Fitzpugh Magna room, no one coming in, and whoever 'boy' was, whether Viv or a servant, he made no reply, or not audibly. Peckover and Twitty negotiated past chintzy sofas, a depressing tea trolley, sombrely Victorian, without tea, and arrived in the hall.

The hall was empty, though only for a moment. At the steady pace which wins the race, in through the front door came the wrinkled woman in the Raj helmet. Twitty feared she was about to sell them a rose from her basket. Would she accept the paltry Belize dollars the Kentucky Fried Chicken woman had handed him at a criminal rate of exchange she had made up in her head? He took off his hat.

Peckover thought: Sir Peter's wife, the Lady May. He cleared his throat.

"Madam?"

The voice of Sir Peter boomed from beyond the open door into a room across the hall. "Ho, by Jupiter! You are, my boy, and you will!"

If Viv was answering his father, he was answering with gestures, sign language.

"Consider your future, boy!"

Twitty started across the hall. Peckover reached out and held his arm. The lady in the helmet walked past the Christmas tree.

Peckover said, "Madam, excuse me. Lady May?"

Outside, the drone of an approaching car. Peckover looked through the front door. He saw a segment of gravel driveway, and beyond the gravel, grass.

"Madam?" he called.

She turned her head and without halting her progress lowered it once towards him, smiling benignly like the Queen Mum. Should he, Peckover wondered, bow from the waist? She looked front again, soldiering on with her basket through the hall.

"What's the matter with you!" Sir Peter invisibly boomed from beyond the open door in the wall hung with oils of galleons on fire.

Slow-marching into the passage which led to the parade ground, or the Roman theatre, Lady May paused, turned her helmeted head back to the policemen, and said, "The Pom-

poms de Paris have such fragrance, don't you think?"

"It's up to you, boy!" shouted Sir Peter. *"Tempus fugit,* what?"

Nothing from Viv. Outside, a car arrived too fast and braked, squirting gravel. Lady May evaporated into the passage. Constable Twitty put on his hat. He stepped behind his guv'nor and towards the front door, through which he saw beside the Lincoln a second car: low, sporty, advertised perhaps as Bahamian sea blue, but beige with dust, and Skip and Shep coming out of it.

Peckover crossed the hall and stepped into the room where trumpeted Sir Peter. Here a reading or smoking room, not that there was smoke, at Boodle's or the Beefsteak, or come to that—White's. Not that he had ever been invited inside a club in St. James's, but everything was wood panelling and leather. A chairman of the board's king-size davenport had a green leather top, armchairs were leather, and the bookcases held leather-bound books on how to swindle people, Peckover supposed, and shoot them. In front of the davenport, Sir Peter was holding out a gun to Viv, pressing it into Viv's hands, then wrapping his fingers round it, a daddy urging on his little boy an unwanted toy, some stupid harmonica, or a racing car which turned into a robot which turned into a shark, which he had played with already and was bored with.

"Lad!" called Peckover, meaning "Come here."

"Guv'!" Twitty simultaneously called from the hall, meaning "Come here."

"Damn you!" shouted Sir Peter. It was not clear whom he was damning. "Do it, boy!"

They heard the front door slam, the top and bottom bolts slide home. Viv, reluctant with the gun, appeared to be of two minds. He looked at Peckover and pointed the gun at him, but without conviction, Peckover hoped.

"What he's always wanted, Viv, isn't it, what we talked about." Peckover's voice sounded peculiar in his ears, as if he were speaking under water. Clammy sweat was gathering on his brow and in his palms. "You'll be put away for ever to rot. He keeps Augusta."

"Boy!" bawled Sir Peter, puce.

Boom! sounded a gun as if in competition with Sir Peter's roaring. It was from outside the house, at the front. *Boom!* again, and splintering wood.

Viv turned the gun on Sir Peter. The father's jaw dropped and his admirable tennis court tan seeped away, to be replaced by a sudsy, dishwatery hue. Father and son stared at each other.

Boom! and smashing glass.

Twitty had advanced deeply through the Fitzpugh Magna chintz to shut and lock the open window before he realised the pointlessness of the exercise. To prove him correct, tall Skip appeared at the adjacent, closed window and signalled to him, a friendly lifting of an empty hand demonstrating that all was forgiven. This was the one he had near throttled on their first encounter, and spruce again, having cleaned himself up and donned a tie and a three-button seersucker suit with a pink stripe which made him look like a side of streaky bacon, though no one not totally wasted on eighty-six proof Duggan's Dew or equivalent would have told him so. Very yuppie suiting, very poncy, Twitty considered. Not my style personally but if that's what you fancy. He threw himself to the floor as Skip fired at him through the window, shooting the glass into myriad sparkling slivers.

You like shooting—windows, people—Twitty thought, barely capable of thought, terrified out of his head, and crawling backwards for his life before Skip could come through the window and sight him among the chintz and chair legs and tea-trolley wheels.

You don't shoot, Peckover realised, watching Viv pointing the gun at roughly the monogram over his father's left tit. You don't shoot people. I understand that. I except it's common, a common failing, though I don't know the figures. Paper targets you shoot, balloons, wild life perhaps—don't your Italians shoot every bird that flies? Why there are no more birds in Italy? But not human life, you don't do humans, though your daddy is barely human. I sympathise because it's hard, hard, for the non-shooters.

Hardly risking breathing, Peckover watched the pointed gun, Viv's vacant profile, his watery eye and dry, red beard. He watched the open mouth of Sir Peter. Sir Peter, too, had frozen except for an involuntary shuddering from bald head to bare feet. Sir Peter wanted his life, loot, and blonde bedmate, not a point-blank bullet. Any movement now, a word, who knew? Viv seemed beyond everything, his mind fused and gone. His finger pulsed on the trigger of a gun forced on him, as his daddy's prick pulsed for Viv's wife, though probably not at the moment. For everyone who had killed there had been a first time. Apart from professionals, wartime infantrymen, bomber pilots—such you didn't count—the first time had probably been also the last, but what of that?

Viv was not after all in two minds. He was in three. He tilted his head upwards, closed his eyes, and put the gun's muzzle to his temple.

TWENTY-NINE

"Viv, no," Peckover said. "Help me."

Help me? Peckover the pig?

The plea did not emerge blurry and reverberating from under water. It was high-fidelity, urgent, demanding to be heard. Viv opened his red, wet eyes and turned them on Peckover. He kept the gun against his temple.

"Viv, they're here, outside, your father's goons—"

Bang! banged a gun outside the front door in verification.

"They're crazy, Viv. You've seen them, remember? They're going to kill us."

"Not us," Viv said. "You."

"The worse for you. I'm the only one can testify you've killed no one, you're not involved—only one who counts. You need me, we need you. So help us, you have to. You can shoot."

Except you can't, you don't, you're as useless as I am. Peckover, sweating, gulped bile, hardly knowing what he was saying, which did not matter as long as Viv heard and believed it. Whatever he was saying, it continued to be impressively high-fidelity.

He said, "What makes you think it's only me they want to kill, and the constable? It's gone too far for them. We all know them now, the word's out, they've got to obliterate us all." He believed that, and his aitches were in place, some of them. What could that mean? That he intended to die correctly, with dignity, his jacket buttoned? "The baby. Your wife. Wipe-out on Andros Island. The bloke in the blazer, the Brit girl, Joanna. Your mother. Do you see them sparing your mother, those two? You want to see her shot to bits, face down in 'er roses?"

"Please, shut up. I have to think." Viv lowered the gun. He did not know what to do with it.

Though the assault on the front door had ceased, somewhere something fell with a crash, or had been pushed. Into the room ran Twitty with a nosebleed and his Panama askew. He flinched at the sight of the gun, tried to take in the situation, and failed. He shut and locked the door.

He said, "One's in the house. Haven't seen the other. Could we phone the police and clear off fast?" He looked from the door to the windows to Viv with the gun. "If that's allowed."

"Haaagh!" cried Sir Peter, and lunged at Viv as at the net he might have lunged to reach a passing shot. Viv hit him on the side of the head with the gun. Sir Peter toppled against the davenport and fell on the floor, his hand to the side of his head, looking up at Viv.

"Boy?" he whispered.

"Where's the phone?" Peckover said.

He had to say it again. Viv, staring down at his father, seemed the more dazed of the two. He looked about him for a telephone but did not see one.

"In the hall," he said.

Peckover stepped to the panelled pecan door and listened. Galactic silence. He had hoped at least to have heard a distant chirrup from Georgie-Porgie. He was aware of Viv's and Twitty's eyes on him. When his thumb and finger arrived within an inch of the key, the oval, porcelain door handle with the squiggly, filigree motif started to turn. Peckover gazed, immobile. After a quarter circle the handle held steady, resting in peace, and exotic egg on its side, exhibited for inspection. Peckover sidestepped to the wall then backed away.

Damn, damn, they were learning, they were getting cagey. The stealth approach. Cunning, surprise, maybe a pincer movement. Not the slam-bang-blast-everything-to-pieces of moments ago, and of Casa Verde. You had known where you were at Casa Verde. You'd known where Skip and Shep were.

You knew where they were here too, one of them. Not that the door had a peephole. So all right, could be the geezer in the blazer. Lady May bringing roses.

Bleedin' wasn't though.

Peckover motioned Twitty, Viv, and Sir Peter to the window. Sir Peter stayed put. Peckover supposed the evil old pus-bag, as patron and paymaster, assumed that whoever else his hit men blitzed, he would be exempt. Likely he was right. Just the same, he wouldn't have cared to be in Sir Peter's shoes, had he been wearing any, if and when Skip and Shep started blitzing. Might be errors, skew-whiff shooting, ricochets. A body could get caught in crossfire. Loonies like those two might think it the giggle of the year, sieving the patron.

Maybe Sir Peter stayed put because he was hurt. Too bad.

Twitty opened the window and put his head out a little way. He saw no one. Man-high, globular bushes barbered smooth as skin flanked the window. More of the same obese bushes grew in clumps between the window and the driveway. On the drive, two cars. The bushes might give cover for a dash to the Lincoln. They might be giving cover now to one or another of the pair. Twitty leaned further out.

"Front door's open," he said.

Someone, like Skip or Shep, had presumably opened it from the hall. Twitty retrieved his head, hat, and torso from the outdoors, looked at Viv's gun, then at Peckover.

"Shouldn't we have that?"

Peckover said to Viv, "You're with us?"

After a spell when he was elsewhere, Viv said, "What?"

"Strictly self-defense, right?"

"All right."

Peckover licked his dry lips. Self-defence, defencive weapons. Meaningless hypocrisy. What he was allowing had to be his most awesome idiocy in a lifetime of idiocies. Viv with a shooter and *carte blanche*. White card for Viv, pink for Our 'Enry. He would know soon. If he were alive to know.

Twitty climbed out of the window. He ran to the first clump of bushes, stopped there, and looked back. Viv came through the window, possibly pressured a little, but did not run. He sauntered, directionless, a weekend guest walking off the roast beef and Yorkshire pudding, smelling garden scents. Peckover ran, and when a gun banged he bent, ran in a crouch, then plunged knocking Twitty sideways.

They crouched behind the useless barbered bush. The bush was elephantine but still a bush, not a bunker. Awaiting the next gunshot, they pressed deeper into the bush, resisted by branches which could pry out an eyeball. Peckover brought from his pocket the Webley Police Model, courtesy of Sergeant Montego and the Belize police. He leaned, dug in his trousers pocket for bullets, and shakingly loaded. *The official Brit revolver for fifty years, you should be at home with it.* Who had said that?

Wotcher, Peachy. Yer, right at 'ome, girl. Snug as a bug. Wish you were 'ere now.

No he didn't. She had done her bit. God love her. Take the rest of the week off, Peachy. Take a month. Viv's turn now.

Where was Viv? Where, come to that, Skip and Shep?

Waiting for gunfire, the policemen heard nothing, saw nothing. Peckover would have liked to have passed to Twitty the loaded Webley, as the buck is passed, as the queen of hearts in that card game with children where you pass your most disagreeable cards to your neighbour. Could he teach Twitty in time? The two-week course shrunk to ten seconds, if they had ten seconds? Sergeant McMaster, suspended pending inquiries, he'd not have said no to having the sarge here. Peckover spat a leaf from his mouth.

"Adjust your muffs and glasses," he said.

"Sorry?"

"Sounds like an orgy, dunnit. Booze and naked ladies. Who fired that gun? Did you see?"

"No." The Panama was more or less in place, though head and body were intimately involved with leafy, springy boughs. "Probably your trusted Viv."

They squirmed round to look about them and behind. No Viv, no anyone. Plenty of manicured savagery, shaved shrubs, blue sky.

"'If you know of a better 'ole, go to it,'" Peckover said.

"What hole?"

"World War One cartoon. Two tommies in a foxhole with shells burstin' all round. You're too young."

"But you remember it well."

Why, wondered, Peckover, only the one shot? If it was them, not Viv, single shots meant they probably weren't carrying MAC-10s. That was something. Not a lot but something.

"Cagey buggers," he said. "They're stalkin' us, we can't sit 'ere."

He had little idea of what they could or couldn't do, apart from sprint to the car, and be shot at. Or what Viv was doing.

Bang!

Peckover's right leg jarred, dirt spattered. He believed he had been shot in the foot, except there was not enough pain. But pain took a moment or two. He looked down. The heel of his brogue had disappeared. He hauled in the leg and heaved himself sideways through crunching bush into Twitty. Huddled Twitty sprawled and craned in search of the source of the shot. Chin in grass, Peckover peered beneath the lowest branches and across the lawn and the driveway. Shep in a laundered, unbloodied white shirt stood at the top of the steps leading down from the front entrance, pointing a gun. He was thirty or so paces away and grinning like a celebrity, avid for love.

"Do you mind?" called someone from somewhere, with a rising inflexion.

The query was put with eminent reasonableness, though with a touch of asperity, as from one who finds in his apple tree a neighbour's child.

"There!" Twitty said, pointing.

Peckover followed the finger. The Honourable Viv, who was not an honourable, stood to one side of a great dirigible of a bush between the library windows and the entrance steps. Wherever he had wandered to, he had returned.

"Viv!" Peckover shouted, climbing to his feet, and cringing that he should have shouted. Distraction was just what Viv needed.

Viv was aiming his daddy's gun at Shep, who was undistracted. His concern was with Viv, not shouting nonentities elsewhere. Shep took aim at Viv.

Shoot, damn you, Peckover urged Viv.

Viv, arm at full stretch, gun steady, opened his mouth and gave song in a tuneful baritone. "'Jolly boating weather,'" he sang, which seemed to disconcert Shep, though only for a moment.

Bang! Shep fired and missed.

"'Swing, swing, together—'"

Bang!

Viv took several steps backwards into the dirigible bush, a bullet in his brain. You horror, you poor bastard, Peckover thought. You didn't shoot, you didn't try, you couldn't.

Bang!

Shep fired at the Scotland Yard bush. Why would he not? Why be satisfied with mere Viv when there were coppers?

Twitty was suddenly dissatisfied with the bush. "See you, guv'," he said, and dashed from the bush in a crouch, to the next bush, en route for the Lincoln. An attempt at topiary appeared to have been made on the new bush, which was shaped like a heart, or two Bardolph noses, unless it was blight.

Twitty sprinted on as if the car ahead were haven, and end to all troubles, as well it might be if he reached it. Shep was aiming but not shooting. Perhaps the gun had jammed or was empty. Peckover cursed himself for not counting bullets. So how many bullets did Shep's gun hold anyway?

Peckover ran for the two-nosed bush, holding the Webley. He ran limpingly over grass which looked as flawless as a championship croquet lawn yet was uneven. He remembered a shoe which had lost its heel. He, not the lawn, was uneven. He waited behind the noses bush, trying to arrange his balance.

Twitty had made it to the Lincoln on the far side of Skip and Shep's car. Good lad. Shep was coming down the steps from the house, stuffing shells into his gun. No sign of Skip.

So, he and the lad got away from all this with no worse than a lost heel and scratches from bushes, then what? Get away where? Were there police on Andros Island? The nearest telephone was right here in the house. Maybe the women in the house were already phoning, if they weren't too terrified of what Sir Peter might have to say.

Sod the telephone. Peckover ran. Twitty had started up the engine. A door opened in the nearer, sporty car, blue overlaid with khaki dust, and low-slung and sleek as a lass looking for a good time, or for trouble. Skip in a summery suit with a pink stripe and a gun in his hand slid from the car, his back to Peckover. Nimble and stooped, Skip set off round the rear of the sporty car, then between the cars towards oblivious Twitty at the wheel of the Lincoln.

Ambush, Peckover realised, running and wanting to scream. They had anticipated it all.

Had Skip not been ducking low, Twitty might have seen him, for what good that would have done. And Skip might have seen galloping Peckover, and paid him no regard, taking the apparition for the Dishevelled Androsian Androphant, an endangered but harmless species. Twitty's hatted head was in silhouette through the open window, bowed as if checking petrol. Skip, advancing, raised his gun.

"Jason!" bellowed Peckover.

If that alerted Twitty, as it did, the silhouette instantly disappearing, Skip also was alerted. He swirled, unfurled to basketball-player height between the cars, and pointed his gun. Peckover swerved, skidded on a deheeled shoe, and fell forward. Falling, he shouted "Police!"

He was aware how absurd, shouting "Police!," how gravel was ripping his knees and one elbow, how his momentum continued, which was fortunate. When Skip fired, he missed, though the distance was only a dozen yards.

Peckover was still in transit through dust, gravel, spouting bug larvae, smoke, and grit, when he shot Skip in the chest.

Bull's-eye.

THIRTY

"Guv'!"

Detective Chief Inspector Peckover lay propped on an elbow, on gravel, looking up at a lonely tuft of white, a smudge, in otherwise cloudless blue. He was too comfy to move. Scraped and probably bleeding a little, but blimey, it was all right here on the ground. Judging from the lad's voice he should be up and active because somewhere Shep was loading a gun. That whisp of cloud was a treat though. Like a chicken feather. He didn't want to look anywhere else because he did not want to see Skip.

"Henry!"

Dammit, I'm coming.

Good bloke, Twitty. Got a career ahead of 'im if he lived through the next couple of minutes. Not that he'd get much beyond inspector, being the shade he was, not unless things changed. Jamaica though, if he were there, they'd make him chief commissioner. Should do.

Peckover sat up and found a gun in his hand. From now on nothing would be the same. His first thought had been that he would not tell Miriam. He couldn't. He would deny it.

She would only have to pick up a newspaper. He would be on the front page tomorrow. Television news, his photograph.

"He's gone back into the house."

Funny, he had been utterly off balance, arm bent, wrist unsupported, finger snatching at the trigger. *She's a lady, responding to a soft squeeze, let her know ye're in control.* The sarge would have had kittens.

For better or worse, a five-star fluke.

Still, he had aimed, best he could. He had intended it, he had no excuse. His ears still vibrated. Ear-muffs did help. Skip lay on his back with sightless eyes, his legs apart, and dark stuff oozing out of the middle of his tie.

"Look," Twitty said. "Sir Peter."

Peckover stood up. Sir Peter came through the door shouting at the policemen. "You'll be sorry for this, you fellows! By thunder, I'll make you sorry!" He ran down the steps and along the side of the house to Viv's bush, to succour his dead son where he lay.

Peckover thought irrelevantly: Your wife, Lady May, she's not going to be pleased about this. All you give her is grief.

Sir Peter was doing little succouring. He pried the gun from Viv's hand.

"Throw it down," Peckover called, and started across the drive. "You're under arrest!"

On what charges he was not sure, but no sense messing about any more. Giving his son a shooter to kill policemen with, that would do for a start, whatever that came under.

"And you're dead, copper," called Shep.

Neither Peckover, who was back on the lawn, nor Twitty, hesitating by the Lincoln, could see Shep.

"Which of you wants it first?" called the voice.

Presumably it was Shep. The voice came from the house.

Boom!

The Lincoln's windscreen shattered. Peckover raced for the hopeless two-nosed bush. Twitty ran behind the Lincoln and dropped to his hands and knees, inching his head past the petrol tank to try and discover Shep.

"What we call a sighting shot," the voice called out. "Here comes another."

The gun fired. Pellets peppered the upper heights of the bush behind which twitched crouching Peckover.

"Fun, you agree?" called the voice. "You having fun, coppers?"

Peckover wiped sweat from his eyes. He fumbled branches apart and saw Shep in a window of the Fitzpugh Magna room, pointing from the waist what looked like a shotgun.

Maybe Sir Peter had an arsenal in his house as Viv did in his—had done. Who would inherit Viv's arsenal? Shep was grinning, happy as Larry. He did not seem perturbed by spread Skip, though perhaps he was. Perhaps the grin was tetanus, a lockjaw rictus. Sir Peter stood frothing and blustering, shielding his eyes from the sun with the hand which held the gun. If he pulled the trigger, he would blow a hole in his house.

"I'll show you fellows!" he shouted, and started barefoot across the drive towards the parked cars.

How he would show was unclear. He was not shooting. Perhaps a jolly good talking to. Peckover would have preferred to have been on the far side of the lawn, the sun at his back, and in Shep's eyes. But he was here, the sun in his own eyes.

The red and white dog strutted through the door and stood on the top step, tail swishing, weighing possibilities. Sir Peter changed his mind about whatever he might have had in mind and altered direction for his front door. Winnie bounded to greet him. Peckover dashed for the window into the library, his closest serious refuge.

"Outa the light, grandpa!" Shep yelled.

Bang!

The bang came from the cars, not from Shep's window, and had a less cannon-like resonance than the shotgun. Powdery stucco puffed from the wall above the Fitzpugh Magna window. Not that Peckover in his unequal brogues saw it, legs bicycling for the library window. Even with one flat tyre, the bicycle travelled well through the din and confusion. The same gun fired again but not from the cars. The shotgun boomed. Sir Peter was shouting, Winnie barking. Peckover returned through the library window, picked himself up, and looked out. The low sun in his eyes, he saw sprinting Twitty fire again towards Shep's window, and vanish round the far corner of the house.

Skip's gun. Bleedin' idiot. The lad had never held a gun in his life. They'll bleedin' court-martial 'im, throw the book at 'im, buggers like Astle. No matter he must have distracted Shep, given him pause enough to save things for the moment. If the lad had hit him, he was finished.

The library door was wide open. As Peckover stepped into the hall, the butler in the blazer backed through a door in the wall festooned with sabres and cutlasses, and slammed it shut. Sir Peter, not looking round, loped barefoot into the passage beyond the armour and out of sight. Winnie pranced, looking from Sir Peter's back to Peckover, and marvelling at the activity. On the marble landing halfway up the staircase huddled blonde August and Nanny Park with the baby in her arms, gazing down. The baby was waving a small wooly creature with a bell round its neck.

"Get upstairs!" Peckover shouted.

He trod forward, watching the open door to the Fitzpugh
Magna room. He paused by the Christmas tree. Shep could
be anywhere.

Could be dead. If the lad had hit him, they would have to
dream something up. He'd hit him himself. Pink Card Peckover. He had just killed one man, another was going to make
no difference.

Not a sound. Even the dog, tongue lolling, was silent.
Then the faintest tinkling of a baby's wooly beast in retreat,
and as if this were his cue, Shep came from the Fitzpugh
Magna room with the shotgun at his waist. From Peckover's
position by the tree, Shep was in profile.

"Shep!" said Peckover.

Whatever his name, it pretty certainly was not Shep. Shep
turned his head anyway, looking for Shep. Peckover was in
the drawn weapons position—facing the target, gun at waist
level, pointing at the target—except that his finger, like
Shep's, was on the trigger.

"Drop it!" Peckover said, though it was plain to him Shep
would do no such thing.

The grin was on Shep's face. Peckover lifted his arms to
eye level, gripping two-handed, thumb on thumb, the Webley. His backside was thrust back, legs splayed, knees bent.
Shep swung through a quarter circle and pointed the shotgun. Without waiting for the sergeant's "Your times starts
now!" Peckover squeezed the trigger. The bullet hit the grin.
The shotgun blast sprayed the ceiling as Shep went backwards and down.

Through the clamour in Peckover's ears, Sir Peter's voice
behind him was roaring, "Great Scott, fellow, that'll be
enough! Don't turn round! Put that thing away! Now get in
there and we'll finish with you!"

Get in where? Peckover did not risk turning. The man
was unhinged, he could almost hear the foaming.

"In the library," Sir Peter commanded. "Go on then,
Peckerbridge, haven't got all day. Capital idea, capital.
Shouldn't take a moment, what? May?"

May? Peckover saw Twitty appear in the front door. The
Panama was in place and in his hand he held Skip's gun.
They were in line: Twitty in the entrance, Shep dead on the
floor, himself, gun obediently in his pocket, and Sir Peter
behind him. Winnie weaved and looked up at people, and
down at Shep. Where was May?

Sir Peter said, "No place for you, May. What're you doing
with that? *May?*"

The last monosyllable was softly said, by Sir Peter's stan-